A JOINING OF SOULS

T.A.CARLSON

ISBN: 979-8-9854229-1-7 (Paperback)
ISBN: 979-8-9854229-2-4 (Hardcover)
ISBN: 979-8-9854229-0-0 (E-book)

DEDICATION

To: Mom
Uncle Corky
Grandma Grace
Uncle Clarence
Uncle Virgil
Aunt Vera
Tom
Sue
Don
Josephine
Clara

And so many, many others who have been afflicted by the crippling diseases (mind and/or body) that diminish your quality of life to nothing and hold you in a vise for what seems like an eternity. You still found a way to touch my heart!!
May you all be known and remembered for your greatness……………..

Also, to all the Caregivers and Relatives who pour their heart and soul into the daily needs and welfare of those suffering.
You are God's angels…………

Where Did They Go? (Alan)

"Consider this, you who forget God, or I will tear you to pieces, with no one to rescue you."

Psalms 50:22 NIV

I believe close to one third of my brain is gone. Not vaporized or disappeared. Rather, a dead mush of Jell-O that is serving no more purpose than filling a cranial void. I know it is still there. Sorta. The other two thirds of my brain tells me thus. It has registered this detail in a memory bank that is becoming more elusive all the time. I am certain my One Third will never return. Even the constant barrage of apps on my phone that want me to complete a puzzle or two every day for brain exercise, will not get my One Third back in shape. It is gone, disse vamos, never to return. I miss my One Third.

This didn't just slowly happen. Not like the brain cells I baked rather heartily in my 20s. Those cells were the weaker ones anyway, and probably needed to be sorted out of the herd. No, these cells packed their bags in the middle of the night and checked out. They might have left one at a time over many years, and the last one to leave on that fateful night was the dude cell that was keeping inventory of the rest of the cells. He let me down. Falsifying records until he realized some cell in the other two thirds was going to notice the vacancy and report to the owner. Thus, inventory cell skipped town. No blame passed there.

So, what does one do when one realizes that his/her mental capacity has decreased by a considerable portion? Does one weep? Are the crying cells still here at home? Why *yes, they are!!* and stronger than ever. Is this a realization of advancing age? Do we cry more freely as we age? I can't seem to answer that because my Wikipedia cells were some of the first to leave.

Maybe you just accept the fact and move on the best you can. After all, studies have shown that if one portion of the brain is damaged, new routes are sewn and necessary functions can return to a semblance of what they were. Sometimes. Other times, the stuff does not come back. It does not repair. An IQ and body function of 144 is now sitting at around 96. I am amazed I can even do that math. The calculating cells must have stayed home.

Can I keep on truckin' with such a diminished thought capacity? We will see. I believe I need to get on the horse and take a ride down memory lane. Record these memories. Share the history. Lock some semblance of a lifetime in. Pass to posterity.

But what if no one really gives a damn? Are the thoughts and words and past actions shared going to be boring and forever stored in a trash can? Maybe the paper used can decompose, eventually supplying some other half-wit with enough biogas to heat his home for an hour or so.

Did God take them from me? Did He finally get tired of my sinful nature and lack of corrective action and reduce my mental capacity to corral me like a frontal lobotomy? Is that still practiced today? I can confirm that most of the front part of my brain feels OK. It is the top rolling off both sides to my ears that is gone. It feels like a dull throb of nothingness.

I believe it is related to the ringing in my ears that magically appeared close to the same time. It very well could be an echo rather than a ringing. It is irritating as hell. The only avoidance is a bombardment of stronger exterior noises that seem to distract the inner echo of dullness. It is a relief to get some time away from the reality that I am knocking on the door of mentally challenged.

Maybe I have always been this way as past actions would support that theory. No, those actions were more from the "idiot" side of my cerebral. When is that part going to pack its bags?

We will press on, keep the story rolling. Possibly find some of those brain cells that went the way of the Ninja. Little bastards anyway.

I miss them.................

2

THE BEST ME (Larry)

Pride goes before destruction, a haughty spirit before a fall.
Proverbs 16:18 NIV

Have you ever experienced that time in your life when you just knew you had the world by the cajones? You put the *Mundo interio* on every day and owned it. Life was good. There was no way it could get much better. People envied you. They wanted a piece of your lifestyle. They listened to every breath you exhaled just to catch a whiff of your success. That is what I have. That is what I have achieved through hard work and little to no help from others. I am a self-made success story that everyone should emulate.

This didn't come by luck or chance. I saw opportunity and grabbed it. To heck with those self-help books. Their only true success is the money made from selling their book of mostly garbage. A book that gives a shot of hope then quickly dies because the backbone isn't as straight as it should be. Luck and shortcuts made for a representation of success. Daddy probably gave it a financial boost. Those book writers would be most fortunate to even copy a small portion of what I have achieved.

Self-made and proud of it. That is yours truly. Don't care if you like me or not. If you haven't made it to my level, that is your problem. No concern of mine. I will allow you to have envy. The rest you can keep your hands off and just admire what I possess.

Sounds good right in front of you, doesn't it? My confidence has paved the way to my fortune. It is MINE. Good for me. People flock to be in my presence. I can swat them away like flies if they irritate me. But they will still cling to my outer realm just to stay connected to success.

Leeches aren't allowed. I can see them coming from a mile away. I stay away from the murky waters that hide these pests. I am talking drugs. Bad drugs. Mind-clouding distractions that let the lower class of life suck the living blood out of you. I am too good to wade in those waters. I don't have time for self-indulgent mindlessness. I have parts of the world yet to seek, yet to conquer.

Onward and upward.

The mirror is my friend. 100% me and dang good if I have to admit. The ladies swoon. I have to sort the true from the just hungry. It is a burden. Attention can be distracting. I need all my faculties to reach my next summit. This constant winning is almost getting boring. What is next?

I am slightly concerned with a somewhat increasing tendency to drop things. With everyone so anxious to get a taste of my achievements, this little flaw of suddenly having my hand release what it is holding for no apparent reason, could be a concern. Most times this happens in my seldom occurrence of being alone.

I think I can hide this. Maybe increase my exercise regimen. Or possibly eat more avocados. One of those "beneath me" books declared that this green fat fruit would be good for my muscle retention. At least that is what one of my groupies said. I think I could handle a daily dose of guacamole. Especially if it was made from the direction of one of my great friends, Juan. He is good for my mental health at all times, and knows how to make the perfect green mush delight. Can't wait to see Juan again someday.

For now, I will stick to using mugs with handles. That way with any semblance of involuntary release from my hands, if held properly, the mug will sit there. Another friend showed me that secret. I am positive that Arthur doesn't have Viking blood in him, but he does know how to grasp a mug through the handle (not grasp the handle itself) so if your hand opens, the mug still hangs on your fingers. My friend can get downright sloshed at times. He is a professional at not dropping his mug.

So, problem solved. Let's move on. NO. Let's move UP............

3

Where to Start (Alan)

If you need wisdom, ask our generous God, and he will give it to you. He will not rebuke you for asking.

James 1:5 NLT

So, I'm committed to recording all that remains in my two thirds of a brain before any of the remaining cells decide to go camping on their own. In processing what is missing and what stories I need to record, I took a break long enough to seek some multivitamins and ashwagandha root powder. If I can't get those deserting little bastard brain cells back, I can at least bribe the remaining ones to stay.

How or where will I even begin? What story is worth telling? Do I share stories of sexual exploits? Do I review all the mistakes I have made throughout my life that have kept me mediocre at best? Should I give advice to others about what road not to travel? Where can I hang my hat in this Godforsaken world that people might continue to remember the name of Alan H. Mers for eternity?

Damn, looking at it from that point of view, I don't think I have anything to brag about. I'd better stick to humor, or love. One of those items will surely capture an audience. If not, at least I can entertain myself until this disappearing act of a brain completely abandons me.

I would pray for wisdom. I do pray for wisdom. I think I pray for wisdom when I remember to pray for wisdom. I want to pray more. I strongly believe in the power of prayer. The problem is that echo

I talked about from those disappearing cells has left a neighbor in the area called distraction. Knee deep in prayer, and I find myself thinking about which contractor is going to let me down this week. This drags on for like, ever. Then, a twinkling spark awakens my echo long enough to pull me back into conversation with my Lord. He's good stuff. I can't believe God didn't put me down long ago. I have failed so often. What did………… damn, can't remember his name……………… Manny……… say the other day?? What was I talking about?

Sorry about the detour. Now you are catching a glimpse of the void in my skull that is kicking my ass. Straight ahead and with assured direction is no longer in my repertoire. Please be patient with my story. I believe it is a good one. Maybe the best parts will sit on repeat. Like an old song that stays in your thoughts for the whole day. "Joy to the world. All the boys and girls now. Joy to the fishes in the deep blue sea. Joy to you and me"……………………………

4

THE TRUTH (Larry)

"And you will know the truth and the truth will set you free."
John 8:32 NLT

I probably should not have been so hard on the "self-help" book genre. But it sticks in my craw. On my way to success, I was sidetracked a few times by people saying they wanted to help me. Telling me they could improve my life. Feeding me the line of bull that claimed a fast track to success. I took the bait. Only to find that their real success was the ability to empty my billfold and make me feel good about it.

The truth is, you must find your own path. Yes, listen to others and grasp what advice you might need. But take the free advice. Don't pay someone to "give" you something. Figure it out on your own and you will succeed to degrees that shadow the "look at me here on this stage with a mic clamped to my head playing on your emotions while I pick your pocket."

I shouldn't just pick on the Carthage Buckleys of this world. There are Evangelical-type preachers who can play this game quite well too. "Give, give, GIVE, and success will be yours. God wants you to succeed. God wants to give you abundance. The only way to open that cornucopia of wealth is to give my Church the money first. I am a steward from God. Trust me to give a portion to the needy when I stop by in my private jet to refuel in a Third World Country."

The first preacher who really grabbed my attention was Oral Roberts, when I was about 14 years old. He was the type of preacher who built your trust, made you feel forgiven, told you the many things God had said directly to him, and had an amazing private university that sported a rather successful basketball team. The perfect combination of outward sincerity and flashy success that made any lower-class citizen feel like there might be a path of gold for them, and that captured a young mind like mine that had a hunger for the charms of wealth.

I had been in trouble at school for various things. Stealing, (we called it ripping off, seemed more justified when leaving the local gas station that peddled mountains of candy). Buy one item, while your pockets just happen to have a couple more things. Then, walking back to school from this quest, comparing our stash for the day. Even stopping in the old abandoned IGA to hit on a cigarillo one of us had ripped off a box of. We were the COOL kids. Yeah, that was brilliant.

Another was destruction of school property. That wasn't deliberate. It was more like the brass weights we were using for some kind of science thing made a really cool sound and dimple in the floor when you dropped them from an accidental height. Yeah, I wanted to fit in. Highwater pants and all. If others thought I was part of the group, maybe they would ignore the five inches I grew in three months, exposing my socks at an unnatural level for a teenage boy in the '70s. I didn't even know it was a problem until some upperclassman from the high school right behind us decided it was time to ridicule a junior high student to make himself look better. Can I blame all my stupid early teen idiosyncrasies on this butt cheese?

Back to O.R.... I had dug a rather deep hole for myself. I had amazing parents who taught me right from wrong. I was easily traipsing down the path of wrong. I felt guilty. There was only one way out. I gave myself to Jesus. I started reading my Bible. I sent Oral Roberts every dollar I had to my name. He would fix it. He was my channel to God and forgiveness. I might even go play basketball for his university someday. I could do this straight and narrow thing.

What did I get? A form letter "Thank you" for my contribution and an assurance that if I would commit to regular giving to that particular ministry, all my sins would be forgiven, and I could be a pillar of God from that day forward. I stayed with that fishhook for a short period. Then, at fourteen, with a world of other priorities combined with a lack of funds, I moved on.

The truth of the matter. God and I could do just fine without Oral Roberts. Oral Roberts could do just fine without my money. I grew up a little that day..........

5

Going Backward (Alan)

*But they did not listen or pay attention; instead, they followed
the stubborn inclinations of their evil hearts.
They went backward and not forward.*
Jeremiah 7:24 NIV

Apparently, I have been rattling on and have not started the story I committed to. I do have some excuses. First, I don't have a clue how to get started. It seems when I tell a story, people tend to get that glazed-over look in their eyes. They check out. My story is using the valuable oxygen that apparently the distracted asshole needs for better things.

How do I engage you long enough to learn my tale without losing you to better entertainment? More importantly, how do I stay focused long enough to even compile words of interest? I think my vitamins are helping. I seem to have more than just dark, vitamin-smelling piss. I think I can pull this off.

Backward is the direction I will take. Start from now and work my story in reverse. Research has shown that my egg head will progressively scramble more and more. Thus, if I work in reverse, I might grasp some of the peak of my life before I revert to a brain that has less function than a newborn. Old to young. Sounds like a plan.

My back is starting to hurt from sitting here writing this dribble. I used to have a strong back. My core was undefeated in Indian leg wrestling. Now things hurt. Damn this aging process. Why haven't the cells that signal pain left, instead of the ones that possess wit and charm I can share with you, my friend? Is bitching and complaining my new strength? Maybe cynicism sells. Plenty of gray-haired old farts who have massive amounts of negative to share on social media. Some of it is quite amusing. Most, annoying. They are always picking on one tree that might be out of place in a beautiful forest. *To hell with nature, let's cut this tree down and dispose of it. Probably won't even make good sawdust. Who cares what this tree has seen. Who gives a rat's ass if it was at one time the birds' favorite tree to roost, nest, and raise babies in. I don't like it. Time to destroy. Will it make a sound when it falls if no one is there to hear it? Stupid tree.*

I'm back. Where did I go? Are all the distractions of life interfering with my promised story? Does this damn cell phone and computer control my thought process? Am I rambling? If I tell my story backward, do I start with what happened yesterday? Maybe what happened a minute ago? Do I have time to count the minutes? Maybe we should back up on a yearly pace. Damn, another message I better respond to.

It was within the last two years that I noticed the ringing echo of the lost portion of my brain. I was previously clear-minded and focused. Except when my eyes caught a beautiful woman, or any woman for that matter. Time to look. Secretly stare. Admire what could be in my grasp. Enjoy the fruits the good Lord put into this world. Why hold back. I have a messed-up history anyway. What the hell, go for it. Another conquest.

Now you know my weakness. My fault. My one crippling leg that has ruined everything I ever tried to build. My reputation chases me down quickly. I have sacrificed more of life's blessings just for a moment of pleasure. I don't want to be this way. I never have. I want to hold to the straight and narrow. I hunger for trust. I have been given another chance again and again. Only to falter, tremendously. Damnit, lust, I hate you.

Can I search backward far enough to find where this fricken black ball of heaviness and chain was clamped on to me? I know I have taken hammer and chisel and hacksaw and cutting disc and torch to continually remove this menace. Then along comes the opposite sex and I am trapped once again. I am good at fixing things. Why can't I fix this?

It is almost funny when you think about your road of life. There are ups and downs, curves and twists, but ultimately you strive to continuously climb the ladder. Whether the climb is to success, to find peace, or to grab your share of happiness, it is always an uphill battle. You continue to keep going up and once in a while get knocked down. That, my friend, is life. Some give up and stay down. Can you recall anyone like that?

Most of us, though, continue to climb. Up and up. Maybe plateau for a while, taking a break to raise a family or build a business. Sooner or later we start climbing again. Always something to achieve.

Not me. Not for a shameful number of years. I climbed. I fought. I attained some respect. My bank account became stable. I bought toys. Really badass toys. Living the dream I've been told. Then, no matter how high I climbed, I decided one day to jump off. Not just a little leap to start on the next mountain. More like skydiving into the pits of hell. All without a parachute. Put me out of my misery. I just f'd up again. Yay me.

Maybe those hard landings at the bottom are what caused so many brain cells to leave...............

6

S & N (Larry)

I must go on boasting. Although there is nothing to be gained,
I will go on to visions and revelations from the Lord.

2 Corinthians 12:1 NIV

So now I am on the straight and narrow. This kid recovered from idiocy and achieved some solid recognition and success within the next few years. Larry G. Stecklin (LG) had some achievements in his youth. Good grades in school were easy. Nothing less than valedictorian. I was class president throughout high school, first team All-State football and basketball, president of National Honor Society, winner of national Voice of Democracy, scholarships coming out from all directions. God was truly blessing me. Tall and handsome. Missed on the dark part. A little too much German heritage. But the blue eyes were a plus.

What other accomplishments do you want to hear about? Maybe I should bring up my appointment to the Coast Guard Academy? That was the BOSS. I originally wanted to go to the Air Force because flying jets would be AWESOME. But I then discovered two things. One, you needed a Congressional appointment to even be considered. And two, my sitting height was above the requirements to fit in a fighter jet.

The Coast Guard Academy. New London, Connecticut. Boot camp in the summer, then sail a ship to Europe as a rite of passage. Play some basketball. Their coach was calling me every week to encourage my commitment. Life was good. I had already started to grab the world. An officer and a gentleman I would be. And fly helicopters. Oh yeah!!

A few loose ends to tie up with high school and my future was starting. No handouts of scholarships and grants for me. My higher education was to be earned. Serve my country and graduate a leader. Yes, that was a perfect fit. Maybe I owed more to Oral Roberts than I thought.

Life was good. I am good. Hope you realize that by now. Dang, my fingers want to get sloppy on this keyboarrrrd. How am I supposed to brag about all my accomplishments if I can't even type at the pace of my success? Maybe I will revert to hiring a typist who will stay quiet and simply record my greatness. God help me if this is leading to something disabling. I have life yet to live to its fullest. Maybe I will take a break and go to Walmart just to look at all the normal people who can't afford my Neiman Marcus lifestyle.

I suppose I could go see a doctor and demand answers. Yes, even doctors will bend to my superiority. Perfection I have attained. If there is a fault, it can be repaired. I demand nothing less than the best. Maybe this possible typist makes a superior cup of coffee as well...........................

7

MA (MayAnn)

This is what the Lord says: "Stand at the crossroads and look; ask
for the ancient paths, ask where the good way is, and
walk in it, and you will find rest for your souls."

Jeremiah 6:16 NIV

MayAnn was at a crossroads. Not just your normal run-of-the-mill crossroads. But one that would forever shape her life and the lives of two precious blessings inside. Leaving the pediatrician's office after the first ultrasound was the heaviest burden MayAnn had ever carried. At six weeks, her babies' heartbeats were strong as ever. Yes, two heartbeats. Vibrant, strong, alive. God's gift to her. Surprise!!

You could say that MayAnn was born on the wrong side of the tracks. But truthfully, in her rural town of 1250+ (that plus is important), the tracks were at the top of the hill overlooking the town.

Even the name didn't achieve a whole lot. Trail City. Not named after someone important or some memorable event. Just a reference to the Ogallala Trail that at one time passed through. My gosh, even the trail had a name/destination of importance. Trail City was a pass-through. Always had been, always would be.

MayAnn had some pretty going on. Probably more of an inner beauty that only came out in her genuine smile. Most definitely, if she had been growing up now, her selfies would have people looking twice. That is, with a pose that didn't accentuate her German nose, or the crook in it from having to start wearing glasses at age two. Pretty was MayAnn.

School was so-so for MayAnn. She had intelligence and humor. This was sadly masked by her being needed at home to help raise her younger siblings. And, amplified even more by having to protect her next in line brother from the beatings arising from a drunk father.

Not once did MayAnn complain of her hardships. Yes, she occasionally longed for nicer, newer clothes that would help her fit in with the My Shit Don't Stink girls' club. But MayAnn had one really, really close friend—Peggy. That was enough.

Peggy didn't help MayAnn carry her books as they walked to school. Peggy did help shoulder the burden that MayAnn carried in her heart. The burden of making sure her four brothers and one sister didn't have to fear their home. MayAnn was the rock. The warm heart to snuggle up to. The protection from shouting and violence that came with an empty bottle tossed at the front door. Peggy was her support group.

Peggy was MayAnn's avid fan of a somewhat hidden artistic talent. MayAnn's first brother had it too. But because of the beatings, his was hidden even deeper. MayAnn would express hers with doodles and drawings when her mind needed to escape the real world of her home.

Every time her grade school class had some type of art project with colored paper and glue and whatever the teacher could rob from the craft supply budget, MayAnn's would always be a cut above the rest of the twenty-four kids in her small class. Most people didn't notice. The adults viewing were only admiring their own kid's creativity. Peggy always noticed though. And would brag to anyone who would listen. "Look, my best friend did this. Isn't it beautiful!!?"

The problem now was, Peggy wasn't here at this crossroads to help MayAnn. Her best friend. The true confidante. Her support had left. Peggy could almost be blamed for these twins. Almost. If MayAnn leaned toward the liberal side of the city of Chicago she was now in, she could justify that the whole thing was someone else's fault. But who could ever blame Peggy?

There is always "the" summer after graduation. It could probably be considered a crossroads of sorts itself. The summer when some graduates leave for a military awakening. Others work hard to save money to live on that first year of college. Some go straight to work in a vocation that will pay well now, and who cares if it is depleted in the future. New car, here we come.

Then there is the young man who graduated. Smart, ambitious, solid future using his brain. Biggest accomplishment so far, perfect attendance at school, K – 12 grades. That would be approximately 12,976 hours of continuous school participation. That is equal to 1,622 days of work on an eight-hour shift. Or 324 work weeks. Or 6.62 years of labor. Continuously. That is impressive. A plaque on the wall at the high school. Except that plaque also remembers his tragic accident that summer. Motorcycle, Wheat Harvest Truck, combination leading to a finality. Sad.

Peggy became one of that type of statistic, too. Hayride, fall, headfirst, done, terrible, sad.

It was the turning point in MayAnn's decision to head to Chicago. She couldn't decide the best route to take pursuing a career as an artist. Thanks to Peggy's continuous prompting, MayAnn knew she needed to do something. Should she start timidly at the local community college, where the professor only had the credentials of "went out and tried but failed?" Or, should she go straight to the Windy City and see what happened? Art school, job in a studio, artistic design company, oh so many options.

With the tragic death of her best friend, the push came naturally. Peggy had been promoting the Chicago idea for years. They dreamt of the possibilities. Peggy painted a picture of success in MayAnn's mind. Her mind said yes. Her pocketbook had another voice.

Take your tuition scholarship offer from the community college. Work part-time at JCPenney or Mac's Drive-In. Stay in the co-ed dorm. Or maybe ride share/commute daily from home. That way she could still protect her brothers and sister from the nightmare. They were all old enough now to either handle themselves or know where to safely hide. Dad finally had a steady job. Maybe this new job would last longer than the alcohol urge.

With Peggy's tragic death, all doubt was erased. You only live once. Timid and perfect attendance got you nowhere if your time was up. Better give it a shot now. Only the good die young. MayAnn was ready to hit the road. Didn't quite see the crossroad coming……………………………………………

8

ANA (Alan)

It bursts forth like a radiant bridegroom after his wedding.
It rejoices like a great athlete eager to run the race.

Psalms 19:5 NLT

Wife number 2 has been my greatest accomplishment. Maybe I shouldn't say accomplishment. Rather, the word blessing would be more fitting. I didn't "earn" Ana; she walked up to me like a gift. Neither one of us had known the other until her task of supplying the office area with its morning coffee met up with my new position in a foreign country sitting at the only semblance of a desk available, which also served as the break table. Most important to my future, it was the table that held the coffee. It was desk size and desk height.

Ana came walking in that first morning. Saw me sitting at her task completion destination. Hesitated. Thought. Decided. Promptly walked up to my desk/table, set the coffee dispenser down, gave me a timid smile, mainly because I was like, staring. Turned around and walked out with a, "This was strange, an Americano at the table, but I have work to do" walk. Of course, I watched that walk all the way to the staircase and down until it disappeared.

I really can't recall what I saw in Ana's first walk away. She later admitted that she knew I was checking out her butt. Truthfully, the first go round, I was still seeing nothing except the beautiful smile that exploded from her eyes as it was launched from her heart. Even if it was timid and with fear, it captured me, tied me up, and forever stole my heart.

From that day forward, Ana brought coffee to my table and sunshine to my day. I soon found the kitchen that Ana made the coffee in, and continually sought excuses to pass by that kitchen's window and wave. Sometimes the window was closed and dark. I waved anyway. Other times it was open, and her friend was busy making the coffee. I kinda waved. Then there were the times Ana was at the window. I waited till she saw me. I gave my "stupid boy" smile and waved like Forrest Gump. Ana waved back and captured even more of my world.

It was a true love that most people never find. Or they think they find it, and for one reason or another ignore/avoid. I know I had been searching for fifty-plus years. I had also been consistently destroying any semblance of a decent relationship in my past. I believe I already shared the reasoning with you. I am flawed. I want to fix. God help this sorry sack of a man who has several times been told to go rot in Hell. I was starting to believe that is where I belonged. If you are going to continually jump into the pit, might as well stay there. Save everyone the trouble.

There was still a semblance of a good side left. I have a huge heart. My one third disappearing brain would have been a concern, but my heart was a full 100%. And Ana took it to a whole other level with that first smile. I now believe I was given one last chance to get it right. God help me if I dive off this cliff. No, God will probably say goodbye. I crossed the last line. My brain at the time, still an estimated seven eighths or better, told me don't f$%k this up.

There was the small problem of a definite language barrier between Ana and me. I quickly learned "Bom Dia"(Good Morning). Followed by the addition of "Tudo Bem" (How are you?). Probably sounded rather lame with my Midwest Americano drawl. It did bring out that much-sought-after smile from Ana, though. That was my daily goal. If Ana had a day off, my heart was sad and silent for that day. The next wave and smile or coffee delivery from my Love erased any memory of negative. I was back in the clouds.

Wonderful, billowy, carrying me like pillow clouds. Kind of stupid for a middle-aged man with faults, but it was still there. Good stuff.

My pursuit was relentless. One of Ana's first questions to me was, "Por que grande bigode?" Or translated, "Why the large mustache?" I had no excuse. My biker/cowboy reputation I was trying to maintain could take a flying hike. Ana didn't like it. Five minutes later it was gone. Period. End of story. If I was ever going to get the chance to kiss those inviting lips of Ana's, it would most definitely be without my bigode. Goodbye, mustache. Hello, Ana!

The courtship was wonderful, confusing, quiet, amazing, and colorful. Our conversations consisted of passing our cell phones back and forth with sentences via Google Translate. Sometimes that didn't quite work as words were confused, and neither one of us could read the other language enough to correct. In a man's world, this was fine. When her hand touched mine, she laid her head on my shoulders, or any form of physical touch, there were no words necessary. I could feel her love. She could read mine. Oh man, is connection without complicated words amazing. We still go to that space to this day. It is still at the level of pure joy and climbing. I will not jump.

Should I share with Ana about the cells in my brain that are leaving on a jet plane? Or do I spare her the misery and complications of this disease that will slowly take me away? Where in the hell did it come from? Why me? Why now? Oh God, please give me a lifetime back with this amazing woman you blessed me with.

Is this my punishment for all the hurt I have caused to others? Is this my form of "What goes around comes around?" Yes, I am over halfway past my average life expectancy. But does Ana need to suffer from my previous life's mistakes? I can't let the love of my life share this pain. Of course, at the rate of my current brain depletion, soon I will no longer even realize what is happening. Somebody make it STOP!!

Instead of focusing on the out of nowhere circumstance of a disease, I decided to move on with making Ana the center of my world. She wanted marriage. We married twice. One and a half years apart. First, a civil ceremony to declare commitment and help with Immigration. The other in the Catholic Church so Ana could once again take the Holy Sacraments. Both weddings made me cry. Both made wonderful memories. Both ceremonies involved her beautiful daughters, humorous and going somewhere son, and her mother. My sister even bought a plane ticket and paid for a Visa to attend the second wedding. That was extra special. We danced, a lot. They welcomed her into their family, too. Somewhere in our complicated and busy lives in the US, we have lost sight of family and the value of such. It is sad. I was not. My tears were from a joy I hadn't realized since the birth of my sons from my first marriage.

Both receptions had limitless food, a bottomless supply of beer and wine, and an extended family of loved ones and friends who welcomed me with open arms even before the beer was opened. The first civil reception struggled with song and dance. I had drawn the line on what we would spend, and the DJ dropped out. I hoped one of the girls' good friends would supply music via pin drive and music equipment, but it didn't quite come to fruition. Instead, we had like ten songs that played over and over and we danced a little, but not in the true Brazilian/Paraguayan style. I knew better. Cheapskate anyway. Guests left early, and we sat and looked at each other. A lot of beer was left over. That should never happen. The caterers "stole" the extra food. Still, my beautiful Ana was by my side. Who gives a damn about the details.

The Church wedding was a different story. Same friends invited. Same family. My sister the special guest. New adventure and eye opener for her. The priest was amazing. He was probably the shortest padre I have ever known. His heart made up the difference. Sole Español did he speak. I could actually understand about half of everything he said. To the other half I just smiled and nodded. God was with him.

The wedding was special. All the women were breathtakingly beautiful and adorned as only an all-day Latina-based hair, makeup, and clothes requirement could produce. The men were dapper but tranquilo, and thirsty for the cold beer later. Ana was on-time. A rarity for any event in South America. Happiness abounded. Tears of joy were shed. A story of our love and its growth was shared. More tears. Amen.

We had a DJ this time. The reception was AWESOME.

Oh, how I love Ana...........................

9

9 LIVES (Larry)

From my youth I have suffered and been close to death;
I have borne your terrors and am in despair.

Psalms 88:15 NIV

If a cat has nine lives, then I must have inherited this trait from some cat, somewhere. Maybe two cats. I have tickled death multiple times in my life. So close on a couple of occasions, I had left my body and was looking down. No big deal. The feeling of that experience gives me confidence that there is an AWESOME beyond. Which one should I share? Maybe a highlight of them all? You should sit in my presence and listen for hours if necessary. Maybe you could gain a sliver of my greatness and feed for a while.

My first brush with the afterlife came at the age of two and a half or so. Probably pushing four, but mom tells it differently. Makes for a better story. Here you go. Hold on.

As far back as I can possibly remember, so, maybe it was in the two plus range, I loved to climb. Anything and everything. The mission was going UP. That has carried through my life. I loved to climb trees. We happened to have some of the best climbing trees in the world, or at least in our south windbreak. Simple pine trees that weren't native to our area, but carefully planted for some reason by my thoughtful ancestors. Maybe my great grandfather had climbed pine trees as a kid. I don't know, but there they were.

What made pine trees so appealing was the branches close enough to the ground that were big, strong, and perfect for that first step up into the tree world. The spacing of the branches enabled an almost ladder-type ascent to the top. Only one's weight and nerve determined how high you could go. And, of course, the height of the tree. At two years old (who cares exact age, remember, the story?) I could easily make it to within five feet of the top. My favorite tree then had me about twenty-five feet high. Awesome.

I was so very proud of my accomplishment, I needed to share. I hollered "Mom"......"mom"....."MOM" until she finally came out to see me. In a typical motherly reaction of panic and fear, Mom's response was, "You get down from there!!" Enough said, mom was the boss. Mom had a wooden spoon. I must oblige. I let go.

Branch to branch, to every ladder step branch, I bounced to the bottom. Mom's description was more like tumbled/cartwheeled. Maybe a Plinko-type scenario. I actually remember bits and pieces. Was kinda fun. I wasn't scared. I made it to the bottom. And abruptly landed on my butt after the last branch. My mom's stomach was a knot of fear slamming into her eyes. Silence.

I got up. Brushed myself off. Reviewed the massive amount of pine sap on my clothes and in my hair. And simply said, "I don't do dat again." End of story. Still climbed trees. Just never made that mistake of asking mom to come see me as I played rocket ship and made the pine tree sway in all directions at an amazing amount of distance. At least in my little astronaut mind.

My occasional visiting friend, Will, had his favorite tree too. It was shorter and had a weird crook at the top. I think it was hit by lightning at one time. It enabled him, twice as big as me (until I was like fifteen), to sit on the very top of his tree. It was awesome. My rocket was taller and better, but he could sit on top of his. This didn't happen very often. Will had better things to do. Like hold pretend track meets and run and triple jump. Or rake hay. Oh, the hours Will as the oldest kid in his family had to work. I felt for him as I swayed in my tree and watched him sweat from a perched distance. I never disrespected his tree, though. That was Will's tree reserved for him. I wished he could join me soon.

On to other adventures and death-defying acts……….. Hard to think back. Lots of cramps in my legs lately. Too many bounces on the tree branches? What is happening, God?...................................

10

The Decision (MayAnn)

You who answer prayer, to you all people will come.
Psalms 65:2 NIV

Somewhere in the storyline of moving to Chicago and getting devoured by the ways of the city, MayAnn became pregnant. Not a time to point fingers or say I told you so. Not a time to judge MayAnn. This is life. This is the way we are made. Men live to conquer and procreate. Women live to nest and produce. It is nature. God did this. MayAnn evolved to this point. The Crossroads.

"Now what" was constantly beating inside MayAnn's head. "Now what" was also racing in her heart. The doctor said twins. Not just one possible interruption of her dreams but two. Double the responsibility. Twice the burden. "My God, I spent my whole life raising my brothers and sisters and now face this?" MayAnn thought.

Another "friend," Windy City type, suggested one option. The sweet-talking sperm donor had already left to pursue other vulnerable females. No help there and never would be. Why try and waste words. POS anyway. MayAnn was on her own.

The friend's option was unthinkable. It had some self-centered arguments, but was morally impossible for MayAnn. She was not built that way. The thought sickened her to no end. Trash-can that suggestion. Never ever, never, trash-can her babies.

What could she do? A starving artist was she. No question about that. Most days she was lucky to have a roof over her head. Some days, food did not pass by her mouth. Life was tough. There were some promises of an art career. But one of those promises had skipped life and the rent payments long enough to disappear and leave her pregnant.

There were women's shelters. There was the food bank. There was welfare. In MayAnn's time, these were not the norm. They were just budding possibilities to an ever-growing problem. The early sixties still had women married, in the kitchen, raising a family, subservient to their man. You know, the good stuff.

MayAnn could find none of the good stuff. No way could she return home to small town America as a pregnant failure. No way could she survive the streets of Chicago as a pregnant wannabe. Where was the answer?

MayAnn could join the ever-growing female head of household statistic of...poor. Because of child-rearing duties and lack of childcare, women could not work outside the home. So, a short-term answer of a decent job that paid enough for food and rent would eventually lead to back on the street as her pregnancy was revealed and empathy was nonexistent.

Sooner or later, she would be an outcast. This was the truth. This was not the life for twins. MayAnn was smart enough to know her predicament, but innocent enough to think this was simply a bad dream. Each day without a decision led to a day closer to the door opening the wrong way and dumping her into abandonment.

It was time to pray. MayAnn's mother had taught her that. When times were tough, when dad came home drunk and started the beatings, the only thing left was to hide and pray. This time, though, hiding was the last thing she could do. A baby, especially twins would not be hidden for long. Maybe a church could help.

And so, MayAnn made her first smart decision since Peggy had died. MayAnn went to church. A big, old, city church. Before the time of megachurches. A neighborhood church supported by the people next door. Open to all. God's church without judgment.

Well, at least without judgment from the clergy and a few people who actually lived Jesus's teachings.

The oversized and heavy doors made you recognize the significance of the step you were about to take. Any doubts were removed with the effort it took to pull the damn door open. Can we say damn and talk about a church at the same time? We are still outside the church, should be fine.

MayAnn went in. A whisper of a child compared to those doors. An echoing of footsteps as her timid self approached the altar, 5000 pews and a mile away. Click, click, click. Surprised that bats didn't come out of the belfry, her determination overcoming fear. God beckoning. Jesus looking down from the cross saying, "I did this for you, my child." A heavy weight almost lifting. The twins moved for the first time. An awakening of the soul to happen. Then Tex walked in..............................

11

Children (Alan)

Behold, children are a gift of the Lord,
the fruit of the womb is a reward.

Psalms 127:3 NASB

Ana wants a child. I am too long in the tooth for this. If we have a child now, my social security plan of sitting under a shade tree and drinking Terere for my remaining days of Tranquilo would be gone. I've already raised a family. I have a butt load of grandkids. I want to enjoy the fruit of my labors, not the fruit of my loins. A child now would push me past my average life expectancy. And that average is elevated due to medical technology that can only extend life. Not a cure, but a treatment to eke out a few more years of mostly pain and loneliness.

This was not part of my Master Plan. The reason I had chosen to retire and die in a third world country was just that. If you get really sick and have sudden emergency problems, chances are, you will die. That is OK. Why hang around as a financial burden to your family just so they feel obligated to visit you on the holidays and maybe your birthday? Life is good. Live it. Get on with living or get busy dying. What movie did that come from? Little fact must have left with the One Third group of abandoning ship brain cells. Bastards.

Having a baby was a new twist to an ever-changing life. I would have to start trying harder. I would have to think about my health. I would need to make life insurance plans. I would have to start praying to God that I could make it as a father for at least another eighteen years. Damn, what is this woman asking of me?

I told you that Ana was my life and adoration, right? Still holds true. I would do anything for my beautiful wife. I tell her that every day. Guess I'd better live up to that statement. Ana wants a baby to profess our love for each other. Ana wants to share a joy that only a mother and father truly in love can share. Then that is what Ana will get. Besides, the quest of making the baby is, well, my secret.

We can skip forward a ways now. Ana is blossoming with child. Pregnancy looks good on Ana. A certain glow. Not just between a mom and her unborn. Oh, did I tell you it would be twins? Don't have a clue where that gene came from. Neither the family I was born into nor Ana's family has a history of twins. Maybe the love we shared was so strong it could only be expressed by doubling? Good thought anyway.

I do know I am overjoyed. My depleting brain has been put on hold. This father must provide. Must clean up the loose ends of unnecessary big boy toys and crap that aren't important to my daughters' security. Yay, girls. It is exciting, but scary for a dad. Boys are easy. I have two amazing sons. Girls. Time to buy a new shotgun. Hell yeah!! I get to buy two.............................

12

1 LIFE (Larry)

*But as I looked at everything I had worked so hard to accomplish,
it was all so meaningless—like chasing the wind. There was
nothing really worthwhile anywhere.*

Ecclesiastes 2:11 NLT

In between the bouncing from the pine tree and my next
tales of near death is a whole lot of everything. A wise man
(probably me) once said, "You will never know the value of
a moment until it becomes a memory. Well, let me tell you a little
secret, I have moments. From awesome, death-defying bicycle and
motorcycle wrecks to falling great distances, to jumping out of a
tree with a bedsheet as a parachute. Being buried alive, once with
rocks, another time with snow, close to drowning, burned badly, on
my wrist/hand (face still perfect), frostbite, sunstroke, smothered,
knocked out with H2S. Ran over by a truck, four broken ribs, one
broken ankle, one broken finger. I have memories. Never had
stitches.

It really is amazing that I am here. Lucky for you, my greatness still
exists. You should be in awe. How many memories do I pluck out
of this awesome tale of a life to share with you?

There aren't too many "bucket list" items set in front of me that
I wouldn't kick over with a better tale. Skydive, done it. With
my jumpmaster scared that I could easily end his life somewhere
between exiting the plane and landing on the ground. Side note, I
landed and carried him strapped to me, back to the station. I believe
I gathered my chute with him papoosed on my back.

Bungee jump, done it. Headfirst, ankles strapped, cowboy hat on. I didn't panic like some idiots and try to grab the cord on my first spring back up. Instead, I reached my hat out and tickled the air mat. Kind of like a bull rider flagging the bull after he passed the eight seconds. Yeah, rode bulls too. Want my moments to keep going?

Jet skied, water skied, slalom skied (even mastered coming out of the water on one ski, barefoot skied, snow skied, cross country skied, snowboarded, snow sledded, snow inner tubed (down the side of a dam), car hood pulled by a jeep sledded, flat sled, runner sled, round sled, snow shovel sled, ice hockey, ice skated, roller skated, inline skated, I am getting bored. Played competitive baseball, football, basketball (college level) track and field, bowling, golf and golf and a little more golf. Car mechanic, motorcycle mechanic, boat mechanic, carpenter, welder, bricklayer, truck driver, bus driver, basketball coach, football coach (loved it). Member of several boards, chairman of boards, president of three boards, COO, CEO, broom pusher, painter, pumped gas, roughneck, roustabout, pumper, driller, pilot, boat captain, snorkel and scuba dive, military veteran. On and on.

I suppose it would be easier to list the things I haven't done rather than enlighten you with my never-ending list of feats. Haven't traveled to the moon, but working on a round trip to the Space Station.

At least in space the lack of gravity might aid in my ever-increasing muscle cramps and failures. I really should go see a doctor. Doctor is one thing I haven't done. I was close as a med aide, nurse's aide, PT aide, vet assistant, rancher and farmhand, bull rider, calf roper, team roper, horse breaker, brander, castrater, vaccinator, and all that fun stuff. (Please note, the branding, castrating, and vaccinating were while being a cowboy and not a medical aide.)

Maybe it is a good thing I have so many accomplishments. My body seems to be resisting any new adventures. Could be the first time in my life I am scared......

13

Tex (MayAnn)

*Fight the good fight of faith; take hold of the eternal life to which
you were called, and you made the good confession
in the presence of many witnesses.*

1 Timothy 6:12 NASB

When MayAnn walked into the enormous, aged, and beautiful old city church, the last thing she expected was this short, wide, bowlegged, cowboy of a preacher. She could just picture the huge Stetson propped on his balding head when he was outside. MayAnn did appreciate his respect for God's house in not wearing the hat indoors. She also appreciated the fact that if that hat had been on his head right now, he would have given the politest tip of that hat as he said, "Howdy ma'am and welcome home."

"My name is Tex, what can God and I do for you today?" said the pastor with the awesome pair of Leddy boots. MayAnn was a long ways from Fort Worth, but she could pick out the fine craftsmanship. She would also bet they had been handcrafted as a perfect fit for Tex's feet. If only she could afford such luxury.

There was something quite warming and welcoming surrounding Tex. MayAnn instantly let go of all inhibitions related to her situation. This cowboy man of God would help. His broad shoulders, though low to the ground, could hold the weight she was ready to unload.

"Pastor," said MayAnn, "I have a problem beyond my abilities. I need guidance. No. I need help." The preconceived response at this point would be, "What can I do for you, my child?" But not Preacher Tex. His reply of, "Ma'am, spit it out" was more relaxing than any rehearsed typical preacher comeback. Oh, how could his Windy City parishioners ever accept such a down-home country boy?

Tears and sobs, bent shoulders and shudders accumulated as MayAnn spilled the truth. "Oh pastor, I am pregnant the sperm donor fled I have no money how can I work and support twins when I can barely help myself I know these are God's precious children and there is a reason for all of this but I am lost and don't know what to do I am ashamed of the hole I have dug myself into and can't find a way out so I came to my last resort this humongous church and pray that someone can fix all these problems and............"

Tex pulled MayAnn into his massive and most gentle arms. "Slow down, little lady," he said as he absorbed her emotions. "God has a plan. Let's start by offering this burden up to Him. Then, with God's guidance we will fix this."

MayAnn could tell this was real. Not surreal. Real. Tex was a gift from God. Tex was God's servant and now MayAnn's confidant. The world might be a decent place after all. It sure felt secure right here. "Can you really help me?" was about all MayAnn had left.

"Truthfully, young lady, I can't help you in the least. But God can help us both."

(Praying)..

"Now, first things first, what is your name?"

"MayAnn, pastor."

"Well, MayAnn, it will be easier for both of us if you simply call me Tex. Formalities are for those with something to hide. You and I are open to each other and now to God. Are you ready for this new journey?"

"I have no choice, Pas..... Tex. Thank you for listening, thank you for praying, now what? Those are sure some awesome boots."

"Yeah, MayAnn, God's blessings to me are a good fitting pair of boots, a full belly, (probably too full at times), and the ability to do His work. And today His blessing is bringing you into this House.

"Now, open your heart. Your brain helped you get into this situation, so let's set it to the side for now. Decisions from the heart are everlasting. People try to blame their problems on their heart, but most problems come from their crotch, or stomach, or mouth. Nothing to blame on the heart. That is where God sits. Even when we ignore Him. He is there right now in your heart, MayAnn. Can you feel Him?"

"I believe so, Tex," MayAnn released. "I can feel a warmth and comfort that has been silent for so many years. Why did I ever walk away from something so strong? So.........................."

"Hard to put into words, God's love from your heart, isn't it," soothed Tex.

"I feel better in my heart. And my burden feels lifted. But I still have these two babies growing inside me. What am I to do, Tex? The last of my money went to pay the doctor to make sure these gifts were doing OK. I am at the mercy of this city, my rent is due, my cupboards are down to a box of Kraft Mac and Cheese but no milk or butter to mix in, I have an extra pack of flavor from last night's ramen noodles cause there were two packs in the package, but I am seeing the end of sustenance with two weeks left until my next pay check, and bills the ex left behind constantly clogging up my phone with nasty threats. And my feet are starting to swell and not fit very well in either of my last two pairs of shoes that are worth wearing in public, and my hair has split ends and now my arms itch constantly and..."

"Now, now, MayAnn. Don't go back there again. We went this route once. Trust me, all will be well. First things first, let's go get some dinner. Maybe 'lunch' in your terms, but 'dinner' to this cowboy.

Supper is in the evening. Lunch is what little ole ladies have mid-morning with gossip, tea, and crumpets."

This statement brought a much-needed smile and even a little giggle from MayAnn. "Oh, how I like this man," she thought. "And I am starving. Do preachers go Dutch?"

Tex assured MayAnn that the only direction moving forward was up. He was buying lunch. Then they would return and raid the church's overflowing food bank. The only share that MayAnn would be required to cover was to attend the morning church service the next Sunday. Tex would be waiting and sit right there with MayAnn during the first part of Sunday morning worship. He would have to excuse himself for a few minutes of "good preachin," but would return to her side prior to dismissal. It would be a "Downright good time with God"..

14

Two (Alan)

*In the same manner the one who had received
the two talents gained two more.*

Matthew 25:17 NASB

I could most likely define my life with the number 2. It seems almost everything I have ever done ended up in second place. Isn't second place the first last? I feel like that most days. Leading the pack of last place people. Son of a bitch, gimme a drink.

Guess I can't say that. Would never win a drinking party. Heck, my ex-mother-in-law could easily drink me under the table. Don't know if it was her incredible ability to drink all night, or my lack of ability to handle more than a few beers without wanting to fall asleep. And now, I drink not much more than a good cold one with a friend occasionally, cause that is required.

It could very well be that if I had put myself second like all my accomplishments ended up, maybe I would still be married to my first wife, growing old and grumpy. I could be anxiously waiting for what might be left of Social Security. The pace that my current mental capacity is depleting, I won't know if I am drawing a check anyway. At least it could pay for my nursing home care so it's not a burden on my family.

Did I tell you my baby girls are BEAUTIFUL!! Effie Viviane and Isabelle Veronica. The names have a little story of their own. Effie from my grandmother. Viviane from Ana's mom. Isabelle because Ana liked the name, and Veronica because it just came to me for some reason. Pretty cool, though. A mix of Latino and Americano will define my daughters. Two of them. A wonderful definition of the number Two.

Oh, how God dumped an amazing set of presents in my lap. They have captured a first place spot in my heart (along with Ana of course). I didn't think I had any love left beyond my sons and grandkids. I really don't deserve these bundles of joy. This happiness is above words. Oh God, how I want to hold them and never let go. They absorb me.

Did I tell you I have two baby girls? I don't know quite when they showed up. But here they are. One in each arm as I try to tell my story. I think they are my daughters. Maybe granddaughters? They are sure amazing little bundles of joy. Wish I could remember their names.............dang............... smells like I need to change a diaper. Now, where in the world is the bag?

It is like I just woke back up. I am standing alone in the living room. Why did I come into this room? Why are my daughters screaming from my office? Oh, how I love those two little bundles of happiness. Better get back and share the love only a proud daddy can. Smells like I'd better take a diaper or two. How did these get in my hand already? Oh well, work to do. Turd buckets anyway...

15

PROGRESSION (Larry)

The fear of the Lord is the beginning of knowledge;
Fools despise wisdom and instruction.

Proverbs 1:7 NASB

inally went to see the doctor. Hard pill to swallow when you have always been so self-reliant. With Google these days, who really needs to see a doctor anyway? I can keep plugging in conditions/symptoms then everybody and their grandma can have a say on the web. But, as a perfectionist, I can't leave a stone unturned or a hill left unclimbed. I needed to speak with a professional, hermano a hermano. Let their overpriced tests and educated analysis get to the bottom of my ever-increasing loss of coordination. This is not what the world expects from Larry. Only the best. Only brilliance.

So, after numerous blood and urine samples, my doctor said he needed more tests. I am not sure if these tests are necessary:

1. My doctor wants a new Lexus LFA Nürburgring, and prefers to pay cash.
2. My doctor is thorough and wants to pinpoint exact diagnosis.
3. My doctor knows what it is, but can only confirm by eliminating every other possibility.

I have a sneaking suspicion that it is #1—can't blame him, nice ride. But my current condition warrants answers, so I will humor the man for a few thousand more. Next test is what he calls electromyogram (EMG). A needle inserted into several areas of my body, through the skin and evaluating the electrical activity of my muscles. Sounds like an experience. Might actually be a kick to a different form of knee-jerk reactions. That old school reflex hammer tap to the patellar tendon gets boring after a while.

In a couple of months, Doc Carson (who is a great man but smokes like a chimney) wants to run me through an MRI. Seems like everything leads to an MRI. Glad I own stock in Siemens. Think Doc Carson already made his down payment on that Lexus.

I do feel a little better now. Just searching for answers is a fun challenge. My brain is firing on all cylinders. My body is revealing a failing suspension. Good drugs and a workout regime should correct this minor inconvenience.

Dr. Carson mumbled something about a possible Mayo Clinic visit. I wonder, does he get some kickback for referrals? Mayo Clinic sounds like a last resort to me. I am man enough to tackle this minor irritation on my own. Doc Carson will be privileged to have me come back for the MRI.

I seem to be tripping over the simplest things. We used to laugh at football teammates who were running with all their might for a touchdown and magically tripped at the 5-yard line, falling short of glory. I'm definitely not a "falling short" type of man. Must be a rare virus I contracted on my last trip for missionary work in the Amazon.

I guess a walking stick could look rather cool. Or maybe an awesome antique cane made from twisted tree root of exotic proportions topped with a polished brass handle. That should give me the appearance of debonair. Wouldn't that be something to add to my awesome list of ME.

I, Larry G. Stecklin, will not let this defeat me. Money is no limit. If I can't beat this with my extreme level of determination, then my fortune will cover needed cures. Can't take it with me. Don't really have anyone who deserves what I have worked for. So, might as well buy a whole fleet of the Lexuses for all the doctors.

Truthfully, I hope Dr. Carson gets his car. He really is a good man. Kinda reminds me of me. Except the smoking thing. That is reserved for the women who are lucky enough to share my bed. Actually, she isn't allowed, but the neighbors crave a good cigarette after my prowess is realized by yet another beautiful woman.

As long as my reward to all good women stays as rigid as the $50,000 cane I just bought, the world is still on axis.................

16

Church (MayAnn)

*The way of life is above to the wise, that he
may depart from hell beneath.*

Proverbs 15:24 KJV

MayAnn went to church that next Sunday. She was at peace. Her belly was full even though half was lost daily from morning sickness., via selections from the four crates of food Tex had delivered to her simple apartment. Someone anonymously paid her rent for the next three months. The landlord should finally leave her alone for a while. Creep anyway. Thought he could get some "favors" for letting her rent slide a few measly weeks. Are all men pigs? Or just the city dude types?

Tex kept his promise. He was waiting at those humongous doors when she arrived five minutes early. (Her dad was strict about punctuality.) Tex guided her toward the front. Not her preferred spot. Sitting in the back behind staring eyes was her seat of choice. But Tex's bull-strength arms led her to a center pew second from the front. Tex somehow knew the very front row would have exceeded MayAnn's limits.

The music was nice. Some very talented people in the somewhat conservative band. The choir was awesome, only second to the pipe organ. MayAnn hadn't even noticed that instrument of grandeur until this Sunday. It reminded MayAnn of her mother talking about her great uncle who played the organ at the Cubs games.

Tex was a decent singer. He was not afraid to let the volume flow out. You could tell he might have had a lesson or two as the music came from his diaphragm instead of his nose. A strong baritone coming from a man of short stature. It actually was fitting. Along with those awesome boots he still had on.

MayAnn wanted to grab Tex and make him stay with her when it was time for him to take over the pulpit. Stronger was the urge that she wanted to hear the Lord's message coming from this man. If she were to put money on it (probably frowned upon in this grand church), MayAnn knew in her heart that Tex would not deliver the Fire-and-Brimstone-type sermon. Rather, it would be filled with love and peace and God, of course.

Tex:

HELL!!

A word not heard all that much in church. We come to church to purposely avoid hell. Deep down, none of us wants to go to hell. Is there anyone here today thinking that hell is exactly where some people deserve to be? Not us! We are here in church, worshiping God, and doing the "right" thing.

But hell is still kind of sitting there in the back of our mind. That is why we are here in the church. We would just as soon never have to think about hell.

Some people worship the Devil and proclaim Satan as king. They do all that stuff because it gives them a false sense of power. It makes them feel special, individual, and different from the normal gathering. But deep down, I believe there is no way in "bleep" they want to actually go to hell. I just can't comprehend a thought process going that far left.

Time to move on. Hell, it is real. No doubts, no questions, no having to use good tax money to study if there really is a hell or not. If needed, they could pay me, and I will give them enough facts to arrive at the conclusion that "hell is real."

Anyone who has been through a war—many of you sitting here today have—know there is a hell. Unfortunately, you lived through some of the worst hell (if there is such a thing as a worse hell versus a better hell). It changed you. With God's grace it has made you better. Without God, you are suffering.

What about hell on a daily basis? The here and now. Where is hell today? Is hell out back just waiting for us to depart from God's church and then attack? Well, truthfully, yes. Hell is brave enough to stand right on the front steps. Hell doesn't have to hide out back. Hell has no trouble grabbing parishioners as they leave this church and controlling their lives clear until next Sunday morning, when they walk back into the sanctuary. Hell knows it is getting more surface time than the church. Hell doesn't mind stepping back for an hour or two and letting us think we are putting hell to rest once and for all. Because hell knows we will be back.

Now that you are all fidgeting in your pews and wondering what on God's Green Earth has gotten into Tex today, I want you to grab this next bit of information. If you don't retain any other words from today, please lock these into your memory bank.

HELL IS REAL. HELL WAS RIGHT HERE ON EARTH YESTERDAY, IS HERE TODAY, AND WILL BE HERE TOMORROW. HELL IS ALWAYS WAITING FOR YOU. IF YOU DON'T GO FIND HELL ON YOUR OWN, IT WILL COME AND FIND YOU! HELL WILL NEVER, I REPEAT, NEVER GIVE UP!! HELL FEEDS OFF ANY LITTLE CRUMB YOU MIGHT THROW IT. AND I PROMISE YOU, YOU WILL FIND A WAY TO FEED HELL.

So, is Tex up here at this pulpit telling you how terrible you are? Am I scaring you into a hopelessness that has no solution? I pray this is not the case. I pray you and I and Jesus and the Holy Spirit and God can overcome what is waiting outside these doors.

We need to realize as individuals, and as a church community, that we can't face hell alone. We need something oh so much stronger than our fragile and faulty human self.

Let's dig a little deeper into this hell thing. Now that we know we aren't alone, we can discuss the truth of the matter. If you consider hell as something that is alive and existing in our daily lives instead of some fairy tale fire and brimstone future thing, then we have already won half the battle.

Earlier, I said, "If you don't find hell, it will come and find you." This is so very true. I personally have gone and found hell on my own. I was selfish and pursued my own desires of unmentionable temporary gratification. It doesn't matter what category you want to put it in. Whether we are talking about addictions, anger, envy, loathing, hate, jealousy, bitterness, blame, deceit, theft, do I need to continue? Each of these and so many more human traits can lead us to hell.

Sometimes it is a long trail. A path forever going down. Back and forth at such a minimal degree that we don't realize the spiral. Other times, we simply jump. Off a cliff, or a bridge, or a mountain, or whatever elevated surface we just happen to be on, we don't waste time with the slow trail. We JUMP.

Is either way worse than the other? Is the slow road to hell a more acceptable route than a nose dive or cannonball into the hells of this life? I don't think so. Same destination. Those who take the leap and hit hell hard are probably judged more harshly by those who are taking their sweet time but will soon join that person who got there quickly.

I know I have been judged harshly like that. I also confess, I have been the one who judged. Yes, the pastor who stands here before you is just as human as each and every one of you sitting here today. Tex is just as human as that junkie sitting in that abandoned building three blocks from this church. This man standing before you is no better than that man who spent his entire paycheck on gambling and drinking and stray women instead of providing wholly for his family. I am no better than that woman who turned her nose up as she walked past the homeless man sitting just down the street. My human nature is no better than that businessman who managed to divert a few hundred dollars from his employer's profits.

We all have our faults. Think about it, my friends. Haven't you found hell itself at one time or another? Maybe you didn't even recognize hell as it had you in its bonds. Then one day, you woke up and realized you were exactly where you never planned on being. This hell thing is not so good.

Then, you had a choice. Do I blame my being in hell on someone else? Surely good ole me couldn't have found this hell thing on my own. I wasn't raised like that. I know better. I go to church once in a while. I give my ten percent when I can. I helped that crippled old lady across the street the other day. There is no way I can be in hell right now. I am too good for that. Somebody else put me here.

Sometimes, there is truth to that. Like I said, hell will come and find you. This world we live in has some ugly. It has some bad. Mixed in with the good is a whole bucketload of people who are a walking hell and don't even know it. Maybe they have never known any better. Maybe abuse took them down that path when they were too young to know what abuse even was.

It really doesn't matter how one got to hell. It doesn't matter if you are a leaper or a trailblazer. What matters most is getting out of hell. Whatever hell that might be. I am not here today to preach to you on the hazards and negatives and ugliness of hell. I know you have already seen it.

What I am here today for is to help you out of hell. I am here to give you the tools to build whatever ladder or climbing device needed to get out of your hell.

> *2Peter1 1-11 ASV: 1. Simon Peter, a servant and apostle of Jesus Christ, to them that have obtained a like precious faith with us in the righteousness of our God and the Saviour Jesus Christ: 2. Grace to you and peace be multiplied in the knowledge of God and of Jesus our Lord; 3. seeing that his divine power hath granted unto us all things that pertain unto life and godliness, through the knowledge of him that called us by his own glory and virtue; 4. whereby he that granted unto us his precious and exceeding great promises; that through these ye may become partakers of the divine nature, having escaped from the corruption that is in the world by lust. 5. Yea, and for this very cause adding on your*

part all diligence, in your faith supply virtue; and in your virtue knowledge; 6. and in your knowledge self-control; and in your patience godliness, 7. and in your godliness brotherly kindness; and in your brotherly kindness love. 8. For if these things are yours and abound, they make you to be not idle nor unfruitful unto the knowledge of our Lord Jesus Christ. 9. For he that lacketh these things is blind, seeing only what is near, having forgotten the cleansing from his old sins. 10. Wherefore, brethren, give the more diligence to make your calling and election sure; for if ye do these things, ye shall never stumble; 11. for thus shall be richly supplied unto you the entrance into the eternal kingdom of our Lord and Saviour Jesus Christ.

Talk about some good news. I won't even try to break this down for you today. Please, take these verses with you. Read them, study them, learn them, live them. There is a way out of the pits of hell. This, my Brothers and Sisters, is it.

If ever there was a rule and guide of faith that would guard our lives as we walk out the doors of this church today, you will find it in the Good Book. Truthfully, it is everywhere in the Bible. These are very strong words here that can help you. There are thousands more. You don't need to come to church to find the path home. (Although, this is a pretty good place to park every so often.) Just open your Bible. This afternoon while it is still fresh. Monday morning to start your week. Every day to give you strength. Saturday night to open your mind for another great sermon on Sunday morning.

Quantity is important here. Quality is guaranteed. Read, read, read read read. Think about this for a second; Do I read my Bible or let hell take me wherever? Hell or Bible?

Let us pray: Dearest Lord, protector of our lives, we come to you today crawling out of the depths of hell. We don't want to be there, Lord. Forgive us for whatever way we managed to go to those depths. We need you today, Lord. We need you every day. We want, no, we need to live for You, Lord. This life of living for ourselves hasn't worked out too well. Forgive us, God, for we know not what we do. We want to do good. We want to live good. But bad keeps trying to cover us over. Only through your Son, Jesus, can we overcome the hell of this world. Fill us today with your Holy

Spirit. Protect us from what is lurking outside. Walk with us, Lord. Carry us when we need it. We are yours today, Lord. We pray that we will be yours tomorrow and every day hereafter until the day you call us home, Lord. In Jesus's most precious and gracious name we pray…. Amen.

When Tex finished praying, came down from the altar, and grabbed MayAnn's hand, a sense of peace and panic surrounded her at the same time. Tex wasn't sitting down beside MayAnn as he reached for her hand. He was standing there, beckoning her to follow him. "Oh no!" MayAnn's brain screamed. The strength of Tex is the only thing that lured MayAnn forward.

Tex simply led MayAnn up the three steps and in front of the pulpit. And once again, he addressed the parish. MayAnn now knew the reason such a revealing sermon was cut so short. She was now part of Tex's ministry for the day. Dang, was she again falling victim to a sweet-talking man? No, this was God's servant. A totally opposite of that %^&(*#$ that got her into this position in the first place. "Forgive me, Lord," was MayAnn's thought as Tex took control.

"My fellow Christians. I would like to introduce MayAnn. I first must apologize for making her feel like she is on display to this church. I want everyone to know and love this beautiful young lady as much as Jesus does. This angel in the rough came walking through our doors the other day. Broken, lost, afraid, emotional, and overwhelmed. Your church, God's church was open for business. She was led to our doors. I had already locked them for the day. God then unlocked the doors, helped MayAnn to open them and guided her into His midst. And then, God proceeded to make my car not start, forcing me to return inside to use the phone in the office."

As I returned into the church, I was not exactly in a positive and angelic mood. Then I heard the timid footsteps echoing off the organ pipes. God was singing to me in a way only God can do. Jesus was leading her. God was pushing me. And here we are."

By now, MayAnn was numb. The words were echoing out from Tex. They were no longer finding connection through her ears. She felt Jesus holding her there, just as He was once on display. God in all his wonder had taken over. His word was taking control of this service. People were coming forward to pray as one. Tex was still speaking. No, God was using Tex as a voice. "Can I just stay here forever?" MayAnn felt.

No church service in her past had ever reached the level that MayAnn was experiencing at this moment. Probably no Sunday in the future would grasp even a glimpse of what Tex and Jesus and God had achieved on her behalf. Good stuff right here. Answers....................

17

Normal (Alan)

Like a bird that wanders from her nest,
So is a man who wanders from his home.

Proverbs 27:8 NASB

Things seem to be back to normal. I don't believe I have wandered out of the house in the middle of the night for no apparent reason, lately. At least Ana hasn't told me about any recent episodes. I have had to start sleeping with at least shorts and a tee-shirt on. The first night downtown in just my skivvies was rather embarrassing. At least that is what Ana said. I truthfully don't remember. It does remind me of a long-lost story I would love to share with you if you have the time. I seem to have a lot of spare time lately. Good thing we have plenty of Terere.

Back in the day, after graduating high school. Salutatorian, second place, "told you," I had decided the best summer job possible would be going on a wheat harvest custom combining crew. I had dreamed as a child every year as I was cleaning the Gleaner A combine after harvest, pretending to operate it as only a custom cutter could do. It took all day to clean that combine. My imagination was fed to the hilt with the glorious task of spending all summer cutting wheat and making money.

So, dad took me to visit a custom cutter who was in our neighboring town. He had advertised for combine operators and truck drivers "leaving soon for Oklahoma." I didn't even realize this man lived so close. I just knew I wanted to be a part of this summer's story. Hope he still had some positions to fill.

Pond Creek, Oklahoma was our first stop. Carl, the harvest crew owner, was getting on in years and had long since decided driving down into Texas a month earlier wasn't really worth the time and effort. Somewhere around the Enid, Oklahoma area was the place to be. So, Pond Creek was where it started.

Our living quarters was a rather cleverly refurbished school bus, painted blue for some unknown reason. Maybe Mrs. Carl's choice. Knowing Carl, it was the cheapest color of paint he could buy at the time. Anyway, it was fricken blue. And not dark awesome navy blue, but rather some faded-out version knocking on the door of baby blue. My God, it was shameful. I had girls to impress. At least it wasn't a "short bus."

So, middle of wheat country. Beautiful, blonde-haired, petite Oklahoma girl in my sights. Things to conquer, wheat to cut, manly things to do. Who cared if the locals called us Wheaties. The girls enjoyed some stray tomcats coming into their closed world little town. Guys weren't too worried. After all, the queer Yankees were living in a baby blue school bus.

The inside of our bus consisted of six sets of bunk beds with a partition wall in the back for a toilet and shower. Almost like camping. Didn't mind the other five guys I was sharing lodging with. They had some definite personality differences.

There was Cliff. I kinda latched onto Cliff as my mentor. He was another combine operator like me. Cliff was old and funny as hell. "Let me tell you a little secret," Cliff would lead into his next story with. Cliff had a terrible shake in his hands due to an accident back in his Army days when some stupid "son of a whore" had run over him with an Army truck. Cliff was rather rotund, so I bet that truck felt some large speed bump pain as well.

Anyway, Cliff's hands shook so badly, he could barely get that first beer to his lips. It was fun to watch as the whole world was shaking but Cliff wouldn't slow down. Eventually, after about the third or fourth beer, Cliff's hands would magically stop shaking and the next twelve went as smoothly as a vending machine rolling that cold beer to his never-ending thirst.

Then there was Bill, one of the truck drivers. Strong as an ox, and a vegan. Probably the first true vegan I had ever experienced. I was curious. How could someone who only ate fruits and nuts lift me and a combine radiator because I hadn't let go soon enough? Bill lived at peace. Didn't get all of Bill's story. I pictured Bill leaving for the Rockies one day, never to return. Living off the land and having a grizzly as a pet.

Then………. Hmmmmm…………why can't I remember his name? Another of the truck drivers. Randy or Paul or something? I do remember that he had pointed ears and a unibrow. Oh, how Cliff detested this dude. Seemed a little off to me, too. He didn't bother me much, though. And was someone with some strange/ interesting stories on rainy days, so all was good.

It was during one of those rainy day stretches. Cliff loved them because we couldn't work, and he could drink beer all day. It was funny when we were on a long stretch of endless wheat cutting that as my combine would pass Cliff's going the other direction, he would lean out of his cab, look at the single little cloud in the sky, hold his hands up in prayer, and beg for rain. It was funny. Especially with the added effect of his shaking hands in a prayerful position.

Back to the rainy days. One of them, I had spent some time imbibing with Cliff until it was his nap time, and then I was off chasing that pretty blonde Okie. After some time, I had returned to our blue bus to get some sleep. Not the least bit intoxicated. A little bit frustrated cause I think my angel in tight jeans was just leading me on, just enough to piss off her jerk of an ex-boyfriend. I was tired, though, and knew I needed sleep in case sunshine returned and we had to go back to work.

The next morning I woke to soaking wet sheets. My first thought was, "I peed the bed." My second thought was, "Even my pillow is wet. I surely didn't pee that much."

Then, Cliff asked, "Where did you go last night?"

Simple reply: "What do you mean, Cliff?"

"Well, let me tell you a little secret. You came in late last night, stripped to your undershorts, climbed into bed, and proceeded to snore within a few seconds."

My thought was, "Snore?" No one could snore to the level of Cliff. He snored breathing in and whistled breathing out. What a trip. Cliff was so funny.

Cliff said, "Next thing I knew, you jumped off your top rack and headed out of the bus like it was on fire. About the time I was going to come looking for you—it was pouring rain you know— your soaking wet dog ass came back into the bus, climbed back in your rack, and starting snoring again."

I was thinking this was another of Cliff's entertaining tall tales, but the truck drivers confirmed it. They also promised not to tell Carl, nor his half-spoiled nephew, who was a damn good combine operator himself, so I wouldn't get in trouble. Or even worse, get a bus ticket home. A few days later, my Oklahoma cutie even asked me what I was doing walking around outside in my underwear in the pouring rain. Oh, how I wished I had had a witty comeback for her giggles.

So, rain, night walks, underwear, public display, nothing new to my story. Same story, different year in my book......................

18

MRI (Larry)

Because in much wisdom there is much grief, and increasing
knowledge results in increasing pain.

Ecclesiastes 1:18 NASB

W ell, that is that. Had my MRI. Would have taken a nap during the procedure, but they kept yakking about me not moving. Didn't think much of the test. They told me with the current backlog, it might be a couple of weeks before doctors would analyze and get back to me. Good grief, do I have to be on a schedule like normal people? Doesn't Dr. Carson know the level of importance I maintain? I have connections. Just a few phone calls and we will expedite this process. LG has things to do. Good day to go golfing.

Golfing is the one relaxing "hobby" in my life I allow. At my level, there is not much time to relax. There are a lot of high-income-type people who enjoy this sport, and it is good for my bottom line to socialize with them. More successful business transactions are completed on a golf course than in any conference room in the country. Dinner parties to hobnob with the snobs, worthless. Except maybe to meet the next delight for my bedroom.

I suppose I enjoy golf so much because it is the one thing in life I haven't mastered, gotten bored with, and moved on. Just when I think my game is coming together, off in the rough I go. Dang that crosswind anyway.

Believe it or not, I started this game with a cheap set of clubs from Walmart. Part of my business success has been frugality. Although it was the best and most expensive set Walmart could provide, it was still of Walmart quality and price. I hate shopping in that store. Too many people with too-small thoughts shopping there. Good business plan, though. Keep the highest percentage of your employees on a part-time status so you don't have to provide top pay or benefits. Work your management like sled dogs with the promise of promotion to plow-horses.

Got off on a tangent there. I kinda like the soapbox status. More people should listen to me. Can't master this new $1,200 pitching wedge if I am standing on said box, though.

I have thought about taking golf lessons. I have a friend, great guy, Tom, who followed his dreams clear from high school and became a professional golfer. He was naturally good at this most difficult sport. I believe we nicknamed him Nancy back in our "punish anyone different" high school days. It was actually connected to Nancy Lopez, who was GREAT at the sport. Tom took it all in stride and kept perfecting his game. I would give up a good portion of my wealth to play the game at the level Tom does. Plus, did I tell you Tom is an all-around fantastic person, diehard Husker fan, and will always hold my respect. "GO, BIG RED" TOM!!

My swing is a little off today. Everything seems to hurt. Club flat out flew out of my hands twice so far. Gotta get a grip. Maybe time for a better glove? New grips for my Callaway's? My shoulders seem to be slouching more today. Keep having to correct my posture. Dang nabbit, just tripped over a piddly gopher mound. Going to have a little chat with the groundskeeper. Man, that cart girl is pretty. Good day to admire her bending over the cooler to get me another cold Sam Adams Utopia.

Just received a call from Dr. Carson. He wants me to come in right away tomorrow to discuss the MRI and my options. WTF. God is abandoning me now? What did I ever do to Him? It's not like

I ever needed to bother God with any of my concerns. I am self-made. Why me now? There went my whole day of owning this golf course. Never faced a challenge I couldn't overcome.

That's right. LG will prevail. Just a small bump in the road. Destroy the bump and move on. Now where did that cart girl go............

19

Again (Alan)

What has been will be again, what has been done will be done again; there is nothing new under the sun.

Ecclesiastes 1:9 NIV

A na found me in the middle of the plaza last night/early morning. Police told her to either keep me confined at night, or pay them a little palm money to start bringing me home...............

20

Good People (MayAnn)

When I am in distress, I call to you, because you answer me.

Psalms 86:7 NIV

After the church service, everything was a blur for MayAnn. There was a potluck with tons of delicious food and desserts that would put the Catholic women to shame. Donations were taken. Silent auctions of things people didn't want and donated so people who did want could pay more than value. People connected. People laughed. It was a grand Christian gathering time. MayAnn tried to hide in the corner, but Tex kept her in the middle of the attention.

After the fanfare and a sum of $1,862 was accumulated and passed discreetly to MayAnn, two couples stayed behind. One couple was middle-aged and wealthy. The other was a young couple with a lot of hope in their eyes. Both couples seemed important to Tex. One could tell they looked to Tex for answers, too.

The first couple introduced was the Stecklins. Wealthy but conservative. Confident, but holding a secret level of pain in their eyes. They were ready to let Tex reveal their secrets to a previously unknown wisp of a stranger. The Stecklins were not anxious. MayAnn could tell that had never been in their genes. Just determined and strong. They could have easily been someone MayAnn admired and dreamed of emulating.

Henry—Hank, he corrected Tex—shook MayAnn's hand with the grip of a man from the Midwest. He carried some attitude, but was quite the gentleman in MayAnn's presence. His beautiful wisp of a wife stayed quiet and let her husband take the lead. You could tell outside the house Hank was in charge. But in the confines of their home, this woman had Hank twisted around her little finger. It was cute. MayAnn felt comfortable with this couple.

The other couple, the Mers, were almost the exact opposite of the Stecklins. The wife, Chris, knew how to take MayAnn into her arms and share a deep and sincere love instantly. MayAnn had never been hugged like that. Even Tex's embrace of comfort that first day fell short of what Chris gave. How could a complete stranger give so much with no reservation? And what was going on, anyway?

After introductions and awkward silence of "Now what," Tex took the lead.

"MayAnn, there are crossroads in life that give us options. One always hopes they can choose the direction that leads to a win-win outcome. The other road may lead to something not quite so good. We will never know where the other road would have led because we chose this road. But win-win is always the goal."

"Now that we have asked God for guidance and direction, the path we are guided to take has more of a triple-win outcome. Like the Triple Crown of horse racing, this is rare. But today, we have that rarity just waiting for the door to be open. Please hear us all out before you close and lock any opinions," Tex gently said as he held MayAnn's hand with that glory-filled comfort that Tex seemed to naturally have.

"The Stecklins and the Mers are offering to adopt one of your babies. There are many reasons for this scenario."

"Yeah," interrupted Hank. "If you have one dog, you have a good dog. But with two dogs, you only have half a dog." That drew a glaring look from Mrs. Stecklin. "Well," continued Hank, "you get my drift, not saying your babies are dogs, just referring to the two at a time.........."

"SHUT UP, HANK," demanded his wife.

MayAnn had to giggle at that. Hank was so strong and honest. He meant no harm by his reference. Just "cut to the chase," as her dad used to say. MayAnn suddenly knew where this was leading. Fear and pain tore at her belly like a scythe. One swing, and her world was forever neatly cut in two. Actually, three, from what MayAnn was perceiving. But Tex's firm and reassuring grip on her hand removed that fear instantly. It was going to be OK. She was going to be OK. Her babies were going to be better than just OK.

The conversations and discussions carried on for a better part of the afternoon. Thankfully, one of the church ladies had left her gooseberry pie for them to take a break with. "Who in the city makes gooseberry pie, anyway?" pondered MayAnn. This whole cowboy preacher and country home cookin' and completely not citified scenario was somewhat surreal. God truly was in charge of the details. Who would have thought?

The Mers presented their side of the solution. They simply couldn't afford to take on twins and provide a stable home. They already had two children, a boy and a girl. They had lost a baby due to a midterm miscarriage. God had told them that He would replace their loss with one baby. One baby who would be welcomed into their home as their own, forever locked in the love of parents as natural as biological.

The most difficult part of this whole story was the fact that MayAnn would be required to walk away after the twins' birth. No coddling, no first breastfeeding, nada. MayAnn didn't know if she was up to being that decisive. She felt like she would have to step into the role of coldhearted. That was not MayAnn. But in the long run, this sacrifice would say more about MayAnn as a mother than if she kept them for herself.

MayAnn let everyone, including the leader Tex, know that this was not a win-win-win. It would forever be a win for the Stecklins, win for the Mers, but a loss for her. They all understood. They all joined hands and prayed. They all became a family together on the path God chose for them. It was decided..

21

Kinda lost here WTH (Alan)

*Trust in the Lord with all your heart and lean
not on your own understanding.*

Proverbs 3:5 NIV

I am having a good day today. Effie Viviane and Isabelle Veronica are growing so fast. They are busy running and playing and giving their dad so much joy. Their mom rarely lets me watch them on my own. For two reasons.

One, I let the girls play outside and get dirty. Mud pies are their favorite to make. If you have not partaken in this delectable treat, you must try one! Not so delicious, but fun nonetheless. At least until their mom came home, caught us, scolded me, and instantly took the girls in for a shower. I didn't see the harm. I received "The Look."

Mom is gone today. We are making clay animals out of the red mud that is so much fun to play with. Maybe if we don't add sugar and try to eat them, mom will let us slide this time. Who cares. The laughter from little girls is worth a hundred of The Looks.

I can't decide if time is moving rapidly, or at a snail's pace. Some days I look at my little angels and wonder how I missed their first rolling over, their first steps, their first word, "Daddy." I know I was here. And there are photos of proof. I just can't find that little room in my brain where these wonderful memories are stored.

Then there are times, like right now, we are locked into a time/ space continuum in slow motion. For all I know, we have been making these clay animals for weeks now. Did we stop for lunch? If so, what did we eat? Who cooked? Where is Ana or her mom Salete in case I go dark again?

I probably shouldn't say dark. Fuzzy would be a better word. Dark kind of defines not so good. Fuzzy sounds too cute, though. I definitely know my brain isn't cute. These two little ladies sitting in the mud and having the time of their lives with Daddy, now that is cute.

It is more like I end up behind a pane of glass marred and scratched to no end. I can see out, but it is a distorted vision. I want so bad to break that glass to see clearly again. I don't want to be on this side of confusion. Even in second place, I could always get the job done no matter what it took. Now, I can't even break through this crinkled plastic wrap of a barrier that is slowly isolating me more and more.

I am not a vegetable. I am not someone to be pitied. I see Ana crying once in a while. I reach out to her to comfort her. She asks me, "Que sou eu hoje (Who am I today)?" If I get it right and say, "Minha linda esposa (My beautiful wife)," she collapses into my arms and lets me hold her. Oh, how I never want to let go.

Other times, I am certain Ana is my mom. I still want to hold her and comfort her through her tears. But not in the same way. I never want to let my mom go, either. Sometimes I think maybe Mom died a few years ago. Other times, I am certain she is sitting right here beside me. But if I look away, and then look back, my mom is replaced by my sister.

What the heck kind of sticky gooey mess is in my hands right now? Is this a cockatiel I am trying to replicate that at one time and forever said, "What did you do?"

I have a brother, and two sons and a stepson. They are all strong, independent men. They have all done well for themselves. I am proud of them. I would be even prouder if I could remember their names on a more frequent basis. I believe there is a Douglas, a Wade, a Felipe, and a Harry somewhere mixed in there. If they were all standing in front of me, I believe I could sort them out. There are fond memories. Many stories. Much love. Maybe on one of my getting rarer good days, I could share our adventures. For now, I just know I miss them, love them, and can't wait to see them again. Maybe for my birthday. Whenever the hell that is.

Back to our clay animals................

Where did the girls go? They were just here seconds ago. Why am I sitting in a mud hole covered in all this red shit that is drying and caking my being? Not only am I once again behind that blurred glass, I seem to be encased in concrete. Maybe if I just pick, pick, pick.........

This isn't so bad, though. It is a safe place. No longer do I have to solve everyone's problems. No longer am I the one pressured to make a decision. The days of leading hundreds of men to completion of a successful industrial construction project are behind me. The pressure is gone. I can relax.

Where is my Terere......................

Ana is crying again. I can hear her on the phone. It sounds like she is talking to either Douglas or Wade. Maybe my dad. I haven't seen him for ages. I love my dad. Great man. Lived his Christian life as an example. Never preached it. Never shoved it down anyone's throats. Just passed the Bible to one of us kids every morning to share in daily devotions. We never discussed the lessons. Dad just lived them. Oh, what I would give to even come close to being the man my dad was. I hope he isn't ashamed of me. I crossed his line a few times.

Why doesn't someone come and talk to me and get my opinion? Why do I seem to find myself in some corner of the world not quite a part of life anymore? Solely observing, rarely partaking. Sometimes I can feel the knots of yarn pulling tighter on what is left of my recognition. Good days, I can untie some of those knots and go back to crocheting a semblance of a normal life.

No one seems to trust me on those days, though. It used to be I could go for years on the straight and narrow. Building a success. Supporting a loving family. Gaining respect and admiration. Then, as shared with you before, I would jump off a cliff. Headfirst. Shattering my world and everyone who depended on me. Sideline observers would just nod and say, "I told you so. Alan was always the scum of the Earth and always will be." Oh, man, how I never intended to be that reference.

Who the hell is Alan, anyway? Today no one trusts me with the most basic tasks. How can I ever bring their trust back? I am a good person down deep. I have a heart that wants to give and give and give. I don't want to be a taker. It just happens. Maybe this quiet corner is the best place for me. I can love everyone deep in the recesses of my being, and never have to worry about shattering their lives because I put myself first for some selfish reason. This blurred glass is as much a protection for them as it is a containment for me. I perceive that I am now part of the Henry Doorly Zoo. Am I viewed as being one of the monkeys? Or maybe more like the baboon that everyone points at and makes fun of their glaring red ass?

Why am I forced to drink this swamp water every day? When am I going to be allowed to display my prowess at the Churrascaria again? A good cold Brahma Chopp or two would hit the spot right now. I seem to be forever thirsty. Is there a football game on today? Will I be watching futebol or football? A goal is a goal, right? Who is that unknown man or boy (can't quite tell) who keeps appearing in my dreams? Do I need to go find him? Why does everyone seem to be running around, kicking their balls of life, while I just sit here scratching mine?.............

22

GIVE IT AWAY (Larry)

Jesus said unto him, "If thou wouldest be perfect, go, sell that which thou hast, and give to the poor, and thou shalt have treasure in heaven: and come, follow me."
Matthew 19:21 ASV

I am forever humbled. God can kiss my patootie. I think I might have bought my way into the everlasting. Realization that ALS is going to defeat me and not with much time to spare, forced my hand.

I gave ALL of my money away. It really wasn't that hard. My whole life of success has been surrounded by people with their hand out. Just because they made nothing from their pathetic little existence doesn't mean all my hard work, dedication, and wins are free for the taking. You want the good things in life, go earn them. Quit expecting father fortune to lay it in your lap. Get off your lazy, "give me what's mine" butt and get to work.

A fair portion of my funds went to this old church in a nameless city. A HUGE church known for its massive doors and even larger heart. Stories have come from this church of all the great works that for years were led by some out-of-place cowboy preacher. They never once stuck their hand out to me. I respected their story. I gave them enough money to have security till the end of time. I hear they are quadrupling the size of their food bank, and building a permanent housing unit for pregnant women who choose life for their babies, but have nowhere to go.

Another bit went to First Tee of North Florida. One of Tom's choices. You should look into this mission. Especially if you love kids and the game of golf. What a noble mission they have. Combining life lessons and leadership skills with playing golf. Win-win situation here. Look into it.

There are other awesome organizations I gave to. First requisite was they established themselves on their own. Second was they provided life lessons. Third was, God had a major role and was at the center. Also, that they weren't ashamed to give God credit. Organizations like Fellowship for Christian Athletes, 4-H Club, Boys Town, Masonic Home for Children, just to name a few.

It was a blast, and probably the most rewarding thing I have ever done. Everything is gone (sort of). My CPA told me to hold on to enough money for private care until my demise. Good advice. But for all the taxes I paid throughout the years, and the Social Security I will never recover, I believe the State can provide nursing home care for me. It isn't going to be all that long anyway.

My lawyers tried a quick move to lock my assets because of "mental duress." I believe they wanted their big piece of the pie they could have billed out trying to locate someone legally deserving of an overwhelming inheritance. One of those "long lost uncle" scenarios. I fired their asses.

I did give another fair amount to the ALS-ONE. If anyone can find a cure, or at least prolong the inevitable, these guys can. Another thing my CPA recommended I do was keep enough for my own care at the Mayo Clinic. No, not for me. Let them put their efforts and hope into someone who still wants to fight. I have already given up. I know when to count my losses. ALS is going to win. Might as well shake its hand.

It really doesn't hurt that much. Just a progressive sense of weakness. I have been lucky that it hasn't touched my thought process. I was told that a form of dementia called frontotemporal dementia was possible. As far as I know, my brain function is quite clear. Not like this poor bastard that is a roommate of mine in this nursing home. He has spaghetti between his ears. Most days, anyway.

He can still run amazingly fast. I cheer Alan on every time he leaps out of his chair, exclaims, "I'M GOING HOME," and gives the nurse's aides a run for their money. I think he does this on purpose. One, to entertain me, and two because he really does want to go home. It is sad to think that Alan doesn't have a clue how to get there. I have heard that he can make it all the way across the highway. Even made it to the Dollar General one day. I was impressed. Wish he would have brought me some Twizzlers.

I like Alan. He would have made a good brother. There were times being an only child kinda sucked the big one. But Dad always told me I could be the Top Dog because there was no other dog in the way to distract me. Never did quite know why he made that reference all the time.

I am trying to decide when I should push to give up my CPAP machine at night and accept that sooner or later, I will need a tracheostomy and be tied to a respirator till my dying day. I think I will stay content for a while getting help breathing while I sleep, and take pride in breathing on my own during the day. Except for the times Alan makes me laugh so hard as he tears through the halls, sometimes in just his skivvies (haven't figured out the story behind that detail), trying to find an unlocked door. The alarms are annoying, but muffled by my breathless laughter listening to Alan "give em hell."

My speech is starting to slur more and more. I am glad I fired my bloodsucking lawyers while I still had all my functions. I do have a good hometown lawyer now that is a brother and a friend. Bryant is good stuff. Don't think he would recognize stress if it came up and slapped him. Laid back and intelligent. Perfect person to oversee some of my assets that are buried deep in the records of some corporate address. I call him BB. He already understands that as my speech worsens, BB will be the best I can do. And that will be more like EE...... this disease sucks. Death sentence while you're coherent. At least Alan doesn't see his coming.

I may have hit the most generous stage. But, I never said I hit the complete idiot stage. God got ninety percent, I kept ten percent. Think that is a fair ratio, seeing how God typically only asks for his tithe. He and I reached an agreement. If I gave my vast wealth to all the causes out there without benefit to myself, He would not hold it against me for blaming Him for allowing this Godawful (excuse me, Lord) disease to overtake my world.

There goes Alan again! This is so frissshhhhen entertaining.........

23

First one here (MayAnn)

This is my command—be strong and courageous!
Do not be afraid or discouraged. For the Lord
your God is with you wherever you go."

Joshua 1:9 NLT

MayAnn didn't really have a clue where she was today. She was woken up this morning to go to the bathroom, change into some decent clothes, and be gently led to breakfast. The nurse who came into her room this morning was an angel. She had the look of heaviness in the back of her eyes. But what looked at MayAnn and talked to her so gently was a dear. A kind soul. MayAnn's favorite.

Not like that half-angry bitch who came in on other mornings. The one who only wanted a paycheck because it would help pay for the sorry life story she had written for herself. MayAnn didn't know why this person of roughness and "don't give a shit" was even allowed to care for her. MayAnn tried to put up her bulletproof haze of glass on the days this Bonnie of a monster entered her world for eight hours. That was what MayAnn appropriately named her, Bonnie, after the Bonnie and Clyde team who ran amok robbing banks and killing people in the '30s. Bonnie was a monster. MayAnn could do nothing about it. When she did have the rare day of clarity, Bonnie was a lost thought locked up in the tangles of her brain.

Today, though, MayAnn had Peggy. Why did the most important and caring people in her world own that name? This Peggy lived right up on that same pedestal with all the other Peggys MayAnn knew. What Peggy gave of herself was an exception to the rule in this place. Most caregivers did their best, and were competent and appreciated by MayAnn. This Peggy, though, seemed to bring the best out of MayAnn. Oh, how she prayed to have Peggy come into her room every day.

With Peggy here, the fogging Plexiglas could be stored and MayAnn could dive into the memories that were good in her life. She might even go see those two younger men down the hall who had a certain draw to her. MayAnn couldn't place her finger on it, but those men felt like kin. Except maybe when the one went half-looney and led the nurses and assistants on a chase.

This seemed to happen most frequently when Bonnie was on the clock. At least when the crazy man was running around, Bonnie wasn't in MayAnn's room sharing her meanness and shitty attitude. "When did I start thinking in terms of profanity?" MayAnn spoke. "Don't mind saying 'shit' out loud. Bonnie is 'shit', I will tell her that."

Not today. Peggy was here. The world was good. Those naughty words unnecessary. Just smiles and love and warmth and hugs and feeling good. Plus, a good laugh if that younger man decided it was a good day for "catch me if you can."

Aside from that, MayAnn was happy. She often would, on her "clear" days, think of the many blessings God had given to her life. A strong and hardworking husband. Three kids whom she had been so enormously proud of. A simple clean life back on the dryland farm. She truly had the best of everything. Not the "most" of everything. They never had much fortune. But most definitely, the best compared to those city folks who wouldn't know a blessing if it slapped a window open to their brain.

MayAnn couldn't remember what date she actually moved into this home. She thought maybe her husband put her here because for some reason he had to go away. He was such a good and Godly man. MayAnn knew that Eugene loved her and always did his best by her. Even if he was a stubborn and slightly male chauvinistic type, he did everything in his power to always take care of her and their family. He must have had a good reason to leave her here. Maybe he believed that everyone in this home was a Peggy. Next time Eugene came to visit, MayAnn would have to tell him about that witch of a Bonnie.

MayAnn knew that forever there seemed to be a huge emptiness that kept her company daily. It was a longing for something lost. A buried memory not quite surfaced. One of those words that sit on the tip of your tongue but refuse to raise its hand and claim acknowledgment. A thing out there that had meaning. An act of God yet to reveal itself. Something that kept her alive and willing to tolerate Bonnie on those bad days.

Then, those two younger men were checked in. MayAnn was sitting in the main junction of two hallways going to rooms and a living area with an aviary and huge TV. MayAnn preferred the aviary and could watch the birds for hours. She was always listening for one of the cockatiels to say, "What did you do?" The other direction led up the stairs to the dining area. At least it always seemed like that hallway was going upstairs.

Back to this intersection. MayAnn referred to it as the crossroads. It was guarded by a nurse's station and Vera. Vera forever sitting at this crossroads, asking everyone who passed, "What day is this?" Vera was old. Maybe a relative of Eugene's. She held that same twinkle of humor in her eyes. MayAnn enjoyed their visits despite Vera's interruption of, "What day is this?"

Back to the crossroads. Ignore the nurse's station. That is where that lazy ass Bonnie hung out until she got bored and decided to go torture some resident for a laugh. "Focus," MayAnn thought. "Emptiness gone when?" "Oh yeah."

The day those two younger men came into this home. First one in a wheelchair. A strap holding his head up and back, for some unknown reason. No family bringing him in. Just a friendly lawyer-looking person MayAnn swore she knew. The gentleman was lucky, as Peggy was in charge. He would be taken care of.

Right behind him came another man. This one was tall, straight, confused, and led by a beautiful lady and what looked like twin daughters. Plus some boys who just had to be his sons. They all looked so sad. Like they had fought the fight to no end, but finally had to concede. MayAnn recognized this as the same look Eugene had had when he brought her to this home.

Half of MayAnn's heart leaped when the first gentleman came in. Just when she was getting that settled down, the other half of her heart joined the first. WHAM. The emptiness was gone. She didn't know why. MayAnn didn't have a clue what these two men had to do with her very heart, but it felt complete. Like maybe a circle had been closed. Vera asked them what day it was....................

24

Exercise (Alan)

Don't you realize that in a race everyone runs,
but only one person gets the prize? So run to win!
1 Corinthians 9:24 NLT

I seem to be in the best shape I have ever been. Or at least the last twenty years. That could be defined as "decades" can't it? I can't attribute it to the physical therapy department because the lazy-ass nurse who runs the little "exercise" room only knows how to fill out the necessary paperwork to bill the unsuspecting families. Those are the families who never seem to visit when all this PT is supposed to be taking place. Wish I could expose her for the fraud. But most of the staff seem happy to look the other way, even if the equipment is gathering dust. Once in a while during state inspections, Miss Lazy Ass puts on a front of running a couple of residents through the regimen. A stretchy band here, a rubber weight there, we're done. Charge an extra $500 a month for these nonexistent exercises.

No, I got in shape by trying to go home. At first it was a casual "Let's just walk out the door because this isn't a prison, after all." Then it progressed to a downright mad dash if I have an inkling of a security breach. I have even figured out how to unhook the alarm from the back of my shoulder, so it doesn't go off when I leave my comfy chair to escape. I can't override the alarm at the doors, but I have figured out that this decoration on my ankle automatically locks doors and sounds alarms. The best part is, most times I can take it off and hand it to my roommate for safekeeping while I dash. He is more than willing to help. It makes him smile. I love his smile. Such a brotherly gesture.

My preferred days of exercise are when Witch Hazel is on duty. I thought she got crushed by a house and melted into a green puddle back in Kansas or Oz or something. Nope, the Bad Bad Witch is here. I can almost hear her broom parking on the days she works. I wouldn't call it work. More like terrorizes. If my roommate had his motor functions, I bet he would "take her out." Not take out like on a date , but rather a right hook to that crooked witch's nose with the appearance of a wart on it. Oh, how I wish Larry would clock her. A baseball bat or golf club upside the head wouldn't be enough for that she-devil.

Best part is, she can't run for shoot. I would have used a more colorful word, but I don't seem to want to be so crude anymore. I would rather run like a chicken with its head cut off and be free. What an accurate description of my disease. Days more frequently coming are like my head has been lopped off. No sense of direction, just the muscle reaction to run and flop and bleed out. I would rather be hung upside down, go to sleep, one pass of the butcher knife, then twirl like a dervish. I do like me some fried chicken!

I have amassed a decent cheering section. What's his name, my roommate starts me out with a bang of laughter as I hand him my anklet and do a few warmup stretches. Maybe I should take him with me one of these days. I think I could push Larry's chair and still outrun Nurse Wretched. If I wasn't scared of, dang forgot his name, not holding on and falling out of his chair, I could never live with myself if I caused Larry any harm.

So, off I go into the wild blue yonder. Or at least past the room of that pretty lady who gives me an "off you go, son" boost. Down to the crossroads. I even know where the calendar hangs at the nurse's station so I can tell that really old lady guarding the intersection what day it is. Costs me a couple of seconds, but seems important to her to know, and my obligation to tell her the date. Wonder if she even works weekends as the crossing guard?

It doesn't matter. But it is also really important which direction I go. There is a door that leads to the outside at every end. I know the easiest door to pass through, but I avoid it if that Ratchet caregiver is around, because "Her Highness of Mean" would find a way to permanently barricade my escape. That way, she could spend more time on her lazy backside pretending to fill out daily charts. How much charting can you do in one day, anyway?

If I take a left, that little hallway seems to go upstairs (some days it does, some days it doesn't), but it always leads through the dining area, by the Sunday church gathering area, right next to the hardly ever used PT room, and out the back door. I enjoy this route because of all the tables I can weave between. Especially if it is Bingo day and more of my fans are gathered. The cheers come in waves as I round the tables. Markers are discarded long enough to clap. The volunteers are frozen in surprise. I can, if so desired, take a hard right and head down another hallway of possible escape. But then, it gives up to the possibility of being boxed in. Made that mistake a time or two.

I even heard the words, "Run, Forrest, run" one day from a gentleman who insisted on his Bingo card always having the O69 on it. He let me in on a little secret one day that the Bingo cards having this number usually won him more quarters and fruit than the other cards. Plus, a twinkle in one eye and a wink from the other needed no more words defining his choice of this number. Maybe his name was Don, or Dave, or something with a "D." I really liked the "Forrest" cheer. Probably one of the greatest movies of all time.

Every rare once in a while, I reach the confusion of the great outdoors. My goal was always to escape and go home. But once I broke past the barriers of confinement, I was hit by an alarming amount of confusion and noise. The real world was still out there, and it didn't welcome me. I could only continue to run blindly like that headless chicken.

One time, I made it to a small crowded sanctuary. It was a store I don't remember existing when I was growing up. I have never seen so much stuff packed into one little space. No passing of two shopping carts down one aisle. One way only. Worst part was, by the time I figured this out, I was in a far corner with no exit door in sight. I sat down with the brooms and mops and new fresh cleaning supplies and waited. The border patrol would come and take me back sooner or later. Glad I snagged some Twizzlers on the way by that candy aisle. Should have grabbed two. My roommate would have enjoyed the treat. Didn't think of that until I had already eaten the whole bag and was back in captivity. Hope they let me go back and pay that friendly store clerk one of these days…………………

Another day—man, the memory bank is open for business today—I went running down this long, long hill. Not extremely steep, but I was glad I wasn't trying to run up it. Nurse Crotch Rot was screaming at me, I do remember. Then, out of nowhere, a train flew over my head. I mean, a for-real full-length 120-car-unit train from Burlington/Santa Fe.

Honest to God's truth. It passed over my head. The tracks were even in the sky. Ghost Rider's herd of fire-breathing bulls had nothing over this freight train. I ducked. I fell. I rolled for like ever. I saw a COOP. What the heck is a COOP doing near flying trains? Why can't that train politely swoop down and carry off Nurse Crotchety? If there ever was a passionate God, this would happen. There would be more cheers from the Bingo gallery on that day.

Dang, another crossroads. Straight ahead leads over more railroad tracks. Maybe I could get to the other side and wait for the show as a local switching train ran over our Wicked Witch of the home. That street looks awful wide, though. Kinda reminds me of the Main Street my classmate David would spend hours on the weekend dragging up and down waiting for something exciting to happen in our small town.

A turn right leads to what looks like a rather large barrier and old nothingness. Been there, done that. A left has promise of freedom and alfalfa. It also runs parallel to that dang nab flying train. I'm a little confused here. Could use some help. Where is Ana, my direction?................

25

FORREST (Larry)

Therefore, since we are surrounded by such a great cloud of witnesses, let us throw off everything that hinders and the sin that so easily entangles. And let us run with perseverance the race marked out for us.

Hebrews 12:1 NIV

I have gained some semblance of confidence back. My body may have gone to hell, but my mind is working overtime. Don't sleep much. Don't need to. Why sleep when your body does nothing but nothing all fricken day? That is not my word of choice, but Alan's beautiful family came to see him today. One of his little girls even shyly worked her way onto my lap.

She touched my heart. Such dark eyes and innocence. I was lucky my hand found enough strength to stroke her long and amazingly soft hair. How did anything so beautiful come out of that running fool "Forrest?" Oh, how I didn't want my newly found angel to leave. Maybe I should have quit pursuing success long enough to raise a family. Alan's wife loves him so very much. You can tell that Alan loves her too Forever. Even if confusion is trying to rear its ugly head in Alan's mind. His heart wins out when Ana walks into the room.

I can see the heavy weight in Ana's eyes. The emotional pain is sitting there on the edge of tears. I can also sense the worry that is suppressed in front of Alan, but still lingering behind her beauty.

I can also tell that Ana has faced adversity before and has always overcome. There is a silent strength that must have grabbed Alan's heart and never let go. Alan is one lucky SOB. I can tell even with his cloud for a brain, he knows the treasure he has.

I wish I could help my roommate and newfound friend. He has always included me in his Forrest adventures. Maybe one day, he will grab the handles on my wheelchair and take me with him on his escape. I need to feel a little rush to my face. Hell, I wouldn't even mind if I fell out of my chair. Forrest and I could have a good laugh. His ox-like strength could easily pick me up, right my chair, and off we would go again.

Damn it, what is Alan doing now? He was having a nice conversation with his wife and girls, looked away, then when he looked back he said, "Hi, Mom, how are you today? And who are these pretty young ladies you have with you?" Come on, Alan, get it back together. Poor Ana's pain. Poor little girls' confusion with their unison reply, "It is us, Daddy, don't you remember??"

Now I have tears in my eyes. If I could roll my chair over and slap Alan, I would. Heck, if ole Nurse Ratchet Ass came in, she would probably slap him for me. I didn't know anyone could be so mean. I am almost scared of her. I see her tease Alan when he is having an off day. I am waiting for her to start her abusive shit with me. I think she knows that my mind is still sharp enough to rat her nasty ass out, even when I can't physically fight back.

Next time BB comes, I will have to check into what recourse we have to get this licensed POS of a nurse's aide permanently fired. She calls herself a nurse, and everyone seems to believe it. I know what CNA on a nametag means. I bet every resident in this facility would cheer as the "black cloud" was escorted out. But then, my Forrest would probably stop running. Don't want that to happen. His physical abilities will soon deplete too. I believe one day we will both be smothered by our own diseases. Alan, because his brain no longer tells his lungs to breathe. And me, because my lung muscles become too weak to function.

I hope God has room for us both. And room for that sweet old lady down the hall who keeps staring at Alan and me. It is a good stare. One filled with confusion, a sixth sense recognition, and a natural love. I remotely feel the connection too. Maybe I will have BB investigate her and discover the magic behind those stares.

While he is at it, we also need to figure out how to make sure Vera always knows what day it is. I hope she doesn't think I am ignoring her as I wheel by. Kinda hard to enunciate the days correctly anymore. Don't want to confuse the clever lady. God, she has to be like ninety-eight or older. And eyes with a never-ending twinkle of humor. I have heard her ask ole Mean Fricken Bitch of a CNA maybe twenty times in a row, "What day is it?" until the abuser left to go torture someone else. Hopefully, she just went out to have a smoke. Lung cancer couldn't grab her soon enough. I really shouldn't be thinking that. Forgive me, Lord...........

26

PEGGY

Let us not become weary in doing good, for at the proper time we will reap a harvest if we do not give up.

Galatians 6:9 NIV

Aww, another day of work here at the nursing home. I can't say why I chose this place to earn my pay four to five days a week. It is sad some days and weighs heavily on my heart. I chose nursing because I need to give. God has blessed me with an overflowing barrel of compassion. Where better to share this than right up the hill from where my family and I live?

I would make more money commuting twenty-two miles one way every day. But these residents own my heart. I could never leave them. They are each so special in their own way. I try to put a little sunshine in their lives when I am there. I do my best. Just holding their hand and talking to them for a couple of minutes is more than most of them get all day. I do feel bad about the amount of drugs I am required to feed some of them on a daily basis. Doctor's orders. I am not "qualified" to question this. We are drug-happy here in the US of A. Drugs to counteract the side effects of other drugs. There needs to be some accountability here. A checks and balances system that would eliminate eighty percent of the drug regimen that is built for the elderly. Then I suppose it would be another bureaucratic government program that would eat more taxes than benefits produced. Drugs or taxes. Hmmmmm, too much of both, don't you think?

This nursing home isn't so bad. At least it doesn't have that lingering smell of urine. My uncle was an administrator of a huge nursing home in the Denver area. When I was a teenager and went to visit, he took me on a tour. As the elevator was going up and stopped on like the fourth floor, Uncle Kork said to me, "I hope you have a strong stomach. This is our incontinent floor." As the door was sliding open, I was drowned in the smell of ammonia. And not the cleaning type. We didn't tour that floor. Uncle Kork simply hit the "close door" button and we proceeded to a more pleasant floor. I will never, ever forget that smell. I will never, ever let this home reach that level.

I suppose it helps that our simple home is on one floor, and those who are cursed with the uncontrollable bladder are scattered throughout. Plus, we have an exceptional cleaning staff. I even saw one of the cleaning ladies, Margie, lying underneath a bed in one room. She was wiping the dust off the bed springs. Either that, or was taking a nap, and made up a quick excuse why she was parked under that resident's bed. No, Margie is definitely one of the good ones. Clean, clean, clean clean clean.

We had one resident; I will call him Gil. He checked himself in one day. Simply walked in and said, "I am tired of living alone. I am not taking good care of myself. Do you have a room I can stay in?" It turned out the only medicine Gil took was a low-dose aspirin every once in a while for a mild headache. He was sharp as a tack, still strong, and just a little stiff in the legs. Gravity had pulled him slightly bending forward. I could tell a cane or walker would soon be needed.

Soon, the system took over Gil. It started with a nurse noticing how swollen Gil's feet were. Ted Hose (extremely tight socks to inhibit water retention in the feet, ankles, and calves) first. Then, a good old daily dose of a diuretic (water pill). Next thing you know, Gil occasionally wet himself because he just couldn't make it to the bathroom fast enough.

Next step, someone caught Gil in his room crying. He had buried everyone he had been close to, except one sister. Of course, he needed to cry once in a while. But whether because of sincere concern, or another way to profit, Gil was prescribed anti-depressants. Then his blood pressure was erratic. More pills. In less than a year, Gil went from a sharp ninety-eight-year-old man to a swamp of a man who continually pissed himself and was stuck cutting wheat somewhere in the '40s. Gil passed on not soon enough. Our system means well, but somebody needs to draw the line on the habit of passing drugs to treat every little thing. Die with dignity. Gil was preserved like a jar of dill pickles. Could sit in a jar forever not doing anything.

As a nurse, though, I am obligated to report every symptom and observation of every resident. That is then passed to a doctor who visits once or twice a month, and moves through resident exams with the sure speed of a quick profit made. He prescribes medicine that is promoted with a little kickback to his practice. Said doctor never quite sees the end results. The worst part, as a nurse, I am obligated to ensure every resident takes their prescribed medicine every day at the exact dose.

Don't get me wrong, some medicines are good. But the level of drugs that pass through a nursing home is unreal. It does make for a subdued home of a false tranquility. Will this ever change? I pray it is so. Let us stop drugging our elderly just to keep them around longer so our hearts feel that we tried, then stick them in a corner to be visited only on a holiday or birthday. We seem to think we have better things to do.

Third world countries have this figured out. Family takes care of the family. They can't afford nursing care, and wouldn't even think of sending their parents away. Drugs are few and far between or too expensive. Do your best by them every day. Find them a nice shade tree to sit under and let God's ensemble of birds bring musical joy to their lives. Life expectancy years are considerably less. But quality of life lived is considerably more. You simply die before you piss and shit yourself every day.

I'd better get off my soapbox and back to these residents. I might not be able to fix it, but I can give the ones here the best of Peggy.

"Yes, Vera, today is Wednesday. How is my beautiful lady today? Do you mind if I sit here with you for a little bit? Maybe we could take your blood pressure today. Today is Wednesday. Here is your afternoon medicine. Thank you for helping me with your pills. Here is some orange juice to wash them down. Today is Wednesday and a lovely day at that. Do you want to go see the birds? They are in quite a frenzy today and singing more than usual. Yes, on Wednesday at 4:00 we play Bingo. I will make sure you make it up those steps and into the dining area. Today is Wednesday. I need to go help catch Alan again. Even the birds seem to cheer him on."

I don't know what will happen with Alan. His bursts of speed and athleticism are amazing for the level of Alzheimer's conditions he is currently at. I am starting to think there is a trend to his escape attempts. It is definitely not on days that his wife and girls visit. Sometimes he runs on days when his adult boys visit. I think he is just showing off then. Most days recorded, though, are when I am off. I have a sneaking suspicion that there is another trigger due to a certain CNA on staff. She could be my polar opposite.

I'd better go check on Larry. Such a sweet man with such a sad story. I was told he had billions at one time and is now close to penniless. When I look into Larry's eyes, though, somehow I know he has a cache tucked away for a rainy day. I feel that Larry is trying to make it right with God. He is recorded as being a tough and unscrupulous man with an eye only for business and profit and little concern for his fellow man. I have a hard time believing that about Larry. His body started failing him sometime back and is progressively shutting him down at a saddeningly fast pace. I keep a close eye on his breathing. He is not far away from needing a breathing tube. It is hard to understand what he is saying. A feeding tube is also soon coming. I hope he knows how much I care.

Now, down the hall to my favorite lady. Little Miss MayAnn. Not too many days we see can relate to this day's events. She is mostly gone to some happy place. At least I pray it is a happy place. MayAnn always has a smile for me. She can only remember my name one day out of thirty. She always knows that I am someone who loves her and cares for her. That seems to be enough.

I see a spark out of MayAnn when she hears Alan running, or sees him fly by her room. She claps her hands like she is cheering one of her children on in a race. A light comes to her face that only a mother has for her kids. I wonder why Alan brings that out of her.

I parked MayAnn's wheelchair next to Larry's one day. MayAnn just blankly stared forward and a little down because her head is getting heavy now. I watched as she reached her hand out and clasped Larry's. She gave a motherly squeeze and held it. Tears came to Larry's eyes. I believe he felt love that he had never known. Oh, how these residents touch my heart.

"It is Wednesday, Vera."......................................

27

Dense Fog (Alan)

Yet I am always with you; you hold me by my right hand.
Psalms 73:23 NIV

I seem to be gliding into a heavy-ass fog. I would turn the lights on if I could find the damn switch. Don't have a clue what the switch even looks like. I haven't been able to get out of this haze for quite some time. F me. I am wandering and pushing and stumbling down this ever-narrowing hallway and the fog is pressing so heavy on me. Two walls closing in like the clamping of a vise on my brain, my life, my sense.

Someone is coming close. Do I know this person? I feel love. That is good. My heart leaps with joy. I think somewhere in the tangle of my fog, this person is important to me. Can I cut my way to a clearing? I need a machete in my hand, chop, advance, chop, advance, chop chop.

I really want to talk to this lady. She is holding my hand now. She is oh so beautiful. The young ladies with her carry the same beauty. My heart is overwhelmed. My hazed-over forest of a brain can go fly a kite. Can you fly a kite in the fog? Would someone bring a big fan and put it beside my head? Maybe if enough wind made it in one ear, it could push the fog out the other. Wouldn't that be a sight. I bet those pretty girls would giggle to see fog coming out of my ear.

My roommate is really quiet these days. He tries to speak, but mumbled garbage comes out. I can relate to that. Except my garbage stays all locked up and piled in my skull. I don't see much of any good left in there to use. People feed me now. I don't know if I am hungry or not. I try to be polite and eat what they shove toward my face. Oh, how I would love to munch on some good ole fried chicken. Or chow down some corn on the cob. Doesn't seem like I get much in the way of chewy type foods. Must have something to do with that choking episode I sprang on them a while back. It wasn't the problem of chewing and swallowing. That bitch aide was feeding me and seemed to find humor in how fast she could shovel food at me. Only reward was when someone grabbed me around the belly, pulled and lifted with a jerk, and I spewed half-digested shit all over that nasty witch of an NA.

Can't wait until I have another chance to spit something else on her. I haven't run much lately. My legs don't seem connected. I can't see them through the fog. They are there.

My wife is here. Oh, what a joy. She gave me a kiss on the cheek and the sun came out. My darling daughters with their big questioning eyes are hugging their mom. I think they are starting to become scared of me. I am glad to see Effie Viviane go talk to Larry again. She seems to have such a natural compassion. Larry always finds a little extra strength to stroke Effie's hair. She even calls him Uncle Larry. Special bond there. Don't know where it came from, but I won't stop it. Hell, I won't stop anything in the rare times the fog is gone.

Isabelle Veronica is talking a mile a minute. She always has so much to say. Most of it comes out so fast I can't understand it. Her energy is addictive. I would tell stories too, but Isabelle doesn't seem to need oxygen to talk. She makes my heart laugh. I am so very blessed to have such love in my life from these three. My boys bring me strength and humor. My girls bring me joy. My wife brings me peace. It is amazing how much better doses of love are versus the damn pills they give me twice a day. I am told they are good for me. Not nearly as good as family visiting.

The days my wife, sons and daughters, or other friends visit are my best. It is impossible to count the days in between. Sometimes it feels like mere minutes. Other times like years have passed. The gap in between is usually filled with a dear old lady who comes to visit often. She insists on holding my and Larry's hands. We can just sit with no conversation and be at peace. At least until that monster-type rag of an NA comes in and insists that MayAnn shouldn't be in our room. WTF is her problem? Is "happy" illegal in her angry world?

Who is this holding my hand now? I should know. The fog came back like a sledgehammer. Please don't give up and leave me. Please, oh, please stay. Young lady, tell me more about your adventure. Sweet other girl, come here and let me stroke your hair too. Amazing woman by my side, just keep your arm around me. Please don't pull away. Kiss me again so the fog leaves. My life has become a swamp. I think I shit myself. When did this start happening...........................

28

Together (MayAnn)

*Behold, this is the joy of His way; And out of the dust
others will spring.*

Job 8:19 KJV

I can tell I don't have much time left. I used to crochet some of the most amazing baby blankets and little doll clothes. Now, I can't seem to ever untie the knots in my yarn. Every day, someone hands me this wadded-up tangled mess of yellow string. It does give me focus. A couple of times I have almost won and solved the puzzle. Then things scramble and I am back to a mass of half hitches and scrambled eggs.

I don't care so much anymore. The hallways are narrow now. I can only focus on a small clearing in front of me. Everything on the sides is a blur. Distractions leap at me from blind directions. If I could just find the right door, maybe I could escape into a room wide and high and open and fresh and open and clear and singing with life. I can't see the doors anymore. Just this long, narrow hallway.

There is an occasional treat for me. Somehow, these two men come from my blindside. One on my right and one on my left. We sit together. I reach past the blur and grab their hands. I hold on for dear life and try to pull them into my little hallway. Neither of them speaks. I don't say anything, either. Our hands talk. A magic starts. We have found that open room.

We dance. We chat. We have cake and punch. It is like a wedding party, but just the three of us. A potluck of emotion carries us as a family. I don't know these men. Why are they almost vegetables but only in the hallway? In this room, we are young. We are happy. I love the time we are able to share together. Oh, if I could just shut and lock the door to that prison of a hallway. Can't everyone see that we belong together here?

It would be even more perfect if my family and these men's families could join us. Oh, what a party. What a reunion we could have. I can taste the joy. My family together with (I think his name is Alan)'s family. And (I think his name is Larry)—he doesn't seem to have any family, just a nice lawyer who comes to visit him. He could come to our party, too. Maybe we could draw up a contract that would be binding enough to keep us in this room of pure love. We might also be able to draw up a restraining order for the evil one who keeps pushing me back into the hallway.

Back to our party. Have to harvest while the crop is ripe. Where the heck did I ever hear that? Can I invite my mom and dad to the party too? Maybe all our moms and dads and grandpas and grandmas. The room would just naturally grow with the sunshine that only parents and grandparents can bring. Oh, how I miss them. Why did they ever leave?

It seems strange that I would want a feast at our party. I don't ever seem to be hungry anymore. Food is nothing most days. Just an exercise that I find confusing. But in this happy room, we are having the ultimate barbecue. People are playing cornhole. Kids are running and weaving amongst our legs. No pretenses. No comparing who has the largest bank account. Just love at its most complex design. And cake. I could eat some German chocolate cake right now. The world would come to a complete stop as I partook of that first bite. "Savor me," the cake would beg.

I feel like this room is going to become a permanent residence soon. The little blind hallway is soon a bad memory. I am ready to meet my Maker. God has blessed me over and over. I feel that blessing when I hold those younger men's hands. Maybe God will explain that to me at the Pearly Gates. I have lots of questions for Him.

I understand, I am old, and due to expire within a reasonable number of years. "But God, why are these two men going through their suffering?" What did they do to deserve their punishment? One has a body that quit and left with a mind that knows every detail of his sentence. The other has pudding for a brain but can run like the wind. At least he used to. Haven't seen that excitement in quite some time. I am afraid he is caught in his own hallway.

I am so ashamed right now. The humiliation of someone having to take me to the bathroom, patiently wait while I do my business. Then have to stand me up, bend me over slightly, and wipe my behind. No matter how dark my day, this has to be one of the worst things I am forced to go through. Pride has left the building. I feel so bad when I make a mess they have to clean up. I don't want to be helpless. I can't even tell them how sorry I am. I can only cry and most of that stays in my hallway too.

Bath day is another adventure. Some of the ladies try their best to be gentle and polite. They seem to sense my modesty and keep me covered as the hydraulic chair lifts my nakedness five feet in the air so they can swing me over a stainless steel tub that reminds me of a horse tank. Then I get lowered into the water that is almost shoulder-deep. The good ones have the temperature perfect.

Then there is Bonnie. Tears my clothes off like she has better things to do. Plops me in that cold plastic chair thing. Straps me in with no concern if she pinches anything. She even giggles when I flinch. The water is always somewhere between lukewarm and cold. I think she enjoys seeing me shiver.

One day, as I was perched five feet in the air waiting to get dunked in her uncaring bath, she got her phone out and took pictures of parts of me that should never be shared. There was an evil behind her eyes as she added text to her ugliness. The joy when she hit "share" was sickening. I could do nothing. I can't even speak now. I know when something wrong and terrible is happening. I pray, "Oh, God, please take me in your arms. Do I deserve this time with the Devil's worker? Can you ever forgive me for giving my twins away?"

Twins. Where did that bomb drop from? I know I had a son, a daughter, another son, and a miscarriage with my husband, Eugene. Did I have twins in a past life? Is there a memory buried so very deep by antidepressants that only the shock of evil makes surface?

I seem to remember a humongous church and overpowering doors. Someone named Tex comes to mind. Fear. Shaking. Helplessness. Reaching. Cowboy. Strength. Calm. Panic. Strength. Calm. Direction. There is a story here somewhere. I can't quite reach it.

SHIT that water is cold. What are you laughing about, you heartless bitch? Did I really just scream that terrible word out? I was in God's house one minute and next snapped back into hell. Hell deserves that word. Forgive me, Lord. Take me away. I want to go to my happy room.

Twins…………………….

29

FIX IT (Larry)

Therefore, prepare your minds for action, keep sober in spirit,
fix your hope completely on the grace to be brought
to you at the revelation of Jesus Christ.

1Peter 1:13 NASB

I don't know how to fix it. For so many years, I could fix
everything. Stock market tumble, make money on the
downslide. Truck broke down, yeah like that ever happened,
but I could have fixed it. Friends with problems, who had time for
friends. Guess I didn't fix that. If there was a problem, though, I
would address, correct, move on and up. That was me.

Now, I see the not so good of life. I see a bad, bad problem in this
facility. There is so much good, but one little spot of mold is trying
to rot the whole basket of apples. That mold has got to go.

I heard a couple of the NAs whispering about a nasty Instagram
they received from one of their fellow workers. It was a photo of
something that should never ever be taken, no less shared. How
ugly does a person's mind have to be to walk in those depths?

People talk freely around me all the time. They might share their
problems. They might tell me a dirty joke. They all seem to like
to share their secrets. I just sit here and take it. My body is almost
useless. I will soon have a tube buried in my throat breathing for
me. I will also have another in my gut feeding me. Not much quality
of life left then. Is the one consolation the fact I have little to no

pain? At least in the physical sense. Mentally, well hell. It has been good exercise to work through that.

God and I have an understanding. I listen to everyone. I absorb their problems. I lift them up to Him Who has answers. Only thing left I can lift, so might as well crank out a good twenty prayers or so daily.

The only thing that bothers me now is I can't figure out how to fix the darkness that lurks these hallways four or five days a week. I throw prayers at God right and left that this CNA might get a terminal illness. Even a bad cold that keeps her away for a couple of days is Thanksgiving for all.

Temporary respite is not the answer. I really, really, REALLY need to fix this if it is the last thing I do with my shortened life. I didn't know I could care about any one person so deeply. Let alone, a whole care facility full of the helpless and old. Most of these people here have nothing left. Just time until. And oh, how many of them look forward to the until.

Each and every day I see the wandering. The miserable. The lost. The only existing. There is no living. I had a 105-year-old sweetness of a lady come into my room one day, looked me straight in the eyes and asked, "Why am I still here?" I had no answer. I slurred out something about, "God must still have a purpose for you." This over-a-century-of-life lady replied, "I think God forgot about me." I cried. Again.

Back to my mission. I heard a scream the other day. It was the S word that rang down the whole hallway. I could tell it was MayAnn. I saw the devil herself pushing MayAnn to the bathing room. I knew how ugly the next half hour would be for poor MayAnn. I had never heard her scream like that. I was glad when I saw Peggy go running by. I knew that MayAnn's torture would be cut short. What can I do to fix this before next time?

I have experienced this cruelty for myself. I can no longer be raised in that hydraulic chair and lowered into the dunk tank. Because my body and head have to be supported at all times, I am strapped to a PVC throne that has a toilet seat for a bottom (in case a bowel movement is necessary). I am then wheeled up against a wall and sprayed down like a 4-H livestock display.

Most of the CNAs try to spare me some dignity. They avert their eyes as they scrub me down, and actually provide a half-pleasant shower experience. They also talk the whole time about husband or boyfriend problems, sick kids, money woes, whatever takes their mind off a grown man being handwashed by a young lady. Thank God that one muscle doesn't work anymore either.

Then there is El Diablo. Those showers don't go so well. She finds humor in the coldest shower she can inflict on another human being who is completely helpless. She even played with my junk one day with a "Come on, big boy, can't you get it up no more." God forgive me, if I had a gun…

A few family members from different residents have had meetings with the administrator. That seems to have led to nothing. There have been grievance officials assigned. Still nothing. Does no one really care? Is the protection of a care facility's reputation more important than the protection of the residents?

Why and how can evil be allowed to lurk here? Are profits or survival of the entity more important?

Don't get me wrong. There are some fantastic and caring people working here. They are doing their best. There are also the others. The ones who have been working here so long they are inbred to the system. They know how to play the game getting the most out of the pay scale with the littlest amount of work. Those, I can tolerate. I would love to fire their smug and uncaring asses for spite. That would feel good. Sometimes, though, one needs to weigh the thought of firing a person.

A wise man who dedicated his soul to the ethanol industry once said, "If you fire your worst employee, someone will always step down and take their place. You must carefully weigh how much of that bad employee you can tolerate before you dismiss them. The next employee that takes his/her place might be worse."

This case is different, though. No one can be as terrible and evil as this CNA. She needs to be locked behind bars. She needs to have a prison shower experience herself. How can administration and people assigned the position to protect residents turn such a blind eye? They need to be reviewed/fired too.

I seem to be ranting here. But until someone has the balls to go into places like this and really see the evil lurking, then I guess all will silently suffer. Even Forrest can't run away from the nasty darkness that keeps visiting this place. How can such good and such evil coexist in a care facility? Who is responsible?

Are the families at fault because they don't want to know the possibilities? Do they really believe that paying $6,000 to $10,000 per month is enough to insure against violations? How did we as a society lower ourselves to pay someone else to care for our family members? Are our careers, social lives, and ambitions that much more important than the people who brought us into this world? I wasn't any better. My world was all about ME. I deserve the place where I am sitting now. But so many of the dear people up here don't deserve the life they are ending with.

Maybe I should get on the medical and pharmaceutical companies for learning how to prolong life for a profit, by treating, not curing. We all flock to CVS to get the latest and greatest medicine for our aches and pains and another five to twenty years in this world. Quantity over quality. We need to fix this.

Alan even told me (on one of his coherent days) that his plan was to retire in Paraguay. Live tranquilo on Social Security. Sit under a shade tree and take Terere with his beautiful Ana every day. Then, when he got really sick, or some organ started shutting down, he would die. Somewhere, his plans went south. Oh, how ugly Alzheimer's is.

I think deep inside some dark recess, Alan knows he is trapped. He knows that he is causing his family more pain than he is suffering himself. At least that is the current consensus: "The family suffers more than the patient because the patient doesn't know what is going on." Pure bullshit, that statement. It is like telling someone going through their own personal hell of loss or suffering that "God will never give you more than you can handle." Another bullshit line. Both those statements simply make the person saying the words feel better, never the victim.

Alan is going through hell, MayAnn is going through hell. Their families are going through hell. Even Vera is going through a hell of not knowing what day it is. I deserve my hell. I can hear hell walking down the hallway. Who will be the victim today? God help me fix this.............

30

An Ending (Peggy)

For the mind of the flesh is death; but the mind
of the Spirit is life and peace:

Romans 8:6 ASV

We closed the double doors to one of the main hallways today. It is always deathly silent on the days the double doors close. No pun intended. It simply means another resident has passed on. The rest of the home doesn't need to share in the solemnity of the designated funeral home coming in to pick up the body. The residents who are trapped in the same hallway have their doors closed. No excitement. No real mourning. Everyone here knows it will one day be their turn. It is a matter of time. Not even who, what, where, and how. Only question is when.

When I first started working in a nursing home, as a CNA, I was reluctant to face my first death. How could I pour myself into these dear people every day and not suffer grief in the deepest level as they moved on?

Then, I came to realize it was a blessing for them to die. The pain was over. The questions were answered. They left. We moved on.

If a death happened on my shift, I always volunteered to be the one to clean up the body prior to being picked up. I wanted to be the one to show them the honor and respect they deserved for making it through life in this sometimes meaningless world.

How better to be with them than to take care of the body left behind?

I always, always felt God there in the room with me. I had tears for my friend who left me. God would gently wipe my tears to the side as I bathed and clothed what was here. I always thanked God for letting me know He had taken them to His Eternal Home. A calmness and completeness would fill me. There is so much better on the other side. Some days, I wish I could have gone with them. Right then.

God would gently tell me that I still have work to do. There are another forty-nine residents under my care that God had put me in charge of. We all have our purpose here in this world, and I was very blessed to find mine. Even through the endless schooling and training and tests and exhaustion at the same time I was raising my own family. To become a registered nurse was a mission I would repeat over and over if God asked that of me.

Am I preaching? I hope so. Are you listening? I pray so.

The lady I am cleaning up today, just she and I behind a closed door. Her roommate out in the dining area having special treats of ice cream and conversation from our activity director, knows of the loss. Today she is counting herself lucky that she is going second and kinda gets spoiled for half a day.

The one with me in the room wrestled with guilt and cancer, each at their own painful levels. Every time I gave care to this lady, I could smell the cancer on her breath. It was eating her alive from the inside. Drugs helped a little. She was such a strong tiny woman.

I think the guilt destroyed her first. She never would quite share her burden. She would sob something about the terrible thing she did with a priest that could never be forgiven. Her Catholic faith would not absolve her of this guilt. Maybe on the outside, confessions and Hail Marys were passed. They must have never reached deep enough for this poor lady to realize true forgiveness. This guilt was so much worse than the black death that ate up every healthy cell in her body. We all have our dark secrets. Hers no worse than any of us. If you think differently, I feel for you.

I do know that Jesus came and gently took her in His arms prior to her passing. Peace had found her. It was time to go Home. There was a Light that revealed the meaning of that cross she had always worn. It was good. She found the Truth. I now have her body ready to leave the facility. Thank you, God...............

31

Memories (Alan)

The slothful man roasteth not that which he took in hunting;
But the precious substance of men is to the diligent.

Proverbs 12:27 ASV

Today I heard a gunshot. It was far off in the distance. Maybe down on the river bottom. Must be deer season. Maybe I should ask Vera what day it is?

That gunshot brought back a flood of memories. Good ones. With one of those friends who just came into my life one day and parked himself there. My friend Dean is an avid hunter. Not a hunting enthusiast. A downright "Let's go" anytime, night or day, always ready, hunter.

I helped Dean move his household a couple of times. I knew he had a fair amount of camo, but the first time I actually saw his walk-in closet packed (perfectly organized though) full of camouflage to fit any and every scenario, I was awestruck. The only thing I could imagine, though, was Dean standing there, scratching his somewhat balding head, staring into that massive closet full of hunting apparel and saying, "I don't have a thing to wear." I told him those exact thoughts of mine, accompanied by a heartfelt laugh.

To get even with my comparing him to a common feminine situation that most men cannot begin to understand, he had me help him move his massive gun safe. Not once, but twice. And, for some reason, both times were out of and back into a basement.

No wonder my left nut hangs halfway down to my knees. I told Dean, "Next time you are on your own. Or you should just buy a new gun safe every time you move." I am positive the last house he built, the gun safe was set first and the house was built around it.

I did appreciate that Dean's massive amount of clothing and number of guns were not just for show. He used every item for one type of hunt or another. Nothing gathered dust. Dean never bragged about what he owned and just had to show off. You had to dig it out of Dean and ask to see his new purchase or collection or "What should I wear today" closet. Sorry, Dean, had to put another shot in there.

Dean was always asking me to go hunting with him. I enjoyed hunting. Didn't think much of the killing part. Kinda tugged at my heartstrings. Dean and I both always made use of whatever animals were in season. The freezer was filled with wild game meat. Perfect jerky was an ultimate goal. Turkey jerky kinda sucked. Deer sticks were the best. Elk steaks could replace a beef T-bone any day. And duck/goose nuggets, Dean cooked up the best.

We always seemed to create a hunting story without even trying. Something we could share at a campfire the night before the next big opening season. Stories that carried us back with a smile for years to come. Damn, which one was my favorite?

Our hunting vehicle of choice for a few years was a 1984 Toyota Land Cruiser wagon. It was the ultimate rig. Instead of four able bodies crammed into the front of a pickup truck (prior to the crew cab years), our wagon could comfortably fit four, plus a kid or two sitting in between us Frontier Freemont type dudes. I usually drove and seldom had a gun for myself. Simply because I liked helping find the game and letting others do the shooting. Plus, Dean was such a good shot and quick fire, I didn't have a ghost's chance of first draw. Dean would have been one of those cowboys in the Western movies who was faster and more accurate with his rifle than any bandito with a six shooter. And shotgun accuracy/

quickness, pheasants, quail, ducks, and geese didn't stand a chance. It was fun to watch. The only gun I was faster on the draw with was, well, that is why I have an ex-wife.

The deer hunting area of choice was right next to the neighboring state line. Due to requested anonymity, I'd best leave exact locations to one's imagination. Let's just say on one side of the state line, deer season (rifle type) started two weeks earlier than the other side. We knew this, The largest, oldest, and trophy-type bucks knew this fact too.

Opening morning, as the greenhorn hunters started firing at anything on four legs and moving, the survivors headed south. Within a bounding of a mile or two, the monster deer could cross the state line to safety. It was amazing how they could lead their herd just below a ridgeline staying out of sight for the most part, and flat out disappear. It was like the black hole theory in outer space. These wise leaders could step through, only to be revealed on the other side of safety.

Dean and I had a tendency to not quite remember where the hell that state line really was. It didn't matter that a straight road took a 1/8th mile jog to the left and then straight again because the surveyors from one state didn't agree with the land markers from the neighboring state. We just never could find a sign telling us the truth. I believe our arguments were true and just. It wasn't our fault that officials only put their "Home of Beautiful Women" sign on the highways and none on country roads. Probably more because these signs made really good targets for wannabe hunter-type assholes. Don't understand the humor in shooting signs or mailboxes. Ignorant city bastards anyway.

Our forays typically consisted of driving around to different outlooks, watching the deer moving south, listening to the smaller version of WWII, and patiently waiting till it was naptime for those who imbibed a little too much Crown Royal the night before. Then, we would head in a southerly direction down some "low maintenance" dirt roads, scanning, looking, using our peripheral vision to catch out-of-place movement. It was the hunt.

No sitting in a tree stand for us. There was maybe one tree in a five-mile radius, and that was only there because some bird had eaten the seed, and then pooped it out as it flew over. Or maybe an old homestead long forgotten on which the original settlers had planted a few precious shade and windbreak trees. No, it was open country. You drove from one area to the next, then parked your vehicle and explored the neighboring draw or canyon. Only when you spotted something from half a mile away or longer, was the hunt on. Dean usually liked to be within 400 yards or so. Anything less than that was too easy and not fair for the animal. My opinion, with Dean shooting, 400 yards in a snow blizzard, thirty-mile-an-hour winds and the only way to pick out the buck was that he would be the one mounting one of the other deer, was still not much of a challenge for my dead-nuts-on marksman of a friend.

There was one day, though, cold and clear. A day that fooled you into thinking it was warm out because of the blinding sun, but when you stepped out and took a breath, your teeth hurt. It was fricken cold. We had made the excuse that our best route to the next preferred hunting area a few sections over was going south a couple of miles, heading west, and then back north. Mainly because there was no road straight over due to some massive rolling hills, rock bluffs, and awesome canyons. Secondly, because we had an inkling of where Big Boy might be.

On our way in the southerly direction, we caught that glimpse of slight movement. Within said movement was a respectable 5 x 5 muley, trailing a sneaky distance behind a good size herd of twelve or more does and one idiot spike buck that still sought mommy's tit. The buck was a keeper and would warrant bragging rights. We drove on past, and Dean hopped out a ways down the road. He cleared the barbed wire fence as only a trained and expert Ninja hunter could do. Dean's outfit of choice that day blended in well with the dried-up pasture grass. Never mind the 40%+ coverage of fluorescent orange we were all required to wear. (Another requirement caused by ignorant hunters who shot at anything that moved.) Even with all that orange, Dean knew how to work the hills, soap weeds, and wind direction to realize the best possible stealth maneuver ever.

I had turned the Land Cruiser around to head back to a location where I could watch the show. Plus, the gold-colored wagon would distract the curious deer long enough to enable Dean to arrive at his predetermined "clear shot" spot. Five minutes later, BOOM. It was done. Time to go help Dean drag his monster back to the hunting rig. Fifteen minutes later and out of breath, we had thrown the 250-pound carcass into the back of the wagon, slammed the hatch, and rather hurriedly headed North.

I told Dean I knew of a field a mile ahead where we could stop and gut his prize for some much appreciative carnivores. It was the perfect spot to maybe peg a coyote or two later when they came to feed. Plus, it was probably back in the same state that Dean's permit was good for. Good plan, off we went.

About a quarter-mile before our destination, I started hearing some shuffling and "Dad".......""DAD"..... "I think the deer is still alive" my son riding in the back seat was sharing rather excitedly. I looked in the rearview to see a set of "more than aware" deer in the headlight eyes staring back at me. His rack was getting ready to destroy the headliner of the Land Cruiser. It was either my son or Dean's brother who grabbed the rack and sort of held the head in place as I took a rather rough shortcut through a ditch and into an open stubble field that would just have to do.

Dean and I both jumped out. I believe we did this before our rig had even stopped. It was our turn to have that same "deer in the headlight" look. We opened the top hatch and bottom tailgate as quickly as we could. Our passengers turned the head of the deer to the opening and released. My cowboy instinct grabbed the buck by the horns as it exited the Land Cruiser. I dug my heels in as the buck was taking off on a powerful last attempt at life. Bulldogging was in play. Dean seemed like he was riding this Buck at the same time I was wrestling it to the ground. Dean's knife quickly came out and ended the rodeo. Man, did we have a story to share. Honest to God, this happened. And it was way before *Tommy Boy* ever hit the movie theater. I believe we could sue for copyright infringement. Good cowboy/hunters like us would never come close to being able to make up a story like that. Just too good. It was fun to point at that little tear in the headliner of the Land Cruiser and reminisce on the evidence.

Which leads into another story involving the same rig. This time, Dean's dad was with us. Turkey season. Warm day. Tough spotting. About ready to call it a day, scenario. But my hard head and Dean's diehard attitude of filling a tag kept us pressing on.

Wild turkey hunting had been a very frustrating and unrewarding experience for us the first couple of years. Wild turkeys somehow magically started to repopulate our area in the mid-'80s. Before that, they were almost extinct. You saw some in zoos, and heard about how hardy and food supplying they were for the early settlers. They were once considered a never-ending supply, and there were no hunting regulations. Open season all year round led to the wild turkey's near-demise. By the 1930s, this bird was extirpated from eighteen of the lower forty-eight. What was once a population in the tens of millions was reduced to less than a couple hundred thousand. The wild turkey came damn close to the history of the dodo bird.

Thanks to the National Wild Turkey Federation and the Net Cannon, these entertaining and hard as hell to catch birds were captured and repopulated from "have" states to "have-not" states. * Now, populations are back up in the over seven million category. It is probably the greatest conservation success story in America.

Back to our hunt. Like I said, the first couple of years was frustrating and predominantly unsuccessful out in our open range. Toward town around the public lands of the local lake, and along the river bottoms, hunters could sit in camouflage or up in a tree and call the birds in. Especially during mating season. Yeah, us males are idiots and will sniff out most any female. Especially if they give us a "Come here, big boy" signal.

But in our part of the woods, or lack of trees thereof, the sitting and calling only led to taking a nap. Invariably, we would post up on one side of the creek, and the turkey would appear on the other side and refuse to cross. I think they laughed at us.

I watched Dean one time spend a couple of hours crawling through an alfalfa feed on his belly, trying to sneak up on these surprisingly elusive birds. Only to stand up for a shot, and they were already too far away. One time, I watched my brother take off running after them. He was a running fool. Only to finally have to give up. If brother Harry couldn't catch them on foot, no one could.

We were driving by an alfalfa field on another "Time to give up" day. Said field was between two creek lines, turkeys (like thirty or so) three fourths of the way up the field. They were just far enough away that it would be impossible to get to them Injun style before they could disappear down that creek line.

Then a simple statement from me, "Let's try this." Landcruiser tearing into the field. Turkeys' heads up but dumbfounded by this gold-colored mass barreling toward them. We actually drove right smack in the middle of the rafter. I stopped. Dean jumped out. Turkey tag filled. End of story. No, actually, new story to tell. New chapter opened. End of frustration. Don't bring up hunting ethics. We have never shot from the vehicle. Well, at least Dean and I haven't. He has an uncle who can brag about two turkeys, one shot, and in flight.

The day in subject, a few years after our new technique discovery was a most sun-filled and beautiful day. We preferred snowy, cold, and shitty when no other hunters were out, but "last day" hunts have no regard for the weather.

As I said, Dean's dad was with us. Same gold Toyota. Midafternoon. Almost ready to say to heck with it when off to the north, Dean spotted around eight to ten turkeys. They were a good half-mile away in a pasture that had small rolling hills and another close to the creek scenario. Dean's dad made the obvious statement of, "We will never get to them." This was followed by Dean calmly saying as he grasped the security handle above the passenger door window, "Hold on, Dad."

Dean and I had been hunting long enough to know each other's habits. Dean knew if I ever heard the words "We will never get to them," it was a personal challenge. And believe it or not, alcohol was never involved. It was never a "Hold my beer" scenario, but simply "HOLD ON, HERE WE GO."

A few bumps and 70 mph later through the pasture, Dean's dad had a good shot at the biggest Tom. Tom went down. Dean ran and snatched. Hatch open, turkey thrown in, hatch slammed shut. Turkey's head hadn't cleared the demarcation line. Turkey blood sprayed all over the outside back of the Cruiser. Hatch opened back up. Head guided inside. We calmly left the pasture. It was a neighbor's ground and I had gained permission to hunt several years prior. But something about the wild chase to the shot had adrenaline flowing and common sense absent. It was so funny. No harm to the turkey, Dean's dad was an excellent shot like his son. Turkey was past dead and pain. Sorry if we offended any animal-rights-type people. No, we're not sorry. Deep fat fried wild turkey is awesome. So is our story of slamming the hatch on a not-quite-inside-the-vehicle turkey. That blood was kind of a bitch to wash off by the time we got home.

Damn, I could tell stories of Dean and my exploits for days. It feels good to have a room full of memories in what is left of my depleting brain. No scrambled eggs today. At least not in this room. I suppose I will be back out in the hallway again. Would be good to have Dean come visit one of these days. He would be the one friend who wouldn't question if I told him to please take me out back and end this. Dean would understand. He would end this suffering only because I asked, and not because he felt sorry for me. Now, that is the definition of friend without question. The world needs more Deans……………………………………..

*Stephen Messenger and The Dodo.com

32

GUILT (Larry)

My guilt overwhelms me—it is a burden too heavy to bear.
Psalms 38:4 NLT

Sitting here strapped to my chair, I have only time to reflect. No thinking ahead. That destination is determined. I know the exact details of my demise. I could say that I am blessed to have the knowledge of how I am going to die. No guessing game there.

I do have time to dig up regrets. I went so long with my "Come what may" approach because I could control every situation. I had absolutely no regard to the trail of pain I might have left behind. You will never see that cluttered path if you don't look back. Maybe that is why God stuck me in this situation of helplessness. It was time to pay my dues. I am now forced to see the damage.

Life's tragedy is, we get old too soon and wise too late. I thought of myself as being wiser than most at a rather early age. There was no regard for others' feelings. Either move over or get run over. I was a dick. I was the ultimate asshole. Who cared, though, I had the American dream in my back pocket.

Now, the conquests are meaningless. I am alone because of my own making. The millions/over a billion, hold nothing in my heart. If you ever want to see the true value of the dollar bill, give it all away. After that, what you thought were your friends disappear faster than nachos at a football game.

Alcoholics and drug addicts at least have an excuse for the lives they destroy. And many clean up, chase down necessary apologies, and seek forgiveness. Theirs is a disease that consumes them. It will never go away. They have to be trained into a new mindset, a different way of life. A set of friends who pick them up and not drag them back down is a must. A higher power is introduced. That is one mistake I still see in rehab. "Higher Power?" What the heck? God is what is needed. No idol. Hell, their drug was a false idol and you want to mask another as a higher power. Call a spade a spade. God is One. There is no other, period. Don't like it, then go back into your perfect little judgmental hole.

In all my exploits, I had the tendency to walk away from my God and my Savior. I have already shared my story of becoming a Christian at fourteen and my life forever changing. That is true. What I didn't tell you was how many times between then and now that I walked my own path, hit a bottom, looked to God, and He was there waiting for me. It was always me who turned my back on God. He never once renounced me with His actions.

Regrets, yeah probably. Guilt, most definitely. From all the women I used simply for pleasure to the small mom and pop stores I swallowed up with my conglomerate of large wholesale-type marketing. And all of this before online shopping and Tinder. I simply ran over anyone in the way. I took whatever I looked at and wanted.

I don't want to share specifics. I apologize to every woman I ever held and discarded. It wouldn't have been so bad if they had been gold diggers. Those types deserve what they get. If money is a higher priority than love, yours truly has no sympathy. But I attacked from a different angle.

I never once used my wealth as a crutch for female conquest. I sought out women of not only beauty, but substance. There needed to be something going on upstairs to spark my interest. If it was easy and free, I didn't want it. No, I went after successful career types. I hungered for other men's wives. They were all a challenge I enjoyed, more than the sex itself.

I was once accused of being a sex addict. I never thought of it as an addiction. See something I like, pursue it, catch, use, then release. I was a fisher of ladies. No addiction. Didn't have to go out and buy. Although, I will admit to visiting a brothel or two just because of curiosity more than carnal need. I didn't know whether to feel sorry for or respect the women of the oldest trade in the world. Each had her own story. Each was trying to survive. It was always respect that I left them with, and a great tip.

Was God proud of me during these times? Well, probably not. Most definitely I hurt my Father. Here He put His Son on this Earth to be killed by self-important assholes and ignorant mobs in the most grueling death possible. Jesus died for me, and I really didn't care. This world brought me all the happiness I needed. Money, recognition and some good lovin'. I didn't need anything else. Even though God bailed me out of bad places on several occasions, I didn't care.

I would toe the line for a while. Even did some lay preaching. I was filled with a sermon for every situation. I was pretty awesome. Give me any subject. Any. And I could whip out a fifteen- to thirty-minute no-notes preaching extravaganza that drove the message of God home to anyone who would listen.

Then, some skirt would walk by. My eyes would lock. My hunger overcame. A new challenge. Sometimes, it was a past exploit I seemed to keep in the background and would easily bring back up front with their hope that they could make that one connection that would tie me down. I probably feel the most guilt for those ladies. I discarded them, gave them time to move on, get married, start a new life, and then simply reached out and pulled them back. Destroying everything about their security, their family, their world. I pulled them back into mine just long enough to prove to myself that I was still Numero Uno in their lives, then discard them once again. What a complete uncaring, horrific person was I. I deserve this death sentence I have received. It wouldn't be a surprise to see crowds dance on my grave.

The worst part, I could probably contact any one of those women and they would drop everything to come and take care of me. They all know I have a heart hidden somewhere within my heartless life. I could even provide a list of names. I remember and cherish each and every one. They all had me trapped. I just kept myself shallow enough not to be permanently snared. No matter how badly I wanted to do right and be right, I continually turned back and failed.

I even had the thought at one time that the only thing to save me from my hunger to consume women was if God struck me blind. I would still be left with taste and smell. At least my eyes being useless would save me from the neck strains caused by the next appetizer to walk by. If I couldn't see them, maybe I could avoid them and get back on the straight and narrow.

Probably the better solution would be to find a woman as beautiful and amazing as what my roommate Alan found. I could see myself locking in permanently and faithfully to a woman like that. She fills our room with a natural love that only the best of the best of all women could. I envy Alan. I am proud of Alan. I know he has his own guilt to deal with. Ana is already like a sister to me. Even the worthless piece of shit I was to so many would never cross that line. Alan is like a brother to me. The brother I never had. Maybe that is why I was such a self-indulgent MF. I needed a brother or some brothers to give me good and timely counsel. What a prick I have been.

Where did I ever learn this completely male chauvinistic attitude? My dad was rough, demanding, and never flinched. But he loved and respected my mother. She was strong, gentle, and tolerated my dad. I didn't learn my disregard for feelings from my parents. Where did it come from? Is there another branch on my family tree I am unaware of? Can I find someone to blame?

No, blaming others, whether an abusive dad, lack of money, drugged-out mother, genetics, or any other shallow excuse is chicken shit. Step up, take responsibility for your own actions. Don't hide behind a past. Determine your own future. Guilty as charged. Live with it.

To all those wonderful and beautiful and innocent ladies, please forgive me.

God forgive me……………………………………….

33

Was I a Good Mother (MayAnn)

Her children arise and call her blessed;
her husband also, and he praises her.

Proverbs 31:28 NIV

MayAnn wasn't around much anymore, though her body was still here. The yarn she so diligently worked with for years was quietly sitting in a basket in the corner. When her children and grandchildren came to visit, invariably one of them would grab the tangled-up mess in the basket and try to solve the impossible puzzle. It would be so much easier to simply cut the string away from the ball and throw it away. There is an unspoken respect for what these tangles represent. Even MayAnn's great-grandchildren knew that if only they could untangle the knots, their great-grandma would return.

What do you say to a person you love who raised you, watched over you while your parents were busy, and held you in her arms with undying love when now she has such a blank stare in those eyes that had always twinkled? Talk about the lights are on but nobody's home. What do you say?

The best answer is to sit beside them and hold their hand. Talk about whatever happened throughout the week. Try to find something that penetrates the fog. Somehow bring a smile out. Just a flicker of recognition would erase the pain slamming so hard on the visitors.

MayAnn's daughter, Sue, was her designated caregiver. If any questions arose about her mom's care, Sue would get the call and come handle matters. Sue didn't want her mom in this care home, but it was close to her work and enabled Sue to stop by often, if not daily to check on her mom.

Once in a while, it would be a "good day" for MayAnn, and Sue would get to enjoy a hint of the wonderful lady her mom once was. Those good days helped Sue return for all the "not so good" days that were prevalent. Sue loved her mother like no other. It tore her heart to know that she couldn't provide the twenty-four-hour care needed. It had been a thought at one time. Anyone who has experienced the effects of this horrific disease gives in to the inevitable. Twenty-four-hour constant care and monitoring are necessary. Being trained to handle the increasing needs as cognizance depletes is a must. It is sad, but it is truth. It is the verdade of life. Alzheimer's is brutal.

It had been seven years since Sue's dad, Eugene, died. His last act of love for MayAnn was to check her into this home and ensure she had the best of care. Once Sue's dad knew that all would be well, he gave in to the cancer that destroyed him so rapidly and without mercy. Sue blamed God. How could such a great man and wonderful woman be handed a plight like this? "Why, God, WHY?"

Sue knew that God had the ability to change the outcome of either of these lives. But He just sat back on His hands and let it happen. "Come on, God, my folks were wonderful people who spent their lives worshiping you and living the best life they could. They served others again and again. No pursuit of *what's mine is mine*. Mom and Dad were always generous with time and money. Proud, but humble. They did not deserve this, Lord."

Now she could only sit with her mom, pat her hand, and wait. It was cruel to the family. No righteous God could ever do this to a family. Her family had its faults. Her younger brother was a wild card. Don't know if he ever will grow up. Her older brother had his own story and was distant.

Sue nursed her dad through the short nine months it took throat cancer to destroy him. She and her brothers all finally accepted their mother would never return to them. This was all on her shoulders. It would be nice if her brothers would give up their ambitions, come home, and help. Sue knew that wouldn't happen. The one thing their dad had taught the boys was "Hard work will take the place of pain or weakness." They were good men, but didn't seem to grasp what it was doing to their sister.

Sue was probably the only human besides her mom to see her dad cry. Many years ago, they were out checking the cows during calving season. A favorite time for the whole family. New life was chasing each other, kicking up their heels and enjoying the sunshine, their mothers quietly and contentedly chewing their cuds.

Her dad stopped the pickup at the top of the hill overlooking their herd, tears slowly welling up and sliding out the corners of his eyes. Sue didn't know what to do. Her dad, always to the point, said, "Your mom found a lump on her breast. The doctor needs to do a biopsy to determine if it is malignant."

At that moment, Sue saw the definition of true love. Yes, her dad had problems with giving romantic gifts and expressing love. That didn't mean he didn't have it. For her dad to be that scared about any possible bad news for her mom, that was love in the deepest sense. It turned out to be benign and nothing but a scare. It permanently locked in Sue's heart to find a man who could love her at that level.

MayAnn had faced some severe emotional pain herself. Only when one of her brothers or sister came to visit the farm would MayAnn talk about how screwed up their childhood had been. They had all suffered. MayAnn carried all their faults with her. She should have been able to do more. She should have been able to protect her brother better from the ruthless beatings. That is another story for another time. Or maybe a story better left buried.

While her children were still young, MayAnn was forced into a level of guilt that only a decent dose of antidepressants could control. She and Eugene had gone to a party one night. A rarity for that couple. They weren't drinkers. MayAnn had already suffered the effects of alcohol growing up. There was no way it would ever be a problem for her children. But a young couple with kids needed a break every now and again.

It was probably a card party that was so popular at the time. A good tournament of pitch with friends was a needed respite. Card tables and folding chairs. Meaningless prizes for the best and worst teams. The evening carried on until late in the night. MayAnn and Eugene arrived home long after midnight. The kids' babysitter was asleep on the couch. MayAnn thought it best to let her sleep. Driving late at night on these country roads was not a good plan. Especially for a teenage girl who wasn't raised in the country. Fifteen miles of dirt roads had taken MayAnn years to master. This young lady could take her time driving home in the morning.

Next morning came, bright, birds singing, a lazy Sunday to sleep in. Even Eugene, who was always up a couple of hours before daylight to smoke, drink coffee, and plan out the day, took care not to disturb the family. When MayAnn finally rolled out of bed and remembered the babysitter, it wasn't that late in the morning, but late enough to cause a small panic.

Their babysitter was also one of the organists for the church they all attended. It was the church MayAnn's children were baptized in. It was the church where MayAnn taught the high school-aged Sunday school class. That was where she had connected with their current babysitter, the young lady who was now in the mindset panic of running late. There was still plenty of time to drive to town and make Sunday school and church services. Their babysitter was driven, though. She insisted on practicing that week's hymn prior to the service. She grabbed her things, ran to her car as MayAnn yelled, "Drive safely and thank you." The car sped off with a teenage urgency.

The babysitter never made it to town. She never played the organ for that day's service. The next organ music was for her funeral.

It was a terrible accident just one mile from town. Over a blind hill, swerve to avoid a washout, high speed, end of a precious life.

It destroyed a part of MayAnn. It tore deeper into her soul than anything before or after. God couldn't fix this. Only a heavy dose of Lexapro and counseling could numb this pain. "If only" was thought over and over and over. For years.

Her children knew there was a loss and pain. But MayAnn never once let that pull her away from being an amazing mom. One time, MayAnn asked her children as adults, prior to the second level of Alzheimer's, "Was I a good mom?" They all teared up. How could they ever let their mom know that they had experienced an almost surreal childhood? Except maybe her haircuts on her sons. Those were a little crooked, but it was still done with love. If the most traumatic experience of their childhood was a ticked ear and extremely crooked bangs, then MayAnn had done well.

Sue thought of all the wonderful things her Mom had done for them since birth. It was like she had to make up for something from a past life. She never smothered them with love and protection. No, there were plenty of scrapes and bruises, but no broken bones, except a cracked vertebra from a fall off a bridge her older brother suffered.

Yeah, Sue would sit here with her mom forever if that was what it took. God had abandoned them, but Sue would hang in there. Maybe she would push her mom down to Larry and Alan's room. That always seemed to light a spark in her mom. It was wonderful to watch her reach out as she sat between the two, grasped their hands and squeezed. All three of them showed a common light in their eyes. It scared Sue a little to see a resemblance that the three of them shared. She wondered if maybe 23 and Me was a possibility. Would it be a violation of nursing home regulations to snatch a hair off each of these men? They weren't much older than Sue herself. She seemed to feel a half connection too. Maybe one little hair that nested on their shoulder wouldn't be any harm. Spit swab was out of the question. Her brothers would probably think she had lost her mind. Still................

This little investigative mission might distract from the letter she had anonymously received a few weeks ago. Someone sent a note that Sue needed to look into some abuse her mother might have suffered here at the nursing home. It included a reference to a nasty Snapchat photo that had been passed from one aide to coworkers. The concerned knew it was wrong, oh so wrong, but was afraid to come forward because of fear of retribution. The writer stated she needed her job really badly, and a rat she never was. The expression of concern was real.

Sue's first inquiry to the administrator was dismissed as nothing more than one worker being mad at another and just wanting to cause trouble. Sue had been brushed off, almost to the point of nervous laughter that anyone could make up such a story. Sue didn't feel right as she was politely pushed out the door. What a lost and lonely feeling. She needed to share this with her brothers. They would know what to do.

There was a darkness coming from her mom that Sue had seen, but had written off as just another level of this ugly disease. Now, Sue was thinking there was another level of ugly that had nothing to do with Alzheimer's and everything to do with evil. And here she was concerned about plucking a hair off those two men her mom had connected with...

34

State Inspection (Peggy)

*Let your light shine before men in such a way
that they may see your good works, and
glorify your Father who is in heaven.*

Matthew 5:16 NASB

I t was a day to wear my best from Scrubs Plus. A new pair of Skechers with a Bugs Bunny sock on the left and Mickey Mouse on the right. Hair pulled back in the most professional style possible for a hairdo short but feminine. No designer or special needs wristbands. My simple gold wedding band. No necklace. The smallest (still cute) earrings, and just enough Cover Girl on my face to erase five years.

We had been hearing rumors for the last couple of weeks about the state nursing home inspectors headed our way. Extra cleaning had already been done. All the paperwork checked by three RNs for accuracy. The kitchen reviewed all of their documentation for diets and food safety. The activities director and her assistant were always involved with the residents and had some excellent programs.

What stood for a sorry excuse of an exercise/physical therapy room was spic and span. Didn't have to worry about proper paperwork because that was all that room ever generated. There were a few residents wheeled into that room for the last week to make them feel like this had been a daily habit for years. The "show" was rehearsed.

Most of this home could easily handle a surprise inspection at any time. The administrator and director of nursing ran a tight ship. At least in the eyes of an inspector. They both knew whom best to have on shift, and whom to encourage to take a few days off. To me, if they needed to ask someone to stay home to avoid mistakes or possible violations, maybe that person shouldn't be on the payroll. That was close to impossible. Especially in the nurse's aide area, where almost any warm body was welcome. Mainly because the pay was typically only a few cents over minimum. Just enough that this work was financially a step up from the gas station/quick stop across the highway. And that was even questionable. The ones who had the most hands-on daily with the residents were the lowest paid in the facility. Yes, good plan there. It is the same at every nursing home. The only chance for advancement was continuing education to medication aide (who could then pass out drugs), to LPN, and the good ones busted their can up to RN. But most were locked in to only have enough time to maybe put in forty hours a week because they had a family to raise/support.

All the residents had been bathed within the last couple of days. It was typically only necessary and mandated that residents be bathed once a week. This was because the elderly's skin can't handle daily baths. The only BO came from those who suffered from incontinence. Our small home had that handled. The residents were always kept clean and looking nice. Nothing to cover up there. Today, though, some of the Sunday best clothes were brought out. Not quite spit and polish, but looking good ladies and gentlemen.

The inspection team came strutting in the front doors around 9:30ish. We had been prepared since 6:00 a.m. This was a good time to start as we had already cleaned up from breakfast, and most residents were taking a cat nap until lunch. Calm was the norm. Our administrator and director of nursing both met the team at the Crossroads and led them to the administrator's office for a closed-door introduction and protocol meeting. The rest of us scurried to our assigned positions, performing each task exactly to standards. A shot of sanitizer and gloves happened at every knock on a resident's door. Even the knock itself was more pronounced than the usual "I am coming in because I have work to do." Respect for the resident's privacy was more pronounced. We were ready.

An hour and a half later, the inspection team came out of the admin office and went straight to their designated areas. One came front and center of the nursing station, grabbed a random selection of residents' daily chart books, took them to a table in the recreation room, and started browsing.

Another went straight to the kitchen with flashlight in hand. Inspecting for dirty areas under stoves, around the dishwashing area, in storage pantries (normal and cold), and everywhere other kitchens throughout the state had given up violations. This inspection was brutal. I felt for the kitchen staff. They really did put out good food every day. And I had never seen a hint of varmints or bugs. Yeah, the grease hood needed attention once in a while, but overall, this kitchen and dining area were as clean as they come.

The kitchen actually was hit with two inspectors at the same time. The other self-important lady went straight to the dietary plans, daily menus, consumption charting, and a mess of paperwork most people don't realize happens in the kitchen. Not just pudding and applesauce here. All meals are planned out and meet a stringent nutritional standard.

Then there was the inspector in charge of just checking the overall function of the home. This lady had a huge heart and could easily converse with the residents. If any dirt was to be dug up, it might happen here. Our prayer as a nursing staff was that it would be a good day that none of the residents remembered the evil actions from one certain aide. She had been given some additional paid time off just to ensure that a few days of space would erase most short-term memories from the residents. If we could only pin an exact violation on this monster, we could rid ourselves. But she was smart as she was bad. One day.......

Three days later, all staff exhausted, the inspection team once again went into the administrator's office, along with the DON, and had their powwow. This took a nerve-racking three hours. With that extended time, there had to be some violations revealed and discussed.

Each department head was brought in one at a time for a "close out" review. Most came out with a relieved look, others with a simple nod of "I did my best."

The Team left. We had a meeting. Even some of the more coherent residents came to listen in. Everyone sat on the edge of their seats. Were we going to be allowed to operate for another year? What changes were we going to be forced to implement to adhere to yet another set of crippling rules that sounded good in theory, but were impossible in practice?

"Do I still even have my job?" was on the minds of most of the staff. No matter how good you are, and how professionally you approach your position, we are all human and make mistakes. Most not on purpose, but still mistakes. How many of these were found? Were we at least good enough to continue to receive state funding to make up for the shortcomings between astronomical medical costs versus what the residents could afford?

The overall summary revealed three minor violations, six recommendations, and one major violation that would be reviewed at the state level, then passed to both sides' lawyers for mitigation and hopefully dismissal of said violation. The worst part was the actual violation could not be shared with the staff until after final decisions on penalties.

One of the minor violations was, one gait belt had been left on a resident when they were left sitting in their easy chair for an afternoon nap. These gait belts are carried by each nurse and nurse's aide, and are used as a means of assisting a resident in sitting, standing, transferring, and walking. They were wide-banded belts that you put around a resident's waist anytime you were assisting them. This belt gave the caretaker a firm place to hold onto and help control a resident. Proper training and use made this one of the best safety tools in a nursing home. Once in a rare while, one of these belts was left on a resident because the caretaker had other distractions and walked away. As soon as said caretaker realized they were missing their gait belt, it would be hunted down and removed. No big deal. Didn't affect the residents. It was a dirty mark on our inspection.

Another violation came from the kitchen. Simple check of the thermostat in the walk-in cooler revealed the reading was five degrees lower than actual temperature. This stayed minor because the true temperature (per inspector's calibrated TI) was at forty-four degrees and the door thermometer was reading thirty-nine degrees. Forty-four was still a safe number. Forty-six would not have been. The five-degree difference could have been critical in food safety. Repair/replacement of said thermometer was going to be around $200. New required weekly cross-checking and monthly calibration fees were going to hit the kitchen's budget for $2500 a year. So much for that special dessert day every Friday.

The third minor violation was a matter of opinion/interpretation of a state mandate of recording steps taken by a resident per day. A lot of the residents were still self-mobile. Who had time to count exact steps? Estimates were used based on trips to the dining area or bathroom and average number of steps/

shuffles taken to get there. The state had been pushing for Fitbits on all residents to record. I think it was simply someone at the state level had been offered a little "incentive" to push through this requirement.

I liked the idea, except for the residents who wouldn't understand why they were required to wear this funny-looking watch thing. And the cost that would be passed to the families to purchase and provide.

As an RN, my step intake in a normal eight-hour shift stayed right at that 2,000 to 15,000 steps a day. I know some of the best nurse's aides average 18,000 to 20,000 steps per day. Others, lucky to get in 8,000. It was always evident in the quality of care given.

We were lucky during this inspection that "Forrest" stayed calm and happy just sitting in his room with Larry and the occasional visit from MayAnn. Oh no...was that the major violation— allowing a woman resident to sit in a private room with two men and hold their hands? Was our act of compassion viewed as something other than that? My goodness, is another set of rules going to inhibit our residents' freedoms even worse? God help us............

35

Another Room (Alan)

*Dear friend, do not imitate what is evil but what is good.
Anyone who does what is good is from God. Anyone who does
what is evil has not seen God.*

3 John 1:11 NIV

I can sense that something isn't quite right. I am sitting at a distance watching the events of my life pass before me with no real control from yours truly. I don't mind this so much. Let someone else bathe and clothe and feed my body. I even have a pretty lady throw a cinch around my waist, help me stand, and guide me to wherever I am supposed to go next.

The bathroom thing is another story. I can't quite connect the urge to pee with the action of walking to the bathroom. Sometimes it is just easier to piss myself rather than go through the stress of not being able to communicate my urgency.

They used to put this button thing in my hand and when I pushed it, a light would go off above my door and a bell would politely ring in the distance. But then, when someone would come to check on me, I couldn't tell them why I rang. I could only sit there and kind of drool on myself, my head twitching a little bit, my eyes not saying a damn thing. So, they took away my buzzer and put me in a diaper. Yay fricken yay.

I always joked with my working buddies that we could all save a lot of time by wearing a diaper when we were drinking beer. No more trips to the bathroom once you broke that ultimate seal. We wouldn't have to interrupt our most intelligent conversations with the need to hit the head. It sounded like the perfect plan. None of us had the balls to actually put it into practice. I'm surprised that on some of our better drunks, we didn't try it. Probably more from the fact that there were no adult diapers available in our immediate vicinity, than the idea we were being childish. Yup, one box of Depends anywhere near us, and I know we would have given them a run. Little did I know that one day they would be a fact of my life, not just something to joke about. Funny how advancement in age changes outcome.

One of my good friends, Deke, had been a participant in one such adult diaper conversation. He was tragically killed a few years ago in a car wreck. I never did understand why we always use the term "tragically killed." Aren't all deaths a tragedy? This one hit me hard, though. Deke was the best.

I have found that having the now two thirds of my brain resembling something close to scrambled eggs and hash browns, has led to a whole avenue of exploration within the confines of my skull. Not having to, or being able to, use my brain to do daily functions has given me freedom from the mundane. Now, I can hike through what is left of my gray matter and visit certain "memory rooms" that had been banked, or hidden. I enjoy these explorations and can check out from reality for days without a care in the world. Remember, I have a diaper on.

One such day, I walked into the memory room with Deke's name written on it. There stood that muscle-bound, gentle man of a soul, with that perfect smile that captured ninety percent of all women. Deke's smile was so white and genuine, that the ladies didn't have a chance. Plus, he was extremely fit, but not in the anal sense. Deke didn't waste his time with self-admiration. That was not his focus. He instead liked how he felt by proper eating habits combined with intense muscle building.

Deke would call me every now and again out of the blue. Usually to just see how I was doing. He cared about people that way. Don't quite know why I received that privilege, but I loved to get his calls. Sooner or later, our conversations would lead to Deke confessing that he broke down and ate a Big Mac or some other fast food "kill you slowly" mass of bad nutrition. He would tell me how Godawful he would feel for hours or days after stepping to the dark side of the food chain, but damnit, a person just needed to "eat that shit" every now and again. It would always make me laugh how he would describe the grease marching down his throat with the mission to invade his disciplined and well-maintained core. "The malnutrition got real," Deke would say. I would be rolling. He would be seriously bothered by the breaking of his health rules. I would offer to buy him some pizza.

Deke and a few mutual friends of ours decided that we needed to go on a weekend motorcycle trip to tour the great Show Me State of Missouri. Simple plan. Skip out of work midafternoon on a Thursday (we of course worked extra hard and long hours Monday thru Wednesday to get our forty-plus in). Ride that afternoon/ evening to our "tour guide's" house that also provided the perfect motorcycle mancave scenario for six wannabe bikers.

Talk about a hodgepodge of motorcycle enthusiasts, we were a mess. Two of the crew borrowed scooters from relatives or friends. Two others had just bought theirs. The lead and I had been riding for a while and had a few good wreck stories to share. We all were from different family backgrounds and areas raised. Not one of us had a sad story; we all knew what hard work was and were reaping the benefits of such. It was going to be a trip for the ages.

The two weeks before this had been a buildup of anticipated freedom. Lots of conversations, lots of plans that went south, came back, got dropped, picked back up, and finally came together as we pulled out of St. Joe on a beautiful Thursday afternoon. A few of the coworkers waved in envy as we roared away from the ethanol plant we had been working so diligently at. "Goodbye, suckers." "Hello, open road!!"

Our ride to Moberly was fun and uneventful. Just a prelude of three days of male bonding and creation of new stories. For the first time in years, we felt like the world was ours to conquer. We owned the road. Hell's Angels better hide in fear. We were the riders of the Cosmic Flow 2009. Don't ask me where that name came from. I believe it evolved from an in-depth conversation in the aforementioned mancave after a beer or twelve. I know exactly who said it, don't remember quite why. But the statement was so far off in left field that it stuck. Glad we never made T-shirts that proclaimed our less-than-manly name.

So many discussions about each motorcycle involved on this trip. Stories from us veterans. Intelligence abound. We found couches and spare beds to sleep in starting at like 3:00 in the morning. Something to be said for adrenaline.

The next morning, we left after a most manly and awesome breakfast served to the Cosmic Flow group. There was a slight sprinkling of moisture, but nothing too concerning. We were born to ride. A little dampness would not inhibit our travel plans.

Three hundred fifty miles later, pouring rain the whole damn time, frustration to the max, our soggy-ass crew stopped for the day. We were able to see some pretty cool stuff at Clarence Cannon Dam/ Mark Twain Lake and work our way around the whole area of Tom Sawyer and Huck Finn's stomping grounds.

Every stop we made consisted of some emptying the water out of our boots, wringing out our socks, telling monsoon stories, and generally deciding that this motorcycle adventure absolutely sucked. No one quit, though. Only because of not wanting to be categorized as a "pussy."

The best part and most laughs came at Deke's expense at every stop. Deke had borrowed his cousin's scooter. It was a wannabe

Yamaha chopper with a cool metallic gold paint job, ape hangers, and no front fender. Badass-looking ride. Not so badass in the rain with no blockage of wet/dirty splatter from the highway.

With the tall ape hangers, single seat, and one position of foot pegs, Deke was forced to sit straight up with his face in a forward position perfect to catch every ounce of road grime available. Having a decent set of goggles was his only saving grace. Every time we would stop, Deke would remove those goggles from an asphalt-black, filthy face, and add his pearly whites to the reverse racoon scenario. It was so funny to see the perfect round circles of white surrounded by all that blackness, that the rest of us forgot our misery. Every ounce of Deke was filthy and soaked through except the goggle area. The rest of us were somewhere less than that.

Deke took it all in stride. There were discussions of stopping and kicking that chopper-looking sorry excuse of a two-wheeled ride into the ditch and walking the rest of the way. Which led to even more laughter as we watched his expression of frustration and humor combined with the ghost white circles around his eyes. Oh my gosh, did we laugh at Deke, and each other. The stories that night are still in that room in my brain containing Deke.

Thank God the next day was sunshine and warm weather. It was a great time. We wouldn't have appreciated it nearly as much if we hadn't trudged through the gates of soggy hell the day before. This day was amazing. Deke and the younger crew bounded heights of the Elephant Rocks that I would have loved to join them on twenty years prior. Deke was fearless. Maybe a tad on the loco side. Must have been his Indian blood.

As great as that trip turned out to be, we never were able to put together another Cosmic Flow. Life happened. We all went in different directions. Deke's car wreck. He had a young son he loved dearly. I couldn't even make the funeral. I wrote a poem and sent it to Deke's mom:

YOU ARE SOMEBODY

One day I was told I was nobody
Not one certain person, not one singular event.
Just a passage of time
Moments of life not well spent.

The next day I was still nobody
Wasting, rotting, and decaying away.
I wanted to climb but continued to fall
Each moment of a passing day.

How long could I remain nobody
Only time would tell.
I knew there was better
I knew I could do well.

Then one day God spoke to my nobody
With the quietest, gentlest voice.
My child, you are somebody
Today I give you a choice.

If you want to become somebody
Here is my word, here is my hand.
I made you to live, to give, to love
Take it, accept it, there is no demand.

For I created you as somebody
To prosper, to grow, to learn.
I made you a somebody
A gift from me I ask you return.

You will be my somebody
To touch the lives of all you should know.
You will bring them joy, warmth, and memories
A child you will help grow.

Now I am living as somebody
So much to do, so much that I could.
I do not rest. I give it my all
I live life to its fullest, just as I should.

But then God spoke to my somebody
Forever too soon. I need you here with me.
Your job done well, so many you blessed.
For now my son, you will always be, their Somebody.

Oh, how I miss my friend and his phone calls. I told him before I left the Deke room in my mind, that I would probably be seeing him soon.........................

36

I WISH I WERE ALAN (Larry)

For the message God delivered through angels has always stood
firm, and every violation of the law and every act
of disobedience was punished.

Hebrews 2:2 NLT

I'm not doing so well today. Have you ever had those dreams where you were running, or wanting to run, but you couldn't quite get your legs to move like they should? You know, the ones that out of fear or desire to catch something, the dream is trying to take you forward but your legs feel like they are tied to the ground. Trying to run in my dreams, my legs were inhibited by the amount of covers I had on my bed. That was my perception. Well, I am living that hell every day now, covers or not.

My mind is sharp as a tack. Probably even more acute than the normal person. Mainly because nothing else works. My brain doesn't have to expend any energy moving limbs that have quit. It does take an added amount of energy and concentration to keep breathing. But not enough to exhaust me or let me sleep. I am sitting here locked in a cage of reality. Observing, smelling, seeing everything. Helpless.

It is like watching a 3D movie with your whole body bound to motionlessness. You have to just sit there and take it. No matter how bad the movie or the soundtrack, you are forced to watch. Your ability to communicate left the theater some time back. Some of the nurses and aides who really care (most of them) have learned to ask me yes/no questions and watch the blink of my eyes. That is about the only movement I have left. It is hell. Trust me. I should have shot myself while I had the ability.

Trying to analyze who is in the worse hell is left to interpretation. Alan has a body that can still do most things, but his mind has checked out. I have a mind that is sharp as a newly ground #2 pencil, but my body is just a stub of useless flesh that is somehow still barely supporting my brain function.

If the body has a soul, where is mine trapped? I think Alan's soul is taking him through a series of stops on memory lane. He will sit there and smile and laugh for no reason. Or his eyes will tear up. Or he just up and goes for a stroll almost like sleepwalking. Alan is always somewhere other than in reality with me in this room. I am filled with reality. And my reality sucks. Fricken Alan is lucky. Wish I could join him in La La Land.

I did have fun observing the nervous tension of the entire staff during their annual state inspection. Everyone was on their best behavior. Well, best that they could remember. Some of their not-so-good habits would come to the surface in front of an inspector. But nothing too dramatic. I could still hear them sharing their minor flubs hours after whatever incident happened. Dang women can talk about the most meaningless things, for hours. And now, I am forced to listen to it.

On and on and on about how one of them remembered to sanitize their hands on entering the room, but forgot to do the same on the way out. Or the one who let go of her gait belt that was on a resident she was helping, just long enough to move a wheelchair out of the way. Lucky the resident didn't fall. I heard all the horror stories. These stories weren't just told to one person and let go. They were shared with every other nurse or aide who passed by. I heard enough of a couple of their stories to be able to repeat them verbatim and backward without missing a single word of the 20,000 words spoken in one day.

I shouldn't be saying all of this. These ladies do their best and most of them are really kind to me. The best part of the inspection was the fact that the Wicked Witch was gone the whole time. It is like every resident is 200 percent happier on those days. The thought of evil is erased. We can enjoy what is left of life. I can listen to repetitive stories without worrying about who might get tortured or abused that day.

I was a little concerned one day about the inspection. One of the aides had brought MayAnn into our room. It has become almost a daily habit of some of the aides to park MayAnn between Alan and me in our room, close the door over, and leave us in peace while we wait to be wheeled to the next meal. All three of us are the happiest at this time. MayAnn, because she can connect with us on a most innocent level. Alan, because someone can join him exploring whatever adventure his mind has taken him on. And me, because I can feel the warmth of MayAnn's hand as she squeezes mine. Even though I can't squeeze back, I hope she can feel my heart skip a joyful beat stronger.

Anyway, same as every other day. Not one of the staff thinking anything of it. Our room door almost completely shut to give privacy I guess. MayAnn sitting between us, holding one of our hands in each of hers, life being good, then in walks Sergeant "I am an Important Person."

She took one look at our perfectly innocent threesome, and I could see the wheels of shock and disapproval coursing clear from her toes to ring the bell between her ears. You would have thought we were having an orgy by the look of judgment on her face. My golly gee, she couldn't scribble in her notebook fast enough. I was shocked that she didn't have a camera to immortalize the moment. It was burned into her brain, though; I could feel the heat. I wanted to laugh. Haven't had that ability for a while.

My urge to laugh was soon erased as I realized the severity of what this self-righteous person was thinking. The number of words she wrote with the force of a small chainsaw tearing through pages of paper was just short of astounding. This was not good. I could not even defend myself or my besties with words. My blinking "no no, NO" meant nothing to this woman. Damn, I wish Nurse Peggy would come in and mellow things out.

Alas, no one came in. Peggy was doing what Peggy always does. She was busy caring for the other residents. Not a thought in the world about us three because she knew that when we were together, our needs were met. It was our happy time in a world of not-so-happy times. Didn't that inspector see that? Can't she at least ask before judging? My disease sucks. Alan and MayAnn didn't realize anything was wrong. They were *gonedy*. I was the only one coherent enough to realize the problem.

And even worse, it was impossible to share this with any of the staff. Even when the aides came in to take us to lunch, no one understood the agitation in my eyes. They were too busy trying to remember if they had properly transferred the last resident from the bed to the wheelchair while someone important was watching and grading over their shoulder.

Family members sometimes didn't understand the inner workings of transfers and the desire to be as gentle as possible moving someone who still weighed 250 pounds when most aides themselves were under a buck thirty. They would question every move and judge. But most of them who visited frequently appreciated the job the aides did and were thankful. Those family members helped make the *close to starving to death* wages worth all that heavy lifting.

But, have a person who is only critiquing your work with a by-the-book mentality, the wages don't even come close. If it weren't for the love of almost helpless residents, these aides would never come back to work. I respect them and the job they do. It takes an incredibly special person to do their job. Their final reward had better be a golden ticket in heaven. Most of them and the rest of the nursing staff deserve the best God can give them.

Then, there are those few who are destined to go the other direction. I don't want to dwell on the Hell they deserve. I would rather praise the ninety-five percent great human beings they are.

Back to that damn inspector. I know her false interpretation is going to show up somewhere in the final report. I would bet it falls under the category of MAJOR VIOLATION. And that bites the big one. If only I had telepathy or something to transfer the truth. If fricken Alan would come back to reality for just a minute portion of a moment, the truth could be told. Damn this disease, I can't seem to fix anything...................

37

I Think I Have Figured it Out (MayAnn)

And join them for thee one to another into one stick,
that they may become one in thy hand.

Ezekiel 37:17 ASV

There's not much left of me. Father Time has done his deed. My mind went (externally) quite some time ago. My body has hung in there, sort of. Now, gravity and longevity are not my friends. Even my head is sagging more and more. It is so heavy some days. I wish I had a special chair like Larry. They keep his head strapped up and straight so it doesn't flop around like a rag doll. Alan's seems to kinda jiggle around like a bobblehead. They will probably start calling him that instead of Forrest. He has long stopped running, except the occasional escape attempt to save the rest of us when The Bitch is working.

You might wonder how I am so coherent and able to remember names and events. Well, my dears, I am in my "Freedom Room" in my skull. Everything in here is clear and coherent. My memories are wonderful. I can talk and visit with people and crochet to my heart's content. Sem problemas aqui. Even learning some Portuguese. Don't know why. I think it is because Alan's beautiful wife is always speaking so very lovingly to him in that language. Portuguese has to be the "language of love." That is the only way I have heard it.

I do have one door in my little Freedom Room that is still locked, and I can't seem to find the key. It is a mystery. Other doors freely open and spill me into a wonderful memory. The front door or return, I stay away from as much as possible. It only leads to that foggy hallway that is shrinking smaller and smaller. No use even going out there anymore. It is like a maze of dense confusion. That hallway is exhausting and there is no clearing in sight. No, I will stay in my room that gives me happiness.

It is awesome when I am parked in between Alan and Larry. I don't have to go out into that terrifying hallway to make my hands reach out for theirs. It is automatic and for some reason is guided by my heart. I don't need my knotted yarn brain to get in the way of our union. My heart is still strong. How many years did I waste letting my gray matter lead me and make life decisions. I should have been following the pull of my heart all along. Oh, how much better my travels are.

I am beginning to realize that there is more to our joining hands than where it started. At first, it just felt good and natural to hold these two strangers' hands. Then, as my foggy hallway forced me into my room of light more often, I was able to invite Alan and Larry to join me. Alan jumped right in. He had many rooms of his own he wanted to share with us. Alan also had his dense corridor that he avoided more and more. He only left his security to enable his apple sauce brain to take control long enough to wander and run. I have learned he only does this most scary exercise only to protect the rest of the residents from Witch Hazel. It is scary for Alan. He fears that he might run too far and not be able to find the way back to Happy Land. Now, though, I have tied my largest ball of yarn to his belt. That way, as he runs he leaves a guiding string to follow back to us.

Larry, on the other hand. Even though I appear as nothing to everyone else, I still have some wit and humor stored away for a rainy day. Did you get my pun? Time for a little LOL?

Larry is harder to bring into Alan's and my world. He hangs outside the door. His hallway is perfectly fine. As a matter of fact, it is not even a hallway, but a whole expanse of a world. Larry's mind is still 100 percent and full of light. He lets me peek out the door to his existence. Larry can't come into mine yet because he hasn't figured out how to follow his heart. His body is still in control and useless. I only had one muscle that failed. Larry has all his muscles failing except one. We need to help Larry.

I think I have it figured out. Right now, we are sitting in kind of a semicircle. Due to the boundaries of our wheelchairs, we are unable to form a triangle small enough to join hands from both sides. I can only hold one of their hands. They cannot reach each other's. We need a fourth or even a fifth to complete a circle. I believe if we could do this, then the circle of life would be completed. No pun here at all. I am serious. There is so much more to life than individuals. There is the strength of a chain in a straight line. Double that strength into a loop, you really have something then. Who could join us?

I am worried that it has been a few days since I was parked in between my saviors. Ever since those few days of complete seriousness. Those days when compassion and friendliness were replaced with "by the book" procedures. I don't quite know what was going on those days. I could feel the tenseness in the caregivers. Even my favorite nurse, Peggy, was on edge. Then the day that pantsuit-wearing, wished she had a penis and balls instead of a vagina, looking thing came into Larry and Alan's room and mentally freaked out, we have not been parked together.

Rules versus happiness. Why can't we residents help make the rules? We have to live by them. What self-important person even has the right to tell us what we can and cannot do? Wait until they get old. Hopefully, the inner light of awareness will come on for them. They will see the error of their ways. They will feel remorse. They will reach out to make changes. They will discover they are ignored and some other "well to do" ignorant buttwipe has taken their place. Ha ha, joke's on them.

Sorry about the soapbox thing. The only platform I have left is this patchwork of thoughts inside my head. Once in a rare while, I can build up enough energy to push out a good solid scream. It takes days of storing my emotions in the gun safe sitting in the corner of my Freedom Room. Nice present from my late husband. He was a firm believer of locking up valuables and guns. Now, I have my own Honeywell Executive to store up my voice. Then when needed, I open the safe, grab everything deposited inside, and use it to produce a scream of death. It is my only Second Amendment right I have left to protect me from The Bitch of Abuse. Only thing I have left.

Enough about my woes. I am running on an emotional high. I know for certain that if we can complete a circle, our worlds will be different. Hopefully, I will soon be returned to my friends' room and we can plot on whom to bring into our circle. Don't know how we can do that since none of us can talk and only one of us has a semblance of an ability to walk. Guess we will figure it out. I miss my boys…………………………………….

38

Some Rules Need to be Broken (Peggy)

It always protects, always trusts, always hopes, always perseveres.
1 Corinthians 13:7 NIV

It was finally passed down and shared with us. The details of our "major" violation. I was in shock when the DON passed it down. I seriously believe that we were innocently oblivious to such a ridiculous and petty rule/law/whatever the heck you call it.

I suppose sometime, somewhere, in this state, some kind of hanky panky happened or even worse a sexual-type assault by one resident on another. Whatever it was established the segregation rule that does not allow women, especially chairbound and noncoherent, to be placed next to a man, or in our case between two men, and left without supervision.

In a dining area, fine. Someone is always present. In an activity room, fine, there is always someone there. But in a private room? Oh my God, the world is going to come to an end.

I will admit, there is that one resident every now and again who falls over to the pervert side. It is almost ironic if you know the person's history and find out for all their lives they were the most straitlaced, bible-thumping, never-do-wrong person in the town. Then, old age snuck up, destroyed any semblance of control, and the suppressed came out. Not just a little cuss word here or there, or eyes staring at others a little too long. They go to the side that would shame *Hustler* magazine.

Every cuss word and pornographic statement possible comes from their mouths. Some even hit the level of masturbating right out in public with no modesty. Their inhibitions are completely gone. Lewd suggestions make passersby scurry with urgency to escape. It is rude, crude, nasty, and sadly, completely innocent. These people don't have a clue they jumped the ship of decency. All the pent-up carnal desires have been set free. Their Vacation Bible School life left the premises. Perversion has overruled.

I try to view it as God gave us these urges. Mainly to procreate. But then, we humans found worldly pleasures being stronger than human will, and we in our infinite wisdom took sex and the acts thereof to an unimaginable level. Bad things happened to good people. Most found control. Some never cared to. But that is a different story for another day.

Poor MayAnn, Alan, and Larry are the victims of something that happened in a different past. We were cited for a major violation of the separation rule. Now it was down to what fines would be imposed and what disciplinary action would be laid on our humble and caring facility.

Would the person responsible for parking the three together get fired? Would that be enough to appease the state? I know our administrator has to think of the good of the whole over one person's career. He is guided by a board of directors from the city, who really don't understand how a nursing home even functions. I shouldn't say that. Some board members do care and do understand. But business is business, and business must move on.

To protect my aides and other staff, I took full responsibility for the placement of MayAnn in the confines of Alan and Larry's room. None of us really even remembers who did the deed on that particular day at that exact time. We have done this for a long time now, with no thought. It was cute. It made three residents who are each suffering in their own definition of misery, happy for a time. Isn't that our primary purpose?

Yes, to care for and protect are higher priorities. Don't compassion and awareness fit in there somewhere? None of us here (well maybe one sick worker) would ever dream of putting an innocent and helpless resident next to one who has lost their ability of control. We don't do that. We are not idiots. We have been well-trained.

We, those who are the creme de la crème, have an added bonus of compassion. If there is one little thing we can do at any given moment to add some sunshine to the darkness of our residents' lives, we will do it.

As a matter of fact, if I am going to get fired anyway, today would be a good day to get back into the habit of letting Larry, Alan, and MayAnn sit together. Maybe I will kibosh the whole *in the room* thing, and park them together in the living area, or dining area. Yeah, that would be a good idea. All three of them need an aide to feed them. They might as well share a table. Maybe they would fit well with Tex and Maria...................

39

Bout Damn Time (Alan)

About that time there occurred no small
disturbance concerning the Way.

Acts 19:23 NASB

I t has been a Godawful long time since I have seen MayAnn. Ever since Tension Week (my definition of whatever the Hell was going on those few days of mass confusion), MayAnn has not come to see Larry and me. As a matter of fact, even Larry has been kept distant. WTH?? What did we ever do to piss someone off enough to deserve this punishment?

Yeah, I can go to my Happy Room/Rooms and be lost for days. No problem for me. Wonderful memories where I can still talk. Fantastic scenarios of conversation and thought. Good stuff from every decade of my life. Kinda awesome that only the doors to good things are open for exploration. There is a bank of really dark doors that I keep closed and locked. I don't want to look there. What is the point? Review the bad parts of my life? Relive having to bury my mom and dad and grandparents and friends and other loved ones? Visit the hurtful things I might have done to others? No, thank you. We will continue to only go to the rooms of sunshine.

Peggy is working today. There are only two adults who can pull me out of my private room and snag me into reality for short periods. It is like they come into my darkest hallway and flip on a light that burns the confusion away. Peggy does this. Ana, the love of my life, does this too. Children do this. Especially my ever-growing-up angels EV and IV. Oh, how I love those girls.

Occasionally, the low voices of my sons will pull me through the mud, too. They don't visit as often. I completely understand. They have man things to do. Their own families, their own careers, their own *I taught them to hold everything in and be a man* outlook, keeps them from coming to see their vegetable of a father. I respect them for that. I am proud of my boys. They are good stuff.

Peggy came into our room all excited. I could feel it. It was like the cloud that had been hovering over her for weeks was finally blown away. The bright sunshine of Peggy was back. The world's axis had been put right. Bout fricken time. I need her sunshine. I feed off of it. All I have left most days.

Next thing I knew, I was being wheeled to a new area somewhere between the aviary and the big screen TV. I don't exactly care for this area. The birds singing is nice for some, but it seems to overpower any of the happy rooms I am in. Noises from the outside interrupt the security of my inside. And the TV, God help us, we have developed generations of bullshit coming from a box. Entertainment and force-,feeding of information have swallowed up most of our self-awareness. TV steals our thought process and replaces it with mostly stupid shit.

Don't take me wrong, there is some good stuff on the tube. History Channel, Discovery Channel, and some of the sports channels are the bomb. And the four majors are ok if they would trash their fricken political views/opinions and just report the news "as is." Most of us are fairly intelligent. Many of us have minds far superior to your twisted thinking. Just because we get our hands dirty for a living doesn't mean you have a right to look down on us. We have saved your liberal asses for lifetimes. Thank us. Don't try to belittle us.

Sorry about my rant. All I really wanted was to say the TV plays hell with my thoughts. It barrages every semblance of control I have trained my spaghetti brain to have. Noise, distractions, different settings, changes in routine, are murderers to those of us locked in the last stages of Alzheimer's. We can't handle anything but quiet and routine. Except love. That form of communication is life-giving and will be our only connection to the world until our last breath. Give us Love. Shut off CNN for like, ever.

Just went right again. On a roll today. Mainly because Peggy wheeled me out to this area. Thank God the TV hadn't been turned on yet. Next came Larry. Still distant, but close. Then, to my delight, in rolled MayAnn. Parked right in between us. I swear her arms were outreached a half a mile before she got to us.

You have to realize that the elderly, and we afflicted with dementia and Alzheimer's, completely lose our depth perception. What is only a few feet away can seem like miles. We stopped reaching out because the distance is too great to overcome. Damn it, climbed back up on another rant. Bear with me please. I will finish this story.

Finally, the three amigos back together. MayAnn and I automatically joining in what we now call our Common Room. Larry hanging just outside, but listening in. One day he will join us. Hopefully soon, I like Larry. He has come a long ways from the prick he spent his life being. He truly is a good man at heart. I can tell this through MayAnn. She seems to be our common bond for some reason.

Peggy wasn't done, though. I almost panicked when she wheeled this other old lady next to me. Oh shit, here is an intrusion. What is Peggy thinking? Doesn't she know we are the three strong whose cords cannot be broken? A fourth will only disrupt our braid of three. Now Peggy is grabbing my free hand, stretching out to this stranger.

WHAM!! "Well, hello lady. Gonna have to boil some more Mandioca to feed everyone."..

40

A UNION OF SORTS (LARRY)

You guide me with your counsel, leading me to a glorious destiny.
Psalms 73:24 NLT

"Well, I'll be!" I heard in my brain as someone grabbed my hand. Yes, I still have all my senses including touch. Just can't do much with the touch thing. It has to come from another person. As a man, this is tough. We by nature communicate better through touch. Our vocabulary and need to talk aren't that strong. (Except in salesmen and politicians, same difference). We men need to touch. I can no longer reach out. My main communication is gone. I feel so alone until someone reaches for me. Then I can connect again. Please, always remember this for your loved ones.

My hand was suddenly gripped by a short-fingered but amazingly strong grip. No piano playing for this guy, but I bet he could tear a deck of cards in half. There was a strength there that was locking on to me with a vise that wasn't going to let go. And, for some reason, that was OK. I had no desire to do a half twist, push forward then escape maneuver. This felt like something that was necessary.

"Howdy, pardner," were the next words slamming through my arm, climbing up my neck, and reaching the inside of my core that only Alan and MayAnn had reached before.

His greeting wasn't a made-up version of cowboy talk. It was original and pure. Who the heck even says, "Howdy" anymore? I believe this hombre is the real deal. He has something special about him that puts me at peace. I can close my eyes, shut out this exterior lifeless chamber I am locked in, and follow this new man to wherever he seems to want to lead me.

I do glance over to see what exactly does have a hold of me. I see nothing but Resistol 7X on top of what resembles a bull in a snap-up shirt. I think maybe only simple old age has landed this man in our home away from home. He still appears healthy as a horse, albeit bent over and stoved up, like only hard work and long years can do.

I am positive there is a halo underneath that cowboy hat. I can feel something so special here. "My name is Tex," he says. It comes across so strong that I don't know if he actually spoke the words, or sent them via our grasp. I could only mutter, "Hi, Tex." I was too overwhelmed by what was now happening.

I could hear other voices in the distance but approaching rapidly, too. Same scenario, I didn't know if those voices on a dead run to me were from the outside or inside. Oh, God, let them be from the inside. The outside is ugly. Except for Peggy. And Alan's beautiful family.

Tex handed me his piggin string. I remember those from my rodeo days. Piggin strings are short but stout ropes with a loop used to tie down calves for doctoring and branding. Plus, they are the main tool in calf roping competition, which is just an extension of the old cowboy ways of tending to their livestock. Tex's piggin string was well worn but stout. It even had a wooden cross braided into the end. I bet that thing would slap you in the face if you were trying to rope and tie a calf in around seven seconds. Ricky Canton would probably have something to say about the hindrance of said cross. Yet again, what cowboy would ever refer to the Cross as a hindrance? They might have some rough edges, but every cowboy ever knows the love of God.

Tex let the loop of the piggin string lap over my hand and cinch around my wrist. I had the most secure feeling like this was OK. I trusted this quiet man whose eyes shared a love from way beyond the boundaries of Earth. Good stuff, this man. I will follow. The old Larry would have probably told Tex where he could put his damn piggin string. But the new person trapped inside this useless shell of a body has again found the lessons from his conversion at fourteen. It is good to be home. Sorry I was running so late.

Tex lassoed my hand with that string because he knew I couldn't hold on with my own strength. He instinctively knew that the best I could do to join anyone else's world, namely MayAnn's and Alan's, was listen from the outskirts and try to speak through a barrier I couldn't break through. Tex was going to drag me through that blockade whether I wanted to or not. I will admit I was apprehensive. I will confess, I couldn't wait for this new journey.

Even if we had to pass through the Gates of Hell, I was ready to follow this quiet man. I have to admit that I had to give up all "self-reliance" not by choice, but by ALS to be able to follow this shepherd of God. Funny how most must find themselves in the depths of their own self-made level of Hades to finally look up and seek His help.

I had been praying for this for a long, long time. Not with "hands clasped and on my knees begging" prayer. I had lost that bodily ability a long time ago. But prayer that I could escape in without distractions. A clear mind with no other skeletal abilities is an amazing mind. A mind capable of most anything. I was blessed to be able to guide mine toward prayer. Now, a few of those requests to God were being answered. Tex was the messenger. Not quite how I had pictured angels, but heck, I will take what I can get.

The only way Tex could lead me to wherever we were headed, was from the beckoning of a voice I didn't recognize. This voice was angelic in the purest sense. It was singing to us. My God, that is a beautiful voice. It reminded me of a voice I heard one time coming from a shack in the middle of poverty. It was the voice of a poor mother trying to soothe her very hungry child. A voice of love that riches and comfort camouflage. Love in the pure sense of love. I wouldn't be a bit surprised if her name had been Angelica.

The voice I heard today, though, I was soon to learn came from a lady named Maria. You could see in her face that life had been hard. Life had been not much more than survival. The ugly of this world had affected Maria. But when she spoke, you could hear the gentleness of her soul that had survived the pain of this world. I don't know why Maria just happened to join us. I do know I was so glad for her beckoning Tex and me to join her. Tex's fingers found Maria's. A circle was formed. I was in the Common Room...

41

The Circle (MayAnn)

Every good gift and every perfect gift is from above, and cometh down from the Father of lights, with whom is no variableness, neither shadow of turning.

James 1:17 KJV

It finally happened. Don't know why it took so long. Don't know why each of us had to suffer so greatly. But here we were. A small ragtag bunch. There was no formal invitation to join. No ad in the local *Weekly Wipe* calling out date and time. No busybody running door to door to spread the news of a gathering. No, it is a gathering led by something far beyond our power to perceive. God is in control of this. I know.

I didn't even fathom what was going on until all hands were clasped in a circle and the union was completed. Suddenly, we were standing in the Common Room together. Each with our flaws. All with our past. Everyone knowing we had a future mission. I recognize that cowboy from somewhere. What was his name?

There was something special about this cluster of minds. We were gathered together by holding hands. The mighty force of us as a collective mind had a power to it that I had never experienced. Something similar had happened to me in a special place long, long ago. I couldn't quite put my mind to it. I believe it was behind that door I kept locked and had no key to. Maybe one day this group would help me find that key.

For now, it was awesome to be together. The newbies to our group had brought Larry into the room with them. Once inside,

Tex (whom Larry introduced), took this funny little rope off of Larry's wrist and let him free. It had to have been a special rope to have the ability to bring Larry past the boundaries of his mind that previously had kept him at bay and out of our Common Room

Now, we were One. It was not necessary to hold hands in this room. Tex had secured the door. No one was leaving just yet. Yes, we were holding hands physically out in the real world, that was a must. In the Common Room, we had the freedom to roam about like mingling through a party. Each person making small talk with others. Lots of stories and introductions being made. I was the host of this gathering for this moment. I felt like we were all leaders from one walk of life or another. If we could find a piano, I was told I needed to hear Maria's voice. She was such a pretty thing. Maybe a bit older than me with a harsh surface she tried to hide behind. A gentle, loving soul sparkled just beyond her recognizing eyes.

Tex took his hat off in our room like all gentlemen should. I have only seen real cowboys adhere to this practice. Even outside when introduced to a lady, they would always stand, remove their hat with their left hand, and reach out to greet with their right. No lifeless fish for a handshake, either. Rather, a strength that was suppressed just enough to not fracture a woman's hand. Greeting made, hand politely removed, hat replaced, and the cowboy rode away. Seemed like they preferred the lonely life on the trail over crowds.

Tex was no different, except he was a servant. A trail boss type. No, I think he might have fit better riding drag. He was more comfortable in the back, eating the dust of the trail, smelling and riding through the natural waste of animals, humans included. Tex knew how to gather and keep things rounded up and moving forward through the trials of life. Trails and trials, oh, how similar.

After much chatter, we silently looked at each other for a few unspeaking moments. Our eyes talking years of experience. We each had a story to tell. A story that took one into the depths of human suffering of many different kinds. A story that was our own and yet connected. It was not necessary to relive those stories. We accepted each other without a background check. We knew we had been chosen for a purpose. A gathering, you might say. Who was going to be the first to admit we were in unknown territory? It sure wasn't going to be simple little me. I could easily feed us. I couldn't lead. I could follow to no end...

42

Together (Peggy)

*Above all, clothe yourselves with love, which binds us
all together in perfect harmony.*

Colossians 3:14 NLT

Yes, Mrs. RN Extraordinaire herself from some unknown urging had put this group of five together. No one on the staff seemed to notice or care. Everyone was busy getting the residents ready for breakfast. It is a huge amount of work, one resident at a time. These five just happened to be the first to be rolled up to my med cart for their morning dose. So many pills. So much treatment. So little cure. We have become a society of "treat the symptoms" not "cure." There is no profit in curing anything. If you cure, the revenue stream leaves. But if one can "treat" them just well enough to feel slightly better, they will always come back for more. Profits did this. I suppose I was part of the problem. It was my obligation as a registered nurse to follow doctor's orders to the very last pill, whether I believed in the process or not.

Alan came to my cart first. A simple dose of an experimental drug called Aducanumab. This drug has shown some promise. And actually seemed to help Alan for a time. Now, sadly, he is past the point of slowing down the progression.

Alan used to be on Donepezil until during one of his care plan meetings, I convinced the team and his wife that this was an expensive drug that should have been used from the onset of Alan's Alzheimer's. By the time he was actually diagnosed, it was almost too late to have any real benefit. Plus, the extreme cost could be better used to support those lovely little girls of Alan's future. We were able to replace it with the Aducanumab that had just been put back on the "trial list." Luckily, the company producing this drug found Alan to be the perfect candidate for their testing. I think it had something to do with their local rep driving through town the same day Alan ran/ stumbled/fell/rolled down the long hill, got up in the middle of an intersection, and couldn't quite decide which direction to run next. The company rep could see that lost and distant look in Alan's eyes that were similar to what his own mother had gone through. Yes, even monster drug companies employ some people who have hearts.

Next was Larry. Every aide wanted to be the one to get those two men up in the morning. Yeah, one was physically helpless and the other mentally gone, but they were always awake and ready to meet the day. Plus, men's clothing is simpler. As long as they were dry, it was get them up, pants and a shirt, socks and Hush Puppies, brush their teeth, comb through the nursing home hair (always flat on the back from lying in one position for like, ever), and wheel them to the nurse or med aide working that end of the floor. Then on to dressing the next. No resistance in this room. No feces smeared to everywhere and back. Nice, kind men ready to greet the day.

It was a daily routine that started sometime around 6 in the morning to enable everyone to be in the dining room by 7:45. Do the easy ones first. Keep the numbers up. Save the challenges for last so you didn't have to be the one who fed three different residents at that meal. Feeding two per meal was fine. Three was a chore that left one mentally drained.

So, as mentioned before, I had already made the decision to put the Three Amigos together plus a couple more, prior to their being wheeled into the dining area. It was a fine dance trying to get so many residents ready but not park them at an empty table for an hour before food arrived. It was either line them up in the hallways like planes waiting for an open runway or circle them in a group in a big Common Room. Circle was my choice. MayAnn should be coming next.

MayAnn was given Memantine (good stuff) which works at blocking the extra glutamate (bad stuff) that is produced because of damaged brain cells. The glutamate damages even more brain cells, in turn producing more glutamate. Memantine protects the living brain cells by blocking the effects of the glutamate. Kind of like a left tackle on offense in football protects the quarterback. But sooner or later, the glutamate always wins. The quarterback gets sacked. Except in the case of Alzheimer's, this quarterback of a brain cell never gets back up for another play. Once down, done. Sad.

MayAnn also gets a multivitamin, one mild antidepressant, and Metamucil to keep her regular. Female thing, not necessarily an age thing. The antidepressant is simply because MayAnn had taken them so long, she still needs a little something to take the edge off. I don't think MayAnn has many edges left. I can relate to the need, though.

So, the Three Amigos were joined once again. It was the first time I have seen MayAnn smile in weeks. Somehow, she could sense she was approaching the two men. A small gasp of glee was let out from some dark place inside MayAnn. I was afraid it was going to build to one of her rare bloodcurdling screams that could reach the north end of town. Not this time. A simple little gasp of pleasure. It warmed my heart. Their hands were joined. The world was right.

For some reason, Tex came next. He had just recently been transferred to us from one of those big-city nursing homes in Chicago. I never did look in his file to see just where. Haven't had time. I liked Tex from the first moment he was wheeled in by what seemed to be a hundred parishioners. They flocked around him like he was the Savior Himself. He had been a special person to all of them, you could tell. They had decided as a collective to get him out of that corporate mill of a care facility and bring him to a "down home" type home that his cowboy self could relate to. Nebraska wasn't Texas, but it was close enough to their city for a weekend drive to come and visit their ancient pastor, who seemed destined to live forever. Tex would shake your hand in the most firm and warming way. I could tell he still had the ability to crush my hand with a single squeeze. I could also tell Tex would never do that to another fellow believer. I would hate to be on his bad side, though. Low-dose aspirin and a multivitamin were all Tex needed. Thin the blood a little and keep it healthy. Good plan. I wish more residents were left to that simple of a medical plan.

Then came Maria. Maria was just old. Not Alzheimer's eating her brain alive but more of dementia caused by age. She had some hand tremors similar to Parkinson's. I believe this was just age too. Maria still had a spark in the back of her eyes. She demanded to be dressed pretty and like a lady. Very proper was Maria. Yet she had a hardness only seen in those who had at one time suffered poverty and hunger. Maria could have passed for a Mother Teresa of sorts. A generous soul with determination. That was Maria.

I had put Tex next to Larry, and then Maria in between Tex and Alan. Maria and Tex grasped the concept of the circle and joined their hands, but not until I had put Alan's hand in Maria's and Larry's hand in Tex's. They seemed to spend a moment bound to their new acquaintances, and then reached out for each other.

I swear to my dying breath there was a glow that formed when this circle was complete. It was a light hovering in the center of their small circle. A pure light that was not made by man but eternal from the heavens. It scared me. It beckoned me. I had work to do. Let them be for now. More useless expensive life-sucking drugs to give to the victims of our society. Maybe I should pursue a nursing job in one of those healthy nest-type places in Denver. I think an all-natural approach is so much better than chemical altering treatments. Plus, I could work baked. No stress there...........

43

The Fix-it Crew (Alan)

My Father's house has many rooms; if that were not so,
would I have told you that I am going there
to prepare a place for you?

John 14:2 NIV

Nothing like coming out of the dark existence of almost hell and stumbling into a path of light. I should say a room of light. I have already told you about all the rooms I had found in my Jell-O pit of a brain that I could get lost in with stories and memories. Those rooms are definitely a good place to hide in for days, and not have to face the demons of where I sat. Then there was the Common Room. Somewhere in between MayAnn's pudding and my Jell-O, where we, if holding hands, could share some sunshine in our lives. It seemed like most of our effort was trying to get Larry to open his entry door and join us. Don't quite understand his hang-up.

This, my friend, was a whole new ball game. It was like a team being put together for the first time. Each was assembled because they had something to contribute to the whole. I have a small hint of an idea who the Coach was who recruited us. I know in my heart it was not coincidence. This was a plan coming to fruition.

We were now becoming the makings of a team. If it was football, we needed anywhere from one to six more. Yes, there is such a thing as six-man football and eight-man football. And more than likely, one played both offense and defense. It is only in eleven-man football that there are specialties. We do have enough residents in this home to put together a decent eleven-man squad with an offense crew, defense, and special teams; we would need like thirty-six players for a decent squad.

If it was basketball, we were good to go with five, unless someone got hurt. So, maybe we'd need six. A starting team roster typically has twelve. Baseball nine, and maybe a couple of extra pitchers to cover. Volleyball six, or sand volleyball two. Soccer, eleven. Rugby fifteen with half again as many subs. Hockey, six. Sorry about that, went on another tangent. Hmmmmmm, wonder when that started happening...

So, we have five right now. I am referring to us as a team because the only athletic activity most of us can muster is inside our head. Maybe we can expand the Common Room to create a gymnasium for us. I guess we might not have room for a full-size football or futebol (soccer) field, so maybe we will start with a basketball or volleyball team.

Or we could go military and have a squad (us), which would be a part of a platoon (this nursing home), which would be a part of a company (all the nursing homes in the state). Is my imagination boring you yet? I could go with a naval-type organization. We could be part of the Old Folks Fleet. Many leaks but not sunk. Yet.

I don't know. Why do I even care what our group will reference? Maybe it is because any group of any kind needs a leader. I liked the football reference because the quarterback is the man running the show on the field. Or the defensive captain. The quarterback typically gets most of the praise and glory for wins, and blamed for losses. Basketball, you might have one player who is exceptional on offense and scores a majority of the points, but the other four typically have to carry him/her on defense. It is a tough call to categorize our newly formed group. Guess I will ask the others.

"Hey y'all, welcome to the Common Room that MayAnn and I started. Just the presence of the rest of you has added an extra light and energy to our room. And most welcome, Larry. Took you long enough.

Now that we have been brought together, I feel we need to organize and get to work on the project 'He who brought us together' wants completed. I am not quite sure what that project is. I just know I am grateful to have us gathered 'as one'. It is an honor to be a part of what I feel is an incredibly special group.

I also realize our time is limited. One, because the nursing staff will soon separate us for whatever our next scheduled activity is. Maybe breakfast this go round? And two, all of us are on the short end of the life expectancy clock. We all know these facts. No changing either one of them. Thus, we should organize, determine needs, and take action. God put us together, let us not grow weary in welldoing."

That little statement helped everyone focus their attention on a purpose instead of us just having a pre-breakfast party and wasting the Light. Tex led us in a short prayer. MayAnn made sure we had treats. Larry stood there like our guardian. Maria brought calmness and a gentle light. And I, who seemed to be taking charge, just because I was here first.

No one argued. There was no vote. It just seemed like we knew who was here, for what purpose. Yes, we were a team. Maybe the "A-Team?" No, that won't work. All of us don't have Alzheimer's. We do have Alzheimer's, ALS, and old age. So maybe we could be the AAA team.

We could be the LTBA team. Lucky to be Alive. That doesn't quite work, either. I know that not one of us feels "lucky" about our situation. We are fortunate to be together. FTBT? No, that is too close to Fitbit, and we have no need for those anymore. Come on, people, give me something to work with here.

Tex said, "How 'bout GC for God's Cowboys, or God's Crew?"

Maria said, "What do you think of NLTL for Not Long to Live?"

MayAnn piped in, "Think of us as NBBGI as in No Body but Great Intelligence?"

Larry grunted, "FOCUS, for Let's eliminate those who abuse our fellow residents."

Everyone had to chuckle at Larry with the acronym that matched no word in his statement. However, we all agreed that maybe it was exactly our purpose and why we were going to really need to "focus" to be able to accomplish anything. LETWAOFR or LETWAR. Now we might have something. Let's Eliminate Those Who Abuse Residents. We are the LETWARs. Sounds a lot stronger than any of us feels. At least as individuals. But as a group? We are Strong. Isn't that a song from the '70s?

We decided to work on the name part. We had a fairly good idea of our mission. We could tell time was almost up for our little team at this exact moment. Tex gave us a parting prayer as we were pulled respectively apart and wheeled to the dining room. Oh, what I wouldn't give for like six eggs over medium, sausage, bacon, and maybe some French toast.

Well, I'll be!! As I was wheeled into the dining area, right past my normal spot, I saw my family sitting at a large dining table all decorated and looking grand. There is hope yet for those eggs and French toast...................

44

HERE WE GO (Larry)

But seek first His kingdom and His righteousness,
and all these things will be added to you.

Matthew 6:33 NASB

That little get-together we just had was pretty cool. Thanks to Tex, I was able to drag past the huge barrier my brain had thrown up. The others had body function, but no brain and it was easy for them to escape into LaLa Land. But I had my faculties upstairs. Just couldn't move any muscles from the neck down. Hardly anyway. My breathing seemed to have improved lately, though.

Every time I had the chance to be together with MayAnn and Alan, it seemed I came away with stronger lungs and maybe a hint of movement in my hands. My heart was slamming away at a good pace still, but my lungs were trying to hang up the coat. It was like I was given some physical strength from my friends' bodies that they weren't using. I sure hope I was giving them some of my mental capacity in return.

After our Light gathering of five, I definitely came away stronger. I could breathe freely. I almost felt like I could speak some coherent words out loud. I definitely could move my arms enough to pat the arms of my caregiver as a gesture of thanksgiving for taking care of me. My gosh, day in and day out, they have to feed me, clothe me, and wipe my butt. I am totally dependent on others to maintain my semblance of humanity. They could leave me naked lying out in the hedgerow and I could do absolutely nothing about it. I couldn't even scream. I would have to just lie there as the bugs slowly devoured me. Damn, what a nightmare of a way to go. My brain needs to go in a different direction. My conscience tells me I deserve a death like that for the SOB I had been for so long.

In our little group, I did not feel the guilt. I only felt welcome. There was no questioning of my past. This was not a church gathering, where intentions were good, but inner faults brought out the ugliness in people.

No, our group was about as pure as it gets. I am understanding a concept here. It is coming from way back in my Oral Roberts days. "Your faith begins to move, to act, when the power of God supernaturally empties you of doubt and fills you with a knowing". At fourteen, one doesn't have a clue what that even comes close to meaning. Now, the light bulb is coming on. As Tex would say, "bout time."

Our doubts had been removed because we had all lost so much of our human distractions that we could accomplish something as simple as a joining of minds. We had been reduced to one-dimension entities that had nothing better to do. No, nothing else we could do, except sit there totally empty until we were joined. Good stuff. God, thank YOU!

I also realized that we had all known this since way back in normal days. Somewhere in our growing up and becoming Christian, we had received the gift to do exactly what we did today. We gathered in His Light as one. We could have done this years ago, but the distractions of either our bodies or our minds or a combination thereof, had prevented us from living/realizing such a simple concept.

The distractions of this world had prevented us from really seeing His Light. Only when we were reduced to something no more than a baby in adult clothing were we able to join, as God had originally intended us to join.

Yes, in a strong enough church group, Bible study, prayer meeting, or revival, we all at one time or another or several others had caught strong glimpses of what could be. Then, life jumped back in the way, and distracted us from His work. Now, in our reduced state, we could do nothing but come, pure and simple, into His room. Our Common Room was God's locker room for work yet to do here on Earth.

WOW, what a revelation for this guy. For once I didn't feel like everyone needed to be admiring me. My tools/talents God had embedded in me were to be used as part of a greater whole. It felt so incredible, and good, and pure, and wonderful, and fulfilling, and simple, and truthful, and happy, and whole, and did I say GOOD?!!

Now, I am sitting here feeding myself. I no longer dread finishing breakfast and then getting set somewhere whoever my caregiver is for the day decides to park me. They could take me out in the freezing cold catching a full face of a Northern, and I would be protected by the lap blanket of warmth our little gathering had left with me.

My aide assigned to feed me almost peed herself when I reached out and stopped her arm. I needed to do this today. Who knows how long this new strength would last? My brain seemed slightly foggy but what the heck. I could capture a little self-dignity back and feed myself like a normal adult. It probably looked more like a two-year-old who has just mastered the spoon thing, and the percentage of successful mouthfuls was in the 60 percent category. Man, oh man, did it feel good. I almost think I could arm wrestle my aide and win.

Did the others feel the same way? Did all five come away with a new strength and outlook on their day? Will we be given a chance to be together again soon? Or is everything I gathered from today slowly going to rot back into my vegetable of a body and destroy all the Light I have spilling out? "Oh, God, don't just give me a small taste of your Glory and then deprive me of the full meal." I am hungry for more.

I can see MayAnn, Tex, and Maria at the next table straight in line with my fixed head view. Yeah, there is a belt across my forehead that keeps my head from flopping around like a worn-out bobblehead. It really is pathetic. But oh, so worth it if I can be a part of the Light again. That's what we will name our group. TLC. The Light Crew in a play on Tender Loving Care. Because we will be carrying a Light, God's Light, because He cares for us, and wants us to care for others. We are assigned the job of carrying the Light.

So, first mission should be addressing the evil in our midst. Flat out get rid of it. Protect our fellow residents. The peace I brought away from our gathering tells me to forgive and forget. The anger I feel when thinking of all the horrible things this woman has done to my friends, is overwhelming. My desire to rid this Earth of her evil far outweighs the goodness of where I want to be.

I need to visit with Tex about this. How can we battle evil with only love and forgiveness? Don't we have to stand up and actually fight the fight once in a while? I am now confused and frustrated. Man, how easy it is to get distracted from God's work.

Is the ratio of this world equal to that classic Clint Eastwood movie, *The Good, the Bad and the Ugly*? Are we outnumbered two to one? Is that why it is so much easier to just stay on the not-so-good side—because the majority of people are there? Why did God give us the option to choose between good and bad? Why does God allow the bad to metamorphose into The Ugly? It seems like once you go to The Ugly, there is no turning back.

Being bad is a part of life. We want to be Good. Most of the time. We are human, though, and the Bad just wants its fair turn. Can't be Good 100 percent of the time. Maybe want to. But can't. We are flawed. I am flawed. I am more flawed than most. How could God even begin to love me?

I'm starting to sound like a preacher. Tex would be proud of my words. He is privileged to have been "called" and not waste most of his life on himself. Rather, he gave it to the service of others. Good man there. If I had only known.

Worst part is, I did know. We all know. Most of us choose to ignore this knowledge. I ignored it because I was in pursuit of the almighty dollar. That God of Wealth is what bought me oh, so many pleasures. It paid for brief moments of what I thought was happiness. It put the deposit on what I believed was envy from others.

I should shut up. You don't really need to hear me preach. My God, who am I to talk anyway? Look at the level of sin I lived. I should crawl into a hole of shame and stay there. That is where I deserve to be, you are thinking.

That is exactly what I am thinking about Witch Hazel. The meanest and most abusive soul I believe I have ever known. Is her evil any worse than mine? Think of the women I have used throughout the years. Isn't that just as bad as what she does to these residents? Were the women under my spell of good looks and money just as helpless as the old and decrepit?

I would like to think not. But maybe I should call a spade a spade. The kettle is black. Damn. I am seeing things about myself that I really don't like. How can God ever even be able to love me? I am evil and ugly. Can I do enough good to ever make up for it?

Do I need to chase down everyone in my life I have wronged at one time or another? Collectively, that would mean EVERYONE. Not just a select few here or there. I used all those I knew, in one form or another. Who is the "bitch" now? I was a terrible person. I am so deeply sorry. I didn't want to be that person. At the time, I didn't have a clue of the pain I was inflicting.

Maybe the Bitch Aide of this nursing home is the same way. Maybe she doesn't realize the suffering she is causing. She has done so many things that even if she were to stop her terrible actions now, the residents would still cower in fear of her, for years to come. Or, rather until their dying breath. Has she stepped past the line of forgiveness? What do you think? What in your opinion should TLC do about this aide who has no heart?

We can't just get her to leave this home. She would simply move on to another one and find new victims. At least here, we know what to expect and could support each other. Kind of like a POW camp. We are prisoners in our own bodies, and this particular guard takes pleasure in torture just because. Full of the worst evil alive.

Was this me too? God, I pray it isn't so. I am afraid there are people who to this day hold that opinion of me. I can't blame them. They will never forget the harm I inflicted on them or on someone they cared about. My reputation will never be fully cleansed, that is for certain. I know there are some who celebrate the condition I am in right now. If they would only forgive me.

"Greater is He who is in me, than he who is in the world" keeps bouncing between my ears. GIHWIIMTHWIIW. A little too long for a group name. I truly felt "He" in me as we gathered this morning. I felt He in me at fourteen when I first accepted Him. Somewhere between then and now, I lived as he who is in the world. Bastard devil anyway, doesn't deserve a capital H on his "he"...............

45

Can't Go Home Yet (MayAnn)

*But when Christ came as high priest of the good things that are
now already here, he went through the greater and more perfect
tabernacle that is not made with human hands, this is to say,
is not a part of this creation.*

Hebrews 9:11 NIV

Oh, what a blessing this morning. It is like a plan coming to fruition. God's hand at work. It was so incredibly powerful. If I had known such an important event was taking place, I would have put on my Sunday best. I would have had a day of hair, makeup, and nails, prior to this gathering. I suppose with only five of us, and with Larry and Alan used to me being just kind of plain, it was ok.

I was never one to get too dolled up, especially as a daily routine. Every once in a while, it is nice to get pampered and feel like a lady ready for the grand ball. Maybe I could suggest that at our next gathering. We could plan a party with formal invitations and RSVPs and a requirement of a certain level of attire. It would be a time of joy and beauty for all.

I can just see "my boys" in their finest suits. The perfect gentlemen giving us old ladies the pleasure of their attention. Younger women swooning after them. They really are fine-looking men if I have to say so myself.

I still am puzzled why they mean so much to me. There is a connection. I know they feel it too. We haven't really talked about it. Doesn't seem to be much of a priority for any of us, though. We just know.

The group Light was amazing. I didn't want to leave. It felt like home. What a lovely group we were. Tex, with his gentleness of character that reaches to the inner workings of your heart. Even in our joint imagined Common Room, he had an effect on me.

I also felt a déjà vu with Tex. I have known him in a past life. Doesn't seem like all that long ago. Special people like him are not soon forgotten. I can almost put my finger on it. Maybe next meeting I will ask. He seemed to look at me with a special "knowing." If we hadn't been so overwhelmed by the immensity of our meeting, maybe I could have figured it out. It will come. I am sure of it. We were surrounded by a Great Light. I feel there is some other Light to be shed, too. God's plan isn't all work and no play. Oh, how I believe He has a sense of humor. His creations tend to be such forgetful idiots. So much of the time, we act like chickens running around with our heads cut off.

I received the feeling/message that we had an urgent order of business to take care of. Next meeting, we will address our primary abuser. Something has to be done. Burning at the stake like the witch she is, wouldn't be good enough. Head cut off, maybe. That is too quick and probably painless. If your head is suddenly chopped off, is there a moment of recollection that you could actually look back and see your body as your head is rolling, your eyes like a tilt-a-whirl gone south? I'm sorry, ladies shouldn't think like that. We should be worried about if our dress matches our purse and shoes. Or rather, "Which shoes should I wear with this dress?" and, "I will never find a clutch that matches this outfit."

Sorry, men, that is how we think. When you catch us standing at the closet, and stating, "I have nothing to wear," we mean exactly that. No matter the size of the closet. Even if we can walk twenty feet in, clothes lining both sides, shoes lined up for miles, we can still have that challenge of finding the perfect dressing for our current emotion. Get used to it, men. That is how God designed us. And it is quite all right.

I need to tell you a secret. Well, not really a secret because Peggy wants to tell everyone about it except the bitch herself. She doesn't need to know because she would find a way to destroy everyone's happiness. The secret: I had a conversation with Peggy just a little while ago.

Coming away from our Light gathering, I felt a clarity I hadn't realized in a long, long time. The fog had lifted from the hallway of my brain. I could think on the outside. I could capture words bouncing in my head, organize them into a sentence and actually release them from my mouth. No *pent-up all I could do today is scream*, for me. It was time to talk. I felt deep inside that this was just temporary. So, I was not going to let it go to waste.

Peggy happened to have her med cart parked right next to our table as we ate breakfast. It is impossible for her to pass all the medication to all the residents prior to breakfast time, and some meds need to be taken with food. So, she has to spend most of the next hour passing out more medications while we eat.

Other meds are a lot easier to swallow if you are eating at the same time. Kind of interrupts our meal. I understand, though. We need what we need. Well, truthfully, we probably only need about ten percent of all the drugs they give us. But they mean well, and the companies that make these drugs love us.

Anyway, back to my long-lost ability to speak. Peggy was her "always cheerful" self, telling each and every resident she cared for "Good Morning." Followed by a "How are you today?" The beautiful part of Peggy was that she meant it. She wasn't just going through the routine. Most of the nurses, med aides, and nurse's aides were the same way. They were born with a special heart. Extra special to be able to care for the elderly and the helpless. Peggy was a master of sharing her heart. Sunshine came right out of every word she gave.

It was my turn for a mixture of some fiber stuff, Metamucil. I was once told it was to keep me "regular." And some other pills. I don't have a clue what for, except they make me sleepy and passive and apparently force me to need Metamucil.

Peggy said, "Well, good morning, MayAnn, you look exceptionally glowing today." I replied, "Thank you, Peggy, and a very good morning to you too!!" The look in Peggy's eyes was priceless. If she'd had anything in her hands, it would have dropped. Maybe not as far as her jaw did, but drop nonetheless.

Peggy's experience with the ugliness of Alzheimer's brought her back to reality quickly. She had seen such "moments of clarity" before. She also knew that these moments were usually brought on by a special event. Like a visit from a family member. Or maybe the playing of a song they knew from their past.

Peggy also recognized this as an even more special event. Something more than emotions was at play here. I could tell she knew that I had found some strength from within. We spent the next ten minutes visiting like only a couple of mother hens could.

We talked and laughed and shared stories. Normally, Peggy has "things to do." But that huge heart of hers knew that she couldn't let this moment pass. She knew I would soon slip away, again.

Oh, how we talked. It was like I had never had an ounce of this terrible disease. It was like we were sisters catching up on all the world's gossip we just "had to share" with each other since the last time we talked.

We talked about Peggy's family. We talked about my family. We talked about each other's hair. We admired each other's outfits. We discussed plans for going to the salon together and doing lady things. We even discussed the men in the room and who was the gentleman and who was just a horny old man. That brought some laughter.

Then, I said, "Thank you, Peggy." She simply replied, "Well, you're most welcome, MayAnn." I then was a little more adamant. "No,................. Thank YOU, Peggy. You are an angel in a white nurse outfit. We are so very blessed to have you here. I, MayAnn, am so very blessed to have you to look after me day after day. I may never get the chance to say, 'Thank you' again. You need to know how we all feel about you. You need to know you are appreciated and loved. You need to hold on to the fact that God is going to give you more than a gold star for your service. You are special, Miss Peggy. Please always know, even if I can't tell you daily, thank you, and I love you."

Then tears started to flow. Peggy's first, then mine. She bent over and hugged me the best she could. I hugged back with all my might, even though my arms felt like useless lead weights. Where did that weakness come from?

We shared something special right then. I still have tears in my eyes thinking about how incredibly special our nurse Peggy is.

Then, the fog started rolling back down the hill. It had almost completely blown away. I knew it would return. I would have given anything to die right there in Peggy's arms. Then I could have gone to that Common Room above. A House not made with hands. Eternal in the heavens.

I guess I was still here for a reason. The fog once again enveloped me. The hallway got so very narrow I was almost held in a permanent state of nonmovement. I quickly escaped to my little clarity room. Slammed the door, and left what others call reality.

Goodbye for now, Peggy. Maybe I will return again someday for another visit. I surely hope so. The girl talk was needed. I fear I will never ever be that coherent again. I do at least have hope, though. Hope had left me a long time ago.

I can still feel the last tear sitting on my cheek. It doesn't want to leave, either. It is a good tear. Can happiness and sadness and love all wrapped up in one package be captured by one little drop of water produced from an eye that has seen so much? I think so. Tears can be good. I wish I could cry the good tears more...............................

46

What Happened Today? (Peggy)

The Lord God has given Me the tongue of disciples, That I may know
how to sustain the weary one with a word. He awakens Me morning
by morning, He awakens My ear to listen as a disciple.

Isaiah 50:4 NASB

Today was a special day for many. As a nurse, we recognized the cycles of the moon and how it affects the residents. Somewhere right before a full moon, the runners run, the screamers scream, the violent bite and hit more. It can be a circus.

Today wasn't that type of day. Today was special. Something different at this home. Something new. Something exciting, actually. Look through my eyes for a moment and you tell me what you think.

Remember, I told you how I had left the five residents sitting together in a circle. I saw a special light coming from their center as they joined hands. I couldn't stand and stare as I had many more residents to take care of. Something told me I had done well. It warmed me inside.

When breakfast time arrived, the aides started grabbing the staged residents and wheeling them to the dining area. Nobody noticed much of anything. Just another day. Get everyone out of bed, clothe them, tidy them up, pass them by the nurse, park them until designated feed time, wheel them in, go back and forth until everyone is at their designated table, sit by whoever needs to be fed that day, and wait for the kitchen staff to bring meals. Same routine, 7 – 365.

Things turned out different today. The aide helping feed Larry gasped as he reached out, patted her arm, and then proceeded to grab his own fork and start feeding himself. Realize, this man suffering from ALS didn't have the strength to even hold his own head up, much less feed himself. It was a sight to see. The poor aide just sat there in awe ready to clean up whatever disastrous mess was about to unfold.

Larry didn't say anything, and his eyes seemed a bit glazed over. It was almost like his brain had somewhat checked out, but his body was functioning again. I think it was taking so much effort to have motor functions running that Larry couldn't concentrate on anything but the task at hand of eating. That was one.

Tex was his same old gentle soul. But he had parked his wheelchair in the hallway. Stood up as proudly as his withered body would let him, and had his boots clomping all the way to his table. He politely asked one of the kitchen staff for a chair, hung his hat on it, sat down and said, "Today, I will dine with some dignity. He even offered to help feed the gentleman sitting next to him who had checked out years ago. The aide assisting at that table thanked Tex, but told him it was a "regulation thing" and she appreciated his offer, but "not this time."

Maria had wheeled herself back to her room after the group of five dispersed. There she worked on her hair a little bit, put some lipstick on, her favorite pair of earrings and a special brooch, and wheeled herself to the dining area. She held her head proud and pretty like she was entering a gala, and all heads turned to watch her entry. There was a glow to Maria that none of us had ever seen. What a lovely lady.

Then my conversation with MayAnn from out of the blue. Understand, this poor lady had not communicated or been mentally present for a couple of years now. Only her occasional scream let us know that someone was still home. Today, she talked to me like a long-lost sister.

We shared family stories. We indulged in a little gossip about the various nursing staff. We talked about girl stuff to no end. We cried. We hugged. MayAnn's arms seemed a little weaker than normal. It was like her brain took all the energy from the rest of her. That was OK, though. We had a grand time. Oh my, did that put me behind schedule for taking care of the other residents.

Today we needed that break in routine. It was like extra sunlight had come into the dining area. I believe everyone felt it to some degree. To be able to capture that moment and hold it in our palm for an eternity would be a story. These special people once again touched my heart.

The most impressive was Alan. I don't know why or how it happened, but most of his family showed up for breakfast. One of them must have notified the kitchen because there was a special table set up in the area where we normally lead church and call out Bingo. The staff had set the table and decorated like a four-star restaurant. There would have been candles if it hadn't been for one more of the thousands of regulations. There were a couple of the battery/LED candles in place that looked very pretty. Rather fancy for a breakfast. Maybe they considered it a social brunch?

Alan's breathlessly beautiful wife, Ana, got up from the table as Alan was wheeled in. You could see the apprehension and weight of a thousand mental pains in her eyes knowing that her husband would probably just sit there like a mindless body. Then, her eyes caught Alan's. They locked in. They said a thousand words to each other as Ana almost ran toward her "awake" husband. Alan's daughters felt the awareness, too, and did run to their daddy. His boys (striking men they were) stood up in respect of their dad. Grandchildren followed their dads' lead. Oh, to have had a video.

That was about all I was able to catch of that reunion. I had everyone else needing my attention, and then MayAnn completely stole it. What an amazing day. Christmas couldn't hold a light to what happened this morning. Well, shouldn't say that. I believe the Light of what Christmas is all about is what was responsible for the joy of this morning.............

47

Kay

"Is not all human life a struggle?
Our lives are like that of a hired hand,

Job 9:1 NLT

This isn't fair. Life in general isn't fair but I was dealt a good portion of many others' "not fair." I am sitting here today tied up with M.S. No constraints for me as my muscles still have strength but are knotted up in a ball of crippling pain. Somewhere in less than 7 years, I went from a lover of arts and crafts to this knotted-up mess confined to a reclining wheelchair.

My husband checked out not all that long after he put me in this care facility. I can't blame him, I guess. He did his best at home until I became too much of a burden. Then, the cost of this nursing home left him no choice but to divorce me so the state would take over. Was it right or wrong? I can't say. My sister, who is here faithfully with me almost every day, hates him and what he did to me. Such is life. Here am I.

Today, things are different in this home. There are a few residents who have escaped from the reality of their life sentence. They are free from their burdens. Even if for just a short time. At least they get a break. My pain won't let up. It is constant and exhausting. My only pleasure in life is eating. And someone in their caring but stupid mind has decided I am getting too heavy and should be limited on my intake. My God, people, can't I have just one pleasure. There is nothing else. HEAR ME.......... NOTHING ELSE!!

Just because my body is a wad of cramped-up pain that tears away my ability to think and converse clearly, does not mean I am not aware of my surroundings. I can see and hear everything clearly. My receptors for intake are just fine, thank you. It is my ability to communicate out that makes people think I am mentally inhibited. No, the thought process is fully functioning. I feel. I understand. I cry. I laugh. I am still alive, damnit!! Only my sisters and a few of my caregivers seem to understand that rather important detail.

The worst part is what I can see in most people's eyes. They are telling me, "Kay, there is no coming back from this one." I can accept that. Doesn't mean I have to like it.

Today, these people who are probably worse off than me and have a more severe and shortened death sentence are having an amazingly good day. I want to be a part of that. I will make sure my sister knows when she comes in today. I will tell her that I want to be a part of that group of Light I witnessed this morning.

Yes, I saw what happened. I was parked in my usual spot in front of the TV. Everyone seems to believe that is where I want to be. Well, yes, most of the time that is just fine. No better way to check out from reality than to be entertained by whatever is going to sell the next best product. Who cares if most of TV is mindless dribble. Entertainment is distraction. I can use all the distraction from this life of mine they will let me have.

The TV was left off this morning. It typically doesn't come on until after breakfast. That is fine. I guess I am parked here because I take up too much room everywhere else. I don't know why they never park anyone else beside me. I am a loving person. I am not mean or angry. I still have a lot of joy to give. Please don't isolate me.

It was a good chance to observe that little circle join hands, create this awesome Light, and form some kind of special communication bond. It was like they joined hands in prayer and then took it up a few notches.

There was no humming or chanting or rocking/swaying in their seats like a séance. It was a simple joining of hands that appeared to be a joining of souls. If I could have wheeled myself over there, I would have asked to join.

Then, seeing everything going on at breakfast was just shy of a miracle. Alan eating a meal with his family, recognizing everyone. Holding those pretty twins in his lap. How fast they are growing. His whole family talking like they hadn't had the chance to in quite some time. Alan absorbing it all and acting like he had never been locked in his mental prison.

I was hoping Alan would take off running like he used to. I loved watching him lead the nursing staff on the wild goose chase of the week. The best times were when he was exhausting that one aide who is just horrible to most of the residents. She keeps her distance from me. I believe she is scared of my sister. That is funny. My sister can be a little intimidating to most of the staff. She loves me to no end, and has made it her life's purpose to take care of me the best she can. I know I will never be able to express my gratitude to her at any level close to the love she has shown me. Maybe if I could be part of that group, though, I could share some of their Light with my sister. That would be so very awesome. . . . .

48

MY LIFE SUCKS (JEAN)

*THE GOOD MAN BRINGS OUT OF HIS GOOD TREASURE WHAT IS GOOD;
AND THE EVIL MAN BRINGS OUT OF HIS EVIL TREASURE WHAT IS EVIL.*

MATTHEW 12:35 NASB

MY POS LIVE-IN BOYFRIEND BEAT ON ME AGAIN LAST NIGHT. I DON'T THINK HE REALLY MEANS TO, IT IS JUST SOMETHING LEARNED FROM GENERATIONS OF ABUSIVE FATHERS. THE ONLY REASON HE IS HERE IS THAT HE IS THE FATHER OF MY DAUGHTER. HAVING HER IS [PROBABLY THE ONLY JOY I HAVE EVER KNOWN. AT LEAST HIS DICK IS GOOD FOR ONE THING, BEAT ME THEN BED ME. IT ISN'T ALL THAT SPECIAL, BUT IT DOES GIVE ME FIVE MINUTES OF ATTENTION WITH PLEASURE.

MAYBE HE WOULDN'T BE SO ANGRY IF HE DRANK LESS AND WORKED MORE. IF IT WASN'T FOR MY FORTY HOURS A WEEK AS A NURSE'S AIDE, WE WOULD STARVE. I EVEN BOUGHT THIS SORRY SHACK WE CALL A HOUSE. I GOT IT CHEAP BECAUSE IT IS AS WORN OUT AS WHAT IS LEFT OF THIS UNINCORPORATED TINY TOWN WE CALL HOME. NO POST OFFICE. NOT EVEN A CONVENIENCE STORE. THE LAST TIME THIS PLACE ACTUALLY HAD A STORE WAS WHEN THEY WERE KNOWN AS GENERAL STORES. HEY, IS THAT WHERE DOLLAR GENERAL GOT THEIR NAME? YOU COULD BUY YOUR NEW WORK PANTS RIGHT BESIDE DUST MOPS. AND JUST DOWN THE AISLE FROM SLABS OF BALONEY AND CHEESE YOU HAVE THEM CUT OFF SLICES OF BY THE POUND.

THE NEAREST SOCIAL LIFE IS TWELVE MILES AWAY. I GO TO THE BAR WITH MY LIVE-IN ONCE IN A WHILE WHEN I HAVE AN EXTRA TEN DOLLARS FOR THE BABYSITTER. MIGHT AS WELL GET NUMB BEFORE THE NEXT BEATING. WE GENERALLY HAVE A GOOD TIME FOR A SPELL. THEN THE HAPPY DRUNK IS REPLACED BY THE BAD DRUNK. BEST PART IS, I KEEP MYSELF JUST SOBER ENOUGH TO SOMEWHAT KICK HIS ASS. REVENGE IS MINE ONCE IN A WHILE.

I HAVE THIS SKIN CONDITION LIKE BEING AN ALLIGATOR. IT IS IRRITATING AF. I CAN'T AFFORD THE OVERPRICED MEDICATION TO TREAT IT. IT WOULD BE GREAT TO BATHE CONSTANTLY IN CALAMINE LOTION. ANYTHING TO RELIEVE THE CONSTANT ITCH. I DO MANAGE TO "BORROW" SOME OF THE PRESCRIPTION LOTION FROM THE MED CARTS WHEN THE NURSES AREN'T LOOKING. I AM GLAD MY UNIFORM AT WORK HIDES THE WORST OF THE SCALING. I AM HAPPY THAT SO FAR IT HASN'T BEEN HEREDITARILY PASSED TO MY

DAUGHTER. THAT WOULD PROBABLY TAKE ME COMPLETELY OVER THE EDGE. I DO WISH IT WAS CONTAGIOUS. IT WOULD BE AWESOME TO PASS IT TO MY BOYFRIEND, WHO LOVES THE ROUGHNESS OF MY SKIN LIKE A WELL-WORN PUNCHING BAG.

I LIKE MY WORK FOR THE MOST PART. THE TRAINING WAS EASY. AND IF LIFE FOR ME EVER MOVED ON TO BETTER PLACES, I COULD EASILY GET AN EQUAL JOB ANYWHERE IN THE STATE. EVERY NURSING HOME IN THE COUNTRY IS ALWAYS LOOKING FOR AIDES. THERE JUST AREN'T ENOUGH OF US AROUND WHO ARE WILLING TO DO SUCH HARD PHYSICAL AND MENTAL LABOR FOR SUCH MENIAL PAY. AND YOU REALLY DON'T HAVE TO BE THAT GOOD. A WARM BODY THAT CAN DRESS AND FEED OLD PEOPLE IS WHAT THEY NEED. COMPASSION AND EMPATHY ARE NOT PREREQUISITES.

THE BEST PART ABOUT MY JOB IS THAT IT IS A GOOD RELEASE FOR MY ANGER. THE ABUSE I HAVE SEEMED TO BE DESTINED FOR SINCE CHILDHOOD CAN BE SHARED WITH THESE HELPLESS OLD PEOPLE WHO CAN'T DO A DAMN THING ABOUT IT. SOME CAN YELL OR SCREAM, BUT MOST JUST SIT THERE AND TAKE IT. THEY ARE ALL QUITE A FEW BRICKS SHY OF A LOAD. OR, THE LIGHTS ARE ON, BUT NOBODY IS HOME. IT IS FUN TO WATCH THE FEAR IN THEIR EYES WHEN I COME INTO THEIR ROOM AND SHUT THE DOOR.

I DON'T KNOW WHY I WAS GIVEN THE "SPECIAL" TIME OFF DURING THE STATE INSPECTION. I AM JUST AS COMPETENT AS THE NEXT AIDE. HELL, PROBABLY EVEN MORE. I CAN OBEY THE FRICKEN RULES. I KNOW HOW TO WASH MY HANDS UPON ENTRY AND EXIT. THAT IS ABOUT THE ONLY THING THOSE DAMN INSPECTORS LOOK FOR IN THE CNAS. IT IS LIKE WE ARE CAPABLE OF NOTHING ELSE. SO MANY THINGS WE HAVE TO DO FOR THESE OLD PEOPLE AND THEY ONLY WORRY ABOUT THE FREQUENCY OF OUR HANDWASHING.

I WISH THE INSPECTORS WOULD HAVE CALLED ME IN FOR AN INTERVIEW. I COULD HAVE TOLD THEM OF SO MANY VIOLATIONS. HALF THE NURSING STAFF WOULD THEN HAVE TO BE LET GO. ESPECIALLY THAT RN PEGGY, WHO SEEMS TO THINK HER ASS DOESN'T STINK LIKE THE REST OF OURS. I WOULD SHOW HER. NOT RECOMMENDING ME TO ATTEND CLASSES FOR MEDICATION AIDE, WHAT A BITCH. AND EVERYBODY THINKS SHE IS SO VERY SPECIAL. IT IS GREAT TO GRAB SOME RESIDENT WHO HAS HAD THE SPECIAL PEGGY TREATMENT AND BRING THEM BACK DOWN TO REALITY. LIFE IS NOT SMILES AND ROSES, PEOPLE. IT IS REALITY. THORNS AND PAIN WITH A LITTLE TORTURE THROWN IN TO KEEP YOU ON YOUR TOES.

I DID SEND AN ANONYMOUS TIP IN TO THE STATE PRIOR TO THEIR ARRIVAL. I LET THEM KNOW ABOUT THAT LITTLE THREESOME IN THE ONE ROOM WHEN THE WHORE MAYANN GOES INTO THE PERVERTS' (ALAN AND LARRY'S) ROOM AND THEY HAVE SUCH A LITTLE HAND-HOLDING PARTY. WHO DO THEY THINK THEY ARE, LIKE 5TH GRADERS OR SOMETHING? HECK, I WAS LETTING BOYS GET TO THIRD BASE AT THAT AGE. OLDER BOYS, OF COURSE. THE BOYS IN MY CLASS WERE ONLY WORRIED ABOUT WHO COULD FART THE LOUDEST AND NOT GET CAUGHT. HALF THE NASTY GIRLS WEREN'T ANY BETTER. THE JUNIOR HIGH BOYS, THOUGH, THEY APPRECIATED MY GROWING TITTIES.

SO, I HEARD THE STATE CAUGHT THEM IN THEIR THREESOME ACT. DOOR CLOSED AND EVERYTHING. OH, HOW I HOPE SHIT HITS THE FAN. WE COULD USE SOME EXCITEMENT AROUND HERE. THE ADMINISTRATOR IS A PANSY ASS WITH NOTHING OF A SPINE ANYWAY. IF I WAS IN THAT OFFICE, HEADS WOULD ROLL. THE DON ISN'T ANY BETTER. JUST A "YES" PERSON WHO KNOWS HOW TO DO ALL THE REQUIRED PAPERWORK. I WOULD TEACH HER.

ON MY LAST SHIFT BEFORE THE STATE WAS SUPPOSED TO MAKE THEIR GRAND "NOSE IN THE AIR" ENTRANCE, I SHUFFLED SOME OF THE DAILY DOCUMENTS AROUND FROM ONE RESIDENT'S BOOK TO ANOTHER'S. NOT A LOT OF THEM. JUST ENOUGH TO MAKE IT LOOK LIKE COMPETENCE WAS LACKING IN THE NURSING DEPARTMENT. I HEARD THAT SEVERAL OF THE NURSES HAD TO COME IN ON THEIR OFF TIME AND AT NIGHT TO GO THROUGH EACH AND EVERY BOOK JUST TO MAKE SURE ALL THE DOCUMENTS WERE IN ORDER. "WELL, HOW DID THOSE PAPERS GET THERE?" I CAN JUST HEAR THEM SAYING. JOKE IS ON THEM. THE STATE DIDN'T CATCH IT, BUT MANY A NURSE LOST SOME SLEEP. ARROGANT AND OVERPAID BITCHES ANYWAY.

IT WAS HELL FOR ME NOT BEING ABLE TO GO TO WORK. MY DAUGHTER WAS IN SCHOOL. MY POS BF WAS OFF HUNTING OR FISHING OR DRINKING EVERY DAY. I SHOULD CALL THE LOCAL GAME WARDEN AND TELL HIM THAT POS DOESN'T HAVE A LICENSE FOR ANY OF THE FRONTIER FREEMONT THINGS HE DOES. BUT THEN HIS ANGER WOULD ONLY BE TAKEN OUT ON ME. AND WHATEVER PATHETIC BANK ACCOUNT BALANCE WE HAVE WOULD BE DRAINED TO PAY THE STATE'S STUPID FINE. I WOULD GIVE ANYTHING TO GET RID OF THAT WALKING DOUCHE BAG. BUT MY DAUGHTER LOVES HIM. SO I GUESS I WILL TOLERATE HIS SORRY WORTHLESS ASS FOR A FEW MORE YEARS. BESIDES, THE BEATINGS GIVE ME NEW IDEAS ON HOW TO TORTURE THE RESIDENTS WITHOUT ANYONE SEEING THE BRUISES. OH, WHAT FUN. I COULDN'T WAIT TO GET BACK AND PUT MY "TOYS" THROUGH JEAN'S MILL OF PLEASURES, ONCE AGAIN.

MY FAVORITE THING IS TO GIVE THEM A LITTLE "POKE" LIKE MY STEPDAD OR EVEN WORSE, MY "UNCLE" WHO JUST LOVED TO HAVE ME SIT ON HIS LAP WOULD DO. YOU KNOW, THE POKE JUST UNDER THE ARM THAT TICKLES ENOUGH TO MAKE YOU SQUIRM JUST A LITTLE. I HAVE FOUND I CAN DO IT TO SOME OF THESE RESIDENTS UNTIL THEY PISS THEMSELVES A LITTLE BIT. THEN I CAN LEAVE THEM SITTING WITH A WET DIAPER UNTIL THE NEXT SHIFT COMES ON. HOPEFULLY, THEY WILL GET A NICE RASH FROM IT. HELL, THEY CAN'T TALK OR MOVE OR DO ANYTHING ELSE ON THEIR OWN. THEY MIGHT AS WELL HAVE SOME DISCOMFORT TO LET THEM KNOW THEY ARE ALIVE.

ANOTHER FAVORITE IS BRUSHING OUT THEIR HAIR AS FAST AS I CAN. NO CONSIDERATION FOR KNOTS OR TANGLES. IF HAIR PULLS OUT, WHAT THE HECK, THEY ARE ALL LOSING THEIR HAIR ANYWAY. OLD RAGS WON'T HAVE TO SPEND SO DAMN MUCH TIME IN THE LITTLE FAKE SALON THING WE HAVE HERE, IF HALF THEIR HAIR IS GONE. I AM QUITE PROUD OF SOME OF THE HAIRBALLS I HAVE EXTRACTED. THOSE PRISSY OLD LADIES WHO THINK THEY STILL HAVE SOME BEAUTY LEFT HAVE ANOTHER THING COMING WHEN I CARE FOR

THEM. PUTS THEM IN THEIR PLACE. THEY REMIND ME OF MY MOTHER, WHO SIMPLY IGNORED THE "QUIET TIMES" MY STEPDAD OR "UNCLE" INFLICTED ON ME.

THE MEN ARE MY FAVORITE TARGET. USUALLY, THE BEST I CAN DO IS MAKE THEM SIT ON THE TOILET WITHOUT THE SEAT BEING DOWN, SO THEIR BALLS DANGLE IN THE WATER. NOTHING BETTER THAN A GOOD OLE T-BAG TREATMENT. OR PUT THEM ON THE SHITTER FOR AN EXTENDED PERIOD OF TIME UNTIL THEIR LEGS ARE COMPLETELY NUMB. THIS MAKES THEIR KNEES CRACK LIKE A BOARD WHEN I HOOK THEM UP TO THE STANDING MACHINE AND CRANK AS FAST AS POSSIBLE. A GROAN OF PAIN FROM THEM LETS ME KNOW I HAVE DONE MY JOB.

DUNKING ANY ONE OF THE RESIDENTS IN A TUB OF ICE-COLD WATER IS FUN, TOO. I ABOUT GOT CAUGHT ONE DAY DOING THAT TO MAYANNDERSOL. SHE NO SOONER HIT THAT WATER THAN A SCREAM OF THE BEST PROFANITY EVER CAME OUT OF HER TYPICALLY QUIET MOUTH. THAT SCREAM WAS SO LOUD AND SHOCKING, I ALMOST PEED MYSELF A LITTLE BIT. AT LEAST I CAN CLEAN MYSELF UP. NOT LIKE THESE VARIETY VEGETABLES WE HAVE HERE. I ALMOST GOT CAUGHT, BUT LUCKILY THE DEEP STAINLESS STEEL HORSE TANK-LOOKING TUB DRAINS REALLY FAST. AND BY THE TIME THE OTHER AIDES CAME RUNNING IN, I HAD MAYANDY SITTING UNDER THE HEAT LAMP AND WAS DRYING HER OFF.

'WHAT HAPPENED?" MY FELLOW CUNT WORKERS ASKED. "OH, YOU KNOW, MAYANN JUST THOUGHT IT WAS A LITTLE CHILLY WHEN I BROUGHT HER OUT OF THE TUB, AND I HAD FORGOTTEN TO TURN THE WARMING LIGHT ON. SHE IS ALL GOOD NOW." I COULDN'T HELP BUT THINK, "HA HA, MADE YOU GET YOUR FAT ASSES UP FROM 'CHARTING' AT THE NURSE'S STATION WHILE I WAS HAVING TO DO ALL THE WORK." MAYBE THEY WON'T PUT ME ON THE 'BATH SHIFT' AGAIN FOR A WHILE. I CAN'T STAND TO SEE ALL THAT OLD WRINKLY SKIN. THOUGH IT IS FUN TO PINCH IT IN PLACE UNDER THE FOLDS WHERE NO ONE LOOKS. MAKES THEM JUMP MORE THAN ANY MOVEMENT I HAVE SEEN FROM MOST OF THEM IN YEARS. GOOD EXERCISE IN MY OPINION. ESPECIALLY SINCE OUR PT DEPARTMENT IS SUCH A MONEY SCAM JOKE OF AN EXERCISE ROOM.

THE GOOD THING IS, THE LESS EXERCISE THESE OLD PEOPLE GET, THE EASIER IT IS FOR ME TO GIVE THEM LITTLE TREATS OF SHOCK THERAPY WITHOUT THEM BEING ABLE TO STRIKE BACK. WHAT FUN IT IS TO RIDE THAT ONE-HORSE OPEN SLEIGH OF TITTY TWISTERS. FRICKEN OLD PEOPLE. THEY ARE LUCKY I SHOW UP EVERY DAY TO GIVE THEM SOME VARIETY IN THEIR MISERABLE LIVES.

THE ONLY ONE I AVOID IS KAY. HER SISTER SCARES THE HELL OUT OF ME. A LOT OF WOMAN THERE. ALWAYS LOOKS NICE, THOUGH. I BELIEVE SHE IS THE DOMINANT ONE IN THAT MARRIAGE. WISH I COULD CONTROL MY MAN THING LIKE THAT. YOU CAN TELL HE WORSHIPS HER. I BELIEVE IF I DID ANYTHING SIDEWAYS TO KAY, HER SISTER WOULD AUTOMATICALLY KNOW SOMETHING WAS WRONG. I WISH I HAD A SISTER WHO LOVED ME THAT MUCH. MY SISTER RAN AWAY WHEN SHE WAS FIFTEEN AND LEFT ME AS THE ONLY TOY FOR

MY STEPDAD AND "UNCLE" TO AMUSE THEMSELVES WITH. OH, WELL, WHENEVER ONE OF THE "SESSIONS" WAS OVER, I GOT SOME CANDY OR NEW CLOTHES OR SOMETHING. AT LEAST FOR A WHILE UNTIL THEY REALIZED I WOULD NEVER TELL ON THEM. IF I WAS ONLY AS STRONG AS KAY'S SISTER. I BET NO MAN EVER CROSSED HER SIDEWAYS.

SO, I WILL ALWAYS LEAVE KAY ALONE. AND ANY OF THOSE WHO MIGHT BE ABLE TO RAT ME OUT. PLENTY OF OTHER WORTHLESS BODIES UP HERE FOR ME TO HAVE FUN WITH. I NEED TO THINK OF SOMETHING NEW AND MORE PAINFUL TO DO. I AM STARTING TO GET BORED WITH MOST OF MY "EXERCISES." I DID TRY FEEDING A RESIDENT FASTER THAN THEY COULD CHEW AND SWALLOW. THAT WAS INTERNALLY EXCITING BECAUSE THERE ARE SO MANY WITNESSES IN THE DINING AREA. NO ONE NOTICED. AT LEAST NOT UNTIL THE RESIDENT PUKED ALL OVER HERSELF. HA HA, KITCHEN STAFF, CLEAN UP THE GREEN PEA SOUP PILE OF VOMIT AND SNOT. STRAIGHT TO THE BATHING ROOM WITH THIS RESIDENT FOR ME. I WONDER HOW COLD THE WATER CAN POSSIBLY BE TODAY?? WIN/WIN FOR ME!!

THIS JOB BARELY PAYS SQUAT, BUT IT IS SURELY ENTERTAINING. I HEARD ABOUT SOME NEW EXCITEMENT AND EXTRA ENERGY FROM SOME OF THE RESIDENTS, ON MY DAY OFF. I WILL HAVE TO SEE WHAT THAT WAS ALL ABOUT AND PUT A STOP TO IT. WE DON'T NEED THE PEOPLE UP HERE TO FEEL GOOD ABOUT LIFE. THEY NEED TO GIVE UP THE GHOST AND DIE. MAKE MORE ROOM FOR NEW ENTERTAINMENT FOR ME.

SMOKE BREAK TIME. I LOOK FORWARD TO MAKING UP STORIES TO ADD TO THE LITTLE GOSSIP TEAM OUT IN THE SMOKE SHED. YOU SHOULD HAVE HEARD THEM CACKLING THE DAY THEY ALL GOT THAT PHOTO OF MAYANN'S COOCHY. GLAD I HAD BROUGHT ONE OF THE POS'S BURNER PHONES THAT DAY. AND THEN WITH SNAPCHAT, THE EVIDENCE DISAPPEARS BEFORE IT CAN EVER BE RECORDED. I AM SOOOOOOOOOOOOO SMART. IF ONLY THIS WORLD HAD MORE PEOPLE LIKE ME, MAYBE THEY WOULD JUST SHUT DOWN THESE OLD FOLKS HOMES AND LET THEM DIE AT THEIR FAMILY'S HOME LIKE IT SHOULD BE. WHY SHOULD THE REST OF US HAVE TO CLEAN UP THEIR PISS AND SHIT ON A DAILY BASIS? ISN'T THAT WHAT FAMILY IS FOR?

I THINK I WILL GO SEE WHAT THAT NEW CHECK-IN HAS IN THE WAY OF JEWELRY AND VALUABLES. I HAVE AN AMAZING COLLECTION OF OLD STUFF. MAINLY COSTUME JEWELRY BUT A FEW ACTUAL FAMILY HEIRLOOMS. I HAVE PAWNED A FEW OF THE ITEMS OFF WHENEVER I GO TO DENVER TO SEE SOME FRIENDS. PAYS FOR MY GAS TO GET THERE. THE BEST PART IS WITH ALL THESE RESIDENTS KIND OF WANDERING AROUND IN A FREE-FOR-ALL, THE BLAME ALWAYS GETS PASSED TO THEM.

A FEW TENS AND TWENTIES SNATCHED RANDOMLY FROM VARIOUS RESIDENTS' ROOMS IS A LITTLE BONUS FOR MY SORRY-ASS WAGE. I DESERVE MORE MONEY. THE STATE CAN PAY FOR THE RESIDENTS TO HAVE THEIR HAIR DONE. THEY DON'T NEED CASH LYING AROUND. I REMOVE THE DISTRACTION. BESIDES, SOMEONE ELSE WOULD JUST STEAL IT ANYWAY. MIGHT AS WELL BE SOMEONE WHO NEEDS A STASH OF MONEY TO MAKE SURE HER DAUGHTER IS FED INSTEAD OF POS DRINKING IT ALL UP. I HAVE MY REASONS.

THANK GOD MY SHIFT IS ABOUT OVER. MISS PERFECT PEGGY HAD MY HALLWAY. SHE CAN TAKE HER POSITIVE ATTITUDE AND SHOVE IT WHERE THE SUN DON'T SHINE.

I HAVE A LIFETIME OF GETTING EVEN TO DO. STAY OUT OF MY WAY, MINIONS. I AM GIVING THEM A TASTE OF THE HELL MY LIFE HAS BEEN SINCE I REMEMBER. THEY ALL NEED TO FEEL MY PAIN. THEY NEED TO UNDERSTAND THAT LIFE IS NOT A BOX OF CHOCOLATES. LIFE IS MORE LIKE A BOX OF TURD BROWNIES AND I AM HERE TO FEED IT TO THEM. OPEN WWWWWWWIIIIIIIIDDDDDDDDDDDE...

49

But For a Moment (Alan)

For His anger is but for a moment, His favor is for a lifetime;
Weeping may last for the night, But a shout of joy
comes in the morning.

Psalms 30:5 NASB

I was in for a treat after our Circle of Light had been snuffed. Wheeling into the dining area, I saw a good part of my family waiting for me. Ana was amazingly beautiful as ever. Effie Viviane and Isabelle Veronica came running toward me. It was as if the lights had been turned back on. I was back. I could hold all my loves in my arms. I could tell them how much I had missed them. I could listen to their excitement as they told me about their days, their school, their world without me.

I wanted to cry as I realized how much I had been missing. I also knew my time of coherence was probably short, so I could not waste it on sadness. No, it was time to be happy and talk and laugh and love. My arms seemed exceptionally heavy, but so what. They could still wrap themselves around all my family and share this grand moment.

"Amor," my wife exclaimed in that voice that still takes my heart up a few notches. "Você está de volta!" (you are back). Those words heralded like a song from an angel. And then, "Daddy, daddy" as the girls launched themselves into my lap. I am so very blessed. Even more so today.

I could write a book on everything that was discussed in that, oh so too little time. But those minutes are for me to store in my memory library. They are my moments. If I was to share, some of the magic would be lost. This might be all I have left to cling on to sanity.

The fog wasn't long in waiting. It came back. But not until I was filled with updates and I had the chance to share my love for each and every one of them. This was a good day. I pray for more of them. I know where they come from.

"Thank you, God. I won't let you down. I am your servant. You rewarded me today and I am forever grateful. I will do your work you have set before me. I will join again with the others. We will invite more. Yes, Lord, your house needs cleaned. We are ready to do that. I know there is no room for anger. No regrets, God. Give me a mission and I will fulfill. Amen."

Life was good today. Oh, how I pray for more Good Days................

50

A SNOWY DAY (Larry)

He spreads the snow like wool and scatters the frost like ashes.
Psalm 147:16 NIV

It is snowing outside today. Big fat white flakes gently gather in a slight tilt as they nestle against the ground. I am lucky today—the aide parked me where I can see outside. Some days it feels good to just stare out the window and let my mind wander where my body can't take me.

Typically, in this part of God's country, the snow comes sideways. It creates drifts of enormous proportion and leaves a blanket of ocean waves across open fields. Any little object that can disperse the wind is extended with additional piles of white pureness. It can be beautiful. It can be a pain in the hind end when it comes to clearing a pathway. The sideways stuff can cause one to stay home for many days. Or, if venturing out, to end up in a blizzard so blinding, interstate highways become a pile-up graveyard of wreckage and death.

I was caught traveling in one such blizzard. According to The Weather Channel, the bad stuff was supposed to stay south of my route home and was moving slowly. Yeah, The Weather Channel pulled an April Fools' on me.

I had spent the night at a good friend's house. I had attended his wedding the day before and of course, imbibed in excess. Mind you, not in excess per wedding reception protocol. Rather, in excess of what I was accustomed to. Not much of a drinker am I. Never was. I was blessed with parents who "got high on life" rather than finding happiness in a bottle. We never looked down on those who partied excessively, just had no reason to join them.

I had spent the night to clear my inebriated cobwebs. Plus, I wanted to share with the happy couple in their opening of like five carloads of gifts. My plan was actually to bail in the morning and drive home. But their offer of an awesome breakfast and wanting me to be a part of the acquired treasure trove convinced me that I should stay. Plus, The Weather Channel convinced me I had NO concerns. Stay I did.

Midafternoon, I had finally stayed long enough. It was time to hit the road. I had important things to do tomorrow, and needed to get to home base to prepare. Plus, my woman "of the moment" who was with me, needed to get herself and her two young boys home to start their weekly routines.

We headed south by west that afternoon, no problem. Sun shining. Slightly chilly, wind out of the northwest, (that should have been my first clue). The Weather Channel was my insurance policy.

As we drove, we could see the storm front headed for us at about the same speed we were headed directly for it. I wasn't too concerned. I had an awesome Land Rover wagon at the time. It was built like a tank, could put most Jeeps to shame, and was the perfect vehicle for what we were about to be swallowed up by.

We were a third of the way home when the first dusting of snow started acknowledging our presence. Kind of like today's snow. Big fat flakes that were carefree with no purpose except looking pretty and making me turn on my wipers to intermittent. It really was pretty.

As we headed west, the pretty transformed to ugly. No in-between. No warning. Pre-cell phone days and portable weather map. We were instantly in a mess. The highway we were on always had a lot of traffic and a decent percentage of trucks. My awesome intelligence told me we should head south and get to the nearest interstate to obtain a little clarity and flow.

Driving south wasn't so bad. Kind of like swimming sideways against a riptide. The plan was to try and get south of the storm and go through safer waters. Good plan, not-so-good results.

We reached the interstate and headed west again. From the onramp, things looked ok. Typical I-80 traffic. People who knew how to drive in these conditions. A little slower. A little more caution. Total awareness. Except of course for that occasional idiot who had some time frame to beat and knew no better than to drive fifteen percent over the speed limit come what may. No regard for others. Their destination was the only goal. Look out, here I come. Hmmm, the same attitude I carried most of my life.

But my dad had taught me that it was more important to actually make it to your destination in adverse conditions than it was to put yourself and others at risk. Slow down, make it there, live to make it on time next time. That was the approach I was taking on this day. Just me, probably more risk. I really did care about my lady and her boys. I wasn't a complete jerk all of the time. At least in my mind.

It didn't take long to realize my wisdom was on the brink of stupidity. There were areas that had trees and other obstructions blocking the sideways snow from the north. This gave one a little confidence. Then, there were the long stretches of interstate that were bordered by open cornstalk or winter wheat fields. Not much to stop the snow there. It was blinding.

We soon found ourselves in a situation that could only lead to disaster. Cars and trucks were starting to pull over on the shoulder to wait out the half-blinding storm. The right lane had people riding their brakes, creeping along, half-deciding to stop and half-keep moving. Some drivers were actually stopped in this lane, unaware of how very stupid they were being. You could not see these cars until you were right on top of them. My hands were putting new imprints deep into the steering wheel. The hammer lane was the only one with confirmable movement.

After only twenty miles and one full hour of white knuckle driving, I had had enough. Next available exit (that I actually saw before I passed by it), we were able to leave the insanity and head south to hopefully a much quieter highway that would take us west.

Life was good. For a while. The home destination looked doable. I could breathe again. The lady friend and boys with me had gotten bored and were napping. Things seemed OK.

After our second trek south and then headed west, there was still a blizzard but not as bad as what we had just survived. We passed through a few small towns and then a rather decent size town, 2,500 people or so. It had a McDonald's, so that defined the size as "not bad" in this remote rural area. I woke the crew up long enough to place orders, pee, and pry my hands from the cramped steering wheel grip.

A double quarter pounder and multiple chicken nuggets later, I was ready to brave the elements once again. My passengers were all fat and happy, ready for another nap. Time to get home.

Just on the western edge of this town, we hit a wall. I mean, an all-out barrier of the most vicious white stuff imaginable. This made the interstate driving look like a picnic. Zero visibility. I mean ZERO. I couldn't make out the centerline nor the shoulder line. I knew one false move and we would either hit someone head-on, or go in the ditch and be stuck where we were. My Land Rover was awesome. The prospect of being buried in a twenty-foot drift of snow, not so awesome.

I considered taking a chance that this area was so bad because a quarter section of farm ground just north of us was bare and not stopping nada. So, simply a quarter mile down the road, if we could make it, there should be a break in this wall and we could keep on truckin'.

I even opened my door and looked straight down on the highway to find the centerline to follow. The snow was passing underneath my Rover as severely as over the top. I couldn't see squat. The fact that looking for a white line with a white monsoon passing by was exceeding intelligence.

I decided that the best course of action was to turn around, go back into town, find a place to hole up, and wait this thing out. I crossed my fingers, whispered a prayer that no one was behind me, and backed up as straight as I imagined until I was back outside the wall. If you have ever navigated through a 3D Model on Navisworks, you will totally understand my reference to being inside a wall.

Back to town we went. This town had like three hotels. No Marriotts or Ritz-Carltons, but more like ranch-style motels that had been around since the '50s, or older. That was OK. A warm place to get off the highway and feel safe was what the doctor ordered for us all. At least me anyway. The boys in the back just thought it was cool, and didn't comprehend the severity of the situation. The blizzard in town was no picnic itself.

I was soon to realize that no matter how much money I offered, there was "no room at the inn." All other travelers had hit the same wall, turned around, sought shelter, and beat me by a few minutes.

I went to the police station to see if they knew of any churches or community centers open that would let us park our bodies for a while. This police department was about as useful as tits on a boar. I don't know where their small-town compassion and hospitality went, but it was definitely out the door. The two people there were only concerned with everything staying quiet while they manned the 911 phones. No help, no suggestions, no offers, no civility from these "servants."

I brushed it off as they were focused on taking care of their own. This was a part of the world where you learned to do everything on your own and not depend on anyone else. My hardheaded father had taught me that. I had used it to be successful. Now, I must figure out what the heck my next move was.

We drove around town a little while hoping to maybe see a bed & breakfast that others had missed, or something with open doors. The problem was, every business had closed or was closing before it got dark, so everyone could safely make it to their domiciles.

After an hour or so of useless nothing, I decided maybe the wind had backed off a little bit and we could maybe make it through the wall and keep on truckin'. I was soon to find out that my reasoning was false. The same wall was there. Maybe even worse as the drifts across the highway were getting deeper. Back to town.

Not too far from the wall was a motel that sported a titty bar. At one time, this establishment was a respectable family restaurant connected to the motel. It was a scenario that appeared to be happening in a lot of rural America. Fast food had replaced full-service home cookin' type restaurants. So, the next entrepreneur decided that some dancing girls with all the delights a working man wants to see, rather than what his wife had given up on, was made available. None of these was a thriving business, but did just enough to get by. Probably would have helped if the customers had more room to hide their vehicles out back.

I had no choice. It was getting dark and we were getting desperate. I left the crew in the security of the Rover while I went in to chat with the manager. The NO Vacancy was the brighest light on the entry sign, but I didn't care. I held the door handle securely in my hand as I knew the nasty-ass wind would easily rip it from my grip. Once securely inside, I was greeted with the warmest smile I had seen all day. I pled my case.

"Good evening. Well, not really so good of an evening, but here I am. I don't suppose you have some place, even here in the lobby that my passengers and I could rest until this storm passes?"

"I have nothing." The gentleman shook his head. "I am not allowed to let any minors even come past this entryway."

He just wanted to hang out and watch his little TV behind the counter. It was also obvious that no dancers and no customers were visiting this fine establishment tonight.

I then asked, "Do you know anyone in town who might at least open their doors and take in a family in need? I have good money to pay." With that statement, I could see his wheels starting to turn.

"I do have the dancers' room empty. The blizzard kept them from coming in from the city, so it could be available for the right price."

"Name your price, my good man," I stated with assurance.

"How about twenty-five dollars cash?" he said. "I feel bad to take advantage of stranded people, so I won't get greedy. I will even split this cash with the cleaning lady tomorrow."

"My good man, I will give you fifty dollars and all three of us will be happy!" I said with a relief I didn't know I possessed. I didn't realize how much I could care about other people's well-being. Self-preservation was always my purpose. Worrying about other people's well-being was just a roadblock. Now, I got a hint of what fatherhood might be like. Felt ok, but would probably just get in the way of my bank account.

The proprietor gave me a well-worn key with an old-school large plastic keychain advertising his fine establishment. I swear the key and chain were original from the time this motel was built. Made me chuckle.

We pulled around the main building toward the back to the last room in a long row of worn-out-looking rooms. There was a car parked in front of every door. I was happy to see the last opening right in front of our #1 door.

As we entered the room, I was struck by the fact that the lovely shag carpet was just as old as the keychain. The room smelled of cigarettes and stale dreams. It was just on this side of nasty. The bedding, though outdated, was clean. I didn't care. It was a refuge. Never mind that you could see light under the front door. With the heater going full blast and some extra provided covers, we were going to be camping in a blizzard. I was exhausted. I had provided. Well, kind of.

About 1:00 in the morning, I could hear someone outside shoveling snow. Scrape, scrape, scraaaaaaaape some more. I had slept like a rock for about four hours, so I felt halfway decent. The next thing I heard after the rudeness of the snow shovel on concrete was... silence.

The calm gave me hope. That meant the blizzard had passed by. We could actually still make our destination in time for everyone's appointed lives starting in the morning.

This first thing I noticed was the two-foot-tall snowdrift inside our room right in front of the door. I had mentioned a slight gap. This was actually quite amazing. It defined exactly how harsh this storm had been. To force that much snow under a door to accumulate in a heated room was quite impressive. If it had been in the more recent cell phone era, I would have posted an awesome photo that might have gone viral. Maybe titled "Snow adrift in dancers' room."

I went outside and found the cause of the annoying shoveling. Every car in this back corner was buried in snow. This poor guy was trying to open a path large enough to get his car out. From the size of the drift and the lack of size of his shovel, it looked like another two hours of work. He wasn't going anywhere soon.

Since my Rover had arrived late, it wasn't quite as buried as this man's car. I offered to help. My Land Rover was up to the task at hand. It plowed its way back out of the parking spot and easily moved into position to assist my neighbor.

After digging a small tunnel to open up his exhaust and to provide access to a decent spot to connect a tow hook (I always carried a chain or a tow rope in all of my vehicles. Another lesson learned from Dad), we let his car warm up for a while and then I proceeded to drag his car like a sled. Soon it was free. He was grateful. The world was right. Helping others for nothing felt good.

As he was getting out his billfold, he said, "You don't know how much I appreciate your help. I would have been here forever freezing my fingers and toes. What do I owe you?"

"You don't owe me anything. Next time you find someone you can help out of a bind, do it. If I took money from you now, then next time I was in a fix, imagine what I would have to pay."

We shook hands, and he jumped into his car and left. I gathered my roommates and we hit the road too. It was a bitterly cold early morning. The stars were twinkling themselves with frost. It was beautiful. The snowplows had already made a couple of passes down the highway. All was well.

I always remember that adventure when I see a heavy snow. Or when I see a forecast from The Weather Channel that is questionable. They try their best, I know.

I also know that a pile-up did happen on the I-80 section we had been on. One couple was killed when their car, parked behind a stopped truck (in the first lane), was slammed from behind by a moving and blind truck. It was reported the couple was simply decapitated as their car was forced under the first truck. I will never forget that I could have been responsible for that happening to an innocent woman and her children, had I not finally had sense enough to abandon the I-80 nightmare.

I probably should have married that woman from this story. Her boys were awesome. Maybe then, I would have someone to come visit me with so much love like Alan has. Oh, the choices we make in life. Most are good. Some tend to lash back at you many years down the road. That sure is a pretty snow today......................

51

Bible Study (MayAnn)

Study this Book of Instruction continually. Meditate on it day and
night so you will be sure to obey everything written in it.
Only then will you prosper and succeed in all you do.

Joshua 1:8 NLT

sense today is Wednesday. Most Wednesday afternoons, a kind soul, Judy, comes into our home for Bible study. I have been attending this little gathering since I was first parked in the "You can't take care of yourself anymore and we don't have time to take care of you" category. Judy knows her Bible. She is always well-prepared and has a magical way of getting us all to participate.

At least that is what I remember. I couldn't tell you if it was last week or two years ago that I started sitting in this study, listening. It always seemed to pull me out of my foggy hallway long enough to hear His word. I can no longer give feedback. My brain put a stop to that. But, the study and ensuing discussions find their way into my existence. God always has a way to be able to reach your soul. Even if your earthly body is a wasteland.

The one day of coherence I had and was able to visit with Peggy, I suggested that the next Bible study should include our Light group. Maybe we could share this Light with all the others who gathered for this class. I even had the thought that Judy, even though distracted with a full life and daily schedule not as open as ours, could come to our Common Room.

Now we are all being gathered in the room used for either arts and crafts or Bible study. They have quit trying to get me to participate in any type of crafts, so today has to be Wednesday, Bible study day.

Our numbers are almost doubled. The regulars are here. Those who are still coherent enough to participate, plus our little group from the other day. This will be a first for Alan and Larry. Maria comes on and off. Tex is new enough here that this will be his first. It seems, though, that Peggy has managed to squeeze a few other "newbies" around these tables, too. What a gathering. Judy is probably panicking that she doesn't have enough handouts for everyone. That is what the copy machine in the admin office is for. I think the nurses have one in their office, too. Tree-killing machines, I call them.

People don't realize that my fog greatly dissipates every time I come to Bible study. They are so used to me being out in LaLa Land that nobody even pays attention to me. Especially considering everyone up here in the resident category has their own monsters to deal with, daily. They don't have the energy to try to help me too. Here I am, though, able to look and count sixteen residents joining our normal group of eight or so. I am very excited.

I had the not-so-righteous thought that if Judy joined hands with us and we gathered in the Common Room of our brains, maybe I could purposely steal some of her youth and energy. That last gathering of Light we had with just the five of us taught us that we could absorb some strength off each other. Imagine what Judy could offer.

Then, I felt guilty. I had already taken something so beautifully pure and was thinking of ways to use it to my advantage. Where did that mentality come from? Sweet innocent MayAnn am I. I don't recall ever having that kind of "What's in it for me?" thought. I must have gained that thought process from one of the others. Kind of like my body feeling like Larry's at the same time my brain was functioning as clearly as his seems to be. Wow, I wonder what ugly traits the others might have absorbed from me.

We seem to have reached into a vast unknown territory. Now we have two options. Run like crazy from said territory, or start exploring with the mindset of climbing Mount Everest. With sixteen of us gathered today, maybe some of them will be our sherpas and carry our baggage for us. I have some "baggage" I would gladly unload. There I go again, thinking of taking advantage of others. Wow, who gave that to me? I don't like it...................

52

Wednesdays (Peggy)

*John himself was not the light; he was simply
a witness to tell about the light.*

John 1:8 NLT

I always like working on Wednesdays. Especially in the afternoon an hour or so before shift change. I try to have all the residents taken care of, my charting complete, and sort of free time on my hands. I park my cart just around the corner from the activity room so I can steal a listen to Judy's Bible study.

If she had this at 3:00 or so, I believe I would clock out and come join the group. But Judy says she has commitments at home in the late afternoon, so her only free time is at 2:00. That is OK, though, I get to at least listen. It is for the residents anyway. I shouldn't intrude.

It is amazing the conversations that Judy draws out of these people who don't have much left except a lifetime of memories. Their experience of going through all four seasons of life adds another level of perception that we younger folk have yet to see. The residents are more open and honest. They are no longer blocked by the appearances regimen. They have nothing to lose. Most everything is already gone. They can be open and refreshing as a little child. Innocence back to innocence. It is enlightening to listen to.

Today, because of the urging of MayAnn the other morning, I decided to try doubling the size of the group. It shouldn't be limited to only those who have been there forever and only those who can participate. All should be welcome. Even those who will probably take a nap through the whole thing. I feel all can benefit.

And just so you know, I am curious to see what kind of Light they might produce with this many in a group. If only five could do what they did the other day, imagine the energy we might capture with sixteen.

So, with permission from the administrator, the activities director, and Judy too, I chose the "extras" to join today. The more the merrier, right? The difficult part was deciding which extra eight above the norm would best be suited for this little experiment. I had to choose from sixty. Kind of like my husband's recruiting day for his fantasy football team. Don't have a clue how football works but am beginning to understand his time spent deciding on the best players for his team.

A few were obvious. Those from the five had to be here. Two of them were already constants, so that added three newbies. I then had to select five more. This was harder than it seemed. Should I grab the ones with the most problems? Or should I choose those with the most strength mentally or physically that could add to the power of the Light those five had experienced?

Most definitely, I knew I would bring in Kay. She has a pretty serious nap every afternoon, but if given something to do, I believed she would enjoy the gathering. Her sister said it was OK. I could feel some reservation there. Kay's sister is super protective. It is almost like a mission. If willpower and determination could cure MS, Kay's sister would have it conquered.

I thought maybe Clara would do well in this group. Miss Clara is 108 years old now. She has a daughter in her early 80s still sharp as a tack and lives close. Clara also has a son, late

70s, who still runs half marathons. Something in the genes, I suppose. Clara is an exceptional lady. She was raised in the time when mothers spent time teaching their daughters etiquette and manners. Plus how to keep a home with skills of cooking, cleaning, washing clothes, ironing, decorating, being a housewife and happy with that. When the proper time came, these ladies also learned the rules of how to take care of their man. Not in a subservient role, but in a more important role of taking care of the family. I sometimes envy those ladies. Women's lib has just opened the door for all of us to have to work now. The family structure is severed. If handled correctly, it's not broken, but strained nonetheless.

Sorry about the tangent. Clara brings the "What might have been" out of me. One of the first days I came to work at this nursing home, Clara, then 100 or so, asked me, "Why am I still here?" That question stumped me. What answer could I give to this sweet old lady to respond to such a deep question? I wanted to say, "Because the Good Lord still has something in mind for you, Clara," but that response didn't feel right. Clara expected more wisdom. My Mickey Mouse socks aside, I needed to give Clara the insight she was thinking. Instead, I simply gave her the most sincere hug I could without cracking her whole rib cage, and said, "I don't know, Clara. I will think about that question."

I thought I would also invite Don. Sweet man. Used to be a rather heavy drinker. Had a stroke or two, is on oxygen, and enjoys a cigarette after meals. An old farmer/cowboy at heart who has a humor hiding inside that comes out as a tease once in a while. He enjoys Bingo more than anything and wins fairly often. Claims there is a secret in which cards you choose. I know he always looks through the pile to find the "right" ones. I believe he is related to Judy somehow. Don't think he cares much for deep religious discussions. I believed he would add some humor to the Bible study group.

I was hesitant to add Willy. He isn't all that old, but fights a serious case of emphysema. He is also on oxygen. Cranked up as high as his lungs will tolerate. Poor Willy has some panic attacks once in a while when he can't breathe. He is given breathing treatments twice a day that add moisture to his lungs to negate the drying out effects of straight oxygen at that level. Seems to help. Willy likes to sleep in if possible. I don't know if it is laziness, depression, or a combination of both. Most mornings, he is one of the difficult ones all the aides ignore until the very last minute. Mainly because he is always wet. Sleeps past the normal time to get up and pee. Really kind of sad.

When Willy is awake, he is one of the most demanding residents in the home. He rides the call button like there is no tomorrow. Some of the aides hide it from him. A no-no per regulations. A person can only take so much of one person's useless and petty demands. Jean seems to like going in to take care of Willy. I believe for some reason, Willy respects Jean. Or he is scared to death of what she might do to him. Probably more the latter.

Willy is very intelligent, though. He has some insight. I gave him a try. If Willy didn't like it, he was welcome to wheel himself away from the group and go find his call button.

I also picked Margaret. I don't know why she isn't a regular at Judy's Bible study. I see her holding her own Bible every once in a while. Never see her read it. Probably can't see that well. And she is on the state's dime, and I don't know if they will even pay for new glasses. Maybe her eyes are beyond reading. That could be why she doesn't go. I will discuss this with our social services director. She will give me an answer. Margaret still has enough of her wits about her. If I ask, she will tell me a straight-up yes or no for joining the group. I believe I can sweet talk her into it. At least for this one meeting.

Over half of the residents here are wards of the state. Nursing homes suck all the funds a person has spent their lifetime earning and saving. They take everything. At an average rate of $6,000 to $10,000 per month depending on level of care and medications, a life's savings doesn't last long. Most families have to separate businesses, farms, and houses from their loved ones before the home takes possession of those things, too. Once all funds are milked dry, the state then takes over for their care. They are allowed a minute pittance (maybe $10 a month) to buy personal items. They have zero independence to go with their zero hope. It is so sad in so many cases. What has our medical profession done except preserve people long enough to suffer an additional ten to twenty years?

I prefer the third world country approach. Kids take forever to leave their parents' home. Most are darn near thirty. Then, about the time they have established themselves and their family, the parents move back in to last out their days. If they get too sick, they die. The doctors try their best, but don't have access to the technology we have. It is a cleaner break. Always with family, then simply die. Next generation's turn.

That gives me the five I need to bring the group to double in size. The other six constant attendees are in for a treat today. Judy is going to have her hands full. I am giddy about what I will witness. Oh, shoot, I forgot to put lotion on Florence's legs, arms, and back. Better get that done before 2:00. Poor Florence loved using Gold Bond medicated powder all over herself. I think it really did soothe her dry skin as advertised. But then she became allergic to it. Florence would probably join the Bible study, but her husband of fifty-plus years is bedridden and still controlling. Florence won't leave his cantankerous side. She was raised a lady, too. Oh, how I love that generation............

53

BS (Alan)

*He has shown you, O mortal, what is good. And what does the
Lord require of you? To act justly and to love mercy
and to walk humbly with your God.*

Micah 6:8 NIV

Ha ha, got you on that title. If you were thinking BS stood for anything except Bible study, I got you. And no, bug spray is not an alternative. Admit it, you were thinking the waste coming from a male bovine. We are all at one time or another, full of BS. Some are stuck in it and BS is all they have to offer. I am sorry, I will get away from this reference. I am a firm believer that God has an awesome sense of humor. He probably chuckled at my rather crude reference to other than Bible study.

This is the first time I have had the privilege to join this group. Don't quite know why I have been omitted before. Probably has something to do with my pudding brain. Mrs. Judy, who leads the group, can only handle so many wasted away minds. If we can't talk or respond, then what is the point of participating? I mean really, save the oxygen in the room for those who can contribute. I fear most people don't realize that being a part of something is far more therapeutic to an Alzheimer's sufferer than being parked in a blind corner to rot. We might not have any light in our eyes, but our ears still work. We can absorb so much more than you realize. Almost like a person in a coma. Everyone tells you that you can be heard. Well, let me tell you a little secret. We can hear you, too. We are starving for stories. We really do want to respond. Just can't.

Even when we are bouncing around in our empty cranium trying to find a safe room to hide in, if someone is talking to us, we can stop, sit down and listen. In the shrinking hallway of deep fog, I have always been able to find a chair and listen to my wonderful wife and amazing family talking to me. I could listen to them from dawn to dusk and back again. It is a welcome distraction from the lost wandering in the woods of confusion. Please talk to me or those suffering from the same as me.

Peggy brought me to this Bible study. I could feel something special about to build. Judy shook my hand and introduced herself. I knew she shared her love for God with palms open wide. Special flowed right through her into my veins. I was suddenly alert enough to see my compadres from our first session of Light were already here. And Peggy understood exactly where I needed to be parked to the left of MayAnn. Larry on her right.

To my left was Kay. I always felt bad for Kay. I had lived a decently full life. Would have liked to have a few more years to help raise our girls, but at least I held them and played with them for a short period before I drifted away. Kay, on the other hand, simply dropped off the edge of life. It was like it had happened all in one day. She still had a sparkle in her eye and a sense of humor that rare few got to experience. The pain throughout her body muffled her enjoyment of much. If it weren't for Kay's sister, Kay would be stuck in the deepest level of hell imaginable. I really felt for Kay. I will never understand why a person should have to suffer like that. One definite question I will ask God on Judgment Day.

Judy told us to join hands in prayer. Peggy stepped around the corner to help us physically challenged people reach out to others. I had it made. MayAnn already had my hand. That gave me enough strength to find Kay's hand. And the circle was formed. It was like a freight train had entered the room. I can't even say if it was only in my mind, or actually in the room. A blinding light, a whistle of awareness. Not warning like a train, but more of an announcement with the volume of the trains I've known.

Then, serenity. MayAnn was already in our Common Room, welcoming each person as they came through their own door and joined us. I could hear some on the outside of the room trying to run away at the same time they were being paged by a fullness of love that only God could have released. It was a calling that couldn't be ignored. No matter how new. No matter how scary. Not one person could ignore. Even the doubtful and mostly angry Willy came rolling in through his door. For once, he was speechless. I think it took him a moment to realize he was no longer tied to his heavy dose of oxygen. He stood there letting his lungs fill in awe of his surroundings.

Judy was the last to join us. It was almost like she had made a complete circle around the outside of our Common Room, making sure not one person from our Bible study was left behind. She peeked in, counted bodies, heads, whatever we were in here, noted numbers were corrected, slipped in and most quietly shut her door. Then with the purpose of any good teacher, locked it. Not to keep us in, but rather to keep distractions out. Reality wasn't allowed in this room. At least the reality of what our human bodies had to face every day. It was awesome. We all turned to her for direction.

Judy simply exclaimed, "Well, isn't this a pleasant surprise." And, "Welcome, everyone. If this isn't the definition of Matthew 18:20, 'For where two or more are gathered in my name, there I am with them.' We could even back up to verse 19, 'Again, truly I tell you that if two of you on earth agree about anything they ask for, it will be done for them by my Father in heaven.' Well, seventeen of us must agree on something. No, I take that back, welcome, Carol, bet you weren't ready for this."

It was awesome. We all were part of something well above anything ever even imagined. As one of the first, and due to a promise from the first gathering, I stepped forward to address the group.

"Welcome to The Light Crew. We have work to do. Each of you is here for a chosen reason. Even if you don't like it, you are here. We have no time to try and answer questions. What, why, and how are not allowed. You have reached an area that is simply 'Here we are, let's get to work.' Larry, as grand marshal of this gathering, what is our purpose today?"

Larry didn't hesitate. I believe he either had been thinking about this previously or was letting God direct his words. Likely a combination of both. Larry simply said in that natural leader voice, "We must address the monster in our home who is a threat to not only us, but every resident in this home."

With that simple statement, everyone groaned. Not so much in fear as in agreement that this was a heavy weight each and every one was involuntarily carrying. The wheels were turning for all. How many hours, days, weeks, years had each of us been wrestling with the abuse this one aide inflicted on us? Indifference from some of the other aides was tolerable. But this abuse was well beyond manageable. And, most undeserved.

Tex said, "As a group representing God from a much higher level, we need to listen to His direction for resolution." Everyone nodded in agreement. We had to use an above-human approach to solve this problem. An eye for an eye was not what we were called here to do.

I could tell several really, really wanted to see pain and torture inflicted back on Jean. Revenge was trying to creep into our room. It was demandingly knocking on several of our doors. We each looked at our doors and back at each other, deciding who was going to cave in and answer their door. The only thing keeping us from taking that step in the wrong direction was the acknowledgment that as soon as one of us opened their door, we would all be sucked back to the real world. Back to a reality that none of us wanted to return to. The Common Room was such a comfort from our lives that, forgive me for saying, really sucked.

The knocking stopped. The ugliness of revenge left in defeat. It was a huge first step for this new group. Our Light grew even stronger.

It was AWESOME. Oh, God, don't let this end. We want to stay here forever.

At the same time Mr. Revenge was leaving, Mother Love joined us. There was no particular door she came through. It was like she was placed right in the middle of us. And as quickly as she appeared, she shattered into a million pieces, filling us each with a sparkle of herself. We had our answer. Our first mission.

Doubts if it could help, yes. We were still human. We all were filled with our human faults. Yet we were filled with a spirit that gave us a higher strength. We had our weapons. Each in a special way.

All too soon it was time to leave our room. After all, Judy had put a lot of work into this week's lesson. It seemed like we had been here for hours sorting through answers. We didn't want to leave. Others depended on us. It felt great to be needed again. To go from helpless, in need of constant care, to take a step back into productive, was AWESOME. I can't speak for the rest, but I was anxious to go to work.............................

54

Please, No (MayAnn)

*He was afraid and said, "How awesome is this place! This is none
other than the house of God; this is the gate of heaven."*

Genesis 28:17 NIV

No, no, no no no............ I don't want to leave our Common
Room. Doesn't everyone realize that none of us in this
room needed our wheelchairs or our oxygen or whatever
apparatus was holding us together for a few more years of
suffering? I could stay here for-e-ver. I feel useful and wanted
and loved and free. Why would I ever want to go back out my door
to the fog? To pain? To abuse? To days filled with nothing?

Please, let me stay. I will keep the light on for everyone else. You
can go do your mission and return here for refreshments. I could
be your hostess. I will keep things tidy.

I will also see if I can find the key to that one door that is locked
from the other side. I don't know if anyone else noticed it. I see a
gold inlaid door with a handle of ivory. Engravings glorified with
every imaginable precious stone. It is an awesomely beautiful
door. Welcome seems to seep out of it into one's soul. I believe I
know where it leads. I am curious how a person opens it. It looks
so very heavy. I have never seen such immensely rich beauty
that hasn't ended up looking overbearingly gaudy. This door is an
exception to all ordained exceptions.

There is a wooden frame around it unlike any I have ever seen.
My dad could probably have told me what kind of wood it is made
from. The colors in the grains seem to change as you move by it. I

just want to reach out and touch the wholeness of this door. I feel like it would absorb me and that would be OK.

The hinges are pure gold. Definitely not polished brass. I am talking 18-carat or better gold. Each pin of the hinge is topped with the most intense red ruby I have ever seen. The rivets holding the hinges on, sapphires so blue the midnight sky would be jealous.

There is no access to a lock from this side. I wonder why that is. I said handle made of ivory earlier, but it is really not a handle to pull on. More of a push plate like a swinging door. The next time I look, though, it is a handle. Maybe this door should make up its mind.

The rest of the doors to our Common Room are decorated with our respective personalities. Mine has roses and irises and orchids and just a whole garden mess of flowers. The men seem to have just plain ole pine doors. Maybe a little carving here or there, but nothing like our ladies' doors display. Maria's has cakes and cookies and pies of all kinds. A cornucopia of desserts. I could eat her door.

Kay's door was covered with arts and crafts. It looks like Hobby Lobby built her door. Margaret's was blanketed in silk of every color. Willy's actually had musical instruments scattered throughout. I bet no one knows that about Willy.

There are no names on any of the doors. When everyone was leaving, though, they went straight to the same door they came through. It is like they parked their marker of favorite things at the door, clearing their minds for the tasks at hand.

I don't want to go to my door. I want to just sit and pull on the strands of my hair looking for split ends. It has been forever since I could care for my hair. In the Common Room, it is no longer white. It has gone back to the golden blond color that could shine a blinding brilliance of joy. I really loved my hair. I know at the home it is just chopped off and unkempt. Because my brain is in a vegetative state, I guess most don't think I still want to look pretty.

Can I please stay in this room? PLEASE...

55

FIRST OUT (Larry)

Because of the privilege and authority God has given me,
I give each of you this warning; Don't think you are better than
you really are. Be honest in your evaluation of yourselves,
measuring yourselves by the faith God has given us.

Romans 12:3 NLT

I was the first to exit our Common Room. I could tell others wanted to stay. Some were gazing at that one "special" door. I personally am not ready for that door yet. Got things to do. There is a mission to complete. No lollygagging around like tenderfeet. Get busy living out the purpose in front of us. Plenty of time to get busy dying later.

I felt for MayAnn. She did not want to leave. I could tell others felt the same. But as it was their first visit to this wonderful room of "back to how we once were," they weren't clear on the rules.

Time does not matter in the Common Room. It could have been days for all we could tell. I knew better because we returned to our cruel lives just moments after we left. Judy was still offering a prayer as we came back. I was ready to say Amen and start initiating my orders. My mission, clear and precise. No use messing around and waiting. The sooner completed, the sooner we could receive new orders.

I did want to stay and listen to what Judy's Bible study was about today. I could almost bet money on the subject. Wouldn't have a clue on what part of the Bible. Never had time to learn the trivial.

Wasn't gonna be a preacher, so why waste time and brain space on memorizing scripture when I could be filling it with profit margins?

So, I felt a little inept at this Bible study thing. The best part was, Judy's questions never once singled a person out by checking for scripture knowledge. Judy read from the Bible. Or asked those of us who could still see and interpret the words to read. Most of this bunch had to just sit and listen. Some I could see mouthing the exact words as someone else was reading. Good stuff right there.

After the prayer was over and hands were dropped, MayAnn was the very last to let go of Alan's and my hand. She really wanted to stay in our room. Judy opened with a verse of scripture that almost knocked me out of my shoes.

"But Joseph said to them, 'Don't be afraid. Am I in the place of God? You intended to harm me, but God intended it for good to accomplish what is now being done, the saving of many lives. So then, don't be afraid. I will provide for you and your children.' And he reassured them and spoke kindly to them. Genesis 50: 19-21," read Judy.

She then slowly looked around the room. All eyes were aware.

How utterly profound is that statement? "All eyes were aware." You must realize most of those sitting in the Bible study hadn't experienced much awareness in quite some time. For some, it had been years. Others' awareness faded in and out. So, when I said we were all aware of Judy's words, that was a miracle in itself.

Judy followed with a simple statement to the group. "Today we are going to discuss the words of Joseph. This was a time when he was addressing his brothers who had thrown him in a pit with intentions of leaving him there to die. They were doing this because they were very jealous of Joseph. He was like the spoiled brat of the family. The youngest child, who seemed to get away with everything. Never had to work. Always had something smart to say. Thought of himself as quite special. Joseph was not someone you wanted to keep around.

"Instead of leaving Joseph in the pit to die, they sold him to a caravan of Ishmaelites coming from Gilead on their way to Egypt. And the rest is history. Joseph went on to be the right-hand man of the Pharoah of Egypt. He ended up saving all of Israel during a terrible drought by providing food to the very brothers who tried to kill him. It is a wonderful story. And we could leave it at that. But let's discuss what the words of scripture we are studying today actually tell us."

Returning from the Common Room with a clear purpose in mind, we all knew exactly what the words said. There was a reason the evil Miss Jean had been abusing all of us. There was a purpose for all of this.

"Kind of a twisted way to make a point, God," I thought as my fists clenched with an anger against the evil that had been suffered by my fellow residents. If it had just been me, no problem. I can take a punch. And I deserved some form of punishment for all the years I had been so indignant to others.

The rest of this group and members of the home did not deserve a single ounce of cruelty. Why would God allow this? To only make his mission look better? I was a little confused.

I asked Judy, "Why did God let Joseph suffer at the hands of his brothers if he was God's chosen one? Why is all this suffering necessary before something good happens? Everyone brags about what a loving and merciful God we have. I don't see a damn thing good about what each of us is going through here in this nursing home. This is screwed up, Judy."

Others nodded their heads in agreement. We all had our personal stories similar to Joseph's. Well, actually I didn't. I was more like one of Joseph's brothers, who didn't care what it took or who got thrown into the pit, as long as I still reigned at the top. Maybe all of us have at one time or another chosen the path of "me first" and "to hell with everyone else." Dang nab it, Judy, you had me thinking now. Is this what Bible study is supposed to be like? Sure wasn't what I had pictured.

Judy said, "You have a valid point, Larry. What do you think about Joseph's suffering, Maria?"

Maria shyly stated, "Joseph's brothers were mean with jealousy. That doesn't say that God is bad. It says that Joseph's brothers were bad."

Willy stammered between oxygen-sucking breaths, "It wasn't anybody's mean brother who put us in the nursing home pit to die. It was God Himself who let this happen to us."

Don argued, "But Joseph had his whole life ahead of him when his brothers disposed of him. At least we have lived whole lives, some good, some not so good. We brought ourselves to this pit we have to call home."

Kay stammered, "I didn't get to live a full life. Look at me. Locked up with all you old people. What did I do to deserve this? Why did my husband and kids dispose of me in this manner? If it wasn't for my sisters, I would have nobody. And, think of how long I am going to face this. At least most of you will die and be rid of this place soon."

"Now, Kay," said MayAnn, as she reached out to pat Kay's hand. "None of us deserves to be here. I don't think God is to blame. Our human bodies have let us down in one form or another. This world is far from perfect. Disease in all forms is a part of life. We are all dealt the cards we hold. It is not God the Dealer's fault. Most is just random chance at life."

Judy sat in awe as all sixteen started chiming in with their thoughts and opinions. Peggy kept peeking around the corner to confirm what she was hearing, and winked at Judy. Never, since she had started volunteering in this home, had this number of residents all been able to contribute. It was almost like a college debate club. Except these people had life's experiences behind them to back up their arguments. Most debates at the younger stages in life are speculation. This was real life being shared. Judy let it flow.

Willy was getting a little too worked up when his next words came out in an exhale of, "Cards my ass. My fate is deliberate. I smoked like a chimney for years, totally ignoring warnings until now I can hardly br............." Peggy came running around the corner to settle him down before Willy's last statement was Willy's last breath.

Tex, having the calming sense to restore order, softly stated, "There is a time for everything, and a season for every activity under the heavens, Ecclesiastes 3:1."

"There goes the old cowboy quoting scripture," said Don. "Give us some more, preacher man."

Tex caught the twinkle in Don's eye with this statement. He could see the others' eyes light up with recognition too. Their generation could already hear the song in their head. Tex continued, "A time to be born and a time to die (We happen to be knocking on the door of the second part.), a time to plant and a time to uproot (Not much planting left in these old bones and my last uproot brought me here.), a time to kill and a time to heal (We all know who we'd like to kill, but we have been given direction to heal.), a time to tear down and a time to build (None of us really has the strength to do either. But others have torn us down, only we can build ourselves back up. And those drugs Peggy passes to us every day, gotta be building something), a time to weep and a time to laugh (If we can't laugh at our circumstances, then how sad are we? Crying is easy. I think we have reached that time.), a time to mourn and a time to dance (Yeah, not much dance left in us and we tend to mourn our own fate too much.), a time to scatter stones and a time to gather them (We would be best to let stones lie. Gathering stones only leads to throwing them at others.), a time to embrace and a time to refrain from embracing (We have to embrace where we are right now. We no longer have time to refrain.), a time to search and a time to give up (We quit searching, we die.), a time to keep and a time to throw away (I keep thinking they will quit feeding me applesauce every day. I am going to throw away the next damn plastic cup if it isn't some good ole chocolate pudding.)." That brought a chuckle and nod from most.

Tex continued, "A time to tear and a time to mend (We have spent our lives tearing our bodies down in one form or another, and we just now caught a glimpse of the only way any of us is going to mend. It will be in another room of life.), a time to be silent and a time to speak (I am living proof that most people can't talk and think at the same time. Most of us only have the ability left to think, except Forrest over there—I heard he used to do a bit of running up here. Wish I could have seen that.), a time to love and a time to hate (We don't have room for hate in our narrowed down existence. Love should be all we have left to share.), a time for war and a time for peace. (Oh what I wouldn't give for a piece of chocolate cake right now.)."

Alan, upon hearing the Forrest statement, just grinned. A huge grin as he relived the legs that took him on so many adventures. Even within the limits of this home. He felt like he could do some serious running right now, but this conversation was too awesome to leave.

The rest of the group silently thought of their own existence and their own paraphasing of these Bible verses. Willy had calmed down and matched his breathing with his machine.

Clara, the ancient one and most wise of us all, added, "What am I still doing here?" In the distant background, we could also hear Vera, "What day is it anyway?"

Life as we knew it was moving on. With or without our solving this world's problems. I was tired. A lot of emotional everything had crashed into our lives within the last half hour or so. Time didn't stop. It was still consuming each of us at our predestined rate.

That chocolate cake sounded like a good plan right now. Maybe one of the kitchen staff had also fired up the ice cream machine. Now, wouldn't that make for the perfect ending to an awesome afternoon......................................

56

WTF (JEAN)

THIS IS ESPECIALLY TRUE OF THOSE WHO FOLLOW THE CORRUPT DESIRE OF THE FLESH AND DESPISE AUTHORITY. BOLD AND ARROGANT, THEY ARE NOT AFRAID TO HEAP ABUSE ON CELESTIAL BEINGS.

2 PETER 2:10 NIV

I DON'T KNOW WHAT WENT ON YESTERDAY UP HERE, BUT I SENSE SOMETHING DIFFERENT. MY BACK IS SCREAMING WITH THE BRUISES MY LIVE-IN POUNDED RELENTLESSLY AS I KEPT MY FACE DOWN BURIED IN A PILLOW. I KEPT TELLING MYSELF, "YOU KNOW, SELF, IF THIS ASSHOLE REALLY WANTED TO, HE COULD HOLD YOUR HEAD SO DEEP IN THIS PILLOW THAT YOU COULD NO LONGER BREATHE." THAT WOULD HAVE BEEN A BLESSING OVER THE BEATING I WAS TAKING. "SON OF A BITCH, NOW HE JUST BURNED A CIGARETTE IN THE BACK OF MY THIGH."

SO, MY DAY YESTERDAY WASN'T SO GOOD. I ALMOST DREAD MY DAYS OFF ANYMORE. IF I CAN KEEP HIS ANGER DIRECTED AT ME, THEN MY DAUGHTER WILL BE SAFE. I CAN'T EVEN SAY "OUR" DAUGHTER ANYMORE. THAT BASTARD DOESN'T DESERVE CLAIM TO SOMETHING AS SWEET AS SHE IS. I GOTTA GET US OUT OF THERE.

ALL THE ENERGY AND HAPPINESS UP HERE AT THE HOME TODAY IS ABOUT TO DRIVE ME BATSHIT CRAZY. I MUST PUT A STOP TO THIS. WHY SHOULD EVERYONE ELSE BE HAPPY WHEN I HAVE TO SUFFER SO MUCH? WHO SHOULD I KNOCK OFF THEIR THRONE OF JOY FIRST? I THINK I WILL VOLUNTEER FOR BATH DUTY TODAY. THE OTHER AIDES WILL LEAVE ME ALONE IN THE BATHING ROOM, AND I HAVE ALL KINDS OF LITTLE SECRET PRESENTS TO GIVE THESE OLD PEOPLE WHO REALLY SHOULDN'T BE ALIVE ANYWAY. EVEN KAY, WHO ISN'T OLD, NEEDS ONE OF MY SPECIAL TREATS. SHE IS JUST USING MS AS AN EXCUSE TO BE LAZY. FIRST UP, HMMMMMMM, YEAH, LET'S SEE IF I CAN MAKE MAYANN SCREAM SOME PROFANITY AGAIN. WHO THE HECK GIVES THEIR KID TWO NAMES COMBINED IN ONE ANYWAY? SHE MUST BE FROM ARKANSAW OR SOMETHING. PROBABLY LOST HER VIRGINITY TO HER BROTHER BILLY BOB OR COUSIN RAY BOB, OR OTHER COUSIN JOE BOB. EITHER WAY, I BET THEY "BOBBED" HER GOOD. MY SHIT DOESN'T STINK BITCH CAN'T EVEN TELL THOSE BOYFRIENDS OF HERS LOOK LIKE THEY COULD EASILY BE HER SONS. PRICKS ANYWAY. THEY WILL BE NEXT.

"OH MAYANN.., WHERE ARE YOU?" .... "YOUR FAVORITE AIDE WANTS TO GIVE YOU A BAAAAAATH!!".......................................

57

Lesson Learned (MayAnn)

When justice is done, it brings joy to the righteous
but terror to evildoers.

Proverbs 21:15 NIV

I heard Jean calling from the distance. My body could only express fear. It had never known any different from Jean. Why did I have to be the first from our group to face the Devil herself? I don't know if I am up to this. I have been praying all morning for this strength to endure. I hope I am ready. I won't have Alan and Larry to lean on. This is only me today.

Typically, Jean doesn't start too much of her antics until after breakfast. She must need her fill of nicotine and caffeine before her Mean Jean comes out.

Poet, didn't know it, feet show it, they're Longfellows. That dates me, doesn't it?

Well, here she comes, all determined and angry. Here I go, ready to spring some shock and awe. Full of references today, aren't I? My mind has been unseasonably clear since yesterday's Bible study. I still wish they would have just left me in our Common Room. But here I am now, ready to tackle the Devil and see what happens.

"Well, Miss MayAnn, you proper little cunt you," Jean said with a perverted grin. "Let's just get you in for your weekly bath. Yes, a nice warm bath with maybe some soothing bath salts and even bubbles to make you feel special, you sexy beast." Jean was on a roll today. This was not going to be a good session.

I could already hear the bathwater filling the stock tank as she wheeled me into the bathing room. Jean at least set some decent clean clothes on my lap to change me into after the bath. I noticed the heat light wasn't on. You would think little Miss Lucifer herself could think of something more creative than an ice-cold bath and watching me shiver uncontrollably for several minutes before she roughly clothed me again. This without any attempt at drying me off. I usually had to sit in this wetness for the rest of the day as Jean kept me "put away" from others' eyes.

As she wheeled me near the lift chair that would elevate me over the tub and then submerge me, Jean set the brakes on my wheelchair. I kept my head slumped and kind of cocked off to one side like the incoherent self I normally was.

When I heard the brake set, I kicked my footrests over, stood up, walked over to the tub, reached my hand in and tested the water. It was freezing. I reached over and shut off the cold water and turned on strictly hot. I then hit the button to turn the jets on. This should stir the cold water nicely with the hot. I stood and watched, keeping my hand in the water until the perfect temperature was reached. Then, I turned the hot water off and walked back over to the lift chair. I held it while I undressed, then sat down, buckled my safety belt, looked at Jean and said, "I am ready for my bath now, Dear. If you do have some bath beads that smell pretty, I would like that."

Jean didn't have a clue what to do next. I could see the wheels of confusion racing in her mind. I could also see a fear of the unknown never expressed by Jean before. It was her turn to scream as she went running out the door. Poor girl. Haven't heard a scream like that since the last time I was dunked in the ice-cold tub.

Wish I could reach the buttons to run this chair. I would raise, swing, and lower myself into my bath before it got cold. I also wish I had walked over and turned the heat lamp on. Starting to get a little chilly here, ladies.

Soon, the other aide, I think her name is Elaine, came in still chuckling to herself. She said, "Oh, MayAnn, I don't know what you said or did to Jean, but WOW, you scared her good enough to pee herself."

I simply sat there, kinda slumped again like nothing had changed. It was a nice bath. Elaine is a beautiful soul. Maybe a little confused. I hope she can pursue her goals of getting her RN certificate. She would be a great one. Hate to lose her as an aide, though. I wonder if Jean will sit around the rest of her shift in her own wetness like she makes me do...

58

AGAIN WTF (JEAN)

THEY SAW IT, THEN THEY WERE AMAZED; THEY WERE TERRIFIED, THEY FLED IN ALARM.
PSALMS 48:5 NASB

WELL GREAT!! I JUST PEED MYSELF. NOT JUST A LITTLE WET SPOT TRAPPED IN MY PANTIES. I AM TALKING, DOWN MY LEG WETTING MY SOCK AND FILLING MY SHOE. I HAVE SPENT YEARS CLEANING UP OTHER PEOPLE AND THEIR INCONTINENCE, NOW I HAVE TO CLEAN MYSELF UP.

I HAVE NEVER BEEN AS SCARED AS I WAS JUST A FEW MINUTES AGO. EVEN WHEN THE SPERM DONOR TO MY CHILD BEATS ON ME, I AM NOT TERRIFIED TO THE DEGREE I WAS TODAY. WHAT GOT INTO MAYANN? SHE IS USUALLY JUST A VEGETABLE HEAD ON A SOMEWHAT FUNCTIONING BODY. NO WAY IN HELL SHOULD SHE EVER HAVE BEEN ABLE TO STAND UP AND DO WHAT SHE DID.

MAYBE WHAT SCARED ME THE MOST WAS THE FACT THAT MAYANN WASN'T IN SOME KIND OF TRANCE. HER DAILY LIFE IS A FRICKEN TRANCE. NO, TODAY HER EYES WERE CLEAR. SHE LOOKED RIGHT AT ME. SHE LOOKED DEEP INTO MY SOUL. MAYANN GRABBED MY TWISTED MIND WITH HER EYES AND SHOWED ME EVERY DEED I HAD EVER DONE TO HER. IF ALL THE RESIDENTS WERE ABLE TO DO THAT, I WOULD GO INSANE. MY GOD, AM I THAT BAD OF A PERSON?

I DON'T KNOW IF IT IS ONLY IN MY MIND, OR IF THOSE BRIEF MOMENTS OF PANIC AND FLIGHT WERE A REAL EXPERIENCE. AS I EXITED THE BATHING ROOM, THE DOOR WAS BEING HELD OPEN BY CLARA. SHE MUST HAVE BEEN NEXT IN LINE FOR A BATH. OUT OF HER WHEELCHAIR, STANDING THERE LIKE SHE WAS TWENTY AND SAID, "WHY ARE YOU STILL HERE, JEAN?"

THEN, AS I TOOK A QUICK RIGHT TO MAKE IT TO THE NEAREST EXIT, THERE STOOD DON. "NOT THIS WAY, YOUNG LADY. YOU MUST FIND THE WAY." WHAT DID THAT MEAN? MY GOSH, HOW COULD DON EVEN POSSIBLY BE STANDING IN THE MIDDLE OF THE HALLWAY? THIS IS A NIGHTMARE BUILDING.

A QUICK TURNAROUND SENT ME IN THE DIRECTION OF THE NURSE'S STATION AND CROSSROADS OF TRAIL'S END. YES, FITTING NAME FOR THIS GODFORSAKEN PLACE. AS I PASSED WILLY'S ROOM, HE WAS STANDING IN

HIS DOORWAY CASUALLY LEANING AGAINST THE JAMB. "WHERE DO YOU THINK YOU'RE GOING, JEAN? SHOULD YOU RUN FROM YOUR ACTIONS, OR SHOULD YOU FACE THEM?" HOW CAN WILLY BE STANDING THERE WITH NO OXYGEN, SPEAKING IN SUCH A FORCEFUL TONE? THIS HAS TO BE A DREAM.

AT THE CROSSROADS/NURSE'S STATION, THERE STOOD LARRY. HEAD RESTRAINT IN HIS HAND. CASUALLY TWIRLING IT LIKE A COACH'S WHISTLE ON A STRING. "TIME TO REALIZE WHO IS REALLY RESTRAINED HERE, JEAN!!"

NEXT CLOSEST EXIT WAS THE FRONT DOORS. LO AND BEHOLD, THERE STOOD KAY. HER CHAIR STILL PARKED IN FRONT OF THE BIG SCREEN TV LIKE EVERY AFTERNOON. HERE WAS KAY, TWENTY FEET AWAY FROM HER CHAIR, INTIMIDATING AS HER SISTER. BLOCKING THE FRONT DOORS. "YOU NEED TO CHANGE YOUR DIRECTION, JEAN."

I DID A FAST RETREAT. HOW ARE ALL THESE RESIDENTS OUT OF THEIR WHEELCHAIRS? WHO PUT THEM UP TO THIS? WHY AM I SO WET? PLEASE, SOMEONE WAKE ME UP.

AS I HEADED IN THE OPPOSING DIRECTION FROM THE FRONT DOORS AND KAY, I ONCE AGAIN PASSED THROUGH THE CROSSROADS AND RIGHT BY WHERE VERA ALWAYS SITS. OUR EYES LOCKED. I WAS RELIEVED VERA WAS SITTING. THINGS MIGHT BE NORMAL AFTER ALL. SHE WILL ASK ME WHAT DAY IT IS. BUT VERA SAID, "TODAY IS YOUR DAY OF JUDGMENT, JEAN. YOU NEED TO FACE YOUR ACTIONS ON THIS DAY." WHAT THE HECK?

I LOOKED RIGHT AS A POSSIBLE TURN TO ESCAPE. THERE, OF ALL THINGS STOOD ALAN BLOCKING THE SOUTH HALLWAY. REALIZE, I PROBABLY COULD HAVE EASILY RUN PAST ANY OF THESE OLD PEOPLE AND BRUSHED THEM TO THE SIDE OR KNOCKED THEM DOWN. THE SIMPLE FACT THAT THEY WERE OUT OF THEIR NORMAL CRIPPLED MENTAL AND PHYSICAL STATE SCARED ME TO AN EVEN MORE PANICKED FRENZY. I HEADED TOWARD THE DINING AREA AND OUR BREAKROOM. I HAD TO GET AWAY FROM THIS VISION OF PERFECTLY HEALTHY RESIDENTS. THEIR WORDS WERE TEARING AT MY SOUL AND MAKING ME WANT TO SCREAM.

OF COURSE, WHAT NEXT. THERE STOOD MARGARET HOLDING THE DOOR OPEN TO THE DINING AREA. "YOU CAN CHANGE, JEAN, YOU CAN BE FORGIVEN."

I COULD TAKE NO MORE. THANKFULLY, TO MY QUICK LEFT WAS THE BREAKROOM. I FELL THROUGH THE DOOR. WHERE WAS EVERYBODY BESIDES ALL THESE SUPERHUMAN RESIDENTS? NO OTHER NURSES, NO OTHER AIDES. I FELT THE BREAKROOM WAS EMPTY. LOOKING UP, I WAS FACE TO FACE WITH TEX. YES, HE WAS STANDING, TOO. NOT SUCH A SHOCK. TEX STILL HAD MOST OF HIS FUNCTIONS. HE REACHED OUT AND PLACED A HAND OF THE MOST AMAZING STRENGTH AND GENTLENESS ON MY SHOULDER. "JEAN," HE SAID. "YOU CAN STOP RUNNING NOW. YOU AND I WILL PRAY. WE WILL PRAY FOR YOUR FORGIVENESS. RIGHT HERE, RIGHT NOW. OR YOU CAN RUN OUT THAT DOOR BEHIND ME, GET IN YOUR CAR, AND NEVER RETURN."

I BOWED MY HEAD.

WHERE AND WHEN DID I EVER CROSS THAT LINE? WILL I EVER BE ABLE TO COME BACK FROM THIS DARKNESS I AM BURIED IN? I DON'T HAVE A CLUE WHERE TO EVEN START EXCEPT FOR THE FACT OF CLEANING MYSELF UP AND PUTTING ON DRY PANTS, SOCKS AND DIFFERENT SHOES. WHAT A MESS.

HOW MANY PEOPLE WERE WITNESS TO MY FLIGHT OF FRIGHT? I JUST KNOW ALL THE NURSES AND OTHER AIDES ARE GOING TO BE TALKING ABOUT ME IN THE BREAKROOM AND SMOKE SHACK. I CAN HEAR THEM ALREADY: "DID YOU SEE JEAN RUNNING, SCREAMING, WITH A STEADY STREAM OF PEE MARKING HER TRAIL OF ESCAPE?" AND "MAYBE WE SHOULD GET HER SOME ADULT DIAPERS OUT OF THE STORAGE ROOM FOR HER OWN SAFETY." OR BETTER YET, "DO WE NEED TO START A PSYCH WARD UP HERE FOR SPECIAL PEOPLE LIKE JEAN?"

UGHHHHHHH, HOW AM I EVER GOING TO FACE ANYONE EVER AGAIN? MY FIRST URGE IS TO SEEK REVENGE ON MAYANN. BUT SOMETHING BURNED BRIGHT INSIDE TELLING ME I DESERVED THIS. THAT SAME BRIGHT LIGHT ALSO TOLD ME I HAD A CHOICE. I COULD EASILY STAY ON THE PATH I WAS ON, OR I COULD CHANGE. I COULD MAKE THE WORLD RIGHT AGAIN. AT LEAST AT MY LEVEL OF SERVICE.

I NEED A SMOKE. HOW CAN I EVER DREAM OF BEING A BETTER PERSON WHEN I DAILY HAVE TO GO HOME TO MY OWN PERSONAL HELL THAT IS WAITING TO ABUSE ME SOME MORE? WHERE IN SMALL-TOWN AMERICA DO I EVER FIND HELP? MY 75 CENTS OVER BARE MINIMUM PER HOUR WAGE WON'T SUPPORT MY DAUGHTER AND ME. I MUST TOLERATE THE HOME ABUSE, SO MY DAUGHTER AT LEAST HAS A ROOF OVER HER HEAD AND FOOD ON THE TABLE. I DON'T EVEN HAVE ANY DECENT FRIENDS I COULD TURN TO. MY FAMILY, WHAT IS LEFT OF THE WHITE TRASH GROUP ARE PROBABLY ALL IN THE SAME DEGREE OF SHIT CYCLE THAT I AM. I NEED AN OUT. WHERE TO EVEN BEGIN LOOKING? THIS CIGARETTE TASTES LIKE THE SWEATY SHOE I JUST PISSED IN...

59

Here We Go (Peggy)

But the angel reassured them. "Don't be afraid!" he said.
"I bring you good news that will bring great joy to all people.
Luke 2:10 NLT

knew something special had happened yesterday more than the awesome Bible study conversation I was privileged to listen to. When Jean came running out of the bathing room like she had seen a ghost, her uniform soaked from the crotch down, I could tell a higher plan was in the works.

Something amazing had just happened and I didn't get to witness. Jean didn't say anything as she headed to the breakroom where our lockers and a private bathroom were. Hopefully, she has a change of bottoms with her. I feel sorry for the girl. I fear she is very much abused at home. I have seen odd bruises in not normal places on her when she has reached high for something. I should ask her about it one of these days. Or at least bring it up to the DON. I think Jean has a heart of compassion hidden in there somewhere. I am afraid it has been beaten down so far, it may never surface again. What did MayAnn do in there, anyway?

"Elaine, please go check on MayAnn. You know we can't leave residents alone in the bathing room. Hurry before something worse happens. I will be in shortly as soon as I give Margaret her meds."

Elaine headed to the bathing room. I turned back to Margaret. She had the biggest most genuine smile on her face I had ever seen. I am talking from the back of her pretty blue eyes burst of sparkle smiles. Realize, most of these residents have little to nothing to smile about. Three-fourths blind Margaret was one of those. She only smiled when her son came to see her, maybe once a month.

This smile was good. It reached the soul.............................

60

Wonderful (MayAnn)

Thank God for this gift too wonderful for words!
2 Corinthians 9:15 NLT

My bath was wonderful. Elaine, after checking on me, quickly exited and came back with some bath beads. I think they were some I had tucked in my drawer since last Christmas. Elaine poured them in. Ran a little more water to get the temperature back to perfect. Gently lowered me in to twenty minutes of heaven.

Elaine didn't say a word to me the whole time. Usually, she has some story to tell about her daughters and their ever-growing little girl antics. Today, though, I think she just wanted to let me enjoy my win over Jean.

It was like Elaine sensed that I had actually done something very much out of the ordinary. Great caregivers like Elaine, Peggy, Carol, Lynn, and so many other ones had an insight for this home like it was a living organism. In a sense, it is. And the infection had just run out the door wetting herself. Oh, what a day. Back to this awesome bath. It is the simple things that can give us the most joy..........

61

It Has Started (Alan)

*He giveth power to the faint; and to him that hath
no might he increaseth strength.*

Isaiah 40:29 ASV

Well, that didn't take long. We knew that one of us would have to be the first to implement our "Let's love the Mean out of Jean" plan. MayAnn had the privilege. From what I could tell sitting here in my room, MayAnn had been successful. I don't know what she did. But the scream and ensuing sprint down the hall from Jean told a thousand descriptions. I wish I could have seen it. Something very special. Something that could have only found its strength from our collective group of Light. Miracles do happen. MayAnn's must have been a doozy.

Unplanned and above the ordinary, most of us from the last Circle of Light just happened to be in the right place at the right time. I with a firm and inner belief know there was a Hand in all of this that we simple residents of Trail's End weren't in control of. Add to that the fact that we could escape the confines of our permanent sitting transportation and stand at assigned positions was a miracle in itself.

This was not just a Common Room in our minds thing. This was a physical miracle. Though brief, and maybe only witnessed by Jean herself, it was a treasure each of us will hold forever. I personally don't remember how I stood up, walked to my designated station, and had the perfect words to share with Jean. One second I was in my usual foggy hallway of a brain, and next I was standing and talking like I was twenty years old again. Then, back in my chair. No fog in the aftermath, but body ready to rest again.

Phase 1 was complete. It was just a matter of time before one of us was next in line to engage with Jean. I hoped it would be soon. I could feel the fog coming from the backside of the mountain of a blockade I had put up. It wasn't going to be stopped. I could only detain it for so long. Hopefully, Ana and the girls will come to see me today. Thursdays aren't their typical visiting day, but one can always hope. Maybe one of my boys will stop by on their way to or from their busy lives. It would be good to talk to somebody from the family.

I wonder if they would believe my story of why things were happening. My first day of coherence in such a long time was never questioned. Everybody just talked and laughed and teased. We didn't want to interrupt the joy with a "why?" I raised them well, my sons. So very proud. My daughters are going to be strong and awesome, too. I can tell it.

I want to tell my wife, "I love you." "Eu te amo, muito muito" needs to be heard by her ears. The burden strapped to her back is not deserved. Ana needs a man to enjoy life with. Not this decrepit thing I am. Was ten years of happiness enough to offset these last years of nothing but pain for Ana? "Oh, God, please give her the love I can no longer express. Let her know it will be OK to move on. But for today, have her stop by so I can once again kiss those delicious lips she shares only with me." Damn, better wheel myself in and brush my teeth just in case. All the staff is so busy taking care of other residents, no one will notice helpless Alan go into his own bathroom and brush his teeth.

This Alzheimer's is such an unknown anyway. It really wouldn't surprise anyone if they caught me. "Just Alan having a good day. Wonder if he is feeling up to a wild goose chase for Jean today," they would all be thinking.

Now, which toothbrush is mine? "Larry, what color is your toothbrush?"

"Hell, I don't know, Alan. Use the dry one. I just had my teeth brushed after breakfast by some volunteer."

Dry brush it is. When the heck did I get this fancy Oral B thing anyway? Damn, been out of touch for a while. What happens when I push on this little bump? Wrrrrrrrrrrrrrrrrrrrrrrrrrrr...............

62

Looking from the Outside (Larry)

And whosoever shall exalt himself shall be humbled; and
whosoever shall humble himself shall be exalted.
Matthew 23:12 ASV

I have been thinking lately. That is an understatement. I have been thinking A LOT lately. When your body has gone off the deep end and given up on normal functioning, one has nothing better to do than think. I don't even have the ability to write down my thoughts. Nobody really wants to listen to me. Maybe BB could bring me a tablet or something that takes all voice commands. Then I could put all of these "thoughts" in a file for someone's future reference.

I had heard that MayAnn had spent time with her mother-in-law's side of the family on a continual basis, asking questions, taking notes, documenting memories. This family had a knack for recalling names, precise dates and events. She was able to put together a family history to share with the upcoming generations so they had an eternal record of their heritage. MayAnn spent untracked hours/ days/weeks collecting data from these living history books. Each had its own story. Each also confirmed certain events on an exact timeline. It was interesting to read the individual versions of the same story as seen from a different set of eyes. Kind of a Matthew, Mark, Luke, and John thing. I suppose the subject matter wasn't quite as profound, but admittedly interesting enough.

I have thoughts that won't go away. I sit here and can sense every part of my body that is quitting. I am going to be completely aware the day my lungs are too weak to take in even one more breath. I will be able to count the pumps of the ventilator that is breathing for me. It will be interesting if I will be aware enough to feel my very last heartbeat.

I think I would be really good at this life coach thing. Or at least able to intrigue an audience long enough to make them buy my book. I'd keep feeding little treats. Just a small taste of big things promised. Not enough sustenance to survive on. You must buy the book for the details. Starting today you will tap into your own source of wealth and prosperity. I promise. Or your money back on a $49.99 book that only costs me $4.99 to publish and promote. And the fine print no one ever reads defines how it is impossible to prove you gained no value from my book. I mean really, who can put a price/value on hope?

I have been thinking a great deal about my experience in the Common Room. It was difficult to get there. Before Tex dragged me in with his "special" rope, I had only made it to the foggy hallway. I could not make it any further. I could hear/feel the others in that Common Room, but I couldn't find it. It was scary wandering around in the fog that is a daily existence for those with dementia and Alzheimer's. Oh, my God, what would it be like to have to take that journey every day? Or worse, be stuck there wandering and wandering until your body finally gave up the ghost. MayAnn, Alan, and thousands of others live this horror each and every day.

I couldn't find my way, or "my door," because my mind was still healthy. I now know, our journey and relationship with God is typically blocked by our own thoughts. God blessed us with free thinking and free will. If and when we chose to love and follow Him, it is real. Our problem is, we have developed intellectually in the opposite direction. The stronger our brain, the further we are from God. We get stuck with the belief that our brain is superior to anything else in this world or out of this world.

I was one of these believers for many, many years. I could take care of myself. I made my own destiny. I was in charge. I didn't need to depend on some entity that I couldn't even see. Just ask anyone with an IQ of over 160, and most likely they will scoff at the possibility of a Higher Power. Their brain is all the power they need. I now pity them. It took my body going to waste to wake up the Holy Spirit who had resided in me ever since my Oral Roberts awakening so many years ago.

I was Number One in my own book. I had the intelligence to take care of myself quite well. Let the poor and uneducated believe in God. Let them depend on Him to bring them out of their own self-made pathetic situation. Prayer was a joke. How many millions have died while in prayer? How many have actually realized prosperity because they prayed the right words, and God decided He would choose to boost their bank account?? Like, NONE.

I know an exclamation point was added when I was finally led into that Common Room. Yes, I had some insight before, but it was clouded by my own intellect. What was in my heart was continuously blocked by the thoughts in my brain. Just try some serious prayer in the middle of the day. You might get a decent start and spew out a few thoughts/words. Soon your mind is going to take you off on a tangent that pulls you away from anything meaningful in the way of communication with God. Next thing you know, you are thinking about which chocolate cake would go best with that Merlot you bought the other day.

I was fortunate to have my full brain capacity when I made it into the Common Room. Most everyone else was still coming out of their own fog and misery, and could not fully appreciate the details of the room. They were all happy to be back to a "normal" state. No time for details. More time for remembering what it used to be like to have both mind and body at "fully functioning."

I, on the other hand, didn't care that I was walking around. I hadn't missed that as much as I thought. What I was interested in was figuring out what this room actually meant. What phase, or rather dimension were we now in? Was this where a person ended up after the big D? Was this as good as it was going to get? Was my eternity going to be stuck with a bunch of people who happened to die in the same place? Maybe at different times, but did being from the same area of your death determine who you shared a room with? Why were there no dead relatives waiting for us in this room?

I have reviewed and reviewed and analyzed and reviewed again every detail of this room. Tex had pointed out the one door that was overly decorated and worth more in precious metals and stones than most people can even imagine. I at one time probably could have bought this door. The important part of this door was that it couldn't be opened from our room. Someone on the other side had to open it. That intrigued me.

I should have realized what that door represented. Remember, though, I was still inhibited by my own stupid brain. Now, I know what Jesus was talking about when He said we must become like children. Get rid of all the adult clutter and get back to a nice clean and innocent thought pattern. That is how we fully find God. Same with this room.

I believe our Common Room was a Waiting Room. A place where you transferred from your life on Earth to a celestial one. That door represented Heaven. If somewhere in your life you had given your life to God in the name of our Lord and Savior Jesus Christ, most likely that door would be opened for you. The Waiting Room was where you sorted out your life story. Cleaned house. Were forgiven for sin. Then the nurse in charge opened the door and called your name. Oh, how I can't wait to see what is on the other side.

I have also thought about my continuous wandering in that foggy hallway when I was trying so very hard to join the others. There was another room I passed by. One that gave me chills clear through to the hair on my toes. Those toe hairs even stood on end. I could feel them pushing through my socks and trying to escape my Hush Puppies. I ran from that room. I could feel arms extending and hands reaching out, trying to get one little grasp on me and pull me into an eternal Hell. Yes, my friends, it is there too. Not all potatoes and gravy waiting. More like boiling hog slop that you were going to join the mix in. I know I pissed myself when one of those dark reaching fingers brushed my shirt sleeve.

I believe throughout our lives; we build a good portion of each room. Whatever path we choose at any given time is furnishing one room or the other. I know I have made choices in my life that were great contributors to that "Room from Hell." And I have visited that room more than once. Choices made by me and only me led into those depths. I figured the sin I was committing was worth the oncoming suffering. At least when I was self-indulging in the pleasures of a woman I shouldn't have been holding. That little piece of heaven was worth time later spent in Hell. Instant gratification was much stronger than any future outcomes. Buy now, pay later.

I now realize the Truth of God will always give you an out when you are faced with sin. He doesn't want you to face the Hell of your own making. God loves you and wants only the best for you. He loves you enough to let you make your own choices and always provides an avenue for the right choice. Good stuff right there. Why did I waste so many years ignoring this? Will I really end up in the Common Room and invited through the beautiful door when my time comes? Is what the Bible says true? Do I have hope? Does God really love me enough to forgive all the wrong I have done in my self-centered life?

I would like to believe this is true. As I said, my mind is still strong enough to have its doubts. My heart is telling me all will be well. My cranium says, "Not so soon, buddy, you have dues to pay for past transgressions." My only option is to give as much as I can now with all of my heart. I have to stop looking back.

Maybe my first step will be getting rid of the "I" that is so important to me. Did you notice every paragraph of this chapter started with "I"? I this. I that. I have a very good chance of going to Hell if I don't change my outlook to: you, them, those, and even we. Now I see an alternate purpose of the Common Room. It is a room created from the heart. It truly defines what love for others can do. Daily, you and I both can visit this Common Room. And when the time comes, we will be there ready for the beautiful door to open.

Those are my thoughts going round and round. I pray you will make use of them.........

63

Do I Tell (Tex)

A gossip goes around telling secrets, but those who are
trustworthy can keep a confidence.
Proverbs 11:13 NLT

Tex here, trying to decide what to do. I have noticed that MayAnn, Larry, and Alan don't have a clue there is a connection well beyond their sharing a nursing home. This connection is the "bond" that pulls everyone into the Common Room when they join hands.

I heard that MayAnn had been visiting Alan and Larry's room on a daily basis, and through some small miracle had always found the strength to join hands. God has brought them back together after all these years. I don't know why they haven't realized the truth of their relationship. It probably has something to do with two out of three of them having the Alzheimer's thing going on. Maybe they have made the connection, and just haven't told anyone.

Larry still has all the lights on in his brain, but his jaw muscles have given up to the point he can't talk anymore. Only after one of their gatherings does Larry have the ability to communicate for the short term. So, I guess if he knew the truth, he would share.

For some reason other than the big A, MayAnn doesn't even recognize me. I know I was only a brief moment in her long life, but I thought it was quite an important moment. Something happened.

Two babies were born and instantly taken away and given to their adoptive families. I could understand Larry and Alan not knowing. What happened to MayAnn? As part of the arrangement, I was banned from being any part of the whole birthing process. MayAnn had set up some stringent guidelines for how this transaction was going to take place. She felt that if my presence was there at the birth, the clean break would never be complete. It had to be 100 percent strangers acting as the go-between. Was there some medical trauma after the birth of the twin boys that erased MayAnn's memory of their existence? Or was it more of the extreme emotional pain that caused a coma of sorts that has never awakened?

Something, somewhere, somehow, provided a protection for MayAnn that was part of her blessing of choosing life for those babies and not the alternative. God's plan was at work. I have thousands of questions for Him when the time comes.

Now my dilemma is, do I tell them or not? Do I state the obvious to these three? Or is it better left untouched? If they are meant to know, then will it happen? If I reveal their story to them, will it cause more pain than good? Will Alan and Larry then want to know who their real father is? Is the story even worth the bother? All three seem quite content with their current relationship. It is more than coincidence that they enjoy each other's company. If I force the truth, will this throw a wrench in the cog? I will need to pray about this. The answer will be interesting.

I have spent all my adult years helping people with their lives and their faith. That was all I could ever do. I actually have ZERO answers. Just belief. That is what puts us preacher types in the position we are in. Belief. Nothing more. Every other part of us is wholly human. We make just as many mistakes as anyone else. We don't want to fall. But we do. ALL of us. Don't let anyone tell you any different. We are definitely not any better than anyone else walking this Earth.

Rather, we are blessed (some think cursed) to have a connection between our brains and our hearts that is called faith. A direct link that is recognized and formed and perfected can be of great service to others. We are a link to hope. A hope that there really is something better.

I will admit that in God's service, our personalities still get in the way. Some preachers take off on a tangent as if they were God themselves. Others I believe just like to hear themselves talk. Some are like banty roosters strutting around and saying, "Look at me." Most have the right intentions. Their human characteristics just jump in the middle of the path they are trying to lead others on.

Now take someone like the late Billy Graham. He was at a totally different level than most of us in God's service. We can only dream of what he achieved. Billy had his stuff together. Whatever human demons that tried to destroy him were well stowed away. It would be interesting to know what Billy's battles actually were. And even more interesting how he controlled them.

You know that famous question of, "If you could spend thirty minutes talking with anyone of this world past or present, who would it be?" My choices would be Jesus first, and Billy Graham a close second. I wonder if anyone would ever say they would like to spend thirty minutes visiting with Tex...........................

64

Now What (Alan)

*Our bodies are buried in brokenness, but they will be
raised in glory. They are buried in weakness,
but they will be raised in strength.*

1 Corinthians 15:43 NLT

It felt good to brush my teeth, comb my hair, and shave myself. I even was able to do my morning chores and wipe myself. Dignity restored for me, today. I can tell it won't last long. I am already starting to slip. It reminds me of a day in my youth that made a permanent imprint on my memory. No matter how many brain cells have expired, I believe this memory is actually more like a cave drawing etched on the inside of my skull. Would be cool to actually see the pictures drawn depicting this life event. Yet again, my artistic skills are well below subpar. Maybe I really don't want to see the rough scribbling of a stick figure in action.

Near where I grew up, there was a pasture with some pretty awesome rock bluffs. Many an adventure was spent "attacking" these bluffs with whatever stick or makeshift thing I had at the time that represented a good cowboy's rifle. And on fortunate days, I had the perfect stick off part of a small branch—a stick that represented a pistol I could carry hanging out of my front pocket.

I never worried about the detail of bullets. Or the need to reload. Heck, I didn't ever have much of a trigger to pull. My dad was a firm believer in the absence of toy guns. If you were going to have a gun, it would be real. You would learn proper handling and respect for this gun and any gun. Fake/toy guns were just a bad lesson in learning how to misuse something that could easily kill someone. He had a good point. Every once in a while, a news flash comes up where some teenager was shot because the police believed the plastic realistic imitation for a weapon was the real thing. Even worse, the story of one sibling accidentally killing their brother or sister because they found dad's gun tucked away somewhere and didn't realize it wasn't just another toy.

I do have a memory of my brother getting an ass whooping more severe than any other of us suffered. My dad just happened to walk around the end of the trees, and saw my brother pointing a .303 British Special at my sister. My brother had taken it off the gun rack that was mounted in the rear window area of our '72 Chevy pickup. It was either that truck or the '48 GMC. Heck, I was fairly young then. Had more serious toy playing to do. I remember it being a dark day for the family. Probably even worse for the backside of my brother. Sometimes words and cautions are not enough. And knowing my dad, it hurt him something terrible to have to whoop my brother that severely.

Past that, past the age of attacking the rock bluffs as a cowboy killing Indians. Maybe TV took me past that stage. Nowadays, it is killing zombies. TV and film have a way of steering a young imagination. By then, I was more into the intellectual stage. Reality had started to hit, and simple imagination was put on a shelf to be replaced by, "I wish I was eighteen and out of school and on my own conquering the world in real time." So much for intellectual. I should have been thinking, "Don't be in such a hurry to move on to adulthood, you idiot."

For some reason, I had picked that day to walk over to the rock bluffs where the county road crew had been removing gravel for a few years. My great uncle had made a deal with the county commissioner that if they kept our road (two miles from the house to the mailbox), graveled and well-maintained, they could have the gravel that was embedded in the base of these rock bluffs, for free.

The area described was a cul-de-sac of sorts. You had one trail/road leading into a semicircle of the rock bluffs. It was a box canyon. A man on a good horse could have made it out the backside if you knew the exact path that was well-hidden. It was an escape route for the mule deer of our area. It also might have been the Indians' escape route when this cowboy was attacking them in my youth. Now I know where they went.

As the county was removing the gravel, it became apparent that this gravel was brought in by glaciers and settled in the Ice Age times. We began to find scattered jawbones (with teeth) and a few other bones. The university came out several times to excavate and catalog the findings. Most were mastodon, camel, rhino, and three-toed horse things. No whole skeletons, just bone fragments. Some very impressive. I found the teeth most fascinating.

Because of the nature of the available gravel going in a downward direction from the rather looming rock bluffs, some awesome and quite high banks of loose material were abundant. Other areas because of a good number of bones, were on hold until the university could sign off that they had collected enough.

I don't quite know why I went on that particular day. Who knows what goes on in a youth's mind. I had walked over to the gravel pit, three quarters of a mile, brandishing a wooden walking stick that had been part of a piece of long-ago-forgotten farm equipment. A few years previous, it would have been an awesome rifle. Now, it was just a stick for destroying rattlesnakes if I found one. Said stick was probably five feet long with a decent point on one end.

That day, after a brief exploration for any newly exposed bones, I was drawn to an embankment a good fifty feet high. There was an overhang to this looming piece of fascination. There was also a decent pile of gravel at the bottom from parts of the face that had loosened and slid down.

So, in my brilliance, I found that if I tapped the looming wall with my stick, a little more gravel would come down. I was then submerged in the world of excavation. The harder I would hit the wall, the more gravel would release and bury my feet. I figured (remember, I was in the intellect stage) that I was killing two birds with one stone.

One, I was doing the county a favor by providing a considerable amount of gravel for their use. By this time, they were starting to express concerns about the good gravel going to depths that made it dangerous for machinery to dig out. They were afraid of the whole bank collapsing and burying their equipment—and the operator.

I, of course, was young and fearless. Didn't have a clue of the finality of mortality. I would live forever.

The second bird was, hitting the wall and having mini avalanches was entertaining. Didn't take much in those days to find self-entertainment when you lived fifteen miles from the nearest town. For some reason, I wasn't even on my dirt bike that day. Must have been broken down. So, big stick, good *knock someone's head off* swing, and I went from my feet being covered to buried clear to the knees. This was fun.

I never once looked up to see the threat of a severe overhang of dirt and rocks. Just calmly walking along looking for the next fissure that would produce the most buck for the bang. Hit, dig myself out, hit, not so good, hit harder, decent avalanche, awwww, here might be the motherlode.

I remember my last good swing. I remember the solid hit. I remember time standing perfectly still. I remember a shudder at my feet. I remember a rumble. I remember instinct.

Then, time came back to reality. I didn't think. Self-preservation made me run. I wasn't the fastest person on the track team, but years of working cattle and other hardened farm tasks had given me an agility and quickness above the norm.

As I ran, I could feel the stick torn from my grasp. I would like to think that my fear-induced speed was so great that the stick was lagging straight back at horizontal. In actuality, my walking stick was probably no more than a foot behind my scamper. Stick torn from my grip. Then feet stopped in place. Then I was flattened and buried. Then quiet.

A large bird flew over. I could hear the heavy wings. Close. My face was planted in rough gravel. Probably a hawk or an owl. Definitely not a buzzard. This was a good sign.

I was awakened to the reality that I might just be ok. Self-analysis let me know that my head was clear of obstruction. One arm and hand were free and in front of me. The stick-dragging arm was behind me and buried. I could feel my toes wiggle inside my boots. No pain was evident. I was too far from home to yell for help.

I owned this situation myself. It was only I who could address the facts. It then became another adventure of imagination. Being buried alive was cool now that I knew I would probably be ok. I couldn't quite turn my head enough to see what was exactly behind and above me, but I could tell it wasn't an impossible situation. Surprisingly, I had enough sense (probably stored up from my previous non-usage of common sense) to take my time and slowly dig myself out with my free hand.

At first, it was like a poor attempt at trying to swim with one arm. I was face down and held somewhat firmly. I could pass the free arm/hand back and pull gravel up toward my head and in an outward direction.

After a bit of time, I was free enough to twist and pull my other arm forward for use. Then, free from the waist up. Finally, I was able to twist around and view my too-close-for-comfort entombment. It shocked me to see how many actual tons of rock and gravel were directly above the lower half of my body. A huge rock was nestled above my legs. As luck would have it, the massive amount of loose gravel that had tackled and buried me also saved me from the crushing weight of the rock.

Just the sheer size of this rock, no, it was a BOULDER, sped up my self-excavation process. No more imagination. It was time to get myself clear of this bone-crushing possibility. I preferred not to add my own fragmented bones to the existing collection. I dug with a fierceness of preservation. I was soon free. I walked home. I thanked God.

A week or so later, the county was back out digging gravel again. The loader operator (a close neighbor of ours, only three and a half miles away by road, two miles as the crow flies) thought it strange that one of his buckets full of gravel included a stick that just didn't belong to the Pliocene Epoch.

Work continued, life continued. A few years later, I shared my story with Mom and Dad. Dad nodded his head knowingly. Neighbor county worker had mentioned to Dad the stick discovery. Dads always know things before we kids ever admit them. Many in the long list of stupidity that I probably shouldn't have walked away from...................

65

Now What "2" (Alan)

*And we know that God causes everything to work together
for the good of those who love God and are called
according to his purpose for them.*

Romans 8:28 NLT

Please forgive my reminiscing distracting from the story at hand. When about all you have to look forward to in life is memories and the review of them, then that is what you will get from the elderly or physically/mentally impaired.

I don't consider myself elderly. Heck, I expected to live at least well into my 90s. Why was I cursed with this endless disease? I can't say. It is what it is. Except for the fact that I am in my early 60s and should be enjoying the first exciting years of retirement and Social Security.

My Master Plan (an ever-changing life outlook that started as a large dream and then life beat it down to a few simplicities) was to retire and live in my house in Paraguay with my amazing wife and daughters and extended family. I could live close to a king's level in that part of the world as the house was paid for and food was cheap. A couple thousand dollars in Social Security benefits would more than cover our needs.

That Master Plan was kind of moved when the girls came along. Timelines were shuffled by about eighteen years. I figured I would have to work and supplement my income until the girls at least graduated high school. We would stay in the good ole USA at least that long to collect the benefits of an Americano education. Then, I could escape to my plan of paradise and sit under a shade tree drinking Terere until my number was up.

Didn't quite work out that way. Most times these days, I don't even realize or know where I am. Or who other people even are. Only after one of our Light episodes and clarity comes to mind, do I remember with regret that I have let my family down.

All the good and excitement that come from the strength I have gathered from the others is soon buried in the thoughts of I am now less than a man. They might as well shoot me and at least collect some life insurance to pay the bills. Did I even buy a good term policy like I had intended to when the girls were born? Damn, I don't remember. I hope so.

Really, though, my question of "Now What" comes down to the next step of what we should do as a collective group of Light. Should we continue to gather, join hands, conference in the Common Room, and what? Are we going to solve this world's problems? Do we need to continue to focus on ridding this home of Jean and her abuse? Why are we blessed with this new ability?

I am starting to think of it more as a curse. If our gathering would offer a cure for our afflictions, then maybe it would be a blessing. But to have temporary relief and then get slammed back into nothingness seems kind of cruel. Is God's plan that we only do our best work when freshly brought back from suffering?

There might be something to this theory. When life is good and better than a box of chocolates, then why should we even help others? Why would we step out of our comfort zone of a good life and do the extraordinary? No, most of us during good times are complacent. We don't want to upset the applecart so we don't even try to push it. Let things sit, nice and calm. Let others come and get their own apples. We will gladly share, as long as the cart keeps self-loading.

No, we must first hit some form of bottom. Whether it is a tragic accident, sickness, loss of a loved one, loss of anything that is providing us temporary happiness. Only then do we wake up to realize there is so much more to life.

Come to think of it, even in "normal" life, are we really just walking around in our own fog? Are we just as blind to the suffering of our fellow man when life is good and we have no problems? Is my current lack of brain function any worse than most people living their daily lives? At least now, I have an excuse. Why didn't I find the clarity and reality that are prevalent in our Common Room earlier in life? What could be better than the gathering of souls and feeding off each other's strengths to improve our own shortcomings?

This new realization needs to be shared with the world. Except, who would listen to the rantings of an Alzheimer's-infested middle-aged man? Especially one who has a few skeletons in his closet. How can we as a collective group get this word out? Have Tex and every other preacher of substance spent their whole lives trying to say the same thing? Is the Bible we typically leave on a shelf the one guide and map to what we are experiencing in our Common Room?

We have some talking to do. I wonder when our next "meeting" will actually be. Maybe if we shared a hint of this with Jean, it would help lead her in a direction she didn't know was available. There is some pain buried deep inside Jean that triggers her abuse of us. I would love to help her remove that pain. Back to the rantings of a mashed vegetable brain of a human. If only there were a way.........................

66

Cold and Flu Season (Peggy)

*Feed the hungry, and help those in trouble. Then your light
will shine out from the darkness, and the darkness
around you will be as bright as noon.*

Isaiah 58:10 NLT

Oh, how I hate this time of year. Actually, it is twice a year with an exclamation point at Christmas time. We are once again fighting the cold and flu season here at the nursing home. Somewhere around when school starts back up and carrying into when it is finally freezing cold out, we are hit internally with a simple runny nose ending in a casket.

I don't know if we will ever find the happy line between the residents' hunger for companionship and family visits, versus the need for survival. I believe that one day family visiting, including grandkids and great-grandkids, or any kids for that matter, will be traded for the reality that the germs shared by the visitors might just end their existence.

We like to tell families not to bring anyone to visit who has a cold, or symptoms of the flu. But discouraging visitors because of what "might be" is just another excuse for people to not come.

There are hundreds of excuses. If I didn't work here, I wouldn't visit. It is depressing. It's not an inspiring reality that if you take care of yourself and live a halfway guarded life, you will one day be rewarded with sitting in the hallway of an almost continuous urine smell as just another lonely person barely existing. That is.... NOT....... inspiring. It is...... downright depressing. People don't want to visit because they see themselves in that same geriatric chair in a number of years. Who would even want to think about that when you have some serious soccer practice to get your eight-year-old to? I make a living caring for these people. I sure as heck don't envy being one of them.

Now, some little germ-carrying angel who came to visit their great grandmother has released a sandstorm of sickness within our walls. More than the normal percentage will die in the next few weeks. We can do nothing to really stop it. Hygiene precautions help lower the numbers, but it can't be stopped.

More temperatures taken. More calls to designated doctors. More not really getting an answer except "Make them comfortable and see what happens." A few get transported to hospitals in the attempt to help them pass through the latest epidemic and extend their misery for a few more years. Others are already gone far enough and have no family support that emergency measures are long past behind them.

It is a wrestling match between my heart and my brain. On one hand, my heart bleeds to take care of them and never to let go. My brain says enough is enough, let their suffering end. My heart wants to agree on this at times, too. So many residents are preserved just so the family doesn't have to feel any pain. Not because they want to visit daily or weekly or even monthly. More, they just have a clear conscience that their family member is taken care of, no matter if the quality of life is gone.

Don't get me wrong, there are some very good daughters and sons who establish a routine of visiting often. They attend the monthly "care plan" reviews. They are very much involved in the remaining days of life. Sadly, these family members are few and far between. Of the sixty residents in our facility, I could list the excellent families on one hand.

Others try, and do what they can, but their attention is captured by the next generation coming on. Or they have their own life priorities. They come and visit more out of guilt than want. I really can't blame them. Who wants to come to visit someone who doesn't even recognize you anymore? It is HARD. It HURTS. It literally tears your heart out. Who wouldn't want to avoid that kind of realized pain?

For today, though, I have forty percent of the residents I am caring for in dire need of some relief. And, for once, I am glad that Jean is working my end of the floor. Ever since her little "episode" with MayAnn, I have seen a new and caring person. Jean was always a good worker, but she had a dark side that carried over to the residents in a bad way I am afraid. Just an instinct because I could never prove it, but I could tell. Now, she is a servant and an angel to the residents in her care. Most still seem scared of Jean. I appreciate the extra care she is giving those I don't have enough time for because of all the sick ones who need my attention.

I wish I could get Jean to talk to me sometime. I feel that her home life isn't so good. There is a suitcase full of darkness still in the back of her eyes that is screaming for help.

Dang it, I am being paged for Josephine's room. Don't know if she is going to make it another day. What a beautiful soul. Heaven will be her home. Soon............

67

What Really Happened (MayAnn)

No, dear brothers and sisters, I have not achieved it,
but I focus on this one thing; Forgetting the past
and looking forward to what lies ahead.

Philippians 3:13 NLT

There is a blank part of my life that I never realized was there until our last meeting in the Common Room. Somewhere in the past, there is a year or so missing. I have never thought about it because my life was so very full after I met my late husband. I was torn from a life of not-so-good and spread into a life of love and family and happiness. Why would I ever want to look back on pre-Eugene?

I have had a good, fulfilling, and happy life. Will anything be gained by digging into the depths of a past that might not be along the same lines as my life remembered?

My daughter, Sue, would probably enjoy finding some mysteries of my past. She likes to do that kind of thing. Family tree and all. I know Sue is up here often because of two things. One, every time I have a good day out of my fog, she seems to be here with me. That can't be happenstance. Two, a mother knows these things.

Maybe I will mention something next time I come clear of my inner trap. Something about that cowboy preacher man who joined us in our Common Room almost opened a long-shut door in my mind. I can't seem to find the right key to open that door. So many good memories I can visit daily. Why does that locked door draw so much curiosity? Why did God ever let us have the desire to go to places that are not good for us?

I should ask why the Devil has spent my whole life trying to take the reins. Why can't the disgusting representation of bad just leave me alone? When we cross the line into Christianity, it should be a one-way road. How much easier life would be if we didn't have the struggles of temptation. I just want to do good. I want to please the Good Lord. I don't want the glimpse of hell that defined my childhood.

Hopefully, we have another "meeting" so I can say goodbye. Our Common Room was a special blessing. I am afraid many people never get to see a Common Room. Maybe we all visit a Common Room? Is this the first time a whole group visited this room at the same time?

There could be churches around the world that experience this on a regular basis during prayer. I've always experienced a fellowship when part of a devoted prayer group, but nothing like what we have found in our Common Room.

I was also thinking about what was inside our Common Room. I think all of us gathered there didn't see the same things. I believe my version of the room contains highlights from my memories. A painting from my brother on one wall. My favorite curtains of all time hanging in front of a picture window that reminds me of our farmhouse. An antique wind-up clock sitting on an old player piano that was such a huge part of my and Eugene's family since they settled that homestead.

Even a shag carpet that was part of a huge remodel after we had a bountiful wheat harvest in 1976. And imitation wood wall paneling. The envy of anyone's house that was still stuck in the '70s. Warmth, Eugene's easy chair, my corner of the room with ten different crochet projects.

And Wilbur. Oh, the family bonding among my children, husband, and me because of the things this stuffed panda bear could say that none of us dared share aloud. My happy is now contained and held forevermore in that Common Room.

I wonder what the others saw. Do they have a monstrosity of a TV stand that held not only our 19", but a reel-to-reel tape recorder, a hand-built Heathkit turntable and amplifier, and an impressive collection of records, many from Columbia Record Club. Eugene was never impressed with the unnecessary expense, but he was husband and father enough to admit that music was a very important necessity for the family. As long as we received an occasional Johnny Cash album, he wouldn't complain about *The Sound of Music*, Simon and Garfunkel, Rachmaninoff, or any number of Disney movie soundtracks.

Or a bookshelf that held a secondhand set of World Book Encyclopedias that we bought when the one-room country school our children attended up until 1966 closed and school buses became the norm for country kids. What a variety of knickknacks and other books that simple shelf held.

If I had time, I believe I would do some remodeling and updating in that room. No, come to think of it, I wouldn't change anything in that room. Nothing but happy memories is contained in those walls. It should stay as such.

I don't feel very good right now. What started as a simple cold that a heavy dose of orange juice could cure, has now moved into my lungs as an almost unbearable weight. I can feel it getting heavier and heavier. Not unlike the fog in my brain. This one is growing at a rapid pace.

And honestly, I have no desire to fight it. I have lived a good life. I have a wonderful husband waiting for me on the other side. I have other family I want to see. My daughter and sons and their children are all doing fine. They don't need to suffer anymore coming up to see an old lady who is a definition of "the lights are on but nobody's home."

If God will have me now, I am ready. My last hoorah was a doozy. I hopefully helped a young lady pull herself from a dark, dark place that I know all too well from my childhood. Different background, same abusive story. I could see it in Jean's eyes.

I need to rest. It takes all my energy to take the next breath...........

68

Please Again (Kay)

I cry out to God Most High, to God who will fulfill his purpose for me.
Psalms 57:2 NLT

Oh my God, that was *AWESOME!* Who would have ever thought that a few people joining hands and completing a circle could lead to such an adventure? A conservative Methodist upbringing never prepared me for this. Yes, It helped me be an expert at potluck dinners and women's gatherings, but nothing like the experience I shared in the Common Room.

It was so very awesome to be able to walk and talk like normal. I was even back to my pre-MS weight. I felt pretty. I was full of energy. I immediately thought of a thousand different ways I could decorate that room.

It seemed like most of the room contained some portion of my personality from some era of my life. I was so busy talking to everyone that I didn't take time to study the details. People I have seen every day for such a long time, and this was the first time I was able to visit. I was a little overwhelmed.

This next chance, and I pray there is a "next meeting," I will be better prepared. I feel there is a lot more than what meets the eye in that room.

The men, of course, were on a mission. Why do men always think they need to "fix" things? Can't we just talk and share feelings? Why wasn't their time spent complimenting the ladies on their outfits? I don't remember changing into my favorite pumps and sundress, but there I was. Oh, how it felt good to be a lady again. This mass of cramped-up nothingness I have become is sad.

What did I ever do to deserve this? Why me, Lord? In the words of my favorite band CCR, "Who'll stop the rain?". I feel like I have been locked in a rainstorm for such a very long time. The only sunshine in my life is when my sister/sisters visit. That is about it. TV and eating are only a temporary distraction.

Life of being normal is long past. I will never be held by a man again. All things female internally have been removed. I have a catheter, so I don't pee myself all the time. Every morning, I am given a suppository and sit on this big open-bottom chair thing made out of PVC. My butt hanging through so once the reaction hits my bowels, I can relieve into a bucket. How humiliating is that?

Then, every other day I am wheeled into the bathing room, parked up against a wall, and sprayed down like a cow being prepped for the fair. Jean the Mean, (what I call her in my mind), took care of me this morning. She actually had the water a very comfortable temperature, and gave me the semblance of a soothing shower. She also took the time to rub some lotion on my back and make me feel special. I don't know what has gotten into Jean the Mean, but it is like she has turned a corner for compassion. Maybe the men did "fix" something right after that last gathering of Light.

Are we actually given a purpose? Almost everything gone from my life is in a physical sense. Having a purpose is what I miss. Just try it sometime. Take away any reason you have for living and then check on your daily happiness.

I want to, no, I NEED to be a part of the next gathering. There is nothing left in my current world. Escape is a must. Maybe the men will have a mission for me, too. Oh, how I long to be part of something. Anything....................

69

The List (Peggy)

That thou givest them they gather: thou openest thine hand,
they are filled with good.

Psalms 104:28 KJV

My goodness, after the last Bible study, the request for participants has doubled. I will need to discuss this more with our administrator, activities director and Judy. We would have to move it into the dining area. I suppose I need to discuss this with the dietary manager, too. Who would have ever thought Bible study would grow into a larger group than Bingo? We will need more volunteers. It is very exciting. Can we call it a revival of the nursing home? Does Trail's End have new life coming forth?

Even Jean was asking me if she could help this next Wednesday. By two o'clock, the residents are usually settled into whatever their afternoon routine is. The CNAs gather at the nursing station to fill out charts, gossip, and generally milk the last hour on the clock the best they can. Jean wanting to be part of some added work and caregiving to the residents is a step in the right direction. The power of this Group of Light is contagious. Amen, brothers and sisters.

Judy has always kept her Bible study nondenominational. She has a special way of presenting the Bible for what it says and not what someone's opinion or religion requires it to say.

As a matter of fact, Judy encourages the participants to give their opinions and views based on their Church. It makes for some fascinating discussions and even an argument every now and again. Imagine that, a group of predominantly women arguing about the meaning of a simple verse. The magic comes when the Bible study is over, and they all leave with a new enlightenment. Judy really is a special teacher.

Now, there is an even more special phase to the Bible study. Word passed quickly through our little home of the benefits witnessed from last week's group. Not only the extra energy and lessened suffering, but the magic or rather miracle of Jean's life changing for everyone's benefit.

It is amazing to see the littlest ray of hope shine a light on the dreary existence of most of our residents. This hope is stronger than the flu bug that is wreaking havoc on our medical care practices. The possibility of these residents gaining even a hint of their previous whole selves is an energy never found in multivitamins or Metamucil. The energy is contagious. If even for a few moments, anything positive to be gained is a blessing.

As an RN, I am concerned about putting that many residents together in a tightly knit group. I suppose not much different from the three meals a day they are required to attend. Only the very sick are ordered to stay in the room and have meals brought to them. Believe it or not, a good portion of them hold on to their meal gathering as a relief from sitting in their room of mostly nothingness.

A few of the residents who requested to attend the next Bible study have a cold and a hint of rasp in their lungs. Not quite the pneumonia stage, but getting there. The benefit of what this Bible study will bring far outweighs the necessity of isolation. These people need all the interaction they can get. It will be a health benefit. I will sell it as thus.

To take it a step further, I believe we will put the effort together to dress each attendee in a more formal, or "special" outfit. Most only have one really nice dress or suit coat hanging in their closets as space is limited. Those with private rooms have the benefit of double the closet space. And those with a residual income good enough to afford a private room typically own a large selection of nice clothes. The rest will have to settle for whatever Sunday best their family provided for them. Maybe we can even have most of the ladies get their hair done special on Monday or Tuesday in our little salon. More volunteers needed. This is getting exciting. I think I will take my nursing outfit to another level on Wednesday, too. Something above a cool pair of Disney-themed socks. I will have to do some shopping......................

70

Wednesday (Larry)

Then adorn yourself with glory and splendor,
and clothe yourself in honor and majesty.

Job 40:10 NIV

I was reminded today of going to a homecoming dance or attending high school prom. Not quite prom as there were no formal dresses or rented tuxedos, but well above the norm for Trail's End attire.

The ladies were adorned and presented as should be, all beautiful in their own sense. The men, well, we did our best. Not much left in the formal wear department. Most of the men's best suits are hung up somewhere in a closet under plastic, waiting for the caretaker to use in preparation for ground planting.

Men in this part of the country only have one suit worn for every occasion requiring formal attire. Weddings, funerals, maybe Easter Sunday, and on occasions when the better half makes them. At one time, I had a vast collection of Joseph Abboud custom-made suits. All had my name stitched inside the left breast. I had my lawyer bring the collection in for the men who needed a suit to wear today. The fancy suits fit decently on the men attending. I was glad one of my favorites fit Alan quite well. His wife had mentioned his wedding suit, but I know she was saving that for "the day." It had gone from a suit coat of wonderful memories to the dreaded suit of goodbye.

I only had to provide six other suits. Yes, there were an estimated thirty-two or more residents going to attend today's Bible study, but the ratio of men to women in a nursing home is pushing it if you have one to four. That would be the definition of heaven to a man in his prime. Four women to every one man is good pickins. By the time you hit the nursing home stage, that ratio doesn't mean very much.

Don't get me wrong. The desire is still there. And can be almost overwhelming at times. Many a story floats throughout every nursing home of some man "visiting" a lady resident's room. Most times due to mutual secret plans. Other times, because their brain is locked in a memory room of the past, and they are simply going to bed with their "wife." Such visits are documented and kept to a minimum as much as possible. Most are so very innocent. And due to the ratio, there is a better chance of one of the women trying to climb into bed with one of the men. We are all carnal, that never leaves. At any age.

Today might have increased that desire from both sides. As our converted dining area to Bible study room started to fill, it would take your breath away. The women had morphed into ladies. The presentation was a sight to see. You could tell they felt "special." Each once again felt pretty to the level of beautiful. It is a sight to store for the ages when a woman goes from everyday level to the princess of the ball.

It reminded me of my time in boot camp. I was fortunate enough, or maybe cursed, to be in a boot camp that also took women through the initial stages of military training. My company had a sister company, literally. A company of eighty-some women who joined us in activities on a daily basis, mainly in a classroom environment. Never really mixed, but in proximity.

The very first time we "met" our sister company; we were already sitting in our half of the classroom when the "others came in. They all sat down. Of course, we eyeballed them, but not with all that much interest. We were buried in our own exhaustion and quick to learn discipline. But heck, you have to look.

Once they all sat down, their company commander quite forcefully stated, "Look, ladies, all the leaves have fallen off the trees." She was referring to our almost bald shaved heads. Compared to just a few days earlier when we had arrived with our '80s personalities, we were completely stripped of anything that defined us as individuals. Our clothes reeked of mothballs. Only a plain wedding band was allowed if you were one of those married types. The only watch was worn by the recruit chief petty officer Our leaves had been stripped.

And yes, the sister company of women laughed. They needed to, because they had been cleaned like a slate, too. Their hair chopped down to just off the neck. Didn't matter what length or style it had been, it was now a uniform haggard mess. No makeup, no perfume, no jewelry (except that plain wedding band if had), and their clothes were just as much of a loose-fitting mothball rag as ours were. We, the brother company, preferred to study that day's subject rather than that ugly group of women who had so rudely joined us.

Two months later, that outlook changed. First, there was the aspect of a young man going two months straight without holding a woman. Second, we were by now almost all in the best physical shape of our lives. Our mental strength had been taken down to "clear out" level and brought back up to a well-oiled machine of like thought. And third, we were on a bus ready to go to our first controlled liberty. The mothball boot camp clothes were tucked away in our barracks. Dress uniform was the requirement of the day. When our sister company walked onto that bus, we men were speechless. Never in our wildest dreams would that nasty mess of ugly women transform into the goddesses that came onto that bus with a light sprinkling of makeup, perfectly form-fitting dress uniforms, and a splash of perfume. Transformation created a hunger. It is amazing we had any semblance of control.

Today was similar, as the lady residents one by one were escorted into our Bible study area. They all looked amazing. Twenty years or more had been erased from their appearance. Ten of that from hair, makeup, and clothes. The other ten from each of them feeling good about their appearance. Feeling pretty easily erases the harsh timeline of life.

I would like to go into a description of each resident as they appeared. I happened to be the first placed in the room. Don't know why, but there I was. Alan was right behind me in a bright blue suit with gold tie and matching handkerchief perfectly mounted in the breast pocket of his suit. Typical of Alan, he had my $2,000 suit coat on with a pair of new Wrangler jeans. Alan also had his dress Ariat boots on. I thought he looked perfect. Even his eyes had a sparkle that matched his tie and hankie.

Then, in rolled Tex. He already had his own selection of suits, being a preacher man and all. Western cut, 5x beaver Resistol to match, and Tony Lama boots. Tex had a sharp-looking bolo tie to complement his ensemble. It was a good thing Tex had his own suit, with the build of a steer wrestler, broad shoulders and enough weight carried on a short stocky frame to enable an easy four hooves up in less than six seconds. I know even in my best of days, I would have never wanted to get on the wrong side of this man. The softspoken words of calm could only contain that bull of a man for so long.

Next, we had Dale, Kenny, and Charlie. They looked good. Not the perfect fit on their suits, but you can only present so much stateliness while sitting in a wheelchair. Kenny walked in. A little skinny and pants a tad long, but even at seventy-nine, still had a strut of confidence to woo the ladies. Dale was brought in by his wife. I felt for Dale. He had had a stroke and was working oh, so very hard to get back into shape to go back home. His wife faithfully came every day before lunch and stayed with him until midafternoon. What a beautiful couple. One day, Dale even surprised his wife by walking almost fifty feet on his own. They could both see the possibility of him coming home, but this latest flu bug set Dale back to almost square one. Their disappointment was only covered by their deep love for each other.

Charlie, don't know how long he had been in this home. He was like a permanent fixture. I think he was inhibited more by some intellectual disabilities than anything else. I really like Charlie; he has such a gentle and happy nature.

Sadly, and I don't know why for sure, Willy was a no-show. Laziness? Flu symptoms? Depression? I can't say. The ups and downs of each resident in a nursing home are very unpredictable. Many still attempt to preserve a semblance of independence, solely by exclusion from group activities. I guess today was Willy's day to make the "self" choice.

Now come the ladies. If my count is correct, there were twenty-six adorned ladies in our presence. I would like to describe the outfits and jewelry for each of them, but as someone from the male species, I would make a confused mess of it. Maybe Peggy could tell this part of the story. You need to picture how transformed most of the ladies were. They all were beautiful. They all shined. They all felt special. I believe that was most important. A lot of work went into the perfect hair, makeup, jewelry, dresses, shoes (some even with heels), and even some had their matching clutch. Nothing like a simple Wednesday Bible study turned into the Trail's End Promenade.

The home ought to do something like this more often, even though it was a lot of work for the nurse's aides and volunteers. After seeing and feeling the energy from so many of the residents who are typically just making it through another day, I believe there are amazingly positive benefits that could be realized from this practice. Maybe we could do this at least monthly?

Anyway, we were all gathered. All looked wonderful and special. All were anticipating something of a miraculous event. Word travels fast. Any hint of hope for most of these residents is like a racehorse receiving a vitamin shot before a race. Expectations to run well were high. Good luck, Judy. You will have your hands full today.........................

71

The Circle of Light (Alan's Account)

I am the door; by me if any man enter in, he shall be saved,
and shall go in and go out, and shall find pasture.

John 10:9 ASV

I will do my best to give you a "play by play" of our little Bible study on this special day. I pray I can describe everything that happened so you all can understand. This is not the easiest picture to paint. Sometimes I can lock the events into slow motion. Other times, it appears as mass confusion, hysteria, or a film clip shot in slow motion and played at regular speed. If I bounce around a little with the events, forgive me. The police are patiently taking my statements as I can present them.

It started fairly reasonably in the manner expected.

Judy read today's scripture:

2Chronicles7:13-15: 13) "When I shut up the heavens so that there is no rain, or command locusts to devour the land or send a plague among my people, 14) If my people, who are called by my name, will humble themselves and pray and seek my face and turn from their wicked ways, then I will hear from Heaven, and I will forgive their sin and will heal their land. 15) Now my eyes will be open and my ears attentive to the prayers offered in this place.

Judy then asked Tex to lead us in an opening prayer. It took a couple of minutes to get everyone to join hands. Larry and I had MayAnn in between us, so that part came naturally. We then reached out to the others. A circle had already been formed, with Judy opposite MayAnn. Judy was the only one outside of the residents who joined us. I could tell Peggy, Jean (the revised version), and Carol the activities assistant, all wanted to be a part of the circle. For some reason, though, they helped the hands join and then stepped back. We bowed our heads. Tex began, "Our dearest heavenly Father……………"

According to the outside sources, those were the last words anyone heard spoken out loud. The LIGHT that many had witnessed before was brilliant in the center of the circle. Enough that anyone not part of the circle could no longer see the faces of the participants. It was almost a blinding light that made one turn away. A good pair of Ray-Bans wouldn't have helped. Maybe if one of the assistants had a welding helmet on, they could have looked within that light.

We were all instantly carried into our Common Room. Thirty-two residents. Judy didn't make it. I felt like maybe Judy was either wandering her own hallways, or she was guarding the entrance to our Common Room to hold back any potential intruders.

I do remember all of us appeared in the clothes we were wearing when brought to the Bible study. I also remember each of us appearing at an age when we had once been in our prime. At first, it was difficult to recognize everyone. If I hadn't seen the clothes they were wearing as they came to the study, I probably wouldn't have been able to identify everyone. Making it even more difficult was the other detail that everyone was walking and talking like it was a garden party. This was a far cry from the daily interactions we residents had at Trail's End.

MayAnn had a table set up with refreshments and snacks. I think she simply did it by picturing these things in her mind and voila, there they were. The food and drink in our Common Room were real, though. I even munched on a couple of red velvet cupcakes, (a weakness of mine). It was a small banquet. And from what I could tell, this table contained at least one of everyone's favorite treat. The investigators didn't really care about this detail. I did. It was important.

I had prepared an order of events in anticipation of our gathering in the Common Room. I planned on everyone's attention staying focused during Tex's prayer and when he finished, I would quickly step in and keep us organized. Too many people with too many different visions and agendas quickly overcame any semblance of a meeting. It was a "free for all" full of joy and celebration. How could I even begin to interrupt these residents' happiness? It was like they had been hibernating for a very long winter and had just come out to a springtime of sunshine and flowers. I can't begin to describe the energy in that room. Saying it was "Out of this world" is a copout. It wasn't of this world. It was extraordinary.

The fact that everyone could eat and drink like normal brought this illusion into a known reality. I remember some Bible verses that used this reference of eating to show that Jesus had returned fully whole and fully human prior to His ascension to Heaven. Maybe those trying to figure out what exactly happened should pay a little more attention to this detail. Why are all of us so very closed-minded when we are in the prime of our lives? Are the distractions so strong, we can't see the Light for what it is worth?

There was no reference to time here. Even though all men had a watch on (that thing men used prior to cell phones to keep track of time), I never once glanced at mine. I did glance at Larry's Rolex and wondered if it was bragging rights to sport a $12,000-plus watch. Or if it actually kept more accurate time than my $120 Bulova. I think even Dale's $24.99 Timex did just as well. To each his own. I would enjoy walking around with a Rolex on. What a gift that would be.

I don't have a clue of the time consumed in our room. Bible study started at 2:05 p.m. on the dot. I returned to the home sometime after that. I didn't look at the clock or my watch upon return. One of the aides or Peggy will have to give that detail. What actually took place in the Common Room was more important than how much time it took.

As we were all talking and laughing and eating, I noticed an additional person walking among us. I did not feel threatened by this person. It just seemed strange that someone other than the thirty-two was able to join us. Like I said, Judy didn't even come in. If Peggy, Jean, or Carol had been part of our circle, I am certain they would not have entered this room either. I felt privileged to be included. Some awesome people here in this group. And one stranger.

I started to make my way to this man for introductions. He looked straight at me as I approached. His eyes presented a love that was equal to the time being tracked. It had no measurement. It had no end. It was strong, welcoming, and almost overbearing. This detail I have kept to myself. The words His eyes spoke to me were mine and mine alone. Maybe someday I will share. For now, I will treasure.

As quickly as this man looked at me and shared a thousand things with His eyes, He turned away and started attracting the group. I don't know if He spoke a word. Most of the people in the room just started gathering around Him. It was like children gathering for Storytime. They all flocked to the Teacher. I wasn't drawn to Him, though. His eyes had told me, "Not yet, Alan, we will talk later." I kept my distance. Besides, on the table I had just found some cheesecake that needed my attention.

While everyone was gathering around Him and I was excluded, I was able to see what else was going on. The highly adorned door I had noticed but paid no mind to last visit, was open. There was a Light behind that door that put our Light as a group to shame. It was the purest, whitest, most beckoning Light I have ever felt. I couldn't say I "Saw the Light." It was more like an invitation. And while I wanted to explore and pass through that door, I knew it wasn't my place. "Not yet, Alan, we will talk later."

As the residents gathered around this man, He would lay His hand on their forehead, whisper a few words into their ear, and then move on to the next. Once each resident received their Word from this stranger, they would quietly exit into that brilliant light. To me, it appeared they almost ran to that door with absolutely NO hesitation. They were not going blindly. The joy and happiness they had been sharing in our Common Room were replaced by a peace and acceptance unequaled with words. (Another detail the police didn't care to hear.) Each one was called. Each person accepted His invitation.

Dale was still gnawing on a healthy piece of fried chicken when he was called. He simply went back to the table, returned what was left to an empty plate, wiped his mouth with a napkin, and presented himself. Me, I probably would have munched as fast as I could on that chicken till the bones were clean, then hurried, found a trashcan, wiped my mouth with my sleeve, and trotted up to Him. Not Dale. It was like, "My time is done here. I will prepare the best I can. I will not delay He who is calling me."

When I realized the room was thinning out and no one was around the table of goodies, I too stepped back with a realization of what was happening. Larry and MayAnn were close by. It appeared that they were waiting for The Call, too. They had stayed at the back of the group to remain with me a little longer.

Some of the dearest, sweetest people I had ever met—Clara, Margaret, Kay, Florence, Josephine, Danny, Dale, Kenny, Dottie, Ruth, Esther, Maria, Jan, Linda, Lois, Terresa, Mary, and another Judy—had all left. I knew they weren't just visiting another room. I knew they weren't coming back. My brain mourned; my heart rejoiced.

Then, there were just the three of us. MayAnn grasped Larry's and my hand tightly. She looked at both of us with a newfound recognition. My being lept with the realization of "I just found my birth mother that I didn't know I was looking for." She looked at us with a lifetime of things to say.........But time had left.

She stepped on tiptoes and gave us each a kiss on the cheek. There was a tear in her eye. A tear of loss at just the breaking edge of a flood. To keep from that, she turned, walked up to the Stranger, and said, "Here I am, Jesus. Bout time you showed up. I have been waiting for you!!" He then whispered into her ear. MayAnn proudly walked to the door. She hesitated, looked back at me and Larry, and winked. Then she was gone. My turn for tears.

Larry didn't give me much of a chance for sadness. He had always been direct. I couldn't have asked for a better roommate. He was the brains and I was the brawn. That is what we had been handed in life. Even as our separate diseases consumed us, we maintained our most prominent attribute. Now, I knew it was time to listen closely to what Larry had to say. I could feel the pull of that door calling him away. He held both of my hands to prevent our separation until he had shared some words that seemed very important to him.

Larry then shared the words that branded themselves in that three-fourths empty cranium of mine:

"Just as the Supreme Architect of the Universe watches the revolutions of the planets and stars in the sky, so does HE, who placed each of us here, watch each of our movements, hears not only our words, but our thoughts, as well....... And it is to HIM that we are ultimately responsible."

Larry then let go his strong grip, gave me a hug that only a true brother could, turned and walked to the Stranger MayAnn had called Jesus. I had never witnessed Larry present himself so humbly. The Larry I had known for such a short time had a pride that kept his back straight and head held high. Even his ALS couldn't rob that from him. Now, though, Larry approached the Man with his hands folded together, looking at his feet. I thought he was going to drop to his knees.

Right before that happened, our Stranger reached out to Larry. The room went from our Common Room that held mainly my memories, to me standing in an old fishing boat. When I say old, I mean OLD, as in Biblical times. We were on a huge lake, or sea, or something. It was dark, so I couldn't tell the size. By the height of the waves, I could tell it was much more than a fishing pond. The boat wasn't much more than a large Jon boat with a single sail toward the bow and two pairs of oars. There was a decent pile of fishing nets at the stern.

From what I could then see, as we were coming down the backside of the next wave, Larry was walking on the water to get to the Stranger. The Stranger had called to Larry. I could hear the words, "Trust in the Lord with all your heart and lean not on your own understanding; In all your ways submit to Him and He will make your path straight." (I later learned that came from Proverbs 3: 5-6.) Apparently, not only was Larry's path now straight, he was walking on water. As Larry arrived within reach of the Stranger, I could see Larry start to sink. Just like it had appeared to me that Larry was going to get down on his knees in front of this man, Larry was sinking in the water. His hands reached out as in "Save Me." The Stranger, no, Jesus, reached out, grabbed Larry's hand, and raised Larry back up. The waters calmed. We were surrounded by millions of the most brilliant stars I had ever seen.

Calm described the water. Calm described the wind. Calm described what I was witnessing. Calm wrapped me in a blanket.

We were back in the Common Room. Jesus, Larry, and I. Larry has lost his humble. His back was straight, his eyes looking directly into Jesus's. The Larry I knew was back. Except, this was also a new Larry. A forgiven Larry. Jesus simply said, "Well done, good and faithful servant; you have been faithful over a few things, I will put you in charge of many things: enter into the joy of your master."

They both turned to the door, Jesus's arm over Larry's shoulders. Like long-lost friends, I watched them leave. They didn't look back. The door closed. The brilliant light was gone. The table was empty. It was time for me to go back through my door and into my fog. What the heck did I do wrong? I felt slighted. I apparently failed. Oh, how heavy is my soul...

72

The Circle of Light (Peggy's Account)

*Then Jesus said, "Come to me, all of you who are weary
and carry heavy burdens, and I will give you rest.*
Matthew 11:28 NLT

A very special day this was. My favorite day as a matter of fact. Wednesday, Bible study. Judy, our Bible study leader, our administrator, and the activities director all agreed that every resident who requested to attend be allowed the privilege. We also agreed this should be taken up to the level of attending a memorable church service. All staff were willing to help the thirty-two residents who in one form or another signed up for this Bible study, to dress up extra special for the event.

We started on Monday with everyone having appointments with the volunteer hairdresser of their choice. We even had an old-school barber come in for the men. Our little salon with two chairs in an open room at the end of the hallway was quite busy. I will say that many of the women came out with close to the exact same hairdo. The "big hair" style from back in the day when our volunteer hairdressers were in their prime, too. Some things won't change. Who wants to grab new age modern when one can reminisce on the good ole days?

Hair coloring was a requisite. I wanted to sit down myself and join the resident ladies in a couple of days of being spoiled and beautified. Two young ladies came from the local beauty school to help with nails. They also helped decide what makeup would be appropriate and easily applied on Wednesday morning. Most of these resident ladies came from the time period when a little blush and some serious lipstick were applied. That was considered "made up."

Only Kay was from the generation that needed eyeliner, mascara, extended eyelashes, concealer, base, blush, and all the other good stuff that turned Kay into the Trail's End beauty queen. Her sister helped with this part. She always made sure that Kay stayed a lady. Makeup application was a huge part of this. For this coming Wednesday, though, Kay's sister took it up a few levels. It was perfect and I know Kay felt very special.

The rest of the ladies had only a slight difference in hair color and lipstick. They looked fantastic. Each had a special set of designer clip-on earrings with matching necklace. Some even sported a family brooch that had been passed down through the ages. Authentic and valuable jewelry was allowed to be kept in the nursing home, but only in the safe in the administrator's office. Too many greedy hands made valuables disappear. Typically, this was from some family member who thought they'd better get "their due" while the getting was good. Other valuables disappeared at the hands of other residents. Mainly those suffering from dementia or Alzheimer's. It wasn't intentional theft. Almost like a young child being attracted to something shiny. Instead of trying to control these things, it was much easier for the nursing home to request that valuable jewelry and large amounts of cash stay either out of Trail's End or inventoried and locked away.

Looking at the entourage while they were coming into the Bible study area/dining room, was like I had stepped back into the '50s. An outstanding generation of women they were.

The nurse's aides, activity director and assistant, a couple of volunteers (the hairdressers), and I helped bring the thirty-two residents into the converted dining/Bible study area. The six men first, and then the twenty-six ladies. We started bringing them in at around 1340. It takes so much time to walk and/or wheel that many residents in. I had all of the afternoon meds passed out and documented by 1300, so I was able to help with final touches of makeup and hair on the ladies.

A debonair group of men it was. And the most elegant group of women I had ever seen at one time here in the home. Christmas and Easter typically put together several families and their resident of name, and was cause for some dress-up, but not to the degree of this day. Cell phones had been banned (except for the breakroom) ever since the little photo incident coming from the bathing room. On this day, though, Carol (activities director assistant) had the home's camera to capture each resident as they entered, and then the group as a whole prior to their completion of the circle.

I wanted to be part of the circle, but discussions with staff led us all to agree that we should assist in the joining of the hands of all, and then step back and allow the residents their special time. It was noted that Judy, as leader of the Bible study, should join the circle, but no one else. I think Jean really wanted to be a part of this. Maybe I should say, "needed" to be a part of this, but she understood the reasoning. We needed to be available to anyone in the circle who might have any problems during the Light.

Little did we know that when Judy reached out and grabbed Kay's hand and the circle was complete, we would be totally blinded by the brilliance of the Light that came from the center. All of us on the outside of the circle had to look away. I am not saying a casual glance in another direction. We had to completely turn 180 and walk to whatever door was nearest. It was blinding.

There was a draw to the Light that I had also felt the last two times the circle was formed. This one was much stronger. The push to leave the area for fear of going blind outweighed the urge to join, though not by much. The two volunteers and I made it to the breakroom. Jean, Carol, and two other aides who were on the other side of the circle probably headed through the doors to the assisted living area. The kitchen staff was out in the smoke shed. In reality, there was a brief moment when no one with licensed qualifications was actually in the room with the residents.

This would have happened around 1405. I propped the door to the breakroom open just far enough that I could at least hear if anything was wrong. I could also see a reflection of the brilliant Light so I could know when it would be safe to return. All I could do now was watch the clock. One minute seemed like an eternity. I was responsible for these residents. I could not sit idly knowing they were alone.

It wasn't like any of them had been brought straight from ICU. As a matter of fact, I had taken the temperature of every one of them prior to their being brought out to the Bible study. Anything above normal, and they would have been sent back to their rooms. Those on blood pressure medicine were also checked for current vitals. Any on oxygen, four as a matter of fact, had their O2 levels checked. All was well. Maybe that is what bothered me.

Out of thirty-two residents, especially with the current cold/flu passing through the home, there easily should have been two or three residents who didn't qualify as fit for a gathering. Not today—ALL were well. I credited it to the general energy that was sparked in each one of them. Whether this was due to being made up to the level of feeling pretty and special, or something inner in anticipation of being a part of the Light, I cannot say. I would speculate a little of both. I was so happy for them. I was so very worried as well.

At exactly 1415, the Light went out, Judy screamed, and Alan yelled, "CALL 911!!" I rushed out of the breakroom at the same time the aides were coming in from the assisted living side, and other nurses and aides came from the hallway leading to the crossroads/nursing station. We had all been nervous. Pins and needles stabbing all staff. The only ones quickly responding were of the medical training sort. All others hesitated as caution/fear of the unknown far outweighed their ability to render assistance. Yes, even within the confines of an elderly care facility, there exist first responders who put others' lives as a priority over their own. That level of giving comes straight from One source. We didn't care what unknown hazard might still be lingering to claim us.

The first thing I noticed was all hands were still held and eyes closed except for those hands that had been joined to Judy and Alan. The second thing I noticed was all heads bowed a little farther than natural. Instinct kicked in superseded by indecision. Who do I even go to first? Closest is best. They all looked the same. I could only help one at a time.

The "help" part didn't last long as a quick pulse check from one resident to another yielded the same result. Nothing, nada, nem uma, not one, had a pulse. Cold was already setting in. My experience told me the 911 call was worthless except to get the police here as soon as possible. The ambulance would only be needed for transporting bodies. I didn't know whether to scream or faint.

I had hopes that maybe Kay or Charlie was just sleeping. They were younger, stronger, and had no reason to suddenly pass on. What had just happened? Our intentions that were so good and so right were now going to be drowned by the situation I was currently looking at.

Alan was up, walking around, talking to every "sleeping" resident by name, shaking them by the shoulders, setting them up as naturally as possible and then moving to the next. Watching him while I was checking pulses reminded me of someone who already knew the answer, but needed to confirm.

Judy was crouched on the floor crying over and over in a shock-filled trance, "I was just outside. They wouldn't let me in. What did I do?" One of us would need to tend to her soon.

As acting head RN, I quickly made the decision to leave them all as found. I told Alan to stop adjusting them. It was best we left the evidence as was. Oh, the questions that were ahead of us. The police, no big deal. Truth, details, simple. The families would be a different story. Somewhere in the back of my overwhelmed mind, I could already feel the lawsuits. The dream event turned nightmare. News stations would be involved. This would easily go national, if not global.

And blame, where would that land? I would take a fair share. Greedy lawyers would make sure several entities would receive a share. The small town that owned this nursing home as a non-profit was going to get slammed, and hard. Even the salons our volunteer hairdressers owned would be sought for compensation. This would get ugly.

Within minutes, the county sheriff and two of his deputies were there. The ambulance, only 100 feet from the home itself in its own ambulance barn, took another ten minutes to back up to the back door of the dining area. This was because of the ambulance crew comprising only volunteer EMTs and drivers. People with other vocations who had to drop everything to come rushing to get the ambulance. Some even lived outside town on one farm or another. Most were women.

Another factor for the delay of the ambulance was the source. Most calls for the ambulance to Trail's End were more of a transport duty rather than a real emergency. The various crews had become complacent. I couldn't blame them. All had taken the EMT course and every year refreshers to serve their community and possibly help save lives. They didn't expect ninety-five percent of their calls to be glorified taxi drivers with a bed and medical supplies.

Don't get me wrong, all on the volunteer crew were very compassionate, every time. Their hearts were huge. They stayed professional. They always did their very best. They received NO compensation except maybe, if lucky, a thank-you from the patient or family.

When the ambulance crew came in stretcher and all, they simply stopped and stared. They had heard "multiple," but none imagined the number to be thirty-one. No one in their wildest dreams thought they would have something like this haunt them for the remainder of their own years on this Earth. They stood there needing direction.

The county sheriff and deputies were at a loss, too. Thoughts of "cause" circled through their whispered discussions. Food poisoning? Medical poisoning? Intentional poisoning? Gas leak? Electrocution? There had to be a physical reason. Their training in this type of case was reason, not reaction. The nearest investigator of any type was a good hour/hour and a half away. Just doing the paperwork was going to take months. How long could everyone simply stare and leave the scene untouched?

As an RN, I never in my own wildest dreams imagined something like this. Thirty-one people alive and well and looking fantastic one moment, then thirty-one people in the next, forever gone. All in a ten-minute time span.

Reports from the other nurses and aides were, all other residents in the home, an equal number to be exact, were doing just fine. Vitals taken, all normal. A couple or three still fighting a slight fever, but other than that, most were in the middle of their afternoon nap. They didn't have a clue what had just happened. For now, we were going to leave it at that.

The nursing home administrator, social service rep, and activities director all arrived at the same time, thirty minutes or so after everyone else. The "management" had a tendency to conveniently disappear early every afternoon. Once in a while, there was a valid excuse of a meeting or need to go procure something for the home or a resident. But mostly, it was salary doing what salary does. Not like they were ever missed. I shouldn't say any more. Enough of that will come forward in the investigation.

Now, we needed to think about the residents. Alan, having previous military training and experience, took charge. For somebody who was on the last legs of Alzheimer's, he sure seemed alert and knowledgeable. I was glad he was here. We definitely needed a leader. I definitely needed some help.

Once Alan was able to settle Carol down and pull her past the first stage of everyone's shock, he had her take photos from every angle possible, and photos of each individual resident. Alan knew exactly what had happened, and didn't view this as a crime scene. He knew it as thirty-one residents passing on, and now their bodies needed the proper care and respect due to any resident who dies in the home.

One at a time, after proper photos and a short brief, written by the Trail's End secretary, excuse me, office manager, they were taken back to their rooms to be cleaned up and prepped for transportation. Every funeral home in a 100-mile radius was contacted to bring their hearses. There was no actual morgue within that 100 miles. They would have to be transported to various locations for an autopsy, if required.

Because of a somewhat similar cause of death for all, Alan arranged it to where in alphabetical order, they would be taken to the hospital that was nearest to the same direction the hearses had come from. It was a smart and correct decision.

The county sheriff and deputies even agreed. They had already spoken to the investigator, who admitted it would be another two hours before he could even get here. He had agreed this was the best course of action. The evening shift had arrived, giving us two additional nurses and four aides. They were a Godsend. Our morning shift crew didn't even question staying, or ask about overtime. They took a minute needed to alert their family that they would be late coming home from work. Arrangements were quickly made. All stepped up to help.

As residents were assigned to hearses and hospitals were designated, Alan had the late-arriving management crew start on the daunting tasks of notifying relatives. All three were perfect for this task. They may have learned to cheat the clock, but they were also professionals with required training in this practice.

Realize, death in a nursing home is a given. It happens, sometimes frequently (especially around Christmas). Every resident file had an up-to-date contact name or number. Ninety-eight percent of the residents also had a do-not-resuscitate order. The one resident (two percent) out of the sixty-four present was currently sleeping calmly in her room. No need for resuscitation, either.

Now, mind you, this home was in a small town. Most of you think of a small town as maybe fewer than 20,000. No, this was a SMALL town. As in, fewer than 600 people. When multiple hearses started showing up, tied in with the radio dispatch after the 911 call, news exploded from the town busybodies who had radio monitors in their homes. Soon, almost everyone in town knew something was up. Several had relatives in the home. A few were even receiving The Call. Word spread fast. It was inevitable. At least Alan had the foresight to make sure all family was notified of what hospital to go to, and not have the whole town invade our Trail's End.

By 1700, all bodies had left, the other residents kept in their room for the evening meal. They were all used to their doors being closed when one of them passed. No questions were really asked. Some were a little concerned as to why their vitals were being taken every thirty minutes and someone was checking on them every five minutes. These residents families were notified too that there had been an emergency in the home, but their family member was OK. They were told it would be good if they would come and visit the day after tomorrow if possible. Those who visited daily were asked to stay home for one day with assurance that all was well. For now, this emergency required twenty-four-hour isolation from any outside interference.

The administrator and social services manager doubted that their requests would be adhered to. They had witnessed many times over that most families ignored their loved ones in the home for most of the time. The only time their interest sparked was if they were told not to come for some reason or another. Always ready to point the finger of neglect or wrongdoing.

Jean was a blessing. I had never seen an aide show so much compassion and respect for the loss as she did. I think Jean personally made sure each and every one of the bodies was clean and well-presented in fresh clothing. Their dress clothes, carefully handled with gloves, were folded neatly, placed in a sealed plastic bag, and sent with the deceased.

The closest doctor available arrived within forty minutes of The Happening. Jeez, we have to call it something. Definitely wasn't an awakening, event, disaster, or mass casualty. Well, maybe the last one, but that just didn't fit with what had actually happened.

The only way I was ever able to maintain my sanity working in an environment like this, where you easily become attached to someone who is soon going to die, has been to have a deep and strong faith. I don't believe an atheist or agnostic could work this closely with the elderly and disabled and provide the care and compassion required. Yes, they could professionally do everything correctly, but in a home environment, it takes more. My faith shares love. My belief also knows they have gone to a better place. For most, it is a relief.

Fewer than two percent who check into a nursing home check back out to go home. Ninety-eight percent either die here or in a hospital their families had them transported to. Usually a broken hip or pneumonia. At times, it is amazing how long we can keep them pickled before they expire to a better place.

Yes, part of my report I filled out for the police included the words, "The Good Lord called them Home". They all left together and by their own will. Judy returned from the joint prayer because of the obvious. She never made it to the Common Room. Alan returned because God had some work yet for him to do. It was A Joining of Souls. They were simply called away.

I am probably going to lose my license over this.................

73

The Circle Of Light (Jean's Account)

To those who use well what they are given, even more will be given, and they will have an abundance. But from those who do nothing, even what little they have will be taken away.

Matthew 25:29 NLT

I won't go into a lot of detail. I already gave my statement to the police. It really isn't much different from Peggy's statement. I know that it was a heavy mixture of emotion that passed through me that day. At the conclusion of the "Circle of Light" or Bible study, or whatever in God's name we must call it, thirty-one residents were gone. Most of them had already been "gone" for years. They were just preserved well enough to keep making payments to this Trail's End.

That, I suppose, is why I had such mixed emotions. I felt very bad for the loss. I hadn't had time to apologize to all the residents I had abused for the years I worked here. I did my best to make amends with as many as I could. How do I even begin to obtain forgiveness for such horrid acts that I did to these people? Most probably don't even remember. The problem is, the few who do remember still cower every time I come into their room. I know Jesus has forgiven me, but more than 100 people (only two had I left alone) in a confined area that at one time or another, I had done some rather unkind things to.

I never thought of it as any type of abuse. More like some teasing that might have gone a little too far. I tried to never leave bruises or marks physically. Apparently, I have left some psychological scars. I can only hope to make amends one resident at a time. Those who left, I hope they didn't carry a grudge with them. The weight I now carry is unreal.

Thirty-one residents GONE in one shot. You want to talk about a complete shit show, this was it. I was able to do my best by their bodies before they left. Each one of them I sent a mental "I am so very sorry" to as they were wheeled out of the home.

What gave me comfort was, every one of them had a natural look of peace on their face. There was an almost smile, permanently glowing from them. I knew they had gone to Heaven. I knew it. Each and every one of them was now in a much better place. Maybe I saw the glow and smile because that is what I believed for them?

I do know after the initial panic and realization that these people were dead, a peace settled over me, too. With direction from Alan, I knew exactly what I needed to do to help preserve the respect of each of them. To heck with any investigation protocol. If there was blame for tainted evidence, I would take my share. It was the least I could do to make some sort of amends.

Enough of that. They are gone now. No going back. Life and death move on in unity.

My direction has strongly gone 180 degrees from where it once was. Exactly fifty days after "The Happening," I was contacted by a lawyer who simply went by the name of Bryant. He told me he would have contacted me sooner but wanted to make sure my name wasn't going to end up on the lawsuits that slammed in from our little "event." I was too low on the totem pole of assets, so I was clear. He did his homework, though, and had each of the representatives from the existing lawsuits sign a very clear waiver that kept me and my daughter from ever being touched. Everyone was so busy chasing the big fish, they dismissed little ole me. Something about not even having a pot to piss in, helped.

Anyway...... Bryant gave me an envelope that changed my life. I had already changed for the better. My home life was still a disaster, though. My boyfriend/provider/sperm donor thing was still continually draining any semblance of a bank account, and was always sharing his form of abuse. I had changed, though, and I think he realized that his being a part of this family was on a very thin line. I just needed an out. Bryant's envelope gave me a very legal and direct out.

The first provision of the contents of the envelope gave that abusive POS $100,000 of nontaxable cash. All he had to do was have a paper signed, notarized, and submitted to the local court that he relinquished all rights to his daughter. He had no problem doing this. As a matter of fact, his last words before he got into his new F-150 King Ranch he bought was, "I have always believed she wasn't mine anyway, you whore." He then slammed his driver's door hard enough that it knocked the dog end off his cigarette. I kinda hoped it burned a hole in his new leather seat.

There was also a court order of restraint that stood for fifty years, barring him from getting within a few hundred feet of me. He had no problem with that as he tore out of our shithole yard. Forgive me, Lord, I am working on muffling my profanity.

I stopped smoking. It is amazing how much clearer my thought process is now. I am going to need it, as the next envelope was a full ride payment to nursing school. A three-year program to obtain my registered nurse certification. And, if desired, I could go into a specialty program after that. We will see how life works out.

The best part of this "full ride" included the quaintest little apartment for me and my daughter that was only a few blocks from her new school, and very close to mine. It had been arranged for someone to always be at the apartment waiting for my daughter if I was tied up with my nursing school. The schedules looked very similar, or close enough that we would leave the apartment at the same time, and I should return a half-hour before she got out of school. This was good.

There was also a provision to give us enough food and spending money that we could be comfortable without me having to work. On top of that was a trust fund for my daughter that would cover all tuition and expenses for any higher education she wanted to take above high school. There were some very strict ties associated with this part, including a GPA requirement and the necessity for a part-time job when she was old enough. It also included that she must be involved in extracurricular activities. This could be band, sport/sports of choice, debate team, or any number of other school-related activities.

Her summers were to involve camps of choice, including at least one Bible camp. There was not a requirement for either one of us to attend church. That was going to be one of my requisites. God had handed us a blessing well beyond anything I ever deserved. The least we could do was be thankful on a more frequent basis than Easter and Christmas.

It didn't take me long to figure out my benefactor. Bryant never told me. But I had seen Bryant only coming to visit one resident in Trail's End. Larry was behind this, I am sure. The only words accompanying this legal documentation was a note:

Jean,

I hope this finds you with the same huge heart you displayed in those last days that I knew you. You and I share something in common that can only be explained with this short poem I wrote a while back;

I CAN WALK THIS PATH NO MORE

I CAN WALK THIS PATH NO MORE.
IT HAS ONLY LED TO DARK.
BY CHASING THE DESIRES OF LORE,
MY LIFE HAS MISSED ITS MARK.

WHY DO I GO SO FAR TO LEFT,
WHEN MY SPIRIT TELLS ME, STAY TO RIGHT?
MY REPUTATION GONE, A VICTIM OF THEFT
NEVER TO BE REGAINED BY OWN WILL OR MIGHT.

THIS DARK PATH WAS NOT THE PLAN,
BUT RATHER MY ATTEMPT AS A GOD.
MY DESIRES HUNGERED AS A MAN.
WHAT I SAW AS "BEST," WAS FLAWED.

THERE IS NO SHORTCUT OFF THIS PATH.
HELP CAN ONLY REVERSE MY WAY.
I MUST RETURN AND FACE THE WRATH
TO ANSWER FOR EACH MISGUIDED DAY.

SOON WITH HELP, MY DIRECTION TURNS.
A PATH OF RIGHT, I CAN ONLY PRAY.
MY GRACE NOT GIVEN BECAUSE OF EARNS.
GOD'S GIFT, THAT I NO LONGER STRAY.

IN JESUS'S NAME I TRY TO FOLLOW
THE GOOD, THE RIGHT, THE TRUE.
MY LIFE, MY PATH, NO LONGER HOLLOW
BECAUSE GOD PROVED "I LOVE YOU."

SO HELP ME LIVE MY FRIEND
ALONG A LIGHTED MOST PEACEFUL SHORE.
ONLY TOGETHER OUR STRENGTH WON'T BEND.
FOR I CAN WALK THIS PATH NO MORE. LG.

I pray this gift helps your path stay true. You are a beautiful soul.
You just needed to get the ugly out of your life. LG.

What can I say? Tears come to my eyes every morning when I open my Bible
and read this little note I use as a bookmark. I would carry it with me, but I
want it to stay for like ever in good shape. Thank you, Larry. I am sorry you
had to see the bad side of me. I promise you will always be looking down on
the best of me..

74

WOW (Alan)

Then they heard a loud voice from heaven saying to them, "Come up here." And they went up to heaven in a cloud, while their enemies looked on.

Revelation 11:12 NIV

don't know where to start and describe the events following my return to the Circle of Missing Souls. I had to name it that to explain to myself what had happened. There was a Joining of Souls, I was sorted out, I picked up Judy on my way back, we opened our eyes, Judy screamed, I felt abandoned.

In those first few seconds, I was filled with a love and peace that could have only come from one place. Jesus had told me we would speak later. Truth be told, I didn't say much in the conversation, I just listened. I could tell you word for word what was said. My brain cells didn't come back. They were replaced by the *now not needed by them* cells of thirty-one other residents. Some didn't have much left to give. Others, like Larry, gave me a few extra that I never had to begin with.

Their memories didn't follow. I believe those stayed with their souls. So, I was not filled with a flood of emotions above and beyond seeing thirty-one people I mostly knew, sitting in that room dead. After the little "chat" with Jesus, I knew to take control and help everyone through the process of handling this Circle of Missing Souls.

Don't get me wrong, the county sheriff and deputies, and Trail's End administrator are well-trained professionals and know their stuff. This was a little different. Having a front-row seat at the event gave me a definite advantage. I knew what happened. I knew they all had passed to a much better place. Dang if I still don't have that urge to go, too.

Yes, I needed to check every one of the bodies to make sure I hadn't been mistaken in what I witnessed. It was a human thing to do. I knew, though. I knew deep in my own soul that their "joining" was a good thing. We should actually be having a party.

Instead, there was some interesting fallout from The Happening. The family members who had come to the home to visit often, accepted the finality of their loved one. They, they went through the shock phase, and had an inkling to want to point fingers. Instead, they personally thanked the nursing home, Judy, and me for giving their loved one an extra special sendoff. Once they heard my firsthand account (I had to tell each one individually the exact details of their particular loved one), they seemed to accept the truth. And yes, that is no misprint. This event was part of God's Truth. He gathered His people. It was a gift for each one of them.

Even Kay's very protective and loving sisters understood and accepted her early passing. I won't call it demise, fate, death, or any other negative word used to describe what happened. There is a reason it is called passing away. They all passed to Heaven. No doubt and Amen.

The family members of those who camped their relatives in the home, never to return except on maybe a holiday or birthday once a year, were a different story. They wanted someone's head. They wanted blood. They wanted blame. They wanted compensation. Besides pushing for an expected inheritance, they could see $$ signs from the nursing home, the board of trustees, and the fine town of Trails City.

The state had no choice except to shut Trail's End down. The remaining residents were all moved to various other facilities. Some close, some to more private and expensive settings, some to one of the large corporate homes in the larger cities where they were likely to outwardly look awesome, but habitually suck any remaining money from the residents' assets. The state made Trail's End pay for all the transfers and one year's care.

To pay for all of this, Trail's End closed, and the property was sold to a developer who thought he could make some pretty awesome controlled environment storage units out of the building. Trails Total Storage was created.

Many thought the home should be turned into apartments, a hotel, or low-rent housing. People realized that death had been a constant in the building since its inception. It was even difficult for some people to consider storing their valuable but apparently no-longer-needed property. If you think about it, Trail's End had always been an environmentally controlled storage unit. Just the contents are a little different now. Park their belongings there. Pay the monthly rent. Only check on their belongings out of necessity. Probably even carry a healthy insurance policy in case of disaster.

The insurance companies that held the life insurance policies of the residents who passed in The Happening fought the hardest. As always, they didn't want to pay. The cost for lawyers to fight said insurance companies was astronomical.

Then, Bryant (Larry's lawyer) stepped in and tore the insurance companies a new one. He had some very prominent backing that influenced the various judges overseeing wherever the suits were. Soon, the insurance companies discovered they'd better simply pay the value of the policy, or they would be tagged for more $$. It was a circus. Greed tried to take over. Justice won. Good won.

Still, Trail's End closed. It was sad. Long before any of that happened, took almost six months to work through all the bureaucracy, I had transferred. Half the families within the first week took their remaining family members out. No new residents came in.

The administrator and board at first tried to promote the extra space and advertised a private room for the normal price of a double. No takers. Word got around fast. Even the residents who fell under state funding were not admitted. This was a hurdle that would not be overcome. Some things just are what they are.

What got me was, this was a good thing that happened. Thirty-one residents were no longer suffering. Each of those thirty-one was given a choice. They chose Heaven. Why couldn't anyone on Earth grasp that concept? If I knew there was a chance that I could choose my path, and be given the option up front, wouldn't that be the first place I would want to be? Maybe you have to live through an experience such as time almost standing still as you are kept alive but not "living," to grasp the concept of the relief it is to be invited into God's Kingdom.

Each of us has that choice. Many professed Christians claim they are excited about going to Heaven. When it comes right down to the nitty-gritty, though, maybe it is our inherent desire to survive no matter the circumstances, that makes us fight to stay alive. Only when that fight is completely defeated do we give in to our passing.

It is both a gift and a curse. Don't tell me God doesn't have a sense of humor. He gave us the gift of choice. He also gave us human instinct to survive. We all have our inner battles.

I guess if we really understood the glory of crossing the threshold into Heaven, there wouldn't be any good left here on Earth. There would be no one left who would appreciate a pretty flower, birds singing, love, a baby's laugh, kindness, charity, a burning sunset, a glorious sunrise, the first flakes of winter snow, the taste of fried chicken, a beautiful painting, music, or the feeling of forgiveness when you accept Jesus as your Lord and Savior.

No, there would be just bad. You can fill in all the words that describe the "Other Side." I don't want to go there. This is a happy story.

Those thirty-one residents within a few moments of each other walked into Heaven. It was AWESOME. I was left to tell the story, I guess. Jesus did tell me a few things, but like all of us going through life, we have to figure out most of our direction on our own. I knew what path I needed to stay on. Plus, I had a heck of a story to tell. This had to be shared. A much-condensed version, yes. Still, an amazing story.

There are doubters, yes. Many. Always have been, always will. Even ministers and leaders of different churches could not wrap their blinded heads around what happened. It was sad. Somewhere between the innocence of a child and adulting, we lose the concept of *Jesus loves Me*. Much like our hearing the truth about Santa Claus, the Easter Bunny, the Tooth Fairy, and all those good things that we cling to as a child.

Someone convinced us different. It is sad. Is reality actually better than possible hope and dreams?

I have a very good friend, Ed, who passed down to his children and I imagine grandchildren, that Santa Claus does exist. Even at his current age of sixty-plus, he believes in Santa Claus. Pretty easy argument to children. He says, "If I don't believe in Santa Claus, or you quit believing in Santa Claus, then how do we expect to receive any Christmas gifts? I still get gifts every year because I still believe." Makes perfect sense to me.

As I sit looking out my window today, I see a mass of little birds feasting on the core of an apple that has been thrown out. With one little wave of my hand, even at a distance and separated by a window, the birds scatter. Rapidly. It takes a while for them to return. Hunger and a sweet treat have to overcome their fear.

We are the same way. Always fearful of disaster. Afraid of death. No matter our beliefs, we are scared of the unknown. We tend to scatter like little birds from even a glimpse of possible danger. We lose sight of the treat. Yes, we eventually come back when we get tired of the normal human life and we know there is better and more. Only after we overcome our fear can we comfortably sit there and enjoy the feast of life that God has prepared for each of us. Sadly, most of us don't realize this until our good years are behind us. Or some calamity has forced us over the line of question into acceptance.

I was fortunate to experience what I did. Think about it. It took a disease as horrendous as Alzheimer's to take me to the point where I could accept the Common Room and be free to enter there without human inhibitions. All the others were the same way. We had been reduced to almost nothing before we found Everything.

This message must be shared. Will anyone listen and truly believe? Will I ever hold hands with a group in prayer and see the Light again? Are there people out there who have crossed that line by choice and not by age or disease whom I can join with and go to a Common Room again?

My name is on a blackball list of ever being allowed into a nursing home again. Not in writing per se. Just by word of mouth. Many people I meet are even afraid to shake my hand. They are more scared of what they might happen to "see" than whatever misery they are suffering at the time.

Don't we all have a certain level of misery in our back pocket? Some carry it in their front pocket. Others wear it around their neck. I truly.... just....... want......... to......... help. The miracle I realized personally scares the ever-living heck out of most people. If I had come from any time prior to the 20th century, I probably would have been lynched in some form or another. At least left in prison somewhere to rot. Thank God I live in a time when people are just too busy to take off on their own crusades. Maybe. We will see.

How or where did I, Alan, transfer to? I walked out of Trail's End on my own two feet. I had a family to raise and support. My end was further down the line. My work was not complete.................

75

Afterword

Brothers and sisters, I do not consider myself yet to have taken hold of it. But one thing I do: Forgetting what is behind and straining toward what is ahead.

Philippians 3:13 NIV

So far, the Other brain cells haven't left. I see/think more clearly now than ever. I do have a twinge of numbness every so often left over from Larry's ALS. I even occasionally have my hands ball up in a grasp of pain thanks to Kay. None of the thirty-one who so generously gave me my life back are ever going to let me completely forget them. It is not so bad. I still believe I came out on the much better side of the trade.

Well, come to think of it, maybe not. They are in Heaven. I am still here on Earth. Their pain is gone. Their sadness, fear, anger, doubt, stupidity, and every negative human nature trait is no longer with them. Those are left out in the Hallways of Fog. Thank God I didn't retain all of that mess, too.

Apart from an ache or pain here and there, I am quite well. More than well. I am truly blessed. I wake up every day to my beautiful wife. My girls are now teenagers doing quite fine. They are at that lovely age when boys are interesting, and Dad is stupid. I understand, though. Birds eventually leave the nest. It is nature at its best.

My sons, Douglas and Wade, from my first marriage, are a strong part of our successful business venture started shortly after I walked out of Trail's End. My Douglas's nine kids are all grown and doing their thing. A couple have spread their wings then returned. My stepson Felipe has his own chain of Christian radio stations, (#1 in all of South and Central America, knocking on the door of #1 in North America).

And the fact of MayAnn being my birth mom and Larry my twin brother; that is my smile carried within. Maybe someday I will further research and know the whole story. For now, it is tucked away most tenderly.

Due to my experiences at Trail's End and some borrowed brain cells from Larry, I decided to try a different type of retirement/nursing home. On our small farm (the original homesteaded eighty acres), we built a state-of-the-art care facility with the idea to provide the best quality of life possible for those who qualify.

Qualifications are thus:

1. You can't afford a private room in an alternate home.
2. Your family has to commit to at least one family member a week visiting. No exceptions.
3. If no remaining family and no money, you qualify even more. Not as a ward of the state, but as a free guest at the Driftwood New Light Center (DNLC).
4. You must have one cognitive function. Either brain or body. Don't need both. If you have neither, then we have a hospice-type center that will do their best to keep you comfortable.
5. You must be willing to use whatever skill you still have left and earn a wage. Even if it is only the ability to talk and tell stories, you are hired.

If you look at qualification #1, you might question our thinking. It is simple. We will help you to set up whatever trust you need, to make yourself poor. Give it all to your family now so you can hear how they enjoy it while you are still alive. That is where qualification #2 comes in. Your family, even if they are no longer being friendly in hopes to gain inheritance, they still must find a reason to come and visit. There could be some ugly repercussions from this, but it really is easy to tell who will adhere to #2 and who is going to try and walk away.

The beauty of the trust funds we help set up is, if the family doesn't adhere to #2, then all the funds go directly to DNLC to pay expenses on those who have no family nor money. Win/win for all. Except the greedy family members.

The inheritances are also tightly controlled by accountants working under BB. Most of the money is invested to earn more returns and control is not given to family members until after the resident's death. There are certain allowances paid as needed to family members.

Qualification #4 seems harsh at first glance. The idea, though, is to not bring anyone in who is just going to be parked in the hallway or in front of a TV and their only thing to look forward to is the next meal or Bingo.

Don't get me wrong, all the meals are excellent. There are some necessary dietary requirements to maintain calories and nutrition, but all meals are designed to be like Mom's home cooking with some good old fast food thrown in for reality. In a couple more generations, it will be more fast food with a little home cooking thrown in.

Bingo is important. That is included weekly, appropriately named Don's BINGO, and we have an amazing turnout. There is probably not a nursing home in this country that could survive without Bingo.

What makes us unique is finding something in every resident that can be of value to the home and to the operating farm/ranch it exists with. To give a person a purpose is the single greatest reward right below giving them faith.

If a resident can only ramble on with the same story over and over, they can do that for one of our residents who are at the hospice level. Having someone to talk to you every day means a lot. And we have found that those who ramble, if given a purpose and someone to try and help, actually come out of their fog enough to tell very good stories of comfort and humor.

Those who can still do something physical, contribute at whatever level possible. They have come out of retirement (as much as able) and thrive on having responsibilities. Even those in advanced stages of Alzheimer's and dementia, we have found ways to pull out of their fog as much as possible. Most is based on what I learned from the Common Room. It is finding a way to direct them out of that crippling hallway and bring them into some semblance of clarity. Each has his or her own way. Some, we are still working on breaking through with. It is fascinating to me.

Those with ALS still tear my heart out. We are working on ways to slow or stop the progression. That and MS. Truthfully, if those it hits are seventy-five-plus years old, it isn't so bad. It is the younger ones who still have a whole second half of life to live that tear at me. I would give anything to have Larry working beside me to help these people. I do have a good portion of his brain cells, which has allowed us to have a very successful business. That, plus a hidden fund that BB passed to me strictly because Larry trusted me to do my best by him and the other thirty residents who were part of The Happening.

I am not personally wealthy. If DNLC never received another dollar from any resident, it would still survive for the next 100 years. Larry was stupid rich. Not one of us at Trail's End knew this. All his money is now going for the good of others.

Our staff consists mainly of the best staff members from Trail's End. The weeds were cut out. Peggy was offered director of nursing. She turned that down. Peggy will always be one who needs to be "hands on" with the residents she is caring for. She is on our board of directors, so she has a strong voice in the decisions we make. Peggy also spends half her time training other nurses and nurse's aides in the ways of DNLC.

We have one neighbor just up the creek a ways that is a big part of DNLC. They have brought the cowboy way of life to be included with our residents. Many times during the year, our residents get to watch calves being born, branding time, fence fixing, or just riding around checking the cows, their water, and minerals. Many take part when the cattle are moved from one pasture to another. There are numerous other animals involved, too.

Even if it is the only possible task a resident will ever realize in their time left and they can scatter a little grain to the chickens, they are fulfilled. Heck, I even enjoy watching and feeding the chickens. They are a trip.

When possible, and if desired, residents are taken on hunting trips. Turkey and deer are the main ones. Some pheasant and quail (we raise our own with half being sent into the wild) are thrown in.

We have built an awesome eighteen-hole golf course that camouflages itself right into the rock bluffs and pastures and Driftwood Creek. Many of the families who come to visit take advantage of the course. The only requirement is, every golfer playing must be accompanied by a resident. It is a great time for all. I wish the season were longer.

Winters are still tough. We have a huge indoor pool and recreation area. Plus, physical therapy is more of tasks to accomplish or build something, rather than rubber bands and free weights.

If repetition-type exercise is necessary, that form of energy is converted into a task that benefits the home. And the residents get paid for it. Even if pedaling a floor-mounted set of bicycle pedals from their wheelchair, generates enough power to blow fresh air into the numerous fish tanks, it is considered of value.

Sounds like a Utopia, huh? We try. Praise God, we are doing our best. We have many preachers come in as guests for a week to provide Sunday and Wednesday services. Judy is in charge of this. I have some who touched my life at one time or another come to give their best. The golf course and hunting rites help.

Each of our "guest" preachers has to sit through my tale. It is then easy to tell if they will be a benefit to our residents. I hope someday we will be blessed with another Circle of Light. We have prayer circles all the time. No Light, yet.

Maybe it is because we have given our residents a purpose again that they haven't reached the level of nothing to lose. Maybe it is because God has a better/different plan for us.

Probably the latter...

www.ingramcontent.com/pod-product-compliance
Lightning Source LLC
Chambersburg PA
CBHW061936170626
46813CB00006B/2425